M000318351

Magnus Heat
A Two Volume Set including
Pack Challenge & Go Fetch!
By
Shelly Laurenston
Triskelion Publishing
www.triskelionpublishing.com

Published by Triskelion Publishing www.triskelionpublishing.com
15508 W. Bell Road #101, PMB #502, Surprise, AZ, 85379 U.S.A.

First e-published by Triskelion Publishing
First e-publishing April & August 2004
First Print Publishing August 2005
ISBN: 1-933471-43-3
Cover art: Kristi Studts for Triskelion Publishing
Copyright © Shelly Laurenston 2004
All rights reserved.

Dear Reader,

Who knew that having a very strange and unexpected conversation regarding werewolf sex would lead me here? But I've realized that sometimes life is all about timing. Meeting the right friends at the right time and being receptive to what they say to you, even when neither of you realize what they're saying will change your life forever..

The fact is, I had Sara and Zach's story pinging around my head for years.. But, I thought, who'd want to read a book about werewolves in love? It would have to be a horror novel, right? There would have to be nightmare sequences and full moons and painful transformations. There would have to be an old curse and a wise woman who explained everything. There definitely wouldn't be sex, comedy, and a loud, rude group of girlfriends who would risk everything to protect each other.. And I definitely wouldn't be able to make a series out of these best friends who were loud, rude, and cursed a lot. Right?

Well, I was thankfully wrong. Really wrong. It's nice after so many years of searching to finally find a place where you truly belong. A place where you find that perfect fit. And although it was a hard journey getting here, it was well worth it in the end.

Now I hope you enjoy Sara and Miki's journey to find their perfect mates Zach and Conall. You know these guys. Those best buds on Harleys, wearing black leather jackets and, at least in Zach's case, a dangerous scowl. These are the guys you could never bring home to mother, unless you really just wanted to annoy the hell out of her. But you would know they were just misunderstood. You would see the sexy wolves underneath and know these were the guys for you and your dangerously unstable friend. The wolves you can't wait to tame…at least just a little.

Enjoy and all my best!

Shel.

Dedication:

Thanks to Maggie R. for putting me on this path by handing me a great book. And to MaryJanice Davidson for writing said great book.

Thanks to Gail Northman, my editor, for giving a first-time author an enormous chance. She proves that the Valkyries still ride.

Thanks to Cypress B. and my California family. You guys may not be blood, but you've supported me and been there when no one else has and for that I will be eternally grateful.

And last but in no way least, thanks to Christina K. aka "Leno Beast.." In high school you somehow knew I'd end up here. Thanks for having more faith in me than I had in myself.

PACK CHALLENGE

Prologue

Waste of his time. That's what this was. Minutes of his life that he would never get back. Zach walked into the club, surprised to find a place like this, called Skelly's, in this dinky little Texas town. Hardcore industrial and tech music tore through the tiny club and Zach let himself relax a little. He assumed he was about to enter redneck heaven. His kind usually ended up in the middle of a shit storm around rednecks. Too much testosterone and liquor always led to trouble.

He moved through the tightly packed club, checking out everyone, until he reached the bar. He watched the bartender pull drinks for a few moments. She was a cute, petite black woman with a shaggy mass of dark curly hair. She was definitely a pro and each drink she made was absolutely precise. She never gave any more or less than was necessary. Plus, she kept up a continuous conversation with a tall, seriously hot Latina at the other end of the bar and she never missed a beat. Never splashed a drop. She was good.

He held up a ten and the girl moved down to him. He caught the last bit she yelled to her friend, "I can't watch her and serve. I thought you were watching her." She turned to Zach and flashed him an adorable smile. "What'cha need?"

"Tequila."

The girl nodded and her hand went searching under the bar, then her face froze. She suddenly disappeared as she crouched down to get a closer look. "Motherfucker!" he heard her snap. She re-appeared, her smile gone. "Gimme a sec." She headed to a door behind her, yelling over at the Latina, "Angelina, she took the bottle."

"Uh-oh." The Latina turned and looked out across the dance floor to a group of tables and bar stools filled with people. Zach followed her line of sight and immediately saw what she was looking at.

She was tall; taller than her concerned friend. Her coal-black hair reached just below her shoulders and brushed across the strap of her black tank top and the Celtic tattoo revealed on her right shoulder. When she turned her head, Zach could clearly see the ragged scar that tore across one side of her face.

She was surrounded by four young men, but she didn't seem to notice them. In fact, she seemed downright bored. He wasn't quite clear what her friends were worried about.

"Here ya go." Zach looked down at the shot of Tequila. "Your change."

He waved it away. "Keep it."

"Thanks." She shoved the cash into the back pocket of her jeans and moved back down to speak to her friend.

"Well, we've got to do something," she was saying. Zach could hear her clearly over the music and even the words she was speaking directly to the one called Angelina with her back to him came in crystal clear. "She's toasted."

"Well, remember what happened last time? I guess we should just be grateful she doesn't drink every day... or year... or decade."

"What's with her tonight anyway?"

"I think her leg's been bothering her."

"Her leg is always bothering her. What makes this new?"

"It's getting worse. And I think she's worried. Worried what it might mean."

"It doesn't mean shit. She reads too much into stuff."

Angelina leaned back and stared at her friend. "Look who's talking. Pot, this is kettle calling."

The girl flipped the bird and deftly made a martini all in one move. He was impressed.

"Uh-oh, Miki. She's on the move."

Zach turned back to the other girl. She slipped off the stool she'd been perched on and in the middle of some guy's sentence simply walked away... well, it was more like she limped away. He'd heard her leg was severely damaged. But as she headed to what he was sure was the restroom, she used no cane or crutches.

He wouldn't have thought another second about the whole thing except for the two men leaning against a far wall. They didn't fit in, although they were desperately trying to. They wore black leather jackets, but brand new ones that looked as if they'd just been bought that day. The shirts they wore were black, but silk. The pants they had on were pleated. And their shoes? They were leather, expensive, and Zach wouldn't put those things on his feet if there was a gun to his head. And as soon as she moved, they followed. Zach shot back his tequila then followed them all.

He'd just pushed his way through the crowd and to the back of the club when he spotted them. One grabbed the girl around the waist, lifting her off the ground. A hand was slapped over her mouth and the three of them were out the back door. It happened so fast none of the other patrons even noticed.

Zach burst into a run, knocking people out of his way, terrified he might be too late. He slammed through the back exit and spilled out into the alley. They'd just thrown the girl down on the ground and one had his hand raised above her. To anyone else it would have looked as if he were going to slap her. But Zach knew one swipe from that hand would rip the girl's throat out. He snarled, forcing his canines to lengthen and grow. The two men turned and one roared in answer.

But before Zach could make any kind of move, the girl pulled a long, thin piece of metal out of her worn cowboy boot and stabbed up into the inside thigh of one of her attackers. He roared again, this time in rage and pain. The unharmed one seemed to realize this was no longer a simple plan of killing the girl. She wasn't going to die quietly. So, he grabbed his partner and the two sprinted from the alley, leaving a trail of blood behind.

Zach went over to the girl who, by now, had slipped the weapon back into her boot and attempted to pick herself up off the ground–clearly it was a chore. Zach sighed and grabbed her arm, easily hauling her up.

"Hey!" She looked up at him. From where he sat at the bar, he hadn't realized exactly how pretty she was. Amazingly pretty. Dark brown eyes peered at him from under black lashes. Her skin a light brown, with a hint of red. And the brutal scar on one side of her face couldn't hide her sharp cheekbones or full lips. In fact, it only enhanced them.

Her dark brown eyes stared straight at him. "Pretty teeth." She had a light Texan accent. Not as hearty as the others he'd heard on his ride from California. "Long." Her right index finger was in his mouth. It suddenly occurred to him he hadn't yet retracted his canines. She smiled at him. "You're pretty, too." Wow, she was *really* drunk. With a sudden surge of strength, she slammed Zach against the far alley wall. Then she leaned into him. "I've never seen anyone as pretty as you." Zach had been called a lot of things in his lifetime, "pretty" wasn't one of them. She growled as she smiled... uh, no... leered at him.

She kissed him. Her soft lips on his mouth; her tongue sliding past his teeth.

Their tongues connected and Zach had the sudden urge to take her right there, in the alley. And when he felt her hand slide down the front of his jeans and take firm hold of the bulge growing by the second, he knew he had to have this woman. Now. This minute. This very second. But before he could even put his arms around her, she was pulled away from him. Torn from him, was how he thought of it.

He'd been so lost to her he didn't even realize her friends had burst into the alley, clearly prepared for a fight. The one called Miki had a baseball bat, probably from behind the bar. The other, Angelina, had removed her high-heeled shoes and seemed ready to handle the situation with her bare hands. He thought she had that take-care-of-herself quality.

"Sara!" Angelina yanked Sara back from Zach, while Miki stared. Zach could only imagine how it must look to them with their friend's tongue down a stranger's throat and her hand on his crotch. "What are you doing?" Zach quickly retracted his canines back to normal human incisors.

Sara pulled away from Angelina and leaned back into Zach. She smiled. "This is my pretty man. Isn't he great? I think I love him."

Miki rolled her eyes and lowered the bat. "You have got to be kidding me."

Angelina moved toward her friend. "Okay, honey, that's the half-bottle of tequila talking. Now it's time to let the 'pretty man' go."

"No!" she snapped, causing her friend to stop in her tracks. Zach watched, startled at her level of aggression.

But her friends seemed completely unaware of how close they were to real danger. Miki burst into laughter while Angelina looked validly concerned. "Sara, honey, you've got to let your toy go."

"Hey!" Zach snapped.

Angelina glared at him. "Work with me," she bit out between clenched teeth.

"Okay. Okay." Sara straightened up. "Don't fight on my account. I can take a hint. I'll go."

Angelina visibly relaxed. "Good."

"But first..." Sara whispered so that only Zach could hear. Then her hand was at the back of his neck and she pulled him down so that their faces were barely an inch apart. "It would be just rude not to say 'night."

She kissed him one more time. And that urge to take her returned in full force, whether her friends were watching or not.

"Whoa!" he heard Miki exclaim.

But before he could slam Sara face down over a garbage can, Angelina had her friend by the waist, dragging her back to the club. "Come on, sassy girl. We need to get some coffee into you before you set somebody's car on fire...again."

"Bye-bye, pretty man." Sara waved at Zach.

Miki pulled the back door open as Angelina, literally, threw her friend inside. "That's it. No more tequila for you, missy. Ever."

Miki followed them but stopped just at the entrance. She turned and looked at Zach. "Look, sorry 'bout that. She's really drunk."

"No problem," Zach forced out. It was taking all his inner strength just to control his dick.

Miki flashed a pretty smile and turned to enter the club. She stopped short. "Jesus Christ, Angie! Get her off the floor!"

Zach pulled out a cell phone and pushed a button. While he waited for the connection, he quickly adjusted his suddenly tight-fitting jeans. "Hey," he answered when he got a pick up. "It's Zach. It's definitely her. But they're already here."

Chapter One

"He's on the List."

"But he just… "

"He's on the List!"

Sara sat behind the counter of Marrec's Choppers, the store she'd worked at since she was fourteen, and watched the now weekly ritual between her two best friends.

"Sara," Miki demanded. "The List!"

"Would you two bitches please stop. I have a migraine."

"No. You have a hangover. Now, the List."

Sara sighed. "No cowboys. No bikers. No criminals of any kind. And no republicans."

"And…"

Sara and Angelina shrugged.

"No rodeo clowns."

"You just added that!" Angelina snapped. A rodeo clown just asked her on a date that morning.

"No. No. They were always on the List."

"He's a nice guy."

"He dodges bulls for a living. He's gonna screw you over!"

"Stop yelling!" Sara put her head in her hands. "Just let me die in peace."

"That's what you get for getting all liquored up," Miki chastised.

Sara felt Angelina slip an arm around her shoulders. "Honey, it's been six months since your grandmother died. Maybe it's time to stop celebrating. Especially since you seem to become quite the whore when you drink."

"I do not!" Yet Sara couldn't help but smile at the faint, drunken memory of attacking some poor guy in the alley of her favorite club. "Besides, I'm not celebrating. I'm just glad that my grandmother's…"

"In hell?" Miki cut in.

"There's no proof of that." Sara rubbed her temples. The pain in her head would go away eventually. Besides, she was used to pain. Her right leg had been in varying states of unbearable pain for more than twenty years. She'd simply learned to ignore it. And she'd probably continue to ignore the pain for the rest of her life. She'd almost grown used to it. Hell, it could be worse. She could be dead.

Or, she could be like the girl stumbling through the front door of the shop. Her face and biker leather covered in dirt and blood.

"Holy shit." Sara quickly limped out from behind the counter. "Guys, call nine-one-one. Marrec!" she yelled toward the back. "Come quick!"

"No. No. I'm fine." The girl waved Sara away.

"Really? You look like shit," Miki remarked.

"Bike crashed." The girl stretched and Sara could hear every one of her bones cracking. "Actually, that's why I'm here. You've got a mechanic, right?"

"Don't you really need an ambulance?" Angelina asked.

"Or a hearse," Miki muttered.

Sara elbowed her friend. She did that a lot when it came to Miki.

"Nope. Just a mechanic...and a bathroom."

"I'll show her." Angelina led the girl to the back of the store.

Marrec appeared, oil and dirt smeared on his face, hands, and T-shirt. The man was supposedly in his sixties but he looked more like a prematurely graying forty-five. He was shorter than Sara but powerfully built. He'd taken Sara under his wing when she was fourteen and had been thrown head-first through his shop door during a fight Miki still claimed wasn't her fault.

"What's going on?" Marrec stood next to Sara, wiping his hands on a rag.

"Some girl just got into a crash."

Miki looked out the large glass window. "Christ, look at that girl's bike. She should be dead."

Marrec looked at the bike and his eyes narrowed. "She's walking?"

"Believe it or not," Sara answered. "Angelina took her to the bathroom."

Angelina returned to her two friends. "She's in there now. I'm patiently waiting to hear a thud."

"I'll go check her bike," Marrec muttered as he moved toward the exit.

After about ten minutes, the girl re-emerged. She had cleaned off her face and hands and rinsed the blood and dirt from her hair. A surprisingly pretty girl–who looked like she could bench press a Buick.

"Much better," she announced. She looked at the three women who stared back. "Something wrong?"

"We're just waiting for you to pass out," Miki admitted.

The girl grinned. "Mechanic?"

"That's Marrec. He's checking your bike now." Sara glanced out the window. "But, honey, your bike is toast."

"Ya think?" The girl walked outside. Sara, Miki, and Angelina following behind her.

Sara marveled at how quickly the girl seemed to be recovering. Maybe she was on some new pain killer. She'd have to ask. She might need it herself soon.

The girl walked over to the mangled remains of her bike. "My poor baby."

Sara caught Miki rolling her eyes. Her short friend never could understand the bikers' love of their Choppers. The passion.

Marrec, who was still crouched beside the bike, slowly stood up and looked at the girl. Their eyes locked and they stared at each other. That's all they did. Just stare. Finally, the girl looked away. She looked back at her bike.

Miki nudged Sara. But Sara blew it off; she'd seen Marrec do that many times before. It was that "weird thing" he did. Hell, Miki did lots of weird things so she had absolutely no room to judge.

"Where did you crash anyway?" Angelina asked.

The girl knelt down beside the mangled metal. "Don't know. I guess about two miles back."

The friends exchanged glances.

"How did you get your bike here?"

"Dragged it." The girl's head tilted to the side as Marrec turned to face the parking lot entrance.

"Wait a minute." Miki didn't even bother trying to hide her disbelief. "You expect us to believe that you dragged that thing here? In your condition? Bullshit," she finished flatly.

Sara and Angelina exchanged glances. As always, Miki was as subtle as a brick to the head.

But the girl ignored her. "Good." She seemed relieved. "They're here." She stood up and walked to the front of the parking lot as four beautiful, tricked-out Choppers, all manned by women, pulled in and halted next to the girl.

"Check it out." Angelina elbowed her friends. "Lesbians. In Texas."

"Would you shut up." Sara chuckled.

"Julie, glad to see you're not dead," spoke the oldest of the women. Her blond hair streaked with gray and her face covered in age lines. She was probably gorgeous once. Now she was just beautiful.

Sliding off her bike, she hugged the battered girl. "You sure you're okay?"

"Yeah, Casey. I'm fine." The girl leaned in and whispered something to the older woman. Casey looked up and straight at Marrec.

"No problem." Casey walked over to Marrec. "This your shop?"

Sara watched her boss's back straighten, his arms crossing over his large chest. "Yeah."

The woman smiled coldly.. "Got a minute?"

Marrec observed the woman carefully. "Sara," he spoke without taking his eyes off Casey. "Go inside."

A startled Sara glanced at her equally startled friends. "Are you kidding?" she asked him. Marrec rarely ordered her to do anything. He especially never ordered her to go away like a ten-year-old child.

The look he gave her clearly told her he was serious. But before Sara could clearly and concisely tell him to fuck off, Casey intervened.

"Julie needs to get a new bike. That one isn't going anywhere. Could you show her what you guys have?"

Sara rolled her eyes at the lame attempt to get rid of her.

"Wow, Julie. Your ride is fucked." This from a tiny Asian woman crouching by the totaled bike.

"I know, Kelly. I know."

"Don't worry about it," the older woman offered. "We'll get you a new one here. Kelly's got the cash and cards. I think it's time to spend a little money."

Miki folded her arms in front of her chest. "Drug money, I assume," she queried smugly.

Angelina's eyes snapped open wide and Sara slapped her hand over her friend's mouth, as Casey raised an eyebrow.

"Why don't you guys go in and check out our stock. Some great stuff just came in," Sara offered.

With a nod of her head, Casey motioned to her females and they entered the store while she and Marrec walked to the edge of the parking lot, out of hearing rage. Once they were effectively alone, Sara and Angelina let out huge sighs.

"Drug money, I assume?" Angelina ground out between clenched teeth.

Miki looked at her friends. "I was just asking."

"Well don't! Don't ask. Don't query. Don't question." Angelina moved toward the door, then spun around to look at Miki. "And try *not* to get the shit kicked out of us by biker chicks. Think you can handle that?"

"Think you can handle that," Miki muttered as she went to follow her friend into the store. Sara watched as Miki grabbed the handle on the glass door, but she pushed instead of pulled and slammed into it. "Motherfucker!"

Sara laughed and felt her headache slip away.

Chapter Two

"So, what happened to your face?"

Sara grabbed Miki by her T-shirt and jeans before she could dive over the counter at the Asian girl they called Kelly.

Angelina leaned forward as Sara pulled Miki back to her. "You know what they say about curiosity? That it stabbed the annoying biker girl over and over and over again until she spit up blood."

Oh, yeah. That was subtle. Sara pushed Angelina back, too. Her friends had always been protective of her. It was sweet, in its own rabid-squirrel kind of way.

Sara looked at the woman. People rarely just came out and asked about her wounds. Not so directly. But there seemed to be no malice to her question. It was just a question. So, Sara gave her a very straightforward answer. "None of your business. So are you taking those shirts?"

Kelly looked down at the six T-shirts she was holding. "Uh... yeah. Sure."

As Sara rung up the sale, Marrec and Casey returned. The tension seemed to have lessened, but she could tell Marrec was still on edge as he walked around the counter, patting Sara on the shoulder. "Everything okay?"

"Yeah." Sara muttered under her breath, "And they're buying a ton of shit. I expect a bonus, old man."

Marrec smiled. "Greedy, bitch."

Casey stood in front of Sara, examining her closely. "Interesting scar."

"Un-fucking-believable," Miki bit out.

"Check this out." Casey pulled her mane of hair off her neck, and turned so that Sara had a clear view.

Angelina and Miki winced.

Sara stared at the healed over and raised rips across the woman's neck. They ran from the back of her left ear, across and down her neck, disappearing under her jacket. Sara sensed they went on well down her torso.

"Mountain lion," Casey volunteered. "Eight years ago. Was a nasty fight."

"You? You fought a mountain lion?" Clearly Miki wasn't buying it.

"It was either him or me. And in the end it all comes down to survival."

Sara thought about her father. He'd fought to protect her all those years ago and it cost him his life, but in the end she survived.

Julie, who seemed to be getting stronger and healthier by the minute, interrupted the moment with an announcement. "The males are here."

Four more bikes pulled up outside the shop. Sara could see the gorgeous chrome through the window. She got all tingly just thinking about having one of those bikes between her legs.

Miki turned to Casey. "Are these men *men* or chicks dressed as men?" Sara closed her eyes and Angelina sighed. Miki grinned. "I'm just askin'."

What walked through the shop door three minutes later, though, were clearly "men *men*."

Chapter Three

"You know," Angelina quietly stated under her breath to her two friends, "I was just thinking I need to stop by the butcher. Pick up some steak."

"I could use some sausage," Sara added. Then she and Angelina began giggling over the "hottie-hots" who just walked into Marrec's store.

"Aren't you two freaked out by these people just a little bit?" Miki quietly asked.

Sara watched the group interaction. She had to admit, they didn't act like any motorcycle club she'd ever met before.

A tall, amazing looking man walked over to Casey. His hair was grayer than the woman's, but it looked premature. There were only a few lines on his face. As soon as Casey saw him she broke into a huge smile. A smile he returned. But he didn't kiss her hello. Instead, he brushed his head gently against hers. Nuzzled her under the chin, pulled her hair aside, and licked the wound on the back of her neck.

Angelina missed the moment. She was staring at her hands and muttering about her chipped nail polish. But Miki saw it.

"Okay. Does *that* freak you out?"

Sara shrugged and answered honestly, "I think it was kinda sweet. Weird, but sweet." She was used to bikers grabbing their women's crotches and shoving their tongues down their throats right in the middle of the shop. It always seemed like they were about to take them right there on the show floor. But what she'd just witnessed, that was affection. Something she herself had never really experienced with the men she had gone out with over the years. They were nice, but she'd only ever let them get so close. There was never a time she didn't have walls up or, as her friends called it, "The Armor." She felt safer with it. But it also kept every well-meaning man at arm's length.

Another male came in. This one was blond and seemed closer to her age. He was as big as a house. Like a blond bear. All muscle and strength. He greeted a few of the females but mostly with a pat on the shoulder or a nod. But when he saw Miki it was like someone hit him over the head with a rock. He looked stunned. He walked into the wall.

Sara looked over at Marrec in an attempt to hide her smile. He'd gone over to greet the older biker as Casey spoke quietly to him. When she was done, the two men stared at each other and, finally, shook hands. "Name's Yates. And I really appreciate this," he said with genuine warmth.

Marrec nodded. "No problem. Just remember whose territory this is."

Yates smiled at that. "I don't think that's a problem."

Sara and Miki glanced at each other. Sara had never known Marrec to be so territorial before. Bikers came in to his shop all the time, but he never seemed concerned about any of them as he did this group. And these people looked positively kittenish compared to some of the hardcore criminals who'd walked through the doors of Marrec's business over the years.

Of course, all this had Miki's major brain power working on hyper drive. And she knew her friend was on the verge of saying something completely inappropriate…again.

Angelina, however, was putting on lip gloss using a mirror customers used to try on sunglasses. Sara had to admit, Angelina didn't let herself get worked up over stuff she couldn't control. Although that rather Zen philosophy did take years of court-ordered therapy to obtain.

Sara was thinking it might be time to take Miki out for a coffee or something. Anything to keep her from getting them all killed. Especially when the blond bear started wandering toward her, with the possible intent of trying to talk to her. Miki turned to Sara with a look of pure panic. "Tell me he's not coming over here."

"Not everyone is loved by Thor, God of Thunder."

Miki glared but still couldn't stifle a laugh. "I hate you."

Sara grinned and would have helped her friend escape true love, but *he* walked in.

He'd been outside checking out the damaged bike. He was tall. Taller than Yates. Taller than any of them, except for the big blond guy who kept silently staring at Miki. And he was big. Sara actually wondered how he possibly got those shoulders through the door. And at six-feet, there were not a lot of men who made her feel small.

Dark brown hair reached to his shoulders and swept across his face, practically covering hazel-colored eyes. He had several days' growth on his chin, and a thick muscular neck she could spend all day chewing and licking. He was dressed in black jeans, black T-shirt, and a black leather jacket.

He was, simply, the most beautiful man Sara had ever seen in her life. And she wanted him so badly she couldn't breathe.

He didn't notice her when he walked in, but everyone else did. The rest of the members stopped talking, stopped shopping, stopped moving. As one, they all lifted their heads and sniffed the air. Then they all turned and looked at Sara.

She couldn't understand it. She hadn't done anything. Hadn't moved. And she'd also stared at Yates when he walked in. Exactly what cued them in to her sudden need to be naked and straddling this guy, she had no idea.

As she pondered this, Angelina leaned over to her. "Um...hon, are we going to need to peel you off that seat?"

Sara, distracted from suddenly being the center of attention, turned to Angelina. "Shut up."

"You don't remember him," Miki chastised, her blond stalker quickly forgotten.

"Remember who?

"Tragic, black leather clad, biker guy over there."

Angelina started laughing. "Oh, my God, it *is* him."

"Who?" Sara snapped.

Sara realized that, after greeting the females of the group, he'd finally noticed her. His eyes locked on her and she actually felt her face get hot and the walls of her pussy tighten.

"The good Samaritan," Miki offered.

"I think your exact words were," Angelina chimed in, "'Pretty man is all mine.'"

"Just before you stuck your tongue down his throat," Miki filled in.

"And I believe there was some crotch-grabbing." Angelina shook her head. "Whore."

Sara growled at her friends when the insanity from the previous evening came flooding back to her. Too much tequila. Asshole club pigs grabbing her. And the classic Sara-drinking stupidity, where she did something she ended up regretting the following morning. Apparently, this time her regret was him.

"Oh, hell."

"But clearly he remembers *you*." Angelina giggled.

Of course he did. When a tall, scarred woman calls you a pretty man, and sticks her tongue down your throat…you remembered her. And if she had any doubt, the sudden grin on his face confirmed it.

"Uh-oh," Angelina whispered.

"He's headin' this way," Miki added.

"I'm in hell." Sara began to search for something, *anything* to do. But she was too distracted to focus. Her nipples had hardened. Her pussy was on fire. And she kept wondering what he looked like completely naked.

Naked with his head between her thighs.

Jesus Christ! What was wrong with her?

"Hi." His voice was so deep she felt like he'd just run a finger up her bare back. He leaned against the counter and lowered his head so they were eye to eye.

"Howdy!" Angelina piped up, a big smile on her beautiful face.

"Hey, y'all!" Miki said, her Texan accent suddenly ten times thicker than normal.

Sara hated them both. A lot.

But she wasn't going to let some guy freak her out. Sara looked up, a greeting on her lips. But it caught in her throat.

He was staring at her—well, more like smirking—with those beautiful eyes of his, and really it was all she could do to stop herself from giving him a hickey on that thick neck.

"Remember me? I'm your…what was it? Oh, yeah, I'm your pretty man. But I never quite got your name."

Sara could actually *feel* her face getting red when the entire room erupted into laughter.

But before she could say a word…or punch him in the face…Yates interrupted. "All right people, let's saddle up. Julie, we'll pick up your new bike tomorrow."

Marrec came back behind the counter and Angelina moved out of the way, so that he could get to the safe her long legs were in front of.

"You three–" Casey stood next to Sara's deepest, darkest fantasy and Sara didn't like it one damn bit. In fact, she wanted to punch the shit out of the bitch for standing way too close to him, which was clearly not a rational response when she didn't even know the guy. "Because you were so helpful today," Casey continued, "I'd like to invite you to a little party we're throwing tomorrow night out near that big park off the state highway."

"Kingsley Park?" Angelina practically knocked crouching-Marrec over to get closer to Casey. The woman did love a good party.

"Yeah, that's it," Casey confirmed. "I think you guys will have a good time."

"Or," Miki interjected flatly. "You could cut our throats and leave us for dead now so we don't have to make the trip."

Sara knew she was no longer the center of attention. Miki and her mouth had thankfully stolen the spotlight once again.

Actually, everyone was staring at Miki. Except *her* pretty man. He was still staring at Sara's face, but he did raise an eyebrow at Miki's comment.

Marrec quickly stood up. "Miki!"

"What?" she asked with that damned innocent smile.

Marrec took a deep breath, something the older man often did around Miki. "You guys, go to the party. Have a great time. I will personally vouch for these people."

Angelina answered for the three of them, "We'll be there."

"Great. Ten tomorrow night. See you then." Casey walked out of the store, the females following her, all loaded down with bags of Harley- and Marrec's Choppers-branded clothes.

"Let's go, gentleman. We've got beer to buy." The men moved out, but Yates waited. "Zach, let's hit it."

Zach stared at Sara for a few more moments, straightened up and followed Yates to the door. "Tequila, right?" Sara watched him as he moved, she couldn't help herself; the man had an amazing ass. "That's your drink of choice?"

Then he was gone.

"Sara's got a hottie on her tail." Angelina was practically frothing at the mouth.

"More like a biker...and they're on the List," Miki pointed out.

"Fuck the List! She needs to get laid," Angelina barked back.

Miki sighed. "Not if her last fuck will be a train pulled by some scumbag motorcycle club."

"Okay!" Sara grabbed each by the shoulder. "Marrec here is as close as I've had to a father since I was eight. I would really appreciate the two of you not discussing me and fucking in the man's presence. Do you think you two could handle that?"

Miki and Angelina were silent for a moment. But it was just a moment.

"Did you see the bulge in the man's pants? He's packing major heat and it's for her!"

"He's on the List!"

*****

She was much prettier than he remembered. And sweeter. She actually blushed when he looked at her. She wasn't all that innocent, though. He smelled her lust from fifty feet away–as did everyone else. What surprised him even more was his body's immediate response to it. To her. What was wrong with him? The woman wasn't anything to him.

Let her fight this battle on her own. Why was he even here?

"Cute, huh, Zach?" Casey sat on the bike behind Yates. Her arm around her mate's torso, her head on his shoulder.

"You're leaving your bike here?"

"Marrec will take care of it. So, what do you think?"

"I think that with all due respect, you should back the fuck off."

Casey grinned. "Don't take it out on me because you're afraid to make a move."

"Afraid to make a move? Really?" Zach shook his head. "I wish I could figure out what you're up to." He turned and looked at Yates' mate. The Alpha Female of his pack. Affectionately known by him as the bitch from hell. "You've never given a shit about what I stick my dick in to before, why do you suddenly care now?"

"I don't. I only care about the Pack. And, unfortunately, that includes you." She flashed him a grin as Yates started his bike.

"So what exactly are you hoping I'll do?"

Casey shrugged. "Follow your instincts."

Zach Sheridan watched them pull out, annoyed his mother raised him not to hit women in the face.

He walked to his bike and stopped. He looked back through the store windows. She was using her arms to haul herself onto the counter. What strength she lacked in her bad leg, she made up for in the rest of her body. She lifted her legs, twisted her butt around, and slid down off the case so that she was in front of the counter. Her friends appeared to be arguing, and she was standing between them. She was clearly trying to stop the fight, but the two women were in full swing. Finger pointing had just begun.

Zach straddled his bike, but he couldn't resist looking back one more time. Apparently she'd gotten tired of the fight. She grabbed both her friends by the face and shoved them in opposite directions. Zach laughed, causing Conall, who had been waiting for him, to stare.

"Those women are crazy."

"Yeah," Conall agreed. "But so cute."

Zach turned to his big, blond friend. He'd grown up with Conall and knew exactly what he liked. "The little black one, right?"

"Zacharias, I don't notice color."

"Maybe not. But you noticed the tight ass in those jeans."

"Yes. That I did notice."

"Did you also happen to notice the mouth that ass was attached to?"

"There's nothing wrong with having an opinion."

"If that logic helps you get through the night…"

"*She'd* help me get through the night."

"Shame she didn't even notice you were in the room."

"Unlike yours. Jesus, I thought she was going to mount you right there."

Chapter Four

Zach and Conall arrived at their temporary den a few minutes after everyone else. The women had done a good job of finding a place with solid hunting, a lake nearby, and thick woods that allowed for privacy. Julie and Kelly were already on their cell phones making arrangements for the following night's festivities. They had the best connections and could have the place set and ready in no time.

Zach was about to head down to the lake and maybe get in some hunting but Yates called him and a few of the others over.

"Well?" He wanted their opinion on the female.

"She's fucking clueless," Jake, a recent addition to the Pack, offered. "How's that possible?"

"We can thank that bitch Lynette. She raised her. So just telling her the truth ain't an option. She'll never believe it."

"But," Conall added, "they're already here. I could smell them on the outskirts of town."

"So then, the question remains. Do we just take her?" Yates looked at Zach. He'd been doing that a lot lately; seeking his council.

Zach shook his head. "I wouldn't. She's squirrelly. We take her now; she might snap on us. And the aggression's already there. She's about three tequilas away from losing it completely."

"Sure we shouldn't just put her down?" Jake asked. "She is seriously wounded."

Zach turned to look at him. He knew Jake was young, but he was starting to discover he was stupid too. And he knew the young wolf wouldn't try and stare him down. Jake knew better. He still had scars on the back of his neck from Zach quietly explaining his place in the Pack.

"That's not an option," Zach stated calmly.

"Fine." Yates nodded. "We watch her and we wait. But remember, we're on Marrec's territory. Be nice." He looked directly at Zach.

"What are you lookin' at me for? I'm a ray of fuckin' sunshine."

"You're an asshole."

Zach shrugged. "It's a flaw."

"I'm glad you're so comfortable with the real you." Yates smiled. "You take first watch tonight with Conall."

"Babysitting?"

"Every princess needs her knight." Yates walked off toward the lake.

Zach sighed. "Princess my ass."

*****

Four hours since they left Marrec's shop and Miki and Angelina were *still* arguing, but now they'd moved on to clothes. What Sara shouldn't wear and what she should wear. The party was twenty-four hours away and most likely she wouldn't wear any of their suggestions. But the two of them were like rabid dogs. Once they started arguing it was really hard to get them to stop. Sara tried to escape them when she closed up the store for Marrec, but they'd argued all the way over to her beat-up white pickup and got in with her. She was really glad she stopped keeping her shotgun in her gun rack.

Sara sighed and shifted on her bed, trying to ease the pain in her right leg. Honestly, the things she put up with. They were extremely lucky she loved them both so much. Otherwise, she might have killed them by now.

All this waiting was making her a bit crazy. It gave her time to think. To worry. Her leg had gotten worse the past couple of months and she didn't know why. It never fully healed after she and her father were attacked, although to the naked eye it simply looked like a badly healed wound. That's why she'd been drinking the other night. It was the only thing that truly dulled the pain and her brain. It had become a constant challenge for her to battle the voices in her head that told her nothing was right. Her body wasn't right. She wasn't right. Her life was a mess. Although it didn't seem messy. Boring maybe. She didn't exactly live on the wild side. That night of drinking was about as wild as she got, and the only thing she remembered doing was kissing a stranger. A really gorgeous stranger. He had the thickest neck, and those beautiful hazel eyes that just seemed to... Sara shifted again. This time not from the pain in her legs but the throbbing between them.

This was ridiculous. She was a nice girl. Not a whore. All men treated her with the utmost respect or they were cruel about her scars. There was no in between. They either treated her like a princess or treated her like a freak. He treated her like she was hot. But she wasn't the "hot friend." She was the sensible friend. Angelina was the hot friend. The reason guys became friends with Sara in the first place. Angelina wore designer clothes and expensive high-heeled shoes. She was the only woman Sara knew who would come to Skelly's on Goth night wearing a champagne-colored dress–her "signature color," as Angelina called it–matching heels, and a purse.

Miki was the brilliant, super-cute friend. She was the one who could diffuse the bomb in thirty seconds with bubble gum, toothpaste, and a binder clip while still looking cute in a belly shirt. Miki was working on her third master's degree because she thought the whole "PhD thing" was so overplayed. Miki was the one in high school who hadn't been able to use a computer or phone for three years "as per court order" and knew all the M.O.s of serial killers from the twentieth century because every woman should know the warning signs of a serial killer. "What if you're dating one," she'd always ask with a smile, just before giving some gruesome detail or two about some murderer.

And then there was Sara. Reliable, dependable Sara. She was like the Golden Retriever of the group. She was always the "good buddy" or the "little sister." She was never the "piece of ass." And after twenty-eight years she'd learned to accept that fate. She accepted it like the pain in her leg and the scar on her face. It was there and it was who she was. Might as well just deal with it.

But then *he* came along. Zach. She thought she'd dreamed that kiss. That amazing freakin' kiss. Part of her wished she had. The reality of it was getting a little too much to bear. It was stressful. She'd been drunk. Drunk-Sara was fun. Drunk-Sara set things on fire. Drunk-Sara grabbed groping men by the balls and squeezed until they passed out. There was no way

Golden Retriever Sara could compete with Drunk-Sara. And Drunk-Sara was a liability. She didn't remember much about the night besides the kiss. But she was almost positive someone had grabbed her while she was on the way to the bathroom. And it was the beautiful man who'd saved her. And for some unknown reason she was obsessed with his teeth. She just couldn't remember why.

Sara sighed. She could still hear her friends yelling. Something about a thong and how she wasn't a slut... unlike some people.

Sara scooted off the bed and stormed into the living room. No use yelling at her friends. Then it would be three crazy women yelling. Instead, she went to her stereo system and turned on some loud techno music from a DJ in Germany.

Miki and Angelina continued to yell for another minute, until they realized they couldn't hear themselves much less each other. They turned to stare at Sara. When she was certain she had their full attention, she turned the music down, but not off.

"Are you two done?"

"She started it," Angelina complained.

"*I* started it?" Miki snapped.

"That's it!" Sara yelled. She walked to her kitchen and grabbed three beers from the refrigerator. "Here." She handed one each to her friends. "You two bitches are making me nuts." Sara opened the ice cold can and took a swig. "Besides, it doesn't matter what I wear." She took another swallow of beer. "I don't have a chance in hell with a guy like that."

Sara went to her front door, determined to sit on her porch and enjoy the cool night. But Miki's cutting voice caused her to trip on the doorframe and stumble outside. "If we'd left the store, he would have fucked you on the counter."

*****

Concealed behind trees, Zach watched Sara's place. "I want you at her house," Yates had ordered after he'd argued. "Make sure she doesn't have any more surprise visits."

He hated babysitting duty and Yates knew it. But he put up with it...for now. Because everyone knew, clearly even Yates, that Zach would be making a move to be Pack leader. He knew he was ready. And he wanted it. He was just waiting for the right time to move. He loved Yates like a brother, but the man was getting weak. It wasn't age either. It was his woman. Casey was tough, but she was toxic. She was too human for the role. Wanting power. Her primary concern, no matter what she said, was not the Pack. But her standing within it. The females put up with her, but he could tell that wouldn't last much longer. His sister, who had been traveling for about a year, had a good shot at becoming Alpha Female, but he wasn't sure she even wanted it or would leave Europe to come get it.

That's why Casey's recent foray into the past was an obvious tactic to keep him busy and out of the way. She never cared about Bruce Morrighan's missing offspring before. They all knew Sara'd been taken by her grandmother after the brutal killing of the girl's father. And although Casey thought she could keep Zach away for weeks "monitoring the girl," as she put it, they never expected the Pride to actually be hunting the woman. Finish off the job they'd started so long ago. But Pride females were notoriously patient. They'd probably known where Morrighan's offspring was for years, but no one, absolutely *no one,* would even think about going up against Lynette Redwolf.

Why? Because the bitch was crazy.

A Native American and a shapeshifter, Lynette rejected both aspects early on. Instead she tried to become a "normal woman." She buried the Beast and stayed human. The fact that she'd come from a long line of shapeshifting shamans apparently meant nothing to her.

And her plan had been to raise her daughter the same. She'd had big plans for Kylie Redwolf. But Kylie figured out what she was by the time she was fourteen. At eighteen, she met her mate and Sara's father, Bruce Morrighan. His family dated back to the sixteenth Century. A tough Scottish clan of wolves that had done some serious damage to the land before they'd gained some control over their need to kill. Like Zach, Bruce was born and raised as part of the Magnus Pack. It was the only world he'd ever known. Until he met Kylie. Their mating was supposedly one for the record books. Their passion scorching the Colorado Mountains were they found each other. Bruce on a camping trip. Kylie trying to escape her controlling mother by working as a waitress in a local diner. Once they were marked and mated, the couple seemed to become more wolf than human. Staying in wolf form for days on end, they slept, hunted, and lived the majority of their lives as wolves. When Sara was born, the Pack's feeling was that she would certainly become Alpha Female one day.

But then Kylie fucked with Annie Withell, head of the Withell Pride, and all hell broke loose. During a confrontation, Kylie somehow killed the four-hundred-pound Annie and started a Pack-Pride war that continued to this day. By the time Sara was one-year-old, Kylie's torn and half-eaten wolf carcass had been dumped at the front door of the Pack's den.

Bruce had been inconsolable. And he, with the help of several Pack mates and against the Alpha leader's orders, attacked the Pride, killing two of its prime breeding males. Then Bruce took his daughter and left. Moved to Arizona. And everything went quiet, until the pair went on a hunting trip in an Arizona state park. No one knew the details, but Bruce's human remains were found beside the campsite.

Sara was missing for a day, but was eventually located twenty miles from where her father's body was found, unconscious next to a riverbank. Her face torn like it had hit jagged rock. Her leg ripped as if hit by an animal paw. She was in a coma for a week and no one thought she would survive. When members of the Pack went to the hospital to visit and protect her, they were greeted by Lynette. She took Pack members outside of the hospital to "chat." But her chat consisted of her attacking them with a thin blade. She got one Pack member in the shoulder, another in the back and a female in the face, taking off part of her ear. She left them all alive, but told them never to come back. That the "bitch" was hers now.

After that, Lynnette took the girl to this tiny town in the middle of nowhere Texas and raised her. The ultimate revenge against a daughter who had abandoned her and represented everything she hated about herself.

But why would Lynette bring Sara here? To a town run by wolves? Marrec was a shapeshifter and so was half the town. He protected and loved Sara like his own daughter. He could have turned her himself. So why hadn't he? Or was it once again the wrath of Lynette, clearly a psychotic bitch to the extreme, which kept him from putting his life and the life of his Pack at risk for a girl who, in the end, was not his blood?

Yet his loyalty to Sara was still strong. Palpable, in fact. Apparently Casey had to do some fast talking to keep the guy from pushing them off his territory. Maybe now that the old bitch was dead, Marrec decided it was time for Sara to know the truth. To know who and what she was. Perhaps he'd waited until he felt the death of her grandmother was far enough away, she could more easily learn to accept what she was. But before he had the chance, they'd shown up. The Magnus Pack. Her true father's Pack. Maybe to Marrec having her turned by her father's Pack seemed only fitting. So, in the end, he'd allowed them all to stay without much trouble.

Now here Zach sat with only Conall to keep him company, watching a house on a Friday night. He could see into it through a window, but all he saw were the two other females still arguing. Boy, could those broads go and go and go.

Sara had disappeared and he was really starting to miss seeing her. Although Conall was enjoying his view of Miki. The angrier she got the more Zach could smell Conall's desire for her. *Twisted.* Conall quietly padded by, his white-blond fur ruffled by the light wind coming from the East.

Zach scratched his muzzle with one paw as German techno music hit his ears. *Good* German techno music. In the boonies of Texas? He looked back at the house. The music died after a few moments and a couple of minutes later Sara stumbled onto the porch. She was wearing baggy sweats and a big hockey shirt. He heard her friends laughing, but he refused to believe they were laughing at the fact she seemed to have trouble walking. He'd hate to have to kick their asses.

But Sara was laughing too and he realized he was getting protective over a woman he didn't know and really didn't want to know. He had no plans of getting all tangled up with a female. Especially not this female.

He was a good one-hundred feet from the house, but he could hear her clearly. "I hate both of you!" she yelled as her friends came out on to the porch. Sara straddled the banister and, boy, did he envy that banister, while Miki hit the swing and Angelina sat on the stairs.

He marveled at how they went from full-on screaming one minute to hysterical laughter the next.

And he wished he could have heard what they had just been talking about in the house because Sara's next sentence completely intrigued him...

"But forget about me, I think Miki's the one with the chance to get laid."

"Don't start," Miki warned.

"He was like the dog," Angelina offered, "and you were like the chew toy that was on top of the cabinet. He couldn't quite reach it but he wouldn't stop staring at it." Sara burst into another round of laughter while Miki looked like she was about to lob her beer at Angelina but changed her mind and took a long swig instead.

"But," Angelina continued, "no one seemed the least bit interested in me."

"Well, of course not," Sara answered. "You have no obvious physical flaws and you weren't balls-out rude. Why would they be interested in you?"

The three women laughed some more at that. Then they drank their beer and quietly listened to the night. Zach couldn't take his eyes off Sara. She was so beautiful. And when she leaned back and stretched, a low growl coming from her throat that he felt more than heard, it took all his control not to charge over there and drag her beautiful ass back into the house and to her bed.

*****

"We should go hunting next week," Angelina offered. "Work off some of that aggression."

"Yeah, Miki."

"She's talking to you, bonehead."

Sara was floored. "What are you guys talking about?"

"Oh, come on. When you told that biker last week you were going to shove your fist up his ass?"

"He touched my tits."

"You've got big tits," Miki muttered.

"And when you threw that helmet at Marrec?"

"I missed."

"Barely," Miki added.

"Would you shut up," Sara snapped at Miki. Both her friends smirked at her, and Sara realized that they were right. She had been aggressive lately. Really aggressive. Perhaps dangerously so. But she didn't know why.

She took a deep breath. "Sorry. I'm sorry. I'm just stressed."

"Your leg," Angelina gently asked.

"It's nothing serious," she lied. "It'll be fine." She smiled at her friends. "Really."

Angelina and Miki exchanged glances, but moved on.

"So," Angelina offered, "that Zach's quite a piece of ass, huh?"

"We are so not having that conversation!" The three friends laughed as Sara felt her face get red. "Bitches."

*****

Zach gave Conall a wolfish grin. He had to admit, it was nice being referred to as a "piece of ass."

He watched Sara lie to her friends. And she was lying. The girl was in a momentous amount of pain, but she hid it amazingly well. She was a lot stronger than any of the Pack, himself included, was giving her credit for.

Sara finished her beer. "I'm thinking about getting a new dog." Well that came out of nowhere. And based on her friends' reactions they were none too pleased.

"Oh, for fuck sake," Miki snapped.

"I thought you guys liked dogs."

"I'm a cat person," Angelina volunteered. Zach had already guessed that.

"I like dogs, just not the dogs you get. You always pick some scraggly-ass stray off the street and try to make it a pet."

"You could get a cat," Angelina offered hopefully.

"Agents of Satan? No thank you. I like my eyes right where they are. In my head."

"Ladies." Angelina sighed. "Is this what we're reduced to? Are we going to be..." She wore an expression of utter disgust. "Pet people?"

"I can't." Miki leaned her head to the side to stretch the muscles, and Zach heard Conall give a low growl. "No pets. No plants."

Sara smirked. "You mean anything that needs actual care?"

Miki gave a dismissive wave of her hand. "It's just too much to remember."

"Please tell me you're not going to breed."

*****

"It's just," Angelina began to whine and Sara knew what was coming, "I don't want us to end up three old maids, living in a house with cats."

"That won't happen." Miki stretched her whole body. She did love to forecast. "I'll be kidnapped by Black Ops. They'll be hoping to use my brilliance against this government's enemies." Sara and Angelina looked at each other.

"Your brilliance?" Sara asked.

Miki ignored her, like she always did during this conversation. "Angelina will marry someone very wealthy but cold. She'll last about ten years, then she'll plot, plan, and execute his murder. Get away with it. And marry a younger man. Maybe even his son."

"Hey!" Angelina never liked that future prediction.

"And Sara..." Miki looked at her friend. "Well, she doesn't like cats."

"I don't like cats? That's the best you can do? How about 'And Sara will live happily ever after with Mr. Doesn't-get-on-her-nerves-too-much.' Why can't I have that?"

"You're too picky."

"It's not my fault that scarred, damaged women aren't high on the market. And I'm not going to take any old thing thrown at me."

"You're too picky," Angelina confirmed. "Because I remember a few interested individuals that weren't too bad. Trevor."

"Too strict," Miki explained.

"Fred."

"Too neat."

"Bobby Joe."

"Too tall."

"Mike."

"Too short."

"Okay. Okay. I get it." Sara didn't need to hear this. All those bad attempts at relationships had happened years ago. The well had been quite dry for some time.

"Wait. There's still my personal favorite. Kenny Ray."

"Too nice."

"Nice? He said I was boring. How is that nice?"

Angelina gave a wicked smile. "Too nice in bed."

"Oh. Yeah. He was." Sara shuddered. "Yuck." She remembered actually throwing him out of bed. Out of bed and across the room. Odd. Maybe she was drinking that night too.

"I bet Zach's not nice." Angelina's smile became more wicked, if that were possible. "I bet he's not nice at all. In bed or out."

"He's on the List," Miki reminded them.

"But he doesn't look like a biker, does he? You know, he actually looks like he bathes. Besides, I'm not talking marriage. I'm talking about getting control of your aggression."

Sara looked at her friend of twenty years. "Dear God, woman! Are you talking about him *fucking* the aggression out of me?"

The three women began to laugh hysterically. "I'm not seeing the problem here, people. You get in. Do what you have to do and get out."

"That's it!" Sara cut them off. "We're not having this discussion anymore."

"You should just think about it. That's all I'm saying."

"No. I'm a nice girl. I'm not a whore." Her friends didn't say a word. "I'm not."

Angelina shrugged. "You just keep believing that."

Sara tossed her empty beer can, just missing her friend's head.

Angelina didn't even turn around. Instead she looked out into the darkness. "It's such a beautiful night."

Sara grinned. "Yup." Her grin widened. "And it's about that time."

Miki closed her eyes. "I hate this."

Sara leaned back. "Sssh. Listen."

*****

A moment later, Zach heard the first howl. Full-bloods. He'd smelled them as soon as he stepped onto her property. He'd been waiting for hours for them to give him a hard time about being in their territory and for not being full wolf but a mystical hybrid of both wolf and human–they were amazingly snobby about that sort of thing. But, to his surprise, they still hadn't bothered him or Conall. Maybe the full-bloods knew they were there to protect Sara.

Because when they howled, their howls were for Sara and Sara alone.

Miki cringed. Angelina looked unimpressed as she still rocked to the German techno coming from the house. But Sara's eyes were closed and she was smiling. Then, she howled back.

"Sara," Miki warned with a laugh. "I swear to God, those things come over here, I'm leaving your ass out here."

Sara's smile didn't change. "Pussy," she muttered. Then she howled again. The wolves answered. And all Zach wanted to do was go to her. To heed her call.

Angelina wrinkled up her pretty nose. "Aren't you worried they'll come down here looking for who's howling back?"

Sara shrugged. "I find them on my porch all the time." At that, Miki jumped up and went into the house. "They never give me any trouble, but I always remember they're wild animals. And this is probably more their territory than mine."

Miki stood behind the living room window. She opened it probably so that she was still part of the conversation, but could easily close it if "they" decided to attack. She had no idea, however, that window couldn't protect her from shit.

"Besides, they've always made me feel safe. And when I had to live here with her, they always made me feel like I wasn't alone."

"Well," Miki advised, "now you've got us." Sara and Angelina turned and looked at their friend. "See?" She held up a cordless phone. "Nine-one-one is just a quick dial away."

"That's it. We're done." Angelina stood up abruptly and brushed off her rear with a well-manicured hand. "Let's meet tomorrow morning for coffee at the bookstore."

"So you can get free coffee from me again, you cheap bitch?"

"And the newspaper. And it's *Mistress* Cheap Bitch to you." Angelina looked over at Sara. "Can we take your truck? Not feeling the walk tonight."

"Yeah. Sure." Sara looked at Miki, "The keys are on the…"

"Yeah, I know. I know." Miki disappeared back into the house after closing the window.

Sara slowly lifted her leg up and swung it off the banister. "Pick me up tomorrow first."

"You got it." Angelina sauntered down the stairs, heading toward the truck. "Let's go, Mik."

Miki appeared in the door, the truck keys in one hand, and a pump-action shotgun in the other. She headed toward the stairs, but Sara grabbed the gun from her as she walked back to the house. "Not on your life, missy."

"You call to animals and then you won't give me anything to defend myself."

Sara slowly limped into her house. "I've found that it's never the animals you have to worry about, Miki. It's the humans."

Miki headed toward the truck as Angelina started it. "I'll remember that when we find your torn, headless carcass."

Interesting girl, Zach thought to himself, and wondered if Conall knew what he was hoping to get himself into.

When the light went off in Sara's house, Zach figured it was time to settle down for the night. But Sara re-appeared on the porch, a can of soda in her hand. She slowly limped to the porch swing and just as slowly lowered herself into the contraption. Once she was sitting, she let out a deep sigh. She drank her soda and rubbed her leg while looking out at the night.

The wolves called to her again and, with a smile, Sara answered. But the wolves did not respond this time–Zach did. He lifted his muzzle and released a howl that tore through the night. He called to her. Zach assumed she would simply respond again as she had for the other wolves, but when he lowered his head, he found her standing. She limped over to the porch rail and leaned against it while she looked out into the forest. She looked right at Zach although he was sure she couldn't see him. She walked to the porch stairs and stood there. Debating whether she should go in search of that howl's owner? Maybe. Zach didn't know. He had no idea what he did would have such an affect on her. To untrained ears, his howl was no different from the wolves now heading back to their den. And yet she still knew.

Her internal debate was cut short, though, when she doubled-over in pain. She gripped her leg and clenched her jaw, holding onto the porch rail until the worst of the pain seemed to pass. When she looked up again, he could see the tears in her eyes from where she stood. She was no longer thinking about that howl and the howl's owner. He knew deep in his gut, she was thinking about death. Her death. Slowly, almost like an old woman, she turned and limped back into her house, barely putting any weight on that bad leg.

This time she didn't come back out until morning.

Chapter Five

"I don't know, guys." Miki poured cream in her coffee and stared at her two friends.

Sara sipped her hot chocolate and stared back. She'd already seen Miki's early morning reading material. A book on the world of motorcycle clubs was lying on the counter.

Miki's second job was in a local bookstore slash Internet cafe. This meant she had constant access to just enough information to make her dangerous.

"I don't think we should hit that party tonight."

"What?" Angelina snapped, coming out of her coffee-induced haze. When Angelina drank her coffee, she had the ability to completely tune everyone out. Especially Miki.

"We don't know these people, Angie. And I think there's something weird about them."

"You think there's something weird about everyone."

"Yes. And there always is."

Miki sat down on a stool by the register, her gaze focusing on Sara. "What do you think?"

"I don't know. I don't feel overly concerned."

Miki shook her head. "It's bugging me."

Sara didn't have time for this. When Miki had one of her "moments," she could analyze something until you begged her to stop. Begged. "Look, Miki, you can come or you can stay home tonight. Your call. But I'm going."

Miki's eyes shifted to Angelina, causing the woman to raise one delicate eyebrow. "Like you even have to ask."

Miki chuckled. "Fine. I'm going then. I can't let you two out on your own. But no drinking, Sara. I need you to be rational."

"Good luck with that." The mug of hot chocolate was halfway to Sara's lips when his lightly sarcastic voice stopped her. "The rational part that is."

Sara looked up and there he was. Leaning against the door jam, quietly watching her. The morning sun was at his broad back, lightening his dark brown hair, and setting off his hazel eyes. He was once again in jeans and a black T-shirt emblazoned with a logo for a band she'd never heard of. His big arms were crossed in front of his even bigger chest and when he smiled at her he showed gleaming white teeth.

The man simply looked gorgeous without even trying. She hated him.

"What are you doing here?" Sara bit out before she could stop herself.

"That's not very friendly. I thought Texans were friendly."

"Texans are. But I'm not."

Angelina quickly cut in, "So that party tonight, lots of people going to be there?"

Sara stared straight at Zach. He wouldn't turn away, so she didn't either. That went on for about a minute until his large blond friend, who was bringing up the rear, slammed into Zach's back. "Where's the coffee? I'm dyin'."

There was no way those two huge specimens were getting through the door at the same time, so the blond simply forced his way past Zach into the shop, making a direct line for Miki at the counter.

It was Sara's turn to smile as Zach was forced to move out of his friend's way. But when his eyes once again focused on hers, Sara's breath caught in her throat and she felt her clit start to throb again and her nipples became rock hard. She couldn't help it. Those damn eyes tore right through her. Sara turned away before he could see how much he was getting to her and took a sip of her now tepid chocolate. She couldn't even taste it.

The big blond bear stood at the counter staring at Miki.

Miki stared back at him. But she looked like a skittish colt that might bolt at any moment. "Do you actually want something?" she asked carefully.

"What?"

Miki looked at her friend. "Okay, Sara?"

Sara heard the desperation in her voice. *Poor thing.* Sara sighed to herself. Miki simply didn't know how to handle someone who actually liked her.

Of course, Miki would probably say the same about her.

"Want something? Oh, yeah." He cleared his throat. "Two large coffees to go. Please."

Miki turned away so fast to fill his order she banged into the counter. Sara could see Angelina's body shaking with silent laughter, while Sara dug her fingernails into the palm of her hand to keep from embarrassing poor Miki any more than she'd embarrassed herself.

"So you guys coming tonight?" the blond stalker asked Miki's back as Zach slowly closed the space between him and Sara. Her back was still to him, but she felt him. Felt him getting closer to her. Felt her body respond. She was terrified he'd touch her. And terrified he wouldn't. And all that "terror" was making her unbelievably wet.

"Wouldn't miss it," Angelina answered, probably because she knew Miki wouldn't. But typical Angelina, she didn't even notice the two gorgeous men right in front of her. Instead, she was flipping through one of those fashion magazines Sara found blindingly boring. Some people called Angelina cold. Sara just called her finicky. Funny thing was, for the first time Sara could remember, neither of these men seemed to notice Angelina. "Thor" couldn't stop staring at Miki. And Zach, for some bizarre reason, wouldn't stop staring at her. Even though her back was to him, she felt his eyes on her. Traveling down her body, her chest, her arms, her legs. But she kept asking herself why? What could he possibly see in her? It was making her crazy and distrustful, which thankfully was helping her control her desire to take his cock in her mouth.

What is wrong with you?

Angelina tossed the magazine aside and stood up. "I've got to get to work." She grabbed her bag and headed toward the door.

"Wait! Don't leave me!" Sara barked loudly before she had a chance to stop herself. They all turned to stare at her. She cleared her throat. "I'm going to be late for work. So I better leave with you."

Angelina looked startled. "Since when do you care about being on time...ow!" Sara grabbed Angelina's arm and forced her out of the store.

"*You're both leaving?*" Miki yelled after them, but Sara kept going. She'd have to apologize to Miki later.

Once Sara dragged her friend to the corner, Angelina snatched her arm away. "*What is it with you?*" she demanded, rubbing the red spot Sara had caused while desperately clutching her friend.

"Nothing," she snapped back.

Angelina gave a dazzling smile. "He's getting to you."

"Who?"

Her friend nodded back to the bookstore. "You know, Mr. Not Nice."

Sara growled in annoyance and turned to make her way up to Marrec's shop.

"Don't worry," Angelina yelled after her. "I won't tell!"

Without turning around, Sara raised her middle finger high into the air and did her best to ignore the laughter that followed.

*****

"She makes great coffee, huh?" Conall asked as he slowly sipped the French-roasted brew. The pair sat on a bench across the street from the bookstore, Zach's body still throbbing from having Sara's hot little ass in his sights. No one had a right to be that cute so early in the morning.

"Yeah. She sure does." Zach took a healthy sip. "But she's still Satan."

Conall smiled. "Then I guess I'll just have to burn."

Zach shook his head. His friend sure did have it bad for a woman who went screaming beyond the realm of blunt. *Well, whatever floats your boat.*

Like Sara. Sara floated his boat. She was such a ripe piece of ass. Well, she was more than that, and hearing her and her friends talk about him last night like a side of beef wasn't helping. Because Angelina was right. He wasn't nice, in bed or out. And he had the feeling Sara could handle that. Would be in to that. Would be in to him. So that he could be inside of her.

But he wasn't about to get caught in that trap. End up like Yates, with some petty, power-hungry bitch as his mate. Why? So he could breed? The Pack hadn't been the same since Casey came along. Not that Zach was considered the fun one of the Pack, but he enjoyed everyone else having fun. Now, no one really laughed anymore. Or just enjoyed themselves, as wolves often liked to do. The situation even forced his sister to move to their European operations just to get away from what she called "that fun funeral feeling" the den now had. Casey brought a pall over the Magnus Pack he would never really be able to forgive the woman for.

He just didn't get it. They were all human enough to just fuck and go. He never understood why Yates hadn't. As much as some of them wanted to believe it, they weren't full wolves. They were human, too. They had the power of choice. He decided he wanted to be Alpha Male. He decided he was going to buy this T-shirt. And he didn't go around attacking every bitch in heat. In fact, he went out of his way to stay away from them. He didn't want kids. He'd be more than happy to let the other Pack mates breed and then raise their little whelps to take over when he was too old or tired to hold the leash. But every wolf female he'd met wanted to breed their mate's kid. So, he'd decided, any mate he chose would be fixed.

But really, in the end, what exactly was the purpose of marking someone as your mate forever? At least full-humans had divorce.

Although he'd never admit it, Zach never thought about mates or mating as much since he came to this fucking little town in the middle of nowhere. All because of her. And it really didn't help she wanted him. Boy, did she want him. He could practically hear her clit twitching from where he stood. But what pissed him off was that his dick kept getting hard every time he saw her. Every time he thought about her. What the hell was that anyway? Even just thinking about seeing her this morning, before he even stepped in to the bookstore, his dick was rock solid. That was unacceptable. He didn't want any woman to have that much control over him. Especially Sara Morrighan.

She wasn't anything like Zach expected. In fact, she wasn't like anyone he'd ever met before. She was insane. Her and her friends. They were loud, rowdy, rude, and dangerously unstable. But they weren't a bunch of sorority chicks either. They were smart. Genuinely smart. But they also cursed like sailors and laughed hysterically over the stupidest shit. He knew he couldn't get attached to her. He wouldn't. He just needed to turn her and go. He had plans to make and a Pack to protect. No time to get involved with some nutty girl whose grandmother probably damaged her more than the Pride that scarred her face and body.

The problem was it sometimes took years to turn someone. To get them to face their true selves. It took years before they felt that surge of power, years before they could shift at will and hunt with the Pack. But, of course, that's what Casey wanted. For him to be distracted by a girl who wouldn't be comfortable with who she was for quite awhile. Twenty-eight years was a long time to be completely oblivious to who and what you really are.

Zach's cell phone went off. He looked at the caller ID and sighed. Casey.

"Yeah?"

"Hey, Zach. It's Casey." Dumb bitch. She knew they all had caller ID.

"Yeah?"

"I need you to pick up Julie's bike from the shop today."

Yeah, of course she did. "Okay."

"Great!" She hung up.

Zach shut his phone off. "Gotta pick up Julie's bike. Wanna come?"

Before Conall could answer his cell phone went off. Conall looked at the caller ID, smiled, and answered. "This is Conall. Yeah. Okay." He hung up. "Can't."

"That was Casey, wasn't it?"

Conall shrugged. "Sorry, Zach. She wants me to help out at the site. For tonight."

Zach sighed again. "Sure she does."

Great. Now he had to go deal with Sara and that old wolf Marrec. Well, maybe Sara was on her own.

Alone with Sara...yup. His dick just went hard again. He would have to do something about that. It was really starting to piss him off.

*****

"You are going to that party tonight, aren't you?"

Sara looked up from her chopper magazine and glared at her boss. He sat on the other side of the counter polishing off his chicken fried rice and beef with mushrooms like he hadn't eaten in three days. The coolest thing about working for Marrec, though...every day she worked at the shop, she never had to pay for food. "Maybe."

"Why maybe? Why not yes?"

"Jesus, Marrec. What is the big deal? It's a freakin' party. Not the prom." Thank God. Her prom turned ugly right quick last time with Miki and Angelina starting that brawl and all. Talk about a long night in jail.

"You know I'm worried about you, right?"

Of course he was worried about her. Marrec was always worried about her. You'd think the man didn't have six kids of his own and more grandkids than Sara cared to think about.

"Why would you be worried? Could my life be any quieter? I mean, nothing has changed for me in like ten years. Actually, I think Lynette's death has been the most exciting time I've had in awhile." Not a lot of wakes turn into a party unless you were in New Orleans, but everyone hated her grandmother so it wasn't really that big a surprise. "So why you should worry about me, I don't know."

"Because. You deserve more than what your grandmother convinced you, you deserved."

Sara rolled her eyes, shoving the chicken chow mein away from her. Maybe it was her annoyance at this ridiculous conversation, but the smell was suddenly starting to seriously bother her. "Come on, Marrec. What exactly are you expecting for me? That my two years of community college will lead to a high life of big business? Or maybe now I can go for that medical degree."

"You are such a smart ass."

"No. I'm a realist. Always have been. I have no delusions. Never could afford them. I just wish everybody would stop worrying about me. You know, I can take care of myself."

Marrec grunted as he closed the lid on his empty container. "Yes, yes. We all know how scary dangerous you can be."

"Well, you don't have to be so sarcastic about it." Okay. So maybe Miki and Angelina were ten times scarier than she was...but she had her dangerous moments. Just ask anyone who'd been around her when she'd been drinking.

"Just do me a favor, okay?" Marrec stood up. "Go tonight. Meet the people there."

Frowning, Sara shook her head. Usually Marrec went out of his way to get between her and a pack of bikers. Now he was practically tossing her into their lap. Strange...very, very strange.

"Look, I'm going. Okay? So just stop askin' me."

"Good." Marrec shoved his empty containers across the counter to her. "Thanks."

She watched the ornery old bastard head to the back of the store. "I guess I'm taking out the trash?"

"Yup. Ya are."

Grumbling, Sara took her and Marrec's lunch containers outside and tossed them in the dumpster next to the shop.

"Is that you, Sara?" she heard Jake, from Jake's Auto, yell over the six-foot-high wall separating Marrec's shop from his.

"Yup."

"Randy's coming over."

"Randy. Randy. Randy," she chanted in a high-pitched voice as a one-hundred-pound red-nosed pit bull came around the corner. His leash and pinch collar were still attached, although Sara never had to use them. His tongue hanging out, he trotted over to her and waited for his daily hello.

As much as it hurt, Sara crouched low beside him. "Is this my Randy? Is this my good boy?" She rubbed her hands along his flank. He growled low and lay down on the concrete on his side. She continued to rub his thigh and back. "Who's my pretty boy? Who's my special guy?" Randy, as always, rolled over onto his back and Sara rubbed his belly, continuing to ignore the growing pain in her leg.   She couldn't disappoint Randy. "Who's my good boy?"

"So, can I be next?"   Sara gasped in surprise at Zach's voice, but she needed to get that under control.   She hated the show of weakness.

"Um..." was all that came out before sweet, lovable Randy jumped up and charged straight at Zach, his teeth bared. Sara caught the leash and yanked Randy back, the dog's jaws snapping shut just inches from Zach's face.   But Zach didn't move. He didn't even flinch.   In fact, he stared at Randy as if unimpressed with the sight of the one-hundred-pound dog trying to turn him into a midday meal.

Sara, still keeping a strong grip on the leash, turned her head to yell over the wall, "Jake! I need you!"   She heard a vicious snarl and when she turned back, Randy had backed off, tail between his legs. He ran behind Sara–whimpering.

She looked at Zach.   He was still in the same position he had been in five seconds before.   Leaning against the wall, his arms crossed in front of his chest, looking completely unimpressed.

"What did you do to him?"

"Not a thing."

Jake came around the corner.   "What in hell?"

"You better take him, Jake."   Sara handed over the leash.

Jake took it, but didn't leave immediately.   "You sure y'all okay?"   He sized Zach up with narrowed eyes.   "Randy don't usually act like this, 'cept when he don't like somebody."

"I'm fine. Really. Thanks, Jake."

Jake gave Zach one more nasty look, and dragged the whimpering Randy back around the concrete wall.

"I've never seen Randy act like that."   She looked at Zach.   "He really hated you."

"But I'm so charming."

Sara gave a short laugh.   "Yeah.   Right."   She headed back to the store.   "So, why are you here?"

"Julie's new bike. I need to get it."

"Well, then, come on."

*****

Zach caught her scent as soon as he'd gotten out of the pickup truck the Pack brought with them just for hauling stuff around. He followed it to the side of the shop, but never expected to find her lathering up some pit bull. Shamelessly, in fact.

Who's my good boy? Was she kidding? Hell, he could be her good boy. Her *very* good boy. Or her very bad one.

As he watched her tight ass move into the store, he knew one of Marrec's Pack—*Jake, right?*—was watching him. He turned and snarled at the nosy bastard, sending his weak-willed pit bull whimpering for safety and causing Jake's eyes to shift away.

When he turned around, Sara was staring at him. "Did you just… snarl?"

"I have a cough."

"A snarling cough?"

"Something like that."

Looking truly distrusting, Sara went into the store and Zach followed behind her. "*Marrec!*" Sara screamed into the back. "Someone's here to pick up that girl's bike!"

"Gimme ten minutes!" Marrec yelled back.

As she perched herself on the stool behind the counter, she caught Zach's look. "What?"

"Are you always so loud?"

"You'd be amazed."

Zach smiled. "Kind of a screamer?"

She blushed and rolled her eyes. "Cute."

He liked it when she blushed—it looked good on her.

Zach leaned against the glass case. "You and your friends definitely coming tonight, right?"

Before Sara could answer, Marrec yelled from the back, "Yes, she is!"

"He doesn't think I get out enough," Sara muttered quietly..

"Do you?"

"Not lately. Death in the family a few months back."

"I'm sorry."

"Don't be. No one else is." Sara winced. "Okay. That was bitchy. Forget I said that. I mean, she wasn't that bad."

"Who?" Although he already knew.

"My grandmother. She raised me... sort of. Died about six months back. The last few months I've been busy sorting out all her finances and business. I just finished cleaning out her house a few weeks back... well, I guess it's my house now."

"Find anything cool? When my father died, my mom and I found a ton of cool stuff at their place."

"Some. Had to give a lot of it back to the government, though."

Zach frowned. "Give what back to the government? Money?"

"No." She started counting off on her fingers. "The M-16. The armor-piercing ammo. The rocket launcher. The grenades."

"Your grandmother had a rocket launcher?"

Sara chuckled. "Apparently she was expecting some kind of attack. She was extremely paranoid. I don't even know where she got that shit from. And you know what, I don't wanna know."

No wonder the Pride waited until the old bitch died. Even they couldn't handle a full-on assault from military weapons. Yates hadn't been kidding–that old woman had been truly dangerous.

"Did you get any money for that stuff?"

"No. I just wanted it gone. I have my daddy's old shotgun, which I use for huntin'. And Miki and Angelina gave me a pump-action shotgun couple of years ago for 'basic home defense.'" She smiled. "So, I don't need much more than that."

"You a good shot?"

"I'm okay. Miki's better. I've seen her nail a buck at two-hundred feet. Right between the eyes."

"That's a lovely story. Learn that in etiquette school?"

"*Texas* etiquette school."

He liked that too. She didn't shrink away from his teasing or get insulted. She just rolled with it.

"You work here long?" He looked around the impressive store. Marrec did some amazing work. There were custom-made bikes here he'd seen on the pages of some of his chopper magazines. They weren't just bikes. They were pieces of art.

"Since I was fourteen. Marrec said it would keep me off the streets."

Zach glanced out the window to what had to be the quietest town he'd ever been in. "Big gang problem around here? Lots of cow jacking?"

"We have all sorts pass through our little town, thank you very much. Bikers. Cowboys. The always dangerous rodeo clowns."

"Rodeo clowns?"

"Don't ask."

Zach shrugged. "I don't want to know."

"So, any other condescending questions about my town?"

"Oh, I'm not being condescending. I'm very interested in your tiny little town, with its tiny little people. I bet you guys even have a movie theater."

Sara barked out a laugh. "You certainly are a charmer."

"So I've been told."

"By who? Your mother?"

"She does adore her son." He looked out the window again. "I thought there'd be desert. Coyotes. Clint Eastwood."

"You're in Hill Country. We have rivers, canyons, and forests. You want desert, you need to hit the Panhandle."

Zach leaned across the counter and smiled at her. "You'll have to show me around some time."

"I have been known to go off alone with strange bikers," she responded sarcastically. "It's a thing I do. Like eating glass." He heard the front door open and she frowned.

"Oh, shit," she muttered under her breath.

"Well, hello, all."

Angelina walked up to the counter, a brown paper bag in her hand. "I'm not interrupting anything, am I?"

"He's here to pick up that girl's bike."

"The one who crashed?" Angelina looked at Zach. "How she doing anyway?"

"Right as rain."

"That's interesting." Angelina was thoughtful. "She's a mighty fast healer."

"That she is."

Angelina turned to Sara. "I just came to drop this off. Didn't want Miki to see." Sara took the paper bag and looked inside.

"Christ!" She slammed the bag shut and tossed it into an open backpack behind her. "I hate you."

"Just looking out for my friends." Angelina turned and strode out of the store. "See ya tonight, Zach."

"Bye." He didn't turn around. He was too busy staring at the blush creeping up Sara's neck and straight to her hairline. "You okay?"

"Fine," she bit out way too quickly. "Just fine."

Zach wasn't buying it. "Can I see what's in the bag?"

"No!" She almost yelled it. "Tampons."

"I'm ready!" Marrec called from his workshop. "Send him back."

"Well, you better go." She tried to shoo him from the room.

"You know." Zach moved toward the workshop entrance. "When my sister and I were teenagers, she always threw out 'tampon' when she didn't want dad to see our bag of pot. But you and your friends seem amazingly straight edge to me. So it just makes me wonder...what's really in that bag?"

Zach backed into the workshop as Sara's face turned a darker crimson. Then he hit a wall and turned around to find that wall was actually Marrec.

"Having fun?" Marrec asked, his arms folded across what might be a normal chest for a bear. The man was short but powerfully built. Red wolves were always a little "stunty," though.

"Loads."

"You know her father died when she was very young." Of course he did. That's why they were here in the first place. "And I kind of took his place. She's as close to me as any of my daughters. And I'll kill any man who fucks with her."

Zach wondered if he already had. "Good to know."

*****

Once Zach disappeared in the back, Sara shoved the bag filled with boxes and boxes of condoms into her backpack. She was going to kill Angelina when she saw her.

She had one friend throwing condoms at her and the other telling her men were nothing but trouble. But as much shit as the three of them talked, they probably knew less about men than anyone on the planet. They all had their own ways of keeping people at bay. Miki had her intense distrust of…well, everyone. Angelina had her fortress of ice. And Sara had her armor. They'd all destroyed potential relationships in record time and without much regret. And although they never discussed it, none of them ever really thought they'd find true love or romance or any of that other crap.

So why did Sara feel like Zach was somehow different? What was it about him that spoke to her on some other level the few men she'd had in her oh-so-tame past just never could? Why did she itch to touch his skin? To feel him touch her? What was it about this man that made her feel like she'd been waiting her entire life for him to come walking through her door?

What was it about this man that made her want to punch him right in the forehead?

*****

Marrec moved over to the bike he'd readied for Julie.

Zach kicked the door to the workshop closed, ensuring Sara couldn't hear the conversation. "I have a question."

Marrec leaned against the bike, his arms crossed in front of his chest. "Why didn't I turn her myself?"

"It would make sense."

"Her grandmother. The craziest bitch I've ever met on two feet or four. When my oldest boy showed interest in Sara, she set my car on fire. She said after that it would be my house."

Zach felt a growing sense of horror for this woman's self-hatred. He couldn't imagine his life without the Pack. Without being who he was.

"If only she would have shifted, I would have snapped her neck. But I wasn't going to kill her as human." Zach didn't blame him. Kill one of them as human, they stayed human. Kill them as beast and they stayed beast. In the end, much easier to explain the dead animal on your territory to the cops. "So, I figured I'd wait until the old bitch died on her own. I just didn't know she'd take so long to do it."

"She's in a lot of pain, you know."

Marrec sighed. A sad one from deep inside his chest. "I know. And her aggression is getting worse, too." Marrec grabbed a sheath of papers off the counter behind the bike. "To be honest, I think it's poison." He handed the papers to Zach.

"Poison?"

"The Withell Pride is known for dipping their claws in poison. Prolongs the agony."

"That's very human of them," Zach noted with disgust.

"But I can't get her near a doctor. Her grandmother made sure of that. The girl's terrified of anything medical."

Zach flipped through the bill of sale and other paperwork Marrec handed him. "What would she need done?"

"It's a little barbaric...she'd have to be bled. But one of the docs at the hospital is one of my Pack so it wouldn't be a problem." Marrec shook his head. "But not until she knows who and what she is. If we just turn her, I'm afraid of what she'll do. Maybe I'll talk with Yates about it. About the timing."

Zach nodded, keeping his expression purposely blank. "Sure. Whatever."

Chapter Six

The arguing about clothes started as soon as Sara picked Miki and Angelina up that evening. The moment they were both in the vehicle, Angelina and Miki started yelling. That was at six. Sara looked at the clock on the nightstand. It was now ten-twenty and these bitches were still at it. Well, she really wanted to go to this party, so she wasn't waiting a minute longer.

"She is not wearing *that*."

"And exactly what is wrong with this?" Miki asked as she held up a long, but very pretty sun dress. Where the hell Miki got that dress from, Sara had no idea. It definitely didn't come from either of their closets…and never would either.

"She's not a nun. She's a horny girl who needs to get laid. The least we can do, as her friends, is help her out. That's why she should wear this." Angelina held up the tiny black hot pants she still had clutched in her hand. Forget the scars on her leg, Sara wouldn't wear that fucking thing on principle.

"That's just trashy," Miki snapped. "She's not going out like that. *Ever.*"

Sara was done. These idiots would go all night if she didn't do something. She pushed herself away from the wall she'd been quietly leaning against and headed toward the door. Her friends stopped arguing as Sara walked by them. She didn't even glance in their direction.

Not willing to leave her wardrobe decisions up to these two psychos, Sara tied her hair into a loose French braid, threw on a green camouflage skirt that landed just above her knee, with a slit up the right side of her leg. Then she added her favorite old pair of black cowboy boots, her thin but deadly weapon concealed inside its leather, and a green tank top. For good measure, she even had on her black cowboy hat pulled low in front of her face.

She stormed out of her house, but not before yelling back, "You two bitches coming or what?"

*****

"*Little* party?" That was the third time Miki muttered that. It started an hour ago as they waited in a long line of cars heading to the park. Then they waited for a parking space. Now they were standing in a long line of people waiting to get into what Sara knew to be a huge all-night rave. A well-organized, well-run rave.

"Christ, would you quit complaining." Angelina was already grooving to the pounding music. "Just relax." Sara shook her head. The girl could enjoy herself anywhere–even in line.

It took awhile but they finally made it to the entrance. Large hulking men took money and checked for weapons, which seemed to relax Miki...at least a bit.

Sara stood in front of them. She was hoping this thing wouldn't cost a fortune. She only had fifty dollars in her pocket.

The largest of the men looked down at Sara. He stared at her and, for a moment, she was worried he somehow saw the blade she'd hidden in her boot. Instead he nodded. "Go on in."

Sara scratched her forehead in confusion. "I... uh..."

"What's up?" Angelina asked from behind her.

"They can go, too."

"But..."

"You're on the list."

Except he hadn't checked his list. He hadn't done anything. Just kind of looked at her.

"Sweet!" Angelina cheered. "Let's go."

Before Sara could ask any questions, Angelina shoved her past the men and into a huge clearing. In the center were a couple hundred people dancing. Booths selling food, liquor, and T-shirts separated the clearing from the dense forest the three friends had hunted in more than once.

Sara had never seen anything like this before. She'd gone to quite a few raves in her less than wild past, but they were always near or in Austin. This was her boring hometown. Raves didn't come out this far.

Angelina stood next to her and, her beautiful face flush with excitement, raised both arms in the air and let out a

"Whoooowho! This fuckin' rocks!" Grabbing Sara's arm, Angie yanked her right into the dancing, writhing crowd. Miki followed and for the first time in a long time, Sara saw her smile.

It had been a couple of years since the last rave they'd gone to together. Miki had school and two jobs. Angelina had her own business, although she never seemed to be there–"That's why I have a staff." And now that they knew there was no biker gang waiting to drug them, rape them, and send them off to Taiwan to be whores–Miki's contention–the friends silently decided that on this clear, chilly night they would relax and just have a good time.

*****

Zach easily caught the beer Conall tossed at his head without his eyes ever leaving the partying crowd.

"Crowd looks pretty good tonight, huh?" Conall walked behind Zach, his own beer grasped firmly in hand.

"Guess." Zach took a long gulp, and went back to scanning the crowd.

"Not here yet, is she?"

Zach glanced at his friend. "Who?"

"Zach, don't bullshit me." Conall smirked.

He was right, of course. Zach *was* looking for her. He couldn't stop himself from looking for her. He hadn't stopped thinking about her since she shoved her tongue in his mouth.

"Oh, her." He tried to sound disinterested. "Yates still wants me babysitting her. That's all."

"Yeah. That's all." Conall could at least *pretend* to buy his brand of bullshit.

"She's probably not coming anyway. Your big-mouthed girlfriend probably talked her out of it."

"I have to ask you not to call the woman I love my girlfriend...she's my future wife!" Zach shook his head at Conall's goofy grin. A goofy grin that successfully hid a predator. "Besides," his friend continued, "that Latina was definitely coming and I'm thinking she's not coming here without 'em."

Zach hoped Conall was right. He needed to see her. To prove to himself she wasn't anything but a distraction. A problem to be solved. Nothing more. *Yeah, right.*

It was the "Whoooowho! This fuckin' rocks!" that caught his and Conall's attention. Christ, these women were loud.

Zach looked through the crowd, his eyes picking up images others would never see. He caught sight of her quickly. The Latina was dragging Sara and the other one to the middle of the rave. This was definitely not their first all-night rave. They had no purses. No jackets. And they were prepared to sweat the night away.

The Latina–*Angelina, right?*–had her long hair in a pony tail, allowing the black bustier she was wearing to be seen in all its tight, form-fitting glory. Plus, baggy blue jeans and sneakers. And the thong peeking out from under her jeans was a nice sexy touch. The one with the mouth had on a tight belly shirt displaying a gorgeous set of abs he could hear Conall growling over, shorts, and hiking boots.

Sara sported a tank top, green camouflage skirt with cowboy boots, and a hat that on anyone else he would have said looked stupid. But it worked for her. Although he figured she wore it to hide the scar on her face, the logic of which completely escaped him.

Sara didn't dance. Her damaged leg prevented that. But she moved really well. Nothing elaborate or fancy, and her moves weren't exactly "stripper-hot," which he and Conall learned to appreciate over the years. But whatever she did, it made his dick bang against the inside of his jeans demanding release...release into her.

Tragically, Conall was not fairing so well. "My. God. She is the *worst* dancer I've ever seen."

Zach had forgotten there was anyone else at the rave until Conall spoke. He glanced over and took in Miki's idea of dancing. It was kind of sad...and frightening. But clearly she was having a good time.

"But," Conall added, "her ass looks great in those shorts."

Zach shook his head, the man was absolutely hopeless.

*****

After about an hour of straight dancing, Miki motioned that the water bottle she'd brought with her was empty. Sara and Miki moved through the crowd, leaving Angelina behind. She'd found herself a nice group of beautiful boys to dance with and seemed happy enough.

"Great music, huh?" Miki asked when they finally extricated themselves from the dancing crowd.

"Amazing!" There were top-notch European DJs here. Sara recognized several of them from music magazines and a few high-level Austin raves. How did some, to quote Miki, "low-life bikers" get DJs like these to come out to the middle of nowhere?

The pair made their way to the edge of the park grounds. The first booth they hit was manned by two tall women.

"Is it me or are a lot of these females mammoth size?" Miki muttered quietly, almost to herself. Almost. Clearly the two women heard her as they turned and glared.

"Two waters." Sara spoke quickly hoping she could avoid one of those fights caused by Miki's big mouth.

One of the women moved over to them and looked at Sara. Looked at her hard for several long seconds. *Uh-oh, I am going to have to fight. Fuckin' Miki!* Sara clenched her hand into a tight fist, ready to use it if necessary, as she closely watched the woman reach under the fold-out table and grab two waters and hand them over.

Sara, releasing a breath, went to pull cash out of her back pocket but the woman stopped her. "Take it. No charge."

Sara looked at the sign clearly listing water bottle prices. And the tiny bottles she held were five dollars each. This was getting weird.

"Why?"

"Take the water and go." The woman turned her back to them and returned to her friend.

"What the hell…"

"Hi." Sara and Miki turned to find Miki's big blond stalker standing next to them. He nodded at Sara but smiled at Miki.

"Hi," Sara answered. "Nice *little* party."

"Thanks. Name's Conall." It was like Sara and the other three hundred people weren't even there."

Miki nodded. "Great."

It was, in fact, physically painful to watch Miki and Conall stand there, with absolutely no idea what to say next. "Well…" Miki glanced at Sara, and Sara let her know with one look she was on her own. Mostly because she found the whole thing funny as hell…and cute. Very cute. Glaring at her, Miki decided to make a break for it. "Bye." Miki took her bottle of water and walked off.

Sara's head tilted to the side as she watched the dejected expression on Conall's face. Nope, she just couldn't help herself. "Well, don't just stand there. Go get her."

"I think she hates me."

"Are you kidding? She really likes you. She's just shy."

"Really?" With that, he disappeared into the crowd, searching for the elusive Miki.

Sara let out a laugh as she realized Miki would make her pay dearly for this tomorrow.

"Having a good time fuckin' with my friend?"

Or she may be paying for it a lot sooner.

He was behind her, his hot breath in her ear, as he leaned into her. He didn't touch her, but her entire body was on fire wanting him to touch her.

"I didn't…" She couldn't even finish her sentence. *This is getting ridiculous!* She forced her body to move away from him. "Look, I don't have to explain myself to you," she snapped as she turned to face him. Great. The sleeveless Harley T-shirt he wore, revealing large tanned muscular arms sporting tattoos on both triceps and his left forearm, so did not help her composure.. "And I'm sure your sturdy friend there can take care of himself."

"Against *her*? Are you kidding? That girl's mean as a snake."

"No, she's… Don't talk about my friends."

"Don't mess with mine."

"Fine."

"Fine."

The two stood staring at each other, and Sara didn't know whether to punch him in the stomach or lick the black tribal tattoo on his right shoulder.

In order to avoid both, she turned and walked away. She'd gotten several feet when she realized he was walking beside her. She stopped. "What?"

"I didn't say a word."

Sara took several more steps but realized he was still there with her. She stopped again, this time turning to face him. "What are you doing?"

"Living life to its fullest."

Sara's eyes narrowed. "Go away."

"Why?" Zach leaned into her, but still didn't touch her. "Do I make you nervous?"

She snorted. "Please. I've known tougher gangs than you people." She started walking again, but stopped short when she realized he was no longer walking with her. It was what she had asked for but she didn't expect him to actually listen. She looked back at him. "What?"

"Well," he stated softly as he slowly moved toward her, his muscles rippling. *Godammit!* Those rippling muscles were driving her absolutely crazy. "At first, I stopped because I didn't know why you were calling me a gang member. Then I was just watching your ass move in that skirt. That pretty much kept me rooted to the spot."

Sara rubbed her nose to hide a smile. "Sorry I insulted you. Do you prefer Motorcycle Club?"

"You do know that we're not some kind of biker gang, right?"

Of course they were. How could they not be? Groups of grown adults in black leather didn't move around in packs, living together and throwing wild raves if they weren't a gang.

"We just like to ride. We like the freedom."

"Then you guys are…"

"Business partners. We own and operate a bunch of clubs."

"Really?" Sara took a sip of her water as Zach dug into the back pocket of his jeans. She would love to dig into the back pocket of his jeans herself.

Jesus, girl! Get a grip.

"Here." He handed her a business card. It was on high-quality card stock and the letters were embossed, but all it had was his name and a cell phone number.

Sara held the card up. "And?"

"Only reputable business people have business cards."

Sara loved his sarcasm. It was so ridiculous. "And the Hells Angels have their own Web sites. They sell T-shirts." Sara started walking again. Her leg started to tighten up, but she desperately hoped she could walk the pain off. She didn't want the night to end. She was, as much as she hated to admit it, having a great time with Zach.

He was a fun idiot.

But she had yet to figure out why this guy was spending any time with her. There were women around this place who would drop to their knees at just a wink from him. She watched them watch him. And yet he seemed to be ignoring them completely. Ignoring them for *her*. She wondered what he was up to. She looked at him out of the corner of her high–dammit, what was the man thinking?

I'd give my eye teeth just to have this woman sitting on my face right now.

"Pole."

"What?"

"You're about to walk into a…" Zach walked face first into a pole between two booths. "…pole."

Zach took a step back and grabbed his forehead. "Motherfucker!"

"Don't be a whiner." Sara turned him so that he faced her, pulling his hands down from his face. "Here. Let me see." She put her hands on his expansive shoulders and lowered him so she could examine his head. "I don't even think you'll have a bruise."

"Will you nurse me back to health if it's a concussion?"

Sara smiled, even as her entire body tightened at his husky whisper. "No. I'll leave you alone. Naked. Food for the wolves."

"Naked, huh?"

"Therapy." She pushed him away or, at the very least, tried. "For many, like you, it's a viable option." She walked past him, hoping he didn't hear her voice catch, or see that her nipples were burrowing a hole through her tank top.

*****

Zach was doing his best to keep some semblance of self-control around Sara. But she wasn't making it easy on him. Letting him walk into poles. Touching his shoulders. Using the word "naked."

And the woman was completely oblivious to the hold she had over him. She was looking at everyone but him. Constantly scanning the crowd, looking for any sign of trouble. He realized while her friends partied and danced she watched their backs and her own.

What an amazing female. The perfect wolf. The perfect mate.

Zach slapped the back of his neck to stop the treacherous errant thought. Sara looked up startled.

"Mosquito."

She blinked. "Bet he's really dead now."

*****

"You know, we should go out some time."

Sara stopped. "So, let me guess. Is this 'get the townie in to bed' or do you and your buddies have a bet about who can nail the cripple?"

Zach turned and looked at her. Simply stared. But when that big grin spread across his face, Sara didn't know whether to run or just scream for help. "You are one mean bitch."

He didn't say it with any malice. In fact, he sounded kind of… turned on. Sara took a step back. He took a step toward her. "I *do* make you nervous."

"Bullshit." Well, at least she sounded like she meant that.

Zach's hand reached for her shoulder. Sara stood her ground even though she felt like high-tailing it out of there and heading home to her nice boring house. His fingers went to the Celtic tattoo on her shoulder, tracing the design with his forefinger. She felt her throat get dry and her pussy wet.

"You know," his voice was low, like a caress across her skin. "You are an amazing piece of work."

She raised an eyebrow. "I'm a bitch. I know it and I've learned to accept that flaw in my character."

"Sounds like you embrace it."

"And if I do, what do you care?" Zach's fingers slid past her tattoo and up to her throat. She fought the urge to flinch, thinking he was going to touch the scarred part of her face. She'd never let anyone that close to her. Not her friends. Not her ex-boyfriends–nobody. And she wasn't about to let Zach get that close either. Besides, she was feeling that desire again. That desire to lick his tattoo or punch him in the stomach.

"Nice hat, by the way," he muttered softly. So, it was going to be the punch in the stomach. Good. That she could handle.

Then Sara dropped to one knee, the sudden flaring pain in her leg nearly blinding her. She gasped for air, trying not to scream. Trying not to die merely from the pain alone.

But this was Texas. Someone must have a gun here. Surely they could shoot her in the head, put her out of her misery. She wanted to yell, "Somebody kill me!" But instead she gritted her teeth against just screaming blindly.

Then she felt strong arms wrap around her and a deep voice in her ear. "Hold on. I got ya."

"Get. Off. Me."

She heard him chuckle. "Get the fuck over it."

*****

One minute she looked like she was about to punch him in the face–he knew that hat comment would get her–looking more and more aroused the more he touched her. Then she just dropped, biting back a scream of pure pain. And before he knew it, he was lifting her off the ground and taking her away as quickly as possible. He saw the others watching her. Smelling her weakness. Hearing the cry of pain she was desperately–admirably–trying to stifle.

He took her away from the rave and into the woods he and Conall had just been hunting in a few hours before. They'd found a small shack that had been deserted for what looked to be decades and it would give her some time to get over the pain and get her strength back. He would be there in case she needed some medical attention or something. He was just going to be there as her babysitter. Just what Yates asked him to do. Nothing more.

Yeah, right.

*****

Sara felt herself being lowered onto something hard and sturdy. She opened her eyes, easy enough now that the pain had begun to subside, and looked around what appeared to be a less-than-pleasing shack.

"Where the hell am I?"

Zach lit a lantern someone left behind. "Feeling better?"

Sara looked down at the dirty, dust-covered cabinet she was sitting on. "Nice digs."

"Well, you know, we try." Zach stood in front of her. "So, feel better or what?"

Wow, he just radiated warmth and charm. "Much better thank you. I'm ready to go back."

"No," he stated simply.

Yup, she still wanted to punch him in the face.

"Does the pain get like that a lot?"

Sara shrugged casually, "No. Not really." He knew she was lying. She saw it on his handsome face. "Look it didn't used to, but lately…" Sara had to stop because suddenly she was crying. For months, she'd been fighting the pain and terror all on her own, not even telling Miki and Angelina. She knew her friends well enough to know they'd worry–and drive her crazy in the process. Besides, they'd insist she go into the hospital. Lynette had always warned her, "Hospitals only kill ya." And, except for the constant pain, she'd been remarkably healthy her entire life.

And what exactly where they going to do for her now, after all these years? So she'd decided to just live with the pain, and had. Quite successfully, in fact. Until now.

Sara buried her face in her hands and quietly wept for several moments...until he touched her. Not on the shoulder or her knee. He touched her scar. Problem was she had successfully hidden it under her skirt. Her sexy slit wasn't even on that side.

With a growl, Sara's hand shot out and grabbed his wrist before it could move further up her leg. "What the hell?"

"I needed you to stop feeling sorry for yourself. Only thing I could think of." She tried to push his arm away, but it was like steel and it wasn't moving. Didn't help he was smiling at her either. And that he had the sweetest smile she'd ever seen. She wanted to slap that smile right off his face. *Smug prick.*

"You know, it's amazing you lasted this long. After what you've been through."

"You being a smart ass?"

"If I were being a smart ass I'd say something else about your hat."

Sara tore the hat off her head. "*Happy now?*"

"Thrilled," he muttered as he pried her hand off his arm. Once accomplished, he pushed her skirt up above her scar.

"What exactly are you doing?"

"Nothing," he lied as he ran his hand over her thigh. For once she didn't feel any pain. Far from it. All she felt was an intense pleasure, although she was doing her best not to enjoy it. The bastard wasn't even looking at her but kept watching his own hand move over her flesh. Eventually, the other hand joined in to move along the back of her knee and the bit of exposed calf above her boot. She watched his hands too, marveling at how big they were. They had light scars, faded over time and were tanned from exposure to the sun. Nails clipped or bitten down as low as possible without hitting the quick. And now these tanned, scarred hands were slipping between her thighs and slowly pulling her legs apart.

She bolted straight up, but he shook his head, still not looking at her. "Don't. You're distracting me."

Distracting him? Was he serious? *She* was distracting *him*?

His right hand moved back to massaging her scar while his left hand went deeper between her thighs. His thumb ran along the seam of her ultra-fancy Jockey For Her bikini briefs, for about three seconds before he simply ripped them off. Sara gasped, her body jerking forward. And, before she could stop herself, she slammed her lips against his. Her tongue slipped into his mouth, while his thumb slipped between the folds of her sex. She leaned into his hand and his thumb slowly circled her clit.

Moaning into his mouth, her arm went around his neck, but he pulled back and pushed her away.

If he stops I'm going to wring his big neck. But he didn't stop, instead his hands went under her hips and roughly pulled her to the edge of the cabinet she was on. He crouched down and pushed his head between her legs. Grabbing the sides of the cabinet, Sara held on for dear life.

She knew she should stop him. She knew she should slap his face and limp off, her head held high. She should be home, safe–and alone–in bed watching another episode of "Seinfeld" for the four-thousandth time. She definitely shouldn't be here, leaning back, letting a stranger bury his head between her legs and ever so slowly swirl his tongue around her clit, taking up were his finger left off. She really shouldn't. But she didn't want to stop him. Instead, she snaked her hands through his brown hair and spread her legs farther apart. And then, to ensure her place as a slut, she arched her back and pulled his head closer into her. She felt him chuckle against her burning flesh and a low growl erupted from her throat.

Big hands gripped her thighs, holding her steady as Zach worked his tongue around and in her. No one had ever gotten her this crazy before. This hungry to be fucked. And Zach was doing it all with his tongue. Christ, what was she doing? Had she finally lost her mind? Maybe she finally had, but who was she kidding? Nothing in her life before had ever felt this good. Absolutely nothing. Her fears of the last few months, her pain, were all forgotten as Zach's tongue fucked her.

It was the way he did it. He didn't rush it or her. He took his time, savoring the taste of her. Eating her out like she had the most important pussy on the planet.

And when he began to swipe his tongue up and down her clit, the low growl he'd steadily pumped out of her exploded into a scream as an orgasm tore from her gut and straight up her spine. She gripped his head tighter as she came and came, and his tongue kept moving and licking, bringing on wave after wave of killer pleasure.

In the same moment, she felt a sharp pain in her thigh where her scar was, but it only lasted a second and was gone. Compared to what she'd put up with the last few months, she barely noticed it.

Panting, Sara slumped back against the wall, her eyes closed, her fingers finally loosening from his thick hair. He slowly pulled away but not before he licked the inside of her thigh which, inexplicably, Sara found really sweet.

Maybe she would go to sleep right here. In this dingy little shack. But the sound of cloth ripping forced her to open her eyes. Zach had taken off his T-shirt and was ripping it into several strips. She marveled at his body. Tanned skin stretched over thick muscles as broad shoulders and chest narrowed into a tapered waist. The bastard simply had no idea how gorgeous he was, or the affect he had on her.

"Looks like I scratched your leg a bit."

She looked at her thigh but he'd already wrapped material around it. But she really didn't give a shit. Right at the moment, she didn't give a shit about anything.

Until she heard Miki screaming her name a few hundred feet from the shack. The thought of having to explain this to her friends was just too much. Without thinking, she snapped to attention, kneeing Zach right in the face. "Oh, sorry," she muttered absently. She pushed him out of the way, slammed her hat back on her head, and charged out the door.

*****

Zach sat on the floor of what even he would consider a hovel. His favorite T-shirt in shreds and his jaw in complete agony from where her knee slammed into it. And he was busy trying to figure out what the hell happened.

He had one simple mission for himself when he brought her here. To stop her pain. It was killing her. He could see that as plainly as her cute little nose. And he figured he needed to try Marrec's suggestion of bleeding her. From there he decided explaining the truth would just scare her off, so he had to distract her somehow. Okay, simple enough. Since his hands on her appeared to make her quite happy, why not a little hand job? Hell, it couldn't hurt. Only five minutes out of his day. At least that was the plan. But the more he rubbed her leg, the more his dick got hard. The more she made that little sound in the back of her throat, the more his dick got hard. And then she kissed him. Like that first night, but she wasn't drunk. She knew exactly what she was doing and that made it even hotter. She wanted him. And before he knew it, he was on his knees, his face buried in her sweet little pussy. He could still feel her hands in his hair and hear that little growling sound she made...

Zach gave a growl of his own and stood up. "Fuck this shit." He angrily yanked off his boots and jeans. Standing naked in the middle of the room, he shifted.

A few minutes later, a two-hundred-pound dark brown wolf silently padded out of the shack. He smelled her scent in the air and knew exactly the direction she'd gone to meet up with her friends–so he turned and trotted off the opposite way.

Chapter Seven

She sailed through the intense question-and-answer portion of the evening: Where did you go? *No where.* Did you see Zach? *Nope.* What happened to your leg? *Just a scratch.*

She flew through Miki's twenty minute analysis on the group's business–some of the hottest clubs any of them had heard of in San Francisco, Seattle, New York, London, Milan–the list just went on and on–and why a bunch of so-called club owners would be in a little dinky town in Texas throwing a rave.

But it was Angelina's innocent "I had so much fun tonight" while they were driving home that Sara simply couldn't take the pressure any more.

"*I'm a whore!*" she screeched suddenly.

Miki hit the brakes of the white pickup, causing the vehicle to fish tail. It stopped in the middle of the deserted highway, across two lanes.

The three friends sat in the vehicle, not moving, not speaking. They stared out at the big, star-filled Texas sky.

Miki, her hands still gripping the steering wheel, glanced at Sara. "You're not wearing any underwear, are you?"

Sara let out a strangled squeal and buried her head in her hands.

Angelina and Miki burst out laughing.

"Bitches," Sara muttered.

*****

It had been a busy night for Sara. A slammin' rave, head from a stranger, and shit from her friends. But she was sure it was the mere three hours of sleep that was making her unbelievably cranky. She'd ripped poor Marrec's head off as soon as she got to work. In response, he ran out and got her a large cup of coffee, like an offering to some evil bitch goddess, then scurried away to his workshop to finish off some guy's order. She didn't blame him. She was being a total bitch and she knew it.

No, she blamed Zach.

That was a stupid name–Zach. He was stupid. Stupid big-armed, big-handed bastard. Both Miki and Angelina assured her she would never see the guy again.

"Honey, he's a biker. He got his wings and flew." That was after they arrived back at her house. During this portion of the conversation, she buried her head in the couch, her hands over her ears, but her friends weren't giving her a break.

"Would you prefer we lied to you?" Miki asked. "Tell you he's going to marry you and take you away from all this?"

"We love you too much to do that," Angelina added.

Yeah, sure. That was it.

Sara flipped through a magazine she found lying around the store. She figured it must be Angelina's since it had all the newest fashions, none of which Sara knew or cared about. But she wasn't really reading anything. She wasn't even seeing the pictures. All she kept seeing were those big hands and those beautiful hazel eyes. She kept remembering how his tongue tasted and the feel of his hands on her legs…between her thighs…and that delicious little "swirly" thing he did with his tongue…

"Hi."

"Nothing!" she snapped, for no reason in particular. She saw Angelina in front of her.

"Hmm, I wonder what you've been thinking about?" her friend asked with mock innocence.

Sara sneered at her. "Why are you here?"

"I was just seeing how my best friend was doing after her recent bout with promiscuity.."

"I'm tired and cranky."

"Clearly." Angelina tugged on her friend's jacket. "Come on. Let's get you out of here, cranky girl. I'll get you lunch or something."

Sara's eyes narrowed. "Did Marrec call you?"

Angelina turned on that dazzling smile. "Well, he's been hiding in the back now for two hours. You scared the shit out of him."

"Honestly." Sara slipped off the stool and grabbed her backpack. "I'm leaving," she yelled at the back door. "You can come out of hiding now."

Sara came around the corner and moved toward the front door. When she realized Angelina wasn't next to her, she stopped and spun around. "Are you coming or what?"

But the expression on Angelina's face startled her. She was staring at her like Sara had grown another head. "What's your problem?"

Now Angelina's eyes narrowed. "Honey, where's your limp?"

"My...what?" Sara snapped.

"I've known you twenty years, Sara Morrighan. And since day one, I've watched you limp that wide ass around this town."

"Hey! It is *not* wide!"

"And now, today, I just watched you practically skip to the front door. Pain free. What the hell's going on?"

Sara looked down at her legs. She took a few steps. Nope. No limp. Because there was no pain. None. Stranger still, even on those rare occasions Sara didn't have pain, her leg was always so weak she still had the limp. Now it felt like her wounded left leg was as strong as her right. And both felt even stronger than that.

Sara bent her knee and raised her leg up. She stretched the leg out behind her and leaned forward. No pain. No weak muscles. Just fluid movement.

Sara had been so late this morning and so busy thinking about Zach, she hadn't even realized it. In fact, when she got out of bed she immediately started limping out of habit.

"I don't know. It hurt yesterday. A lot."

Angelina was next to her now, concern written all over her face. She knew what her friend was thinking. Stuff like this just didn't happen to people like them. Random events of good luck, is what Miki always called it. In their world, people didn't win the lottery, meet the perfect man, or suddenly get better. And that meant only one thing...

"Oh, my God. I'm dying."

"What?" Angelina shook her head. "You're not dying, you idiot."

"Everything okay, ladies?" Marrec had re-appeared and was watching them closely. Sara opened her mouth to tell him she was clearly dying because her leg suddenly felt better and people always felt better just before they died and she just felt he should know. And to make sure her funeral was a tasteful affair, but Angelina cut her off.

"Everything's fine, Marrec. Thanks." Angelina pushed her out the door into the parking lot.

"Where's your truck?"

Sara pointed. "Over there."

Angelina took the keys sticking out of Sara's baggy khaki pants and pushed her over to the vehicle. "Get in," she ordered.

Sara looked at her friend. "I don't want a big funeral, ya know. Just something simple."

"Would you get the fuck in the truck," Angie snapped.

*****

Zach had just gotten back from hunting, stopping briefly at the nearby lake to wash the blood off his fur and paws. He'd since shifted back to human and, leaving most of the Pack by the lake's edge, he returned to the campsite to get dressed and track down Sara. He convinced himself it was simply to see how she was doing. To find out if opening her old wound helped her as he thought it might. But he really wanted to see her. He thought about her all night. Her smell, her taste, her hands in his hair. Her cries of passion and her growls of desire. He couldn't stop thinking about her no matter how hard he tried. Not that he tried all that hard.

Already in his jeans, Zach had just pulled on his boots and T-shirt when Marrec arrived. A few of his Pack was with him and as soon as he jumped out of his truck he made a direct line for Zach.

Zach stood to his full height, but didn't make any aggressive moves. Nor did he back down. But he knew they were in this man's territory because of Marrec's goodwill, so he wasn't about to risk that by ripping the old bastard's throat out. At least not yet.

But before Marrec could get his hands on Zach, Yates and Conall, who had yet to venture down to the lake, stepped in front of their Pack mate. Yates, being Alpha, snarled, his canines extending.

"Back off, Marrec." They may be in Marrec's territory, but Zach knew Yates would never let the man get near one of his own Pack.

"You tell that bastard to keep his hands off her!"

Yates didn't need any clarification as he and Conall turned to look at Zach. "Tell me you didn't?" Yates demanded with a sigh.

Zach shrugged. "It depends on what your definition of 'didn't' is."

At that Marrec went for Zach again, but Conall pushed him back.

Yates glared at Zach before turning back to Marrec. "Is she yours? Did you mark her?"

"No!" Marrec looked truly appalled. "She's like my daughter!" He looked at Zach again. "A very protected daughter," he growled out.

Yates sighed. "I understand that, but..."

Marrec cut him off, "Who's not ready to be turned yet."

Yates frowned in confusion. "Marrec, that usually takes years. No matter what Zach did or didn't do."

"Then why was she trotting around my store today like she was about to run a marathon? No pain. Just power. And guess what? Her friends noticed."

Yates sighed again, his canines smoothly disappearing back into his mouth. "Shit, Zach, what *did* you do?"

Zach wasn't ashamed of what he did, he just didn't know Sara would react to it so strongly or so quickly. "I bled her old wound, just like you suggested."

"I didn't suggest shit to you!" Marrec stared straight at Zach. "And exactly how did you bleed her without her knowing what you were up to?"

When Zach didn't answer, Marrec again went right for his throat. Yates and Conall pulled Marrec back.

Yates was clearly losing patience. "Marrec," he snapped as he pushed the man back for what seemed the hundredth time. "The bottom line is she's not yours. By blood or mark. So, I'm not exactly sure what your problem is."

"Did you ever see someone turned quickly? It's rare, but it happens." Marrec took a deep breath and once he seemed to be under some kind of control, Yates silently allowed him to walk over to Zach and face him. The two men stood toe to toe and, although he was a good five inches shorter than Zach, Marrec's power and why he was Alpha Male of his Pack was more than clear. "If something happens to her because of this," Marrec warned in a deadly low voice, "no one will be able to protect you from *me.*"

The men locked eyes for a few more seconds; then, with a snarl, Marrec turned and walked away. The three men watched Marrec's truck pull out of their campsite.

Conall gave his friend a sympathetic look, and headed off to the lake to meet up with the rest of the Pack. When he was gone, Yates rubbed his tired, blood-shot eyes and looked at Zach. "Let's not bullshit around, okay, Zach?" When Zach didn't reply, Yates went on. "We both know what Casey is up to. But I know that it's time for me to step down, no matter what she thinks or wants. I'm tired. And I'm burnt out. I just want to be part of the Pack. Not worrying about who is doing what. And I want you to take over. But if you fuck this up, and that girl goes down because of you... there's no Pack in the world that will have you."

"I don't care," Zach answered honestly. "You didn't see her in pain, Yates. She was dying." Zach paused for a moment. "And I wasn't going to let her."

Yates looked mildly surprised. He slowly nodded in understanding. "Fine." Yates moved next to Zach so that he was right by him, his voice low. "Then you better watch her. Because if she turns as fast as I think she might, she *will* go down and she'll take this entire town with her."

Yates left Zach standing there in the middle of the campsite. And for the first time in Zach's life, his first thought wasn't about the Pack or himself. It was about Sara. The thought of anything happening to her caused his insides to clench up and his brain to shut down, leaving only one thought. He had to find her. He had to find Sara now.

Shit. Dick went hard again. He would really have to do something about that.

Chapter Eight

Sara paced back and forth inside Miki's tiny apartment. She was anxious, tense, and extremely horny. This seemed odd, considering her current situation.

As soon as they left Marrec's shop, Angelina dragged her to Miki's. After banging on the door for several minutes, a clearly just-awakened Miki answered, snatching the door open. "What?"

Angelina blinked in surprise. "My God, where you actually asleep?"

"Yeah," she replied sarcastically. "I was actually asleep."

"Well, isn't that rare," Angelina stated honestly as she pushed her way past Miki, dragging Sara behind her. "You're not going to believe this shit," she announced. And before Sara knew it she was forced to act like a runway model, parading back and forth in Miki's tiny, book-filled living room to demonstrate how her limp had all but disappeared.

By this point, Miki was fully awake. "Honey, exactly what did that guy do to you?"

"I'm not answering that question again." Sara had given them the barest of details on her sexual exploits the night before. So she wasn't about to go into how she'd screamed and writhed under the man's tongue like a horny dog.

"Would you focus," Miki snapped. "There has to be a reason you're suddenly...okay."

Sara stopped modeling and faced her friends. "But I'm not okay. I'm dying."

"*What*?"

But Angelina cut off the potential insanity. "You are not dying, you idiot." Staring at her friend from the safety of Miki's old couch, Angelina looked Sara up and down. "In fact, you look as healthy as a fucking horse."

"Which brings us back to the point," Miki cut in. "What did he do to you?"

"I don't know. Nothing?"

As if rehearsed, both Angelina and Miki raised one eyebrow each as they stared at their in-denial friend.

Sara sighed and crossed her arms in front of her chest, hoping to hide her hardening nipples. *Christ, just the thought of him!* "Look, I'm not telling you about… you know."

Miki rolled her big brown eyes. "I don't want to know where his tongue was…"

"Dude!"

Miki barreled on, "But did he give you anything? Any pills? Anything to drink? I mean, fuck, Sara, it was a rave."

Sara thought back to that night. She remembered him rubbing her thigh, kissing her thigh, licking her… *shit.*

Sara turned and charged into the bathroom, Miki and Angelina close behind. As they walked in, Sara already had her khakis down around her ankles and was turning to the mirror to examine the wound she had cleaned off and slapped a large bandage on just that morning. With one move she tore the bandage off, revealing her old scar, ripped through with four new ragged lines.

"Holy shit," Angelina gasped as Miki knelt by Sara and looked at her thigh. After several moments her eyes locked with Sara's.

Miki shrugged. "They look like animal marks."

"Bullshit!" Sara barked. "How would you know that anyway?"

Miki looked exasperated. "Hello. I read *everything.*"

She left the bathroom, and Sara could hear her rummaging around her apartment, pawing through the huge number of books. After a few minutes, Miki returned with a huge, dusty tome. "Here."

Pushing the book at Sara and Angelina, the two friends examined page two-hundred-and-thirty-four of the *Encyclopedia of Mammals* and saw a huge paw print. "Front paw print of six-year-old gray wolf, actual size," read the caption.

"You see?" Miki demanded.

"See what?" Sara demanded back.

"It can't be," Angelina muttered, still staring at the book.

"Exactly." Sara momentarily felt vindicated.

"The paw mark on her leg is much bigger."

"It is not a paw mark!" Sara raged as she reached down to pull her pants back up. "You are both insane!" She pushed past her friends. "I'm outta here."

Sara headed for the door, but both Miki and Angelina grabbed her just as she stepped outside.

"Oh, no you don't, missy." Angelina pulled her back in while Miki slammed the door. "Until we know what's going on, you're not going anywhere."

And that had been four hours ago. Her friends still had no answers, although a lot of ridiculous theories were running rampant. So, Sara paced and paced and paced. The walls were closing in on her–at least that was how it felt. Like she was trapped. The apartment was so tiny. And she had all this energy. She just wanted to go for a run or something. She just needed some fresh air. What could be the harm of that?

With Angelina and Miki arguing in the bedroom in whispers, a few minutes on the porch wouldn't hurt anybody.

Moving silently to the door, she eased it open and slipped out into the night.

*****

Zach was about to howl in frustration when he got the call. For hours he searched for her. He knew she was with her friends, but he lost her scent once she left Marrec's. He tried her house, the two restaurants in town, and the local movie theater.

Then Conall called. "You better get over here."

It turned out "here" was the club he first saw her in. He had gone there earlier, but it was a quiet evening with just a few patrons hanging out.

But when he rode his bike up, Conall was standing outside with Kelly and Julie. Standing with them was a small group of patrons, wearing their requisite Goth black and leather. They all looked like they were waiting for something, but he was afraid to ask what.

He got off his bike and walked up to Conall. "Well? Where is she?"

"In there." Conall motioned to the club. "But you better hurry up. The owner's about to call the cops. I'll hold him off as long as I can."

Heading toward the entrance, he heard Conall's voice behind him. "Be careful, Zach."

Zach walked into the club and right into a bar fight. Several men already knocked out and bloody on the floor. But at least six other men still fighting. He looked for Sara assuming she'd be in the middle of it. She wasn't.

But in seconds he picked up her scent. How he hadn't caught it five miles back, he'd never know–it was that strong. He looked across the room. She sat on the stool watching the men fight. It hit Zach like a thunderbolt. They were fighting over her. And she was letting them. Actually, she looked as if she were thoroughly enjoying herself.

The men fighting were bikers. Gang members she'd probably known over the years who never paid much attention to her. Until now.

Okay. This is bad. But it could be worse.

Sara looked up from the men fighting in front of her. She cast around and he realized she'd picked up his scent. She turned and looked right at him and Zach felt his heart stop. The woman had been beautiful before but now...

Sliding off the stool she'd been perched on, Sara walked toward him, expertly avoiding the tangle of bloody men.

As she came close to him, she licked her lips and Zach wasn't sure how much more he could take before he lost the control he was barely holding on to.

Sara stood in front of him, a smile sliding across her full lips. She reached up and kissed him. Nothing fancy. Just her lips touching his. Then she abruptly pulled away from him.

"Have fun," she spat. As she moved away, Zach was hit from every side by six bikers who hated his guts.

*****

Okay. That was really *bitchy*, Sara thought as she watched Zach hit the floor. Every man she'd touched that evening had somehow ended up in this huge brawl in the middle of her favorite club. And she knew kissing Zach would send the remainder of these idiots his way. And yet she felt he kind of deserved it.

Christ, what was wrong with her? She had been out of control since she walked out of Miki's house.

Well, actually, it started off innocently enough. She went for a walk along the highway, enjoying the chilly night air against her skin and the smell of the trees. Hearing music down the road a-piece, she realized she was nearing the club. She figured she should go back to Miki's first; let her know she was okay. But, she reasoned, a soda would really hit the spot after such a long walk. So she went to the club first. But as soon as she walked in she knew something was different.

In the past, she'd walked in and out of Skelly's without anyone ever noticing her unless she was with Angelina. But as soon as she walked in tonight, all activity stopped. And every man in the place turned to look at her.

At first, she panicked. She wasn't used to being the center of attention. But as she forced herself to move through the club, she realized she wasn't scared. In fact, she felt remarkably confident. She walked with her head held up and looked every man looking at her straight in the eye–daring them to make a move.

That started off pretty simply, too. A couple of bikers she knew bought her a round of drinks she didn't touch. But rival gang members pushed them out of the way to talk to Sara. And that was all she wrote. She worried guns might be drawn, but it seemed that all the men felt the need to fight *mano y mano*.

So she'd sat on a stool and let them. Until she saw Zach. No, that's wrong. She didn't see him at first. She *sensed* him, and then she smelled him. And he smelled primal and oh, so male. Her mouth actually watered.

She debated whether to ignore him but, she thought, W*hy shouldn't the fucker fight for me, too?"* And that's where the kiss came in. She knew she had him as soon as she licked her lips.

Now, however, she was starting to worry. Zach wasn't coming up out of the throng of men. And she had no intention of going home with anyone else tonight.

She was about to start dragging men off him herself, until she heard an angry snarl and saw a biker she knew only as Ray fly by. Then another, and another.

In less than three minutes, Zach had wiped the floor with the biggest, toughest bikers she'd ever known.

When done, he turned and faced her. He was breathing deeply, his face battered and bloody, and already starting to swell in some spots. His lip split and dripping blood, she had the overwhelming desire to lick that blood away.

Looking at his handsome face, she had the intense feeling he was about to take her right there on the dance floor. Fuck her brains out in front of everybody. Not that she'd complain.

*****

Zach didn't know whether to fuck her or soak her head in the toilet. Both seemed like reasonable reactions to what she pulled.

But he smelled his Pack behind him, watching them both.

"Well, well. What a mess, huh, Zach?"

He gritted his teeth at Casey's smug voice. Maybe he would fuck Sara and put Casey's head in the toilet.

Casey leaned against the bar and stared at Sara.

"How ya doin', honey? You doin' okay?"

Sara didn't answer her. Instead she stared. At first Casey was smiling, but when Sara didn't turn away, Casey lost that smile. And Zach knew she wanted, no *needed*, Sara to turn away.

Without turning from her, Casey spoke to Zach. "You better put a leash on your girl there, Zach. I'd hate to have to break her in so soon."

He'd kill Casey first before he let the bitch touch Sara. "Breaking her in" being the euphemism they all used for grabbing a Beta around the throat and bringing them down until they showed their belly and learned their place. But apparently Sara wasn't about to be anybody's bitch. He caught the woman in mid-flight as she dove over the bar; her hands outstretched and reaching for Casey's throat.

Sara didn't like the way Casey was looking at her. Like she was challenging her or something. And she was standing a little too close to Zach for Sara's liking. In fact, the bitch was just pissing Sara off. She wanted to hurt Casey. She wanted to see the bitch bleed.

So what's stopping you? Her last thought before she went for her.

But Zach stopped her, his big hands grabbing her around the waist. "Sonofabitch!"

Casey didn't move, but she was clearly rattled. Her eyes wide as she watched Sara. And Sara seemed enough of a threat that Yates stepped between them.

Zach luckily had a good grip on her, because Sara was losing it. "You fucking whore! *Break me in? Fuck you!*"

Zach pulled her back, wrapping his arms around her body. She was shaking, but it wasn't from fear. "Easy," he whispered in her ear. "Easy."

His voice seemed to soothe her. He thought he might just be able to get Sara out of there without any more problems. But not wanting to show weakness to her females, Casey continued to stare at her.

Sara pulled away from Zach and went for Casey again. He caught her on the bar and dragged her back, tossing the woman over his shoulder and heading to the exit. Sara was still screaming and banging her fists against his back demanding to be let go so that she could "...*finish the little bitch!*"

He motioned to Conall who tossed the truck keys to him. He caught them in mid-air, went outside to the truck, threw Sara in, got in after her, and tore out of the parking lot.

*****

Sara wasn't exactly sure when she turned feral, but she was curious to see where this would lead. She'd never actually "lost it" before. Miki lost it all the time. She popped off continually, like a little firecracker. Angelina seemed like the most rational of the three, but everyone in town knew she had a temper that had caused some men to actually move out of Texas. No, it was a well-known fact Sara was the rational one. The one people came to for sage-like advice. The one people knew they could rely on since Miki might forget and Angelina just wouldn't care. She was Golden Retriever Sara.

Until tonight. Tonight she was Drunk-Sara without the liquor. And she finally had to admit, Drunk-Sara was fucking scary.

When the pickup truck pulled up to her house, Sara was immediately disappointed. She wanted to hit another club. Maybe go to Austin and scare some city-folk. She sure as hell didn't want to slip into her comfy clothes and watch TV for the rest of the night.

Now, if Zach wanted to keep her busy for a few hours... well that was completely different. But by the look on his face when he stopped the truck, his staying might be a remote possibility.

Sighing, she waited to see his next move.

Chapter Nine

Zach turned off the motor and pulled the keys out of the ignition. Clearly the woman wanted him dead. She'd thrown him under the proverbial bus, and she knew it, too.

Now what to do? Simple. Dump her ass and go. If he fucked her tonight, he was going to keep her. He knew that as securely as he knew she was crazy. And he didn't want a mate. He especially didn't want *her* as a mate. His whole life would be spent trying to keep her pretty ass out of trouble, and he had much bigger plans than that.

Pushing open the truck door, he stepped out. He reached back in and dragged her across the seat, ignoring her plaintive, "Hey!"

He pulled her to him and tossed Sara over his shoulder again, walking up the porch steps to her house. He was tempted to drop her on her head, but instead he carefully lowered her to the ground. "Keys," he ordered. She pulled them out of her pants pocket and handed them over. He unlocked her front door and pushed her inside, following behind her.

While she stood in the middle of her living room, he double checked the house to make sure they were the only ones there. He wasn't worried anyone was really there; he would have smelled any Pride members before he even walked in. But doing that kept him from thinking about how good she smelled or hot she looked in those khaki pants that were clearly too big for her. They kept slipping off her waist and she kept hiking them back up.

"Everything looks safe."

"Why wouldn't it be?"

No, probably not a good time to tell her there was a whole Pride that wanted to see her dead. The mood she was in right now, she'd go looking for them.

"Never hurts to check." He headed toward the door, making sure not to touch her as he left.

"You want a drink or something before you go? I think I have tequila around here somewhere." Kicking off her sneakers, she disappeared into her kitchen.

Zach slammed the door and quickly followed. *"No!"*

Sara turned around startled.

"And you don't want any either." The last thing the woman needed was tequila.

"I don't?"

"No. No drinking. And don't go anywhere tonight. Just stay here. Be quiet. Watch TV or something."

"I see." Sara, using only her legs, hopped up on to the counter. Zach was amazed how fast she was changing. Every second she seemed to be getting stronger. "You don't want me to drink. You don't want me to go out. You just want me to sit here quietly. Like a good little girl."

Zach swallowed. "Right."

"Interesting." Sara leaned back, her palms resting on the counter top behind her. Her back slightly arched, her breasts pushing against her white T-shirt. She kicked her legs out, the heels of her feet banging against the wood cupboard. "You know, my friends think you did something to me."

"I *did* do something to you." She actually blushed at that.

"Something other than that. Something bad."

"What do you think?"

"Me? Oh, I think I'm dying."

Absolutely psychotic. "You're not dying." Zach couldn't help but laugh. "Why would you even think that?"

"My mother died when I was a baby. My father died in an actual *animal attack* when I was eight. My grandmother was a very unpleasant woman. And I've been limping around this town for the last twenty years. Do you really think I believe in good fortune?"

She did have a point. "But how do you feel? Do you feel like you're dying?"

She was quiet for several moments, and when she spoke her voice was low. "No. I feel strong. Powerful. I feel amazing."

"You are amazing." Okay. Where did that come from? How did those words just leave his mouth? And she looked as surprised as he felt.

"Why, thank you tall, dark, stranger."

"You forgot handsome."

"No I didn't."

Looking into those beautiful brown eyes, Zach realized he could see his future in those eyes. Everything he'd ever wanted to be or wanted to have were in those eyes.

I gotta get outta here. "I better go."

"That's not fair."

Uh-oh. "What's not fair?"

"I'm bored. I'm anxious. And you say I can't leave and I can't drink." She looked at him. "So I'm thinking you better come up with a way to keep me occupied or who knows what kind of shit I'll get in to."

Zach had no response for that, although his dick certainly did. But he ignored it. "I better go." *That was feeble,* he thought desperately.

"Then go." She didn't sound hurt or disappointed. In fact, she sounded rather smug.

Zach got as far as the kitchen door that led into the dining room.

He turned and looked at her. "If I go, you're out the door, aren't you?"

"Well, you're not giving me a reason to stay, now are you?"

He growled. He couldn't help himself. This woman was bringing out every base instinct he had. And she knew it, too. When he growled; she smiled. She was playing with him. Playing with the beast and on some subconscious level, she knew it.

So maybe it was time to show her this was not a game she was ready for. Maybe it was time to show her what it meant to touch the beast within.

One minute he was standing across the room. The next he was standing in front of her. Grabbing her legs, he yanked her forward, and she slammed into that brick wall he called a chest.

Sara wrapped her legs around his waist and her arms around his neck. It was the only move preventing her from hitting the floor.

Her breath was coming in shallow gasps, like she ran several flights of stairs. And everywhere her bare skin touched his, she felt her flesh burn. She'd never wanted anyone or anything as much as she wanted this man at this moment. Clearly she'd found an edge and she was about to go over it.

His hand reached into her hair and grabbed a handful. "You have no idea what you're doing," he growled at her. And it was a growl–like an angry pit bull. "I'm not nice."

Yup. There's the edge. And this is me leaping off it. "If I wanted nice," she growled back, her hand reaching into his hair and snatching his head back. "I'd fucking ask for it."

Then his mouth was on hers in a crushing, bruising kiss that left her breathless and fearing he might crack her front teeth. Laughing at the thought, her body was suddenly moving. While his tongue slid around hers, he carried her through the house, releasing her once they were in the bedroom.

Slowly, Zach let her slide down his long body until her feet hit the floor. He kissed her again, stopping only long enough to pull her T-shirt over her head.

The bra went with one tear, and his mouth was on her nipple as he pushed her pants over her hips so that they puddled at her feet. She knew after her bra, her panties didn't stand a chance. *Yup. There they go.* He ran his hands down her back and across her now-naked ass as his mouth moved to her other nipple. Sara let out a small gasp as his teeth slid across her sensitive flesh and his hand slid between her thighs. But his hand stopped short of touching her pussy and in frustration she slapped his shoulder. Zach laughed and stood to his full height, looking down at her, his hand gripping one of her nipples and squeezing. "Thought I told you I wasn't nice?"

"Asshole," she ground out as the sensation of his tightening grip on her nipple went straight to her clit and stayed there.

"Bitch all you want, but you made it pretty clear...you like that I'm not nice."

Sara stared up at him. He didn't really think she'd actually respond to that statement, did he? Not when she really did like the fact that he wasn't some sweet teddy bear guy. True, she had no use for assholes who made her want to stab them in their sleep, but she did like her men edgy. She always had. There was something about a guy who didn't get scared about her habit of biting during sex that simply turned her on.

Zach chuckled. "You're staring at me."

"So? Are you suddenly shy?"

He grinned at that and her knees almost buckled. *Christ, what a smile.*

Sliding his hands up her body, his fingers gliding across her breasts, brushing her nipples. "Yeah. I'm very shy. Can't ya tell?" Then his hands were at her neck, holding her steady as his lips took hers. Oh, man...no one had ever kissed her like this. This man's tongue *owned* her. And he knew it, too.

While still kissing her, Zach moved her back until she felt the wall against her shoulder blades. He continued kissing her, possessing her, making sure no one else would ever be good enough for her again. Really, who the hell could live up to this? And this was just a kiss.

Sara wrapped her left leg around his waist, enjoying the fact she actually could without pain. Then any thoughts of pain disappeared as Zach thrust his jean-clad hips into her. Sara moaned at the contact. It wasn't lost on her she was completely naked and Zach fully clothed. Actually, she was thoroughly enjoying it. He still wore his leather jacket and she loved the sounds it made as he moved against her.. Add in that his T-shirt kept rubbing against her hard nipples while his jacket kept rubbing against her bare arms and chest and her whole body had become one throbbing, sensitive mess. And Sara knew the only one who could make it right was "big-armed, big-handed bastard" Zach.

Without warning, Zach pulled away from her but only so he could turn her around and push her back up against the wall, the palms of her hands slapping against the cold surface. He leaned into her, his body pushing against her, then he thrust his hips real slow, but this time against her ass...*oh, yeah...that works..* His erection felt like hard steel through his jeans and she had no doubt it would feel unbelievably good inside her. But he was making her wait. Taking his time. She admired his control and hated him for it.

His tongue connected to the flesh at the back of her neck and Sara closed her eyes, leaning her forehead against the wall. As his tongue trailed down her spine, his hands slid around and gripped her breasts. His tongue reached the cleft of her butt and went back up the way it came. He kept going until he reached her ear.

"Give me your hand," he whispered, sending a deep shudder through her entire body.

He placed his hand on top of hers and brought it down to her waist, slipping both between her thighs. Her body gave another, more violent shudder as he led the tips of her fingers to her clit and used them to slowly stroke her. A harsh breath burst from her lungs as her whole body tightened up and an intense heat began to spread from her lower back and up her spine. She felt him growl against her flesh as he nudged her hair off to the side with the tip of his nose and began to gently nip the back of her neck. *Oh, God! Biting!* She loved biting. Not too hard and definitely not too soft–just enough pressure to make her wince and groan at the same time while not causing any unnecessary screaming.

Her knees gave way and she would have hit the ground if Zach's other arm wasn't around her waist holding her in place. Her fingers, led by his, continued to firmly circle around her clit until her head fell back against his shoulder and a brutal spasm rippled through her. Gently pulling her hand away, he brought it up so that they could both see it. Sara watched as he, still holding her hand wet with her own juices, slipped her middle finger into his mouth. He swirled his tongue around it and Sara used her free hand to push herself away from the wall. She turned in his arms and looked at him, her finger still in his mouth.

"Clothes. Off. Now." Zach was still fully dressed and she wasn't having it. She wanted him naked and inside of her. Now.

*****

Zach pulled her finger out of his mouth with a loud, wet "pop." Then she was pushing his leather biker jacket off his shoulders. He let it drop to the floor as she snatched the black Tee off his body. She unzipped his jeans and shoved his hard body back on the bed. Raised up on his elbows, Zach watched her with a smile as she snatched off his boots and pulled off his jeans. She chuckled over his boxers and then dragged them off his body, leaving scratches along his thighs. She stood back and stared at his erection. Just stared at it. He wasn't sure exactly what she was thinking until she looked up at him, and smiled. "Rock on."

Laughing, he wondered how in hell he ended up with this crazy bitch. Well, this hot crazy bitch.

"Wait." She ran out of the room, leaving Zach and his desperate erection lying there.

He could hear her tearing through the living room of her house, muttering "Where is it? Where the fuck is it?" to herself.

"Get your tight ass back in here," he ordered.

"Keep your balls in check. I'm coming."

"You will be if you get your ass back in here."

"Here." Sara tossed a brown paper bag on the bed beside Zach as she moved purposely into the room.

As the bag landed, it opened and boxes of condoms fell out. Zach smiled triumphantly. "I knew that's what you had in that bag!" He laughed as Sara dropped to her knees at the foot of the bed.

Zach's smile faded as a groan escaped his lips. She ran her tongue along the underside of his dick, the tip gliding along the thick veins. She reached the head and swirled her tongue around it like he had her finger. Slowly she took him in her mouth and he dropped back against the bed, fighting for control. He wasn't going to take her. He'd fuck her, but he wasn't going to take her. No matter what she did to him or his dick.

He just kept repeating that thought to himself over and over again, like a mantra.

But Sara had no idea what she was doing to him. If she had she wouldn't have deep-throated him, her left hand wrapped around the base of his dick, until he could feel the back of her throat with the tip. Then the bitch growled–*Fuck! Not the growl!*– and he felt the sensation all the way up the shaft to his balls, which she'd firmly gripped in her right hand.

She rode him with her mouth, the sound of her sucking and growling and his moaning the only thing that could be heard in the room. And that's when he decided...she was his. He was going to claim her and claim her now.

He grabbed her by the hair, roughly pulling her off his dick. She looked at him, surprised but definitely curious. Taking her by the shoulders, he threw her onto the bed, slipping the condom on the last rational thought he had as he sat up and flipped her on her stomach. Zach knelt behind her and, grabbing her by the waist, pulled her back until she was against his dick. He didn't waste any time with coaxing words or sweet endearments. She was wet and he was ready. He slammed into her and let her throaty scream wash over him, making him harder and more desperate to bury himself inside her.

Growling, he slammed back into her with such force she let out a gasp that sounded suspiciously like "Fuck!" So he slammed into her again. Leaning forward, he kissed her back as he mercilessly pounded into her. He found a muscled spot just below her right shoulder, kissing and licking it as his hand reached around and found her slippery wet pussy. He clamped onto her clit as he bit down onto her back, his canines extending to tear into the flesh.

An animalistic scream ripped out of Sara's throat as she continued to bring her hips back to meet his thrusts. He felt the walls of her pussy tighten around him and he knew she was coming. Knew she was his. He held on to her shoulder with his teeth as his tongue licked at the blood and his fingers worked her clit. He slammed into her hard again. And again. That's when she screamed out his name and he felt her juices flow over him and down her thighs, her body shaking as the orgasm spread through her. Releasing her, his teeth slid out of her skin. Then he couldn't hold back anymore and with a roar he came inside her.

When the last shudder passed through them both, they collapsed on the bed and the last thought Zach had before falling into an exhaustive sleep was simple. *Goddammit.*

Chapter Ten

Sara forced her eyes open. At first she wasn't quite sure where she was. But quickly she realized that it was her bedroom, in her house–with one large arm thrown possessively over her waist.

Tell me I didn't. But she knew she had. It all came flooding back to her–the club, the bar fight, that bitch Casey. And the best sex she'd ever had in her life.

Well, at least when she lost it, she really lost it.

She looked over her shoulder at Zach. Out cold, his dark brown hair fell across his face, but she could still see the bruises and cuts from the bar fight.

Sara couldn't believe that was her last night. She'd been completely out of control. Although, the more she thought about it, the more she realized she hadn't been out of control–at least not in the usual sense. In fact, she'd been completely aware of every move she'd made. Almost hyper-aware.

She glanced over at the clock on her night table. Still had a couple of hours until she had to be into work, but she just couldn't face Zach when he woke up. He would, naturally, think her a big ol' slut. Probably want to pass her around to his friends. And she couldn't really blame him. She didn't merely throw herself at the guy. She practically tackled him. The thought made her cheeks burn.

She slowly slipped out from under his arm and off the bed. Throwing on some clothes she left lying on the floor, she quietly escaped her own house.

*****

Zach knew the minute she was awake. He felt her whole body tense up. She slid out of bed, grabbed some clothes, and was gone.

Part of him wanted to stop her. Grab her fine ass and drag her back to bed; he wasn't near being done with that body. But he was too busy kicking himself in the ass. She was his. Even if she had no intention of letting him near her again, no other woman would ever get close to him. He wouldn't let them. Bound to her for the rest of his life, the realization did not make him happy. Forget that he never wanted this in the first place. Forget that he was convinced she was possibly clinically insane. The bottom line was, she ran. She didn't kiss him awake or make him breakfast. She didn't even stop to shower. She woke up, saw Zach lying next to her, and took to the hills. Not a good sign when one was just starting out in a relationship.

Zach turned over with a sigh and looked up at the ceiling. "You are an idiot, Sheridan."

*****

Sara unlocked Miki's apartment door with her key. They each had a set of the other's keys for safety reasons. Theory was it was for emergencies only; otherwise, you knocked. But Sara was convinced this was an emergency.

She found Angelina asleep on Miki's incredibly comfy couch and Miki asleep in the recliner. Neither moved when she walked in, so she slammed the door shut. Angelina didn't move, but one eye opened and focused on Sara. Miki, however, flew out of the recliner, the book she still had in her hand raised as a weapon.

Sara looked at her two closest friends. "Well, I'm a whore."

"Oh, please." Angelina turned over and closed her eyes again.

Miki looked equally unimpressed. "Not again." Miki threw her book on the old coffee table. "Give us a break. And what the fuck happened last night anyway? We leave you alone for two minutes and you up and disappear on us."

"We were worried sick," Angelina added from the couch. Her voice muffled because she buried her head into the cushions.

"I just went for a walk. *Then things spun out of control!*" She yelled the last sentence.

"Skelly called last night. He's unbelievably pissed at you. And he said to tell you that you are going to pay for the repairs."

Sara didn't blame the man, she felt like the whole thing was her fault.

"So are you going to tell us what happened or not?" This from muffled-Angelina.

"I need a shower first."

Miki took a step back. "You haven't showered?" She pointed an accusing finger. "You're still covered in his DNA, aren't you?"

Sara started to say something, and then thought better of it. She needed her friends right now. Instead, she stalked off to the bathroom, while Miki and Angelina burst out laughing.

"And throw out the soap when you're done!"

Once clean enough for Miki's standards, Sara changed into sweats she had left over at Miki's and filled her friends in on the last sixteen hours, while they ate bacon and eggs cooked by Angelina. Although she was once again extremely sketchy on the fuck-of-a-lifetime details.

"So basically," Angelina analyzed, "you were the bone and they were the dogs fighting over it... uh... you."

"I am really starting to hate your analogies."

"Whatever. And his cock was huge?"

Miki choked out past a piece of toast, "So don't need to hear that."

"Enormous." Sara held her hands up to give an approximate length.

"Rock on." Angelina gave the thumbs up and pushed herself off the couch. "I need coffee. Anyone else?"

Both Sara and Miki nodded and Angelina moved off to the tiny kitchen right next to the tiny living room.

"Still hungry?" Miki asked quietly as Sara sopped up the last of the egg yolk with her toast. Sara shrugged. She could eat a ton of bacon and never get full. She loved bacon. Miki's eyes narrowed as she looked at her friend. "Perhaps you'd like a steak? Rare?"

Sara put her plate down on the coffee table. "Uh... no. Why?"

Miki shook her head. "No reason."

"Okay." Sara knew that tone–years and years of experience. "What's going on?"

"Well, we have a theory."

"No," Angelina called from the kitchen. "*We* do not have a theory. *You* have a theory."

"Whatever," Miki snapped back. "It's just that I've been analyzing the situation." *Uh-oh.* "And based on your recent body change..."

"Body change?"

"Increased muscle mass, tone, and strength."

Sara looked down at herself. She *had* liked the shape of her abs this morning when she was showering.

"And increased senses."

"Senses?"

"We practically had to leave the apartment to have a discussion you couldn't hear."

"You mean when you went into the bedroom? No. I heard you clear as crystal and my feet are not inordinately big."

"Not if you're a man," Angelina interjected.

"Shut up!"

"Mhhm. Interesting. You could hear us." Sara could see Miki clicking off some checklist firmly planted in her head.

"Increased aggression."

"I'm not aggressive."

"Maybe we should ask Casey about that." Wow, Miki could be smug. How did she never notice that before?

"She looked at me funny."

"Uh-huh." Check. "Increased sexual drive." Sara opened her mouth to protest that one, but Miki cut her off, "When I asked you how you felt yesterday, your response to me was 'Horny. Very, very horny.' "

"Oh. Yeah. I did say that, didn't I?" Check. "And what does all that prove?"

Miki folded her arms in front of her chest. All she needed now was the lab coat. "Werewolf."

Sara choked out a laugh. She couldn't help herself. "Have you lost your mind?"

"I have proof."

"What proof?"

Miki handed her the book she'd thrown on the coffee table earlier that morning. Sara read the title out loud, "The Truth About Werewolves?"

"Really good book. Factual. It's all in there."

"That's your proof?" Sara threw the book down. "All right. No more reading for you."

Sara went into the kitchen. She grabbed several more pieces of bacon and hopped on to the counter, again using only her legs. Angelina looked at her from the corner of her eye. "That's new."

"Cool, huh? Must be my new super powers."

"You keep joking, stretch," Miki snapped. "But wait until the next full moon."

Sara looked at Angelina. "Full moon?"

"Don't worry." Angelina pulled coffee mugs out of the cabinet. "You've got a good three weeks before that happens."

"Okay, when your body starts morphing at the full of the moon. Don't call me." Miki disappeared into her bathroom.

"We've got to get her out of that bookstore."

"Wouldn't help." Angelina pulled milk from the refrigerator and set everything up on the counter beside Sara. Staring at the coffee maker, they both waited for the coffee like it was elixir from the gods. "Are you still going to work today?"

"Yeah. Why?" Sara knew where this conversation was going.

"Just wondering…" Sara waited for it. She wasn't disappointed. "…if you'll be seeing Zach."

"I don't know. I doubt it. I don't know." Christ, she sounded like an idiot.

Angelina smiled softly. "He loves you, you know." That wasn't what Sara expected. Not by a long shot.

She burst out laughing again. "Oh, my God. You're crazier than Miki is."

"But you know I'm right." Angelina pulled the glass pot out of the coffee maker and poured two mugs full of the steaming brew. She handed one to Sara.

"Look. He came over, he fucked me. I'm pretty confident that's the extent of our relationship."

Angelina shook her head. "He didn't 'come over.' Skelly told us everything. He came there to get you. He was looking for you, he heard that blond guy on the phone with him. And he protected you from that girl Casey. He fought for you, Sara."

Sara stared down at her mug of coffee. "I can't believe that right now." Putting the untouched coffee down on the counter, she slipped off.

"Why not?"

Sara headed to the front door, snatching up her backpack on the way. "Because when he leaves, it'll kill me." She opened the door, but looked back once at her friend. "And you said it yourself. He will leave."

Sara had gotten down the stairs of the apartment complex when she heard Angelina's voice from above her. "Sara." Sara stopped at the foot of the stairs and turned to look back at her friend.

"You're right. He's going to leave. But whoever said he'd leave without you?"

Without waiting for Sara to answer, Angelina turned and went back into the apartment.

Chapter Eleven

The conversation with Angelina kept replaying through her mind. He couldn't love her. Not somebody like him. And she absolutely refused to love him. It didn't matter how gorgeous he was or how well he fucked. What did matter was that she just didn't have any faith in love or lovers or people who said they were in love or any of it. So, she wasn't about to be led down that path. Not for anything or anybody. And especially not for Zach. Never for Zach.

"Hi."

"Nothing!" she snapped, for no reason in particular.

Conall stood there, staring at her. Looking a little concerned.

"Everything okay?"

Sara took a breath. "Just fine."

"Good. Where's Marrec?"

Sara motioned to the back room with a nod of her head. Conall headed in that direction. "So, is it just you today?" he asked, almost innocently.

Sara bit the inside of her lip to stop from smiling. "Yeah. Just me."

Shrugging, he disappeared in the back. Sara grinned. That boy had it bad for her brutally honest friend. Poor thing. Miki would eat him for breakfast.

"What a beautiful smile you have."

Again Sara was startled out of her thoughts, but she had no idea who this was. He was handsome enough. Tall, powerfully built, golden blond hair, green eyes, and clothes straight out of GQ.

She should call Angelina, because he wasn't doing a thing for her.

"Thanks." Sara went back to her magazine. She figured the guy was just there to look around to say he had. He didn't exactly seem like the Harley-Davidson type.

"I smell him all over you," he whispered. "Did he fuck you well, little girl?"

Sara felt her mouth go dry and a jolt of fear go down her spine. But she controlled it. And slowly, oh so slowly, she looked up into those beautiful, cold green eyes. Smiled. And punched the prick in his face. The man's head snapped back, but he looked more surprised than hurt. Then he looked pissed. He grabbed Sara by the throat and hissed, "Dog's whore." Which seemed an odd turn of phrase. But before Sara could react to it or this stranger's hand on her throat, she heard a growl coming from behind her.

It was Conall. The big, sweet bear chasing after her friend a few minutes ago was gone, and in his place was a man that on a dark night she'd cross the street to avoid. Behind him was Marrec, and Sara couldn't remember ever seeing him so angry or dangerous looking. But it was the growl that came from the front door that completely shocked her.

He stood there. Beautiful as ever, frothing with rage. Zach's hazel eyes almost black. His lips curled back as he snarled his obvious displeasure. Sara was torn between being scared to death and wanting to fuck his brains out.

The stranger looked back at her and their eyes locked. His hand tightened on her throat ever so slightly. "I do hope he's not too attached to you," was all he said. Then he pulled her close and forced his mouth on hers. Sara screamed and grabbed his face, digging her nails into the tanned flesh, trying to hurt him enough so that he'd release her. But the kiss lasted only a few seconds, then he was gone. Over the bikes and out the side door. Zach and Conall went after him while Marrec came to stand beside her.

"*Who the fuck was that?*" Sara screamed as she repeatedly wiped her hand over her mouth.

"A problem," Marrec answered. Then he did something that was going to freak Sara out for the rest of the night. He sniffed her. "Oh, boy," he sighed. "Zach's gonna kill him." With that, he turned and disappeared back into his workshop.

At that moment, things just got too weird for her. What did Miki say? Werewolf? Sara grabbed her backpack and left.

*****

They tracked him to the forest. Then, once safely protected by the trees, Zach and Conall ripped off their clothes, shifted, and tore after the bastard they were tracking. They caught sight of him heading through the trees and up an embankment. He, too, had shifted, and was moving fast. Zach circled around while Conall went straight for him.

The little prick charged up one of the old trees, but the branch he jumped on wasn't sturdy. It broke and he fell. Landing on his feet, he took off again, but he'd lost precious seconds. Zach latched on to his leg while Conall went for his neck. But the big cat wasn't going down without a fight. He slashed at Conall, ripping into his muzzle before he could get to the soft flesh of his throat. But Conall kept coming. So he spun on Zach. But Zach wouldn't let go. Not with the bastard still having Sara's smell on him. He was going to kill him. But they were near the edge of the embankment. When Conall tackled him to get at his throat, Zach was pushed back to the edge. He saw Conall snap the cat's neck just as he lost his footing. The ground gave way, and Zach's body slid down the hillside.

The last thing he heard before hitting the ground was Conall screaming his name.

*****

Sara's pickup truck arrived at her house well after midnight. She'd headed over to Angelina's house when she left the shop. She knew she couldn't go to Miki's. Tell her Marrec was now sniffing people, and all hell would break loose.

So, instead, she and Angelina drank iced tea, watched the sunset from the porch, and obsessed over what the hell was happening in their tiny town. Raves. Strange bikers. Guys randomly attacking shop girls. It was simply getting weirder and weirder every second.

Angelina offered to let her crash at her place, but Sara just wanted to go home. Besides, she had her basic home defense, so she wasn't too worried. But Angelina insisted she take her shotgun to keep in the truck. She was worried about Sara just getting to her house safely. Not surprising, considering the last few hours.

Sara jumped out of her pickup and landed on both feet. It took her a second to realize she felt no pain. It was the most glorious feeling in the universe. She just couldn't get too worried about her weird life when her body felt so wonderful.

She grabbed her backpack, leaving Angelina's gun in the gun rack–*I do love Texas*–and slammed her truck door by doing a little spin and bumping it with her hip.

She was heading toward her porch when it caught her attention. It was laid out by her door. At first, she was terrified that it was dead, but as she got closer, she saw it was breathing. So, moving slowly, she quietly went up her porch steps and stared.

The wolf was huge–a good two hundred pounds or so. The largest dog she ever owned was about one-hundred-and-twenty-five pounds. But when he dragged her across a river bed to catch a rabbit, she decided never anything that large again.

Leaning down, she ever-so-gently touched his back paw. No movement, and she could see he was wounded. He had a deep gash on his side and his fur was matted with blood and dirt.

Briefly, Sara debated whether to go back to her truck to get Angelina's gun, but instead cautiously moved around him and, after quickly unlocking the door, went into her house. She grabbed the phone and dialed four-one-one. She eventually got through to animal control, but was immediately put on hold. While she was waiting and watching the wolf from her porch, she saw headlights heading up the path to her house. She watched those, too, until they disappeared. Just like that, which meant someone shut them off to avoid being seen. Probably not good.

"Shit," Sara got out as Angelina's concerns and the day's past events flooded her mind. Stuffing the cordless phone into her back pocket, she was about to slam the door shut and leave the wolf to fend for himself, but for some completely irrational reason, she couldn't. She felt she had to protect him. "Fuck. Fuck. Fuck."

She ran to her closet and grabbed the muzzle she'd used for her largest dog, Rocks, and her own always-loaded pump-action shotgun. She went back to the wolf. His eyes still closed, he seemed to be out cold. Burying all her fear, and any logical thought, she carefully knelt beside him, placing the shotgun at her feet. She put the metal basket muzzle on him, tightening the leather strap that would hold it in place should the wolf try to take her arm off. She grabbed him under the shoulders and dragged him into the house. It should have been harder, but... well, maybe he wasn't as heavy as she originally thought. Once she had him settled, she went back out to her porch and retrieved her gun.

She watched an extremely expensive car pull up to the front of her house. Four men got out. All well-built and all well-dressed. Okay. So, the guy in the shop seemed to have brothers. Not a problem. They began to head toward the house, but she pumped the weapon once and aimed at the first guy she saw. They stopped moving. They may have even stopped breathing.

"You're trespassing. Get off my property."

The one she had her weapon aimed at decided he would charm her. He opened his mouth to speak, so Sara shot the ground at his feet. All four men stumbled back.

"Welcome to Texas, gentlemen. Now get the fuck off my property!"

They dove into their car and were gone.

Sara took her phone out and dialed a number,

"Sheriff's Office," a deep voice drawled. "Deputy Fogle speaking."

"Hey, Eddie. It's Sara Morrighan."

"Hey, Darlin'. How you doin'?"

It was true, Sara was always a sucker for the cowboys and the cops. But her weakness and general kindness to them also helped her. Like right now.

"I'm not bad. Look, I was wondering, though, if you and your boys could do me a favor tonight. Some strangers were round my property just a few minutes ago. Never seen 'em before. *Not from around here*, if you know what I mean?"

"We've been seeing a lot of that in town the last couple of weeks." *I just bet you have.*

"Well, I was wonderin' if y'all could check my house from time to time tonight and make sure they don't come back."

"For you? That's not a problem, darlin'. I do hope you gave them strangers a Texas-sized welcome."

Sara laughed. "I sure did. But I gotta sleep sometime. Be nice to know you guys will be watchin' my back for me."

"You bet. I'll send a car out there right now."

"Thanks, Eddie. Tell the Sheriff I said hey."

"Sure will. You sleep well now."

Sara turned off her phone, looked out again into the darkness, and finally went back inside. She locked and bolted her door.

Her wolf friend was still out cold on her floor. Once again, irrational behavior took over. She hauled the poor thing up on to her couch. Cleaned off his wound, realized it wasn't as deep as it initially looked, and wrapped it in a clean bandage. Then, to top it off, she covered him with a blanket.

Yup, I am clearly losing what is left of my mind. Soon I'll be as crazy as my grandmother.

Sara made sure all her doors and windows were locked, took a shower, and went to bed.

*****

It was three a.m. and Sara still couldn't fall asleep. All that obsessing over *everything* did not make for a good night's sleep. Well, it started off she was obsessing over everything. Until she just began to obsess over Zach. He looked so angry when he saw that scumbag touching her. He actually snarled. Snarled! It was kind of cool.

"This is ridiculous." Sara tossed the covers aside and slipped out of bed. She padded out of her bedroom, through the hallway, through the living room, into her kitchen. She poured herself a glass of ice cold water and headed back to her bedroom. She'd just gotten to the hallway when she stopped dead in her tracks, the glass of water gripped tight in her hand. Eyes staring straight ahead, Sara slowly walked backward until she was standing in her living room. Taking a deep breath, she turned her head until she was looking at the couch. And there he was, laying on it. His wound bandaged. The blanket she'd placed over him, pushed down so that it was around his hips. The muzzle still on his face.

She stared at him…just stared.

After a few moments, his eyes slowly opened. Looking around in confusion, he pushed the muzzle off his face, and stared at it. Then his eyes looked across the room and focused on Sara.

"Sara?"

"Zach?"

Then her water hit the floor and she bolted. He was off the couch, charging after her. She ran into the dining room and around the large oak table. Zach was a second behind her. He stood naked on one side of the table while Sara stood on the other. She took two steps to the left. He shadowed her. She took three quick steps to the right. He did the same.

"You… you're…" She couldn't even think straight.

"I need you to remain calm."

"Fuck you!"

"That's not calm." Sara growled. "Okay. Okay." Zach held his hands up, fingers spread wide. "I know you're confused. And scared. But everything's cool. If you just give me five minutes, I can explain everything to you."

"You can explain to me why last night I went to bed with a big shaggy dog on my couch and four hours later I find you? You can explain that to me?"

Zach was silent for a moment. "You're right. Why bother?" He lunged across the table for her. Sara stumbled back and slammed up against the wall behind her. He missed her, so Sara jumped onto the table, over him, and tore across the room. But he was so fast. She'd made it to the hallway when she felt his arm grab her around the waist. She struggled desperately, trying to get away from him, but he continued to easily control her with one arm.

She screamed in frustration and kept screaming. Zach brought his other hand up to cover her mouth, but Sara saw it coming. Grabbing his arm, she wrapped her mouth around his flesh, and bit down. She heard him grunt in pain but that was all. So she bit harder but still he made no sound. Now she was getting pissed. She wanted to hear him scream. That's when she felt it– her canine teeth grew. Just like that they burst from her gums. The other teeth in her mouth re-adjusted to accommodate their new length as they easily sank deep into his flesh.

Zach pulled her tight against him and he buried his face into her hair. "I hate to tell you this," he muttered, his voice thick in what Sara assumed was pain. "But we consider what you're doing foreplay. You're making my dick hard."

She was so startled her canine's immediately retracted and she felt the rest of her teeth adjust back to their old position.

Then Zach lifted her like a load of laundry and carried her into the bathroom. He looked around, seemed satisfied she couldn't get out through the tiny, high window, and tossed her into the tub.

Sara's ass hit the hard linoleum. "Ow!"

He didn't even look at her, instead grabbing a towel and wrapping it around his waist. Then he slammed the bathroom door closed and opened her medicine cabinet. Pulling out alcohol and bandages, he ran his bleeding arm under the faucet.

"You know, this is why I didn't tell you earlier. I knew you wouldn't be rational."

Sara wiped Zach's blood off her mouth with the sleeve of her sweatshirt. "What did you do to me?"

"Nothing. You are what you are without my help."

"What does that mean?"

Zach poured rubbing alcohol over his wounded arm. "It means I didn't *do* anything to you. You just didn't know what you were. You can actually blame your parents for what you are."

Sara took a large, dramatic breath. "I am a werewolf then?"

Zach looked at her as if she were insane. "There's no such thing as werewolves."

Sara stood up, her aggression coming off her in waves. She could feel it. "Then what the hell are you?"

"A shapeshifter!" He seemed truly insulted. Like she'd called him cracker or redneck or said his mother wore combat boots. "The whole Pack are shifters. So was my father. And his father. And on and on. I can trace both my father and mother's families back to the druids. Werewolves," he spat out in disgust as he turned back to his wound. "And at night the boogeymen comes and gets us."

"Don't give me attitude."

"Then don't ask me stupid questions." He re-adjusted the bandage on his arm. "This isn't about things that go bump in the night. It's about a gift handed down to us through the ages. I live my life in this world and theirs. And I wouldn't change it for anything."

"You're a freak."

"Yeah. Probably. But I'd take one of us over what you'd call normal. At least I always know where I stand with them."

He may know where he stood, but she was completely lost. "Why are you here, Zach?"

"It involves me falling off one of those goddamn hills you're so proud of, but that's a very long story."

"Why are you *here*?" She didn't mean tonight. She meant at all.

She saw that Zach understood.

"Your parents were part of our Pack. But we had to wait until the old bitch died before we could come for you." Zach tied off his bandage.

"So last night…"

He brutally cut her off, "Don't even go there. I didn't have to fuck you last night."

Sara winced, but stood her ground. "That's good to know. I'd hate to think you were just following orders."

"Wait." Sara hadn't moved, but he seemed to think she was about to. "That's not what I meant to say." Zach touched Sara's arm. She looked down at his big, strong hand. She'd gotten finger-fucked with that hand.

She didn't even know she was going to do it until her fist actually made contact with his jaw. His head snapped to one side, but he swung back with a snarl and Sara took a step farther into her tub and away from him. His canines extended and his hazel eyes glinted in the dim bathroom light.

"Holy shit." Then she had her finger in his mouth–she couldn't help herself. He stopped and stared at her as her forefinger ran over the white enamel. "That's amazing. Now I remember why I've been so obsessed with your teeth. Do mine look like that?"

Zach pulled her finger out of his mouth. "You're crazy."

She stepped out of the tub and went to the bathroom mirror. She raised her lip and carefully examined her face.

"What are you doing?" Zach seemed almost afraid to ask.

"Seeing what my scary wolf face looks like."

Putting the palms of his hands against his eyes, he sighed–deeply. A cleansing sigh really. Sara was sure with a little effort she could make him do that all the time.

"You can't stay here," Zach suddenly announced.

"Why?"

"They're after you. Remember the guy that attacked you today in the shop?"

"It was more like a kiss." She heard Zach growl but kept her face completely neutral. *Fuck him.*

"Whatever. But he's one of several. Like the guy's at the club that first night I was here. He's Pride."

"You mean proud."

There was that sigh again. "I mean he's *Pride,*" that stated through gritted teeth.

"Pride? Lions have prides."

"Yup."

Sara spun around. "There are lions, too?"

Patient Zach made an entrance. "Yes. And tigers. And mountain lions. There's an array of shifters."

"Bunnies?"

Sara watched him swallow. "No bunnies," he bit out through clenched teeth. "Think predators. Our ancestors became one with the predators. Bunnies are low on the food chain."

"Sharks?"

"*What*?"

"Don't get huffy. They're the ultimate killing machine."

"I can't have this conversation." He leaned against the bathroom wall.

"Zach?"

Another sigh. "Yes?"

"How many are in a Pride?"

He shrugged. "Ranges. But about eight or nine."

"Male and female?"

"Yeah."

"And they killed my parents?" Zach's face softened. He nodded. "And now they're here for me." Again Zach nodded.

With that she was out the bathroom door.

*****

He never thought she would run. And he was right. She didn't. Instead she grabbed the well-oiled shotgun leaning against the hallway closet. He smelled gun powder and realized she'd recently fired it. She snatched a box of ammo from the top of a bookshelf and moved straight to the front door.

Zach caught her in his arms before her hand reached the doorknob. But she was in full aggression mode and she easily pulled out of his grip and swung the shotgun back, aiming for his head.

Instinctively he caught the weapon before it struck him; although the human side of him was startled and a little hurt she would attack him. Luckily he wasn't depending on that side of himself to stay alive.

"Christ! What is your damage?" he snapped angrily as he tried to pull the gun away from her.

"They were here."

That stopped him. In fact, it froze him to the very spot where he stood. "What?"

"They were here," she repeated. "Probably looking for you. And I let them go. I should've killed them. I should've killed them all."

"How many?"

"I don't know." She pulled at the weapon, trying to get it out of his grasp. "Three. No. Four."

"Females?"

"No. Males. Give it!"

Zach let the weapon go and Sara, surprised he let it go so abruptly, stumbled back. The only thing that stopped her ass from hitting the floor was the old chair she fell into.

"And that's the only reason you're still breathing. You, and your little gun, wouldn't have meant much against four Pride females." Zach rubbed his tired eyes. "Stupid. I led them right here."

"You're an idiot."

Zach took a deep breath and looked at the only woman he would–tragically!–ever love. "Why?"

"Because you didn't *lead* them here. They already knew where I lived. They probably just figured you'd come here. Now move." She stood up. "I gotta kill some cats."

One minute she was completely logical. The next a raving lunatic. She really just plucked his last goddamn nerve.

Snatching the shotgun from her, he tossed it across the room, praying it wouldn't hit the wall or floor and accidentally go off. The ammo followed right after.

She stood there in front of him with her baggy flannel pants, no shoes, and a Dallas Cowboy football shirt, just itching to kick some Pride ass. He guessed it would just have to be his ass.

*****

That was it. Sara was just going to have to kick his fine ass. Right here and right now.

Her fist reached back to punch him again and hopefully break his nose, when he grabbed her around the waist and lifted her off the floor. High enough that she had to look down at him. She had to admit, she was impressed. Not simply because he risked getting that close to her when even she could feel herself going "feral" again, but because at six feet tall and...well, rather curvy, she wasn't the first chick guys looked at to lift over their heads–unless they were football players and really drunk.

"Do I have your attention now?"

His voice was so soft and so seductive–she should have known he was up to absolutely no good. Because when she nodded yes, Zach with an evil-sounding "good" chucked her–yes, *chucked her*–across the living room into her old, but thankfully sturdy, couch.

Sara let out a surprisingly girlish squeal as she landed on her side and felt her ass hit the back cushions. To Sara's further astonishment she wasn't hurt, mostly just stunned. And when she opened her eyes, which she slammed shut as soon as she took flight, Zach was walking calmly toward her.

"Honestly. The things I have to do to keep you from killing anybody."

And there went the towel. The only thing between her and his mammoth cock.

She scrambled up onto all fours and tried to go over the arm rest, but he grabbed her arm and swung her around to face him.

"Oh, no you don't, beautiful."

"Don't even think about it...aye!" He'd snatched her off the couch and wrapped her legs low around his waist, his hands under her ass and his lips on her throat. He pushed his hard erection against her leg and it all felt so freakin' good.

"Don't," she begged. "I can't think when your hands are on me."

"Good. Then we're even."

She started at that. Could she actually have the same effect on him that he had on her? She didn't want to believe it. Instead she wanted to hate him. Hate him for breaking through that armor she'd spent her whole life building around herself so she could be safe.

He pulled at her jersey and she grabbed his hand. "Hey! There will be no yanking or tearing of the Cowboys. Ever."

First he looked surprised. Then he looked really amused. "You better get it off then...or it's shredded."

Sara swallowed as she realized that as "amused" as he may look, he was as serious as a heart attack. At least she convinced herself that taking off her shirt was to protect her Cowboys and not because she wanted his hand and mouth on her tits.

She leaned back and pulled the jersey over her head, dropping it to the floor.

"Now the pants." He placed her back on the couch so that she was standing over him, his hand still possessively on her hip.

"I..." was all she got out, but he tugged at her favorite comfy pants with an expression that said "either you take them off or I take them off."

"Okay. Okay. Christ, I'm runnin' out of clothes." She untied the drawstring and let the pants fall at her feet. She heard a definite change in his breathing as he stared at her body, his hand running over her flesh. Sara looked at the ceiling, completely uncomfortable with anyone staring at her naked. So many scars. So many flaws. No, no, he needed to look at something else right now. Right this minute!

"You going to look at me?" he asked her quietly.

"Nope."

He kissed her stomach. "You sure?"

She cleared her throat. "Yup."

"Okay. If that's what you want." His finger slipped into her pussy.

Sara let out a surprised gasp as his thumb caressed her clit, while his forefinger slowly stroked in and out of her. She wanted to ignore him. Wanted to keep looking at the ceiling and pretending he wasn't giving her a hand job right in the middle of her living room. But when his middle finger joined the other inside her and his thumb made lazy circles around her clit, she couldn't pretend anymore. Her hands gripped his shoulder and her eyes locked with his.

Zach smiled at her. That sweet smile she had so grown to love. "Tell me what you want, Sara."

What she wants? She closed her eyes. How was she supposed to know that? Five minutes ago, she wanted nothing more than to kill somebody. Now, at this very moment, she could care less. She didn't know what she wanted.

"I don't know."

"Liar." He licked a line across her belly. "Tell me what you want, Sara."

She could feel warmth spreading from her groin and up her back. She could feel blazing heat building. She held onto his shoulders because it was the only thing that kept her standing.

"You, Zach." She opened her eyes and looked down at him. "I want you."

Was that surprise on his handsome face? She wasn't sure. But it was gone in a second as he kept working her clit, while his other two fingers slowly fucked her. She dug her own fingers into his shoulders as the first spasm tore through her. She gasped and let out a moan as she came.

*****

Zach felt her orgasm when her tight pussy practically snapped his fingers in two during the first spasm. But it was watching her face that made it all worth it. Her eyes closed, her bottom lip gripped by one of her incisors. Add in that fucking amazing growling sound she made when she came and he was in wolf heaven.

She spasmed again and then her knees gave out. He made sure she dropped onto the couch as opposed to the floor. Her breathing came out in ragged gasps and her fingers still gripped his shoulders. He laid his hand gently on her mound, until the spasms eased down.

Finally she loosened her grip on him. But, to his surprise, she wrapped her arms around his neck and leaned her forehead against his chest. "When, exactly, did I become such a fucking whore?"

Now Zach was completely confused. "What are you talking about?"

"Me. I'm a whore." Zach wasn't sure if she wanted him to start calling her that during sex or if she was serious. Instead of potentially sending her spiraling into depression, he decided to go with her possibly being serious.

"Do you do this sort of thing with everybody in town?"

"No!" She looked up at him, completely insulted.

"Then you're not a whore. Psychotic? Absolutely. Whore? No. Now…" He brushed against her smooth, tight body as he laid back on the couch, his erection standing at full attention, as the damn thing always seemed to do in her presence. "I think you've got some unfinished business here."

She frowned, clearly confused. So he motioned to his cock. "Hello? You didn't finish the job last night."

She smirked, her arms crossing in front of that gorgeous chest of hers. "If I remember correctly, you practically ripped the hair out of my head getting me off it."

"I called rain check."

Sara exploded into laughter. She had the sweetest laugh and, unlike the entire Pack, actually found him funny. "You are so full of shit!"

"No. Really. I said," he covered his mouth with one hand, still smelling her scent on it, " rain check."

"Really? 'cause I thought I heard 'flip over.' "

"I was *thinking* rain check?" he asked hopefully.

"Pathetic." She ran one long finger the entire length of his shaft. "At least not all of you is as pathetic." Running her finger along the tip, she cleaned off the pre-come. He watched as she slipped that finger into her mouth and sucked it clean. He clenched his jaw tight as she leaned into him, her naked body pressing against his. She swept her tongue around and across his nipple, then softly sucked. Zach felt the tension from the past day slip away as her tongue led a brutal trail down his chest and across his abs, stopping briefly to lick his recent wound. Reaching out with both hands, he gently touched her black hair, marveling at how beautiful it was. How beautiful she was.

When his dick slipped into her mouth and that evil tongue of hers swirled around the tip, he forgot about everything but her. The Pack. The Pride. The war. He forgot all of it as he became lost to the scent of her body, the feel of her mouth on him, the way the silky strands of her hair felt on his naked flesh. He wanted this to last forever, but his body couldn't hold out that long. Not when he looked down and saw his dick being sucked by the most beautiful woman he'd ever known. The woman he loved.

Zach, his body screaming toward orgasm, grabbed Sara's head in both hands and roughly fucked her mouth. She didn't get mad. She laughed, her lips smiling around his dick and her hands gripping his thighs until his come flooded her mouth, and he let out a roar that shook the couch.

As the last spasm rippled through him, Zach laid back and tried to remember his name. Sara moved back up his body, kissing him as she went along. He felt her tongue slide across his neck and over his jaw. Then her lips were on his and he gripped her to him. He tasted himself as she sucked on his tongue and he immediately got hard again.

She pulled away from his kiss and looked down as his dick nudged at her sex. "Hold it!" Suddenly Zach was staring at her crotch as she bent over him to grab at her backpack. And since he was there anyway…

"Hey!" That after his tongue darted out and swiped her clit. "Cut that out." But she didn't sound half-convincing. She lowered herself to his lap and handed him the box of condoms.

He looked at it and smiled. "You do know you just licked my very recently opened wound?"

"So? Oh god, what's wrong with you? Mange?"

"There's nothing that a therapist couldn't cure."

She nodded knowingly. "You could use a good therapist."

"I was talking about you."

Sara whipped that middle finger out like she was fast-drawing a gun. "Besides, it's not disease I'm worried about." She leaned close to him. Her face filled with the most serious expression he'd ever seen from her. "The fact is, I don't want children. Ever. And when I'm thirty, I'm going to get fixed."

Zach frowned and leaned back. Could he have heard her correctly? She didn't want children? Ever? She didn't pine to be a mother? To know the joy of childbirth? Blah, blah, blah?

He grabbed her tight by the shoulders and stared straight at her. "My God, woman, I've been waiting for you all my *life!*" Sara was so startled by his shout, she reared back and fell off the couch.

"Shit, are you okay?" Zach looked down at her as she raised herself up on her elbows.

"What the fuck was that?"

"That…" he quickly slipped the condom on and was off the couch and between her legs. "Was utter fucking joy. That's what *that* was." He kissed her neck, her breasts, sucked on her earlobes.

Sara laughed at his loving onslaught. "You're insane."

Zach grabbed her thighs and yanked her down while he thrust forward. His dick slammed into her and Sara stopped speaking. He was going to fuck the hell out of her and he just wanted her to enjoy it. He didn't want her to think about another goddamn thing while he was inside her.

Zach pulled back and slammed into her again. He marveled at how wet and tight she was. How sweet she smelled. And he was really glad she wasn't into "nice." Because he had no real idea how "nice" worked. He equated "nice" to "boring" and neither of them were boring in his book.

Sara's teeth bit into the lower part of his neck where his throat and collarbone met, as her hands ripped ribbons of skin from his back. But he didn't mind. He barely felt it. And every time she bit into him or tore flesh from him, she was marking him as her own. Forever. Whether she meant to or not.

When her hands dug into his ass and her teeth bit down into his shoulder, he buried himself inside her, pumping into her hot, wet pussy, the sounds of her moans and growls filling his senses, making him love her more and more. And when his canines clamped onto the side of her breast, her pussy clamped his cock into a vise-like grip as the first orgasm hit her.

He could have come then. Could have let her go, but he wasn't about to. He wasn't nearly done with her.

*****

Sara knew she had to be causing him some serious pain. He was bleeding from several spots on his neck, and under her fingernails she had flesh that once belonged to his back. But every time her canines extended and tasted flesh and blood, he slammed into her harder. She was turning him on, and everything about him was making her wetter. Every time he said her name in her ear or against her flesh, she clenched, taking him deeper into her.

When she came, she thought he'd come too and then they'd lay around and do that "afterglow" thing Angelina always talked about. But he didn't come. Instead he kept going. Kept slamming into her with the same level of ferociousness she'd come to expect–hell, demand–of him. But when his hand slid across the old wound on her thigh, Sara gasped, her entire body clenching.

Zach stopped. "God, did I hurt you?"

"No." She shook her head and stared at him. She couldn't tell him. She couldn't give him that much power. That's the kind of thing that could make a girl like her into some guy's love slave. But he read her like a book. He glanced down at her leg, his hand hovering just above it. With the lightest of touches, he ran his finger across the damaged flesh, and Sara grabbed his hand as her body jerked in response. She couldn't explain it, but her old wound had somehow become a giant G-spot on her leg. Those fucking cats had somehow given Zacharias Sheridan the keys to the kingdom–namely her–and now Zach knew it. She wasn't comforted by the evil grin he gave her.

And when he pinned her hands above her head with one hand, she knew she was in serious trouble. Using his free hand, he slowly moved across her thigh; moved along the ridges left by those who'd tried to kill her as well as the paw marks he'd just made a couple of days before. Sara's body arched in response as her pussy was flooded.

She knew Zach watched her face. She couldn't hide the pleasure he was giving her as her thighs clamped around his waist, the sensation almost too much to bear. She tried to pull her arms out of his iron grip, though she wasn't sure once her hands got free whether she'd knock him off her or simply rip more flesh from his back.

He began to fuck her again, while his hand continued to move across her skin. Trapped while he basically forced unbearable pleasure onto her. She'd kill him if it hadn't been the best fuck of her life. It didn't take long for her to come again. And she was grateful for the control he had over her hands. She came so hard she wasn't sure she wouldn't have ripped all the flesh from his body. Instead she buried her teeth just under his chin and bit down. She felt his body jerk in response and then he was coming, right behind her, slamming his cock into her, his hand gripping the flesh of her thigh.

They both screamed out as the last spasm shook them. After a few moments or years… whatever… Zach leaned back and looked at her. "I'm *so* going to have fun with that," he taunted as his hand tapped the tender flesh of her thigh.

Sara rolled her eyes. "Prick."

*****

Zach shoveled another spoonful of Fruit Loops cereal with milk into his mouth. "It is *not* possible!"

"How do you know? Just because there's no proof to prove it, there's no proof to *dis*prove it either."

"You're trying to make me crazy, aren't you?"

"Not at all." Sara put her bowl down. "I'm just saying there could be bunny shifters."

"There are no bunny shifters!"

Shaking her head she accused, "You're a bunny bigot.."

Zach threw his spoon back in the near-empty bowl. "And there is no such thing as bunny bigots."

"Bunny bigot," she accused again.

How exactly did he get here? Lying naked and stomach down on the living room floor beside a naked Sara Morrighan, bunny advocate?

"We're not having this discussion anymore."

"If you're going to be that way about it…" Sara climbed up on his back, wrapping her arms around his neck and grinding her hot crotch against his tight ass. "I guess you'll have to find some other way to keep me occupied."

"You're damn demanding." Zach closed his eyes and did his best to control the lust stampeding through him. Good God but the woman worked him like no one ever had before. Just the way she touched him made him absolutely crazy.

She licked the back of his neck. "You know what I like about you?"

"What?" He really wished she'd stop grinding herself against him. The ability to think clearly was quickly slipping away with every move she made.

"That you're so easy to torture." She nipped his ear. "You're like a cranky Rottweiler."

Zach sat up abruptly, causing Sara to roll off his back and hit the floor. "Hey!"

"We need to get something straight right now." He sat up, pushing his hair out of his eyes. Pulling herself into a sitting position, she stared at him as he worked hard not to look at her tits. Not easy when all he wanted to do was bury his face right between them. But this was important…really important.

"Do not...and I mean never...compare a wolf with a dog. We *hate* that."

Sara said nothing for a good long time, then she leaned forward, staring deeply into his eyes. "Arf."

She burst out laughing and fell back on the floor, legs kicking up like she was ten-years-old. Rolling his eyes, Zach took firm hold of her legs and yanked her over to him. The woman was silly, exasperating, and so damn beautiful his back teeth ached.

"Ow! Rug burn, dude!"

Ignoring her, Zach slipped his hands under her back and lifted her off the floor. "Kiss me, lunatic."

She turned her face away. "No. You're mean to me."

"You haven't seen me mean." Leaning down he grasped her nipple between his lips and sucked hard. Sara's hands slapped against his shoulders as her head fell back and her back arched, pushing her breasts closer to his face.

Shit, where did he put those condoms? Without releasing her breast or her body, he quickly glanced around the room. Spotting a box under the couch, he picked her up and moved them both closer to the couch–still without releasing her breast. What could he say? He really liked having her nipples in his mouth.

Reaching out, Zach grabbed hold of the box and brought it over. Glancing up, he found Sara'd raised herself up on her elbows and was staring down at him, one eyebrow raised.

"What the hell are you do…" He sucked her nipple hard and Sara's head fell back, cutting off her question. "Oh, my God, that feels so fuckin' good."

He smiled to himself. He liked that he wasn't the only one out of control. The condom was on him in seconds and he was inside her.

Damn, but her pussy was tight. Tight and hot and all his. He ground his hips against hers and Sara reached up blindly, her hands digging into his hair.

Wrapping her legs around his waist, she pulled herself up so that their bodies rubbed together. "Do that again. Please, Zach."

"Kiss me first, you evil little tease."

Tilting her head to the side, Sara smiled just before her lips mated with his. They both moaned as their tongues swirled around each other.

Man, he was in way too deep. Lost in this erotic haze with a crazy woman who felt the compulsion to fight for the rights of non-existent bunny shifters.

Pushing her back to the floor, Zach ground his hips against hers again. Sara tore her mouth away and gasped loudly.

He must be hitting her clit just right. *Nice.* What a piece of ass. An ornery, crazy piece of ass, but a piece of ass just the same.

He kissed her cheek, then said against her ear, "Come for me, you crazy bitch."

Her eyes closed tight, Sara grinned. "Arf, arf, arf." Then she exploded, screaming out her orgasm and probably scaring the poor full-blood wolves lurking around the woods. Before she even stopped convulsing, Zach began fucking her with long, deep strokes. He took his time, enjoying the feel of her muscles contracting around his dick. Good thing they'd eaten something to tide them over, because he had no intention of stopping anytime soon.

*****

At least now, it all sort of made sense. Zach had given her the quick Morrighan family synopsis, promising more when they weren't still covered in each other's DNA and panting from exertion. At least he'd filled her in after they'd fucked in practically every room of the house. He told her about who and what she was. He explained how her aggression was normal since she'd never shifted. And that helped her understand her grandmother. She still didn't like the old bitch, but at the very least, she now understood her. She even understood herself, and why she'd always felt like a freak. Because she was a freak. But she found herself liking that. This was a freakiness should could get used to.

Of course now she had to apologize to Miki. She'd been damn near close to right. And there was no way she'd ever let Sara live that shit down.

Sara settled back against the headboard of her bed, and gently ran her fingers through Zach's hair. He gave a low growl as his hands slowly moved up and down her legs. He was lying in between her naked thighs, his dark head resting against her chest, and she felt as if he was always meant to be there. Lying comfortably between her legs, making that low growling sound that absolutely curled her toes. She wanted his place to be there forever. But, she knew, eventually he would leave and she'd be on her own again, no matter what Angelina said. She'd be on her own just like always. She held no false hope what they had was anything more than great sex. She couldn't afford to hope for anything more. She couldn't handle the disappointment.

"Do you ride?" he asked her.

She smiled as her fingers lightly slid around his ear. "Not since I hit that barn."

Zach's hands paused on her flesh. "You hit a barn?"

"I had to avoid the cow."

Zach burst out laughing and Sara couldn't help but smile wider. She liked making him laugh. She got the feeling a lot of people didn't.

"Okay. Okay. I guess you'll just have to ride with me. No bike for you."

Sara frowned in the darkness. What the hell was he talking about?

His hand began to move again against her flesh. Slowly, seductively, as if he just enjoyed touching her. God, how she would miss that. "Do me a favor, and don't bring a ton of shit with you. It's a long enough trip without having to worry about a bunch of bags."

Sara tensed and cleared her throat. "What are you talking about?"

"Don't panic, we'll send for the rest of your stuff."

She grabbed him by that glossy mass of dark brown hair and snatched his head back. "What are you talking about?"

"What do you think I'm talking about? You're coming with me." It wasn't a question, or even a demand. It was simply a statement of fact.

"I... I didn't agree to that." He turned his big body over, but never left his place between her thighs.

"There's nothing to agree to. You're mine."

"What? Like a dog? I don't think so."

He smiled in the face of her anger as he placed his big arms on either side of her. He dragged his large body against hers until their eyes met. She took in a ragged breath as she became moist. Christ, she *was* a horny dog, and she fought the urge to grab his cock.

"You don't get it, do you? You're not in this alone. You belong to me, but I belong to you. Even before you marked me, I belonged to you... as much as it annoys the shit out of me."

"Marked you?" He glanced down at his bandaged arm and she realized what she'd done. Not just on his arm but all over his body. The man looked like a used chew toy. Then she realized what he'd just said. "And you annoy the shit out of me, too. You're an asshole."

"And you're a psychotic bitch." His head dipped down and he dragged his tongue across her nipple, causing her back to arch. "But I'm pretty sure I could fuck that right out of you."

"Well," her hands grasped the headboard as her body stretched out underneath him and her legs inched farther apart. She stared at him in an open challenge. "You can *try*. But I'm not holding out any hope."

He smirked at her. "Really?" Then he ran his hand across her wounded thigh and her body jerked in response.

Her hands tightened on the headboard as she shook her head. "Those fuckin' cats."

Chapter Twelve

Yup, she could actually *hear* her phone vibrating and it was in the other room, buried in her backpack. She had to admit it, she was starting to really enjoy this "freak thing."

"Either you shut it off or I break it in half."

Zach was lying on his stomach, his arm thrown possessively over her naked waist, his face buried in the pillow. And clearly he was not a morning person.

Sara slipped out of bed and silently padded into the living room. She found her bag by the couch, the dog muzzle right next to it. She couldn't help but smile as she remembered Zach having that thing on his face.

She found the phone buried, as usual, in the very bottom of her backpack. Pulling it out, she quickly answered it before the caller hung up.

"It's Miki," was the reply. And she knew just by the sound of her best friend's voice something was wrong. "You better get to the shop. The cops are here and I just saw an ambulance pulling away."

Sara hung up the phone and moved.

*****

The slamming door woke him up for the second time that morning. But it was the banging on the window an hour later that actually made him move.

Zach literally dragged himself up and out of bed. He sleepwalked to the window and pulled the shades open. Conall stood on the other side. Leave it to his best friend to wake him from one of those great sleeps. The kind of sleep you only get after fucking the woman you love throughout her entire house.

Zach opened the window. "What?"

"We've got a problem. They went after Marrec this morning." Conall shoved Zach's saddle bags from his bike through the window. "Get dressed. And thanks for letting us know you weren't dead."

Zach stared at his friend, seriously confused. Then it all returned to him–that bastard touching his female, the fight, and the falling. The last thing he remembered was Conall calling his name, but not much else... except gunshots.

"I'm really sorry." Zach pulled his jeans out of the bag. His friend didn't answer. "But if it makes you feel any better, she put a muzzle on me last night."

Conall started laughing and didn't stop until they got to the hospital.

Sara was already there when the two men arrived. She glanced at Zach when he and Conall walked in to the room, but quickly turned back to Marrec.

The look on her face said it all. She blamed herself for what happened. Blamed herself for bringing the Pride to Marrec's territory. Blamed herself for putting him and his Pack at risk.

Marrec, though, seemed to be seriously enjoying the attention of three beautiful women. Miki was fluffing his pillows, Angelina was reading his medical chart, and Sara was holding a water cup to his lips so he could drink. Zach and Conall exchanged glances. They both knew this was ridiculous. Marrec had clearly been attacked. Zach wouldn't–couldn't–deny that. Half his face and throat covered in bandages that were ready to be changed, and his hands were bruised and torn. The man was a mess. But he was also Pack. In two days he'd be fine. At the moment, as bad as he looked, he was probably just feeling a dull ache.

Zach turned and tested the air. Marrec's Pack was around here somewhere, probably the cafeteria. And Zach's Pack had just arrived. Unfortunately, Casey was with them. "Shit," he muttered to Conall.

Yates came in first, stopping in the doorway to observe Marrec. "Comfortable?" he asked with obvious amusement.

"A lot of pain," Marrec forced out.

"Oh, come on!" Yates sneered in return.

Zach would have laughed too, except Sara was pushing the red and grey hair off Marrec's face. Balling his hands into fists, Zach wondered what it would feel like to beat the shit out of an old man.

Casey entered the room then, her females following behind. Sara didn't even look up. Zach smiled–she'd smelled Casey coming.

Moving across the room, Casey's attitude was one of complete dominance. Her females didn't follow; instead they stood back and waited. He knew Casey well enough to know she was about to show Sara exactly who was Alpha Female and although Zach could step in, he wouldn't. He needed Sara to start fighting these battles on her own. Even the ones she would lose.

"Excuse me, honey." Casey grabbed Sara by her jacket and hauled her up and off the bed. Sara spilled water on the floor as she stumbled out of the way. Casey sat on the bed beside Marrec. "Oh, you poor, baby. Are you okay?"

The room grew quiet. Even Angelina and Miki weren't speaking, clearly too stunned. But they did take several steps back, the whole thing feeling a lot more dangerous than it probably was. Sara wasn't ready to take on Casey and, from what Zach could tell, Sara knew it.

Zach watched his woman take a deep breath and place the empty water cup down on a nearby table. She turned away from Casey and stared down at her sneaker-covered feet.

He saw the struggle on her face. Knew what she wanted to do. And knew what she could handle. He expected her to walk away, and she didn't let him down. She walked away...for about five feet. Then, with a snarl, she spun back around and grabbed Casey from behind. One hand in the woman's hair, the other grabbing the denim jacket she wore. She snatched her off the bed and slammed her, face first, into the wall. She yanked her back, leaving a splash of blood on the white paint, and slammed her again. Then she threw her. Across the room and out the door, an arc of blood slashing across Marrec's bed. Zach heard Casey hit the wall with a sickening thud.

Sara was about to go after her when Miki and Angelina, not Pack and not knowing better, jumped in front of her.

"Hey! Hey!" Miki pushed her friend back. "Sara, *no!*"

Sara halted in her tracks, looking at her friends as if debating whether to tear their throats out or not. Instead she took a deep breath and looked over their heads at Zach. He glanced at the rest of the Pack females and, to his growing pride, Sara picked up on it immediately. Her head snapped around and she nailed the four other women with one look. "What are you bitches looking at?" she snarled.

Zach watched them all look at the floor, the door, the ceiling. They looked at everything but Sara. He bit back a smile and thought about mounting her right there in front of everybody.

That's when Miki grabbed Sara's jacket and dragged the woman from the room. Angelina following after them.

Once gone, Yates went over to see the damage to his woman. They all knew his time as Alpha Male was now over. And the man looked relieved.

Conall shook his head. "Your woman is a major bitch."

Zach grinned. "Isn't she, though?"

*****

Sara let Miki drag her out the hospital and around the back. Eventually stopping in the doctors' parking lot, the forest behind them. She was *letting her do it*. Sara couldn't quite believe how strong she'd gotten in just a few days.

Miki finally released her. *"What is going on with you?"*

Sara looked at her friends. Tired and worn from worry over Marrec, they wouldn't be up to hearing the truth. Hell, even Angelina was wearing sneakers and sweats. So what was Sara supposed to say? *Apparently I'm Pack now and I was exerting my dominance. You wouldn't understand..* That would play well. These pushy, tiresome, sometimes psychotic women were her best friends. They had been there when no one else had. She didn't want to lose them, and she knew if she told them the truth she'd lose them forever. Wouldn't she?

"Nothing. I'm fine." Boy *that* was lame.

Angelina and Miki exchanged glances. Sara had a feeling whatever they were about to say to her was something that had already been discussed between the two of them. Angelina leaned back against an expensive car with MD plates and smiled.

"Miki and I were reminiscing on the phone last night. And I forgot how much my grandmother hated when I went over to your house. At the time, I just couldn't understand why because she liked you so much. So I asked her. And she said it was because your grandmother was *lobo del diablo*. Roughly translated, 'devil wolf.' I just figured it was my grandmother's way of calling Lynette a bitch because of the Church Bake Sale Incident of 1984. But it wasn't that, was it?"

Sara, staring down at her feet, shook her head. She just couldn't face her friends. So, instead she studied her feet and marveled at how big they were. She wondered what they would look like furry.

"You've gotten really strong," Miki noted. "You threw that blond chick around the hospital room like a rag doll. Which, by the way, was so many levels of cool."

"And that growling thing you've been doing lately," from Angelina.

"And the snarling," Miki continued.

"Bottom line is," Angelina finished. "Maybe they're not werewolves. But they're not quite human, are they?" The women locked eyes. "And neither are you?"

Scratching the back of her neck, Sara looked down at her feet again. "I... uh..."

"Why don't you just tell her? Tell her what you are."

The friends spun around at the sound of a strange voice. It was the man she'd shot at the night before. And, as before, his three friends were with him. All golden and beautiful, and so cold Sara felt her stomach drop. Why, oh, why hadn't she killed them?

"Hello, pretty. Now, why don't you be a good little puppy and come with us."

"She's not going anywhere with you." Miki stepped in front of Sara, but one of the men backhanded her. She flew across the hood of a car, landing on the other side.

There was a brief moment of silence as Sara and Angelina looked over at their fallen friend. Then they slowly turned back to face the four men standing in front of them.

"Angelina?"

"Yes, Sara?"

Sara was staring straight at the leader. "Go," she bit out as she punched the man closest to her in the groin.

Angelina turned and ran; sliding over the hood of a car and charging flat out back to the hospital.

Sara charged off into the woods. Hoping, praying, they would be more obsessed with getting her then going after Angelina.

She couldn't hear them, but she could smell them. If they shifted she probably didn't stand a chance. She was pretty sure she was slower as human. And she had no idea how to change to anything. So she ran, and she prayed. Prayed her Pack would come for her before it was too late.

Chapter Thirteen

Zach smelled them before he even hit the parking lot. He, Marrec, and both their Packs were already out the door of the hospital when Angelina ran into them. Silently, panic and fear for her friend coming off her in waves, she grabbed Zach by the hand and dragged him to where she last saw Sara.

He caught his woman's scent immediately and within seconds shifted and took off into the woods, shaking his clothes off as he went. His Pack right behind him.

At first, the bastard cats didn't shift. He could still smell the human. Besides, they couldn't taunt and terrify her as cats. Only men could do that. But then, they must have realized she was a lot faster and stronger than they'd expected. About two miles from the hospital, they changed. And Zach knew it wouldn't be long before they caught up with her. Before they killed her.

Soon he figured out where she was heading. Home. She was going home. To where she felt safe. To where she had guns.

Good girl, he thought. Anything she could do at this point to buy him time.

*****

Sara knew as soon as they shifted, but she kept moving. If she had a moment to think, she would be marveling at the fact that she hadn't run since her attack when she was eight. And now she'd run almost five miles and felt–no, she *knew*–she could go another twenty. But they were gaining on her. She'd been right– they were much faster once they shifted.

Sara cleared the woods and made a mad dash for her house. She leapt over a car parked in front of her porch, which bought her precious seconds, flew up the stairs, and through her front door. She turned and slammed the door just as the cats made it up the stairs. She could hear them throwing themselves against the wood and she wondered how long before they forced the heavy oak off its hinges? She wondered where Zach and the rest of the Pack where?

She wondered how long before the bitches behind her actually said anything?

Sara looked over her shoulder at the four women standing behind her, one holding her shotgun.

They were beautiful females. Tall. Powerful. Blonde. Really blonde. Impeccably dressed, sporting four-hundred dollar gold-colored shoes and gold jewelry she could never afford.

"They were right. You do look like your mother."

Talk about having a bad day. Sara sighed and stepped forward to face the leader. She wasn't the tallest, but clearly she ran these females.

"She killed my sister. Now I'm going to kill you," the woman stated simply. "I'd hoped to do it long ago, but that bitch grandmother of yours moved like lightning."

"Then let's end it." Sara was so tired of the bullshit. "Here. Now. Anything to get you to shut the fuck up."

The woman hissed her displeasure and Sara snarled back, her lips pulling back over her growing canines.

Then the bitch's hand was around her throat, dragging her close. Sara grabbed at the hand cutting off her oxygen, panic spreading through her. Panic, fear, and anger. Definitely anger. The female leaned in and smelled her. "How sweet. Just turned. Just marked." A tongue that should not have been able to fit in the woman's mouth lashed out and swiped up the entire side of Sara's scarred face. It wasn't really wet, but dry and painful. "I bet he'll miss you when you're gone." Then she lifted Sara off the floor and tossed her across the room and through the closed glass window.

*****

Zach skid to a halt in front of Sara's porch, Conall practically slamming into the back of him. He watched her body flying toward the window and his mind howled in anger and pain. He was going to lose her. Lose the only woman he liked much less loved. But as Sara's body cleared the glass, he watched her change. Her limbs smoothly shifted to hind and front legs, her hands and feet into paws, black hair spreading over her body. To finish, her beautiful face elongated into a muzzle and snapping jaws.

Then she hit the porch, bounced and flipped off it; sliding across the grass in front of her house and coming to a halt when she slid right into Zach's long front legs.

And just like that she'd shifted, officially becoming one of them. One of the Pack. But this was her first shift, and she'd need time to come to terms with it. Time to learn to use her new body. Time none of them had.

*****

Sara felt her body go through the window. Felt the glass shredding her clothes, tearing her flesh. She briefly wondered how long she could fight if she lost a lot of blood.

She hit the porch, bounced once, and flipped off it into the air. Then she felt grass and dirt against her body as she slid into Zach. He wasn't the Zach she was used to seeing. He was the wolf she'd set up on her couch. But she recognized those beautiful eyes. Those beautiful hazel eyes. If she'd seen them that night, she would have known it was him. No one else had eyes like that.

The cats were coming closer. She could smell them and hear them moving, surrounding her and the Pack. Quickly, she scrambled up on all fours, ready to fight.

It took her a good five seconds to realize she was no longer human. She realized she'd shifted when she went through the window. That explained why she'd bounced so easily from the porch. She shook herself out of her clothes as the power of the wolf coursed through her new body. The strength of centuries of breeding and the lust for the hunt and the kill. She turned to the beast behind her father's death. A golden lioness stood on her porch and roared in rage. And Sara realized that as a lion, the bitch was huge.

All the cats were. She stared in awe at their size and beauty and tried to figure out how, exactly, they were going to fight animals that weighed a good three-hundred to four-hundred pounds more then any of her Pack did? Then she felt Zach brush up against her. She felt his strength. His power. And his utter confidence in her. Confidence in the psychotic bitch he'd come to love.

He was right. She was a psychotic bitch. And these heifers had murdered her father. She was probably going to get herself killed today, but she was going to hurt, maim, and kill as many of them as she possibly could first.

She turned to face them; her lips peeling back to bare her teeth, a snarl angrily forced out of her. And that's when they burst out of the woods–thirty-strong. Marrec and his Pack. People she'd known most of her life. She knew each one even as wolves. Jake. Fogle. Lana from the hair salon, and so many more. She recognized their scent. The rest? True wolves. Wolves and descendents of wolves that had watched over her since she was a child.

Sara turned back to the lioness. Things had just evened up a bit. And being the psychotic bitch she was, she charged her head-on. The lioness let out a roar that shook the trees and went up on her hind legs, but Sara kept coming. She collided with the female and clamped her jaw around the beast's throat. Three of her Pack joined her. Two went for her groin while the other wolf gripped the lion's head in her mouth. They all bit down and wouldn't let go. Even as the lioness fought for her life, Sara still wouldn't release her. Big paws clawed at Sara, tearing her fur-covered flesh. Sara simply ignored the pain and the blood she could feel running down her side and muzzle. Instead she dug her teeth in deeper and, using all her new-found strength, yanked out the bitch's throat. Sara stood back to watch the lioness struggle to get back on her feet. But blood gushed from her wounds and eventually she stopped fighting.

Sara spit out the remains of the lioness and turned to see Zach, Conall, and Yates dispatching one male. Marrec and six of his Pack were fighting another. The full-blooded wolves had taken on two male lions. Her Pack had taken on another female.

Two more females came at her, so Sara tore down the steps of her porch and slammed head first into one of them. The two bounced off each other into opposite corners. The other lioness was slower and became the tragic victim of a white pickup truck driven by a crazy Latina.

Angelina hit the brakes and violently turned the steering wheel so that the truck spun out; the side of the two-ton vehicle hitting the lioness and knocking her across the temporary battlefield. Miki leaned out the window, Angelina's shotgun in her hands. Sara watched that expression of cool detachment Miki always got when she was hunting. She pulled the trigger once and the beast gave a pained roar, landing in a heap, a large part of its skull gone. Sara saw that classic Miki smile and knew her friends were as much predators as she was.

Assured her two friends could handle themselves, Sara turned back to see the last female scramble to her big feet. She roared out in anger and frustration. And when she did, Sara attacked, wrapping her maw around the back of the lion's neck and twisting the beast around so that they both hit the ground. Then Zach was there beside Sara, grabbing the lion's throat, Conall took hold of the beast's rear right leg. Marrec grabbed the rear left. Casey, Yates, and Julie all took a firm grip on exposed flesh. Zach crushed the lion's windpipe and as it struggled to breathe, they all tore her to pieces.

Sara released the animal and trotted over to Miki and Angelina. They looked down at her, but their eyes widened. At first Sara thought they were simply afraid of her as wolf. But she quickly realized she was freezing cold and shaking. Looking down at her crouching form, she saw blood-and-dirt-covered skin. She'd changed back.

"Oh, honey." Angelina reached into the truck and pulled out a blanket.

"I'll take it." Zach, now human, took the blanket and moved toward Sara.

"Dude, some clothes!" Miki, the entire left side of her face already black and blue from the punch, turned away to look at the truck, the ground, anything but her friend's naked boyfriend. But then Miki saw Casey prance by with her muzzle wrapped around a hunk of lion leg. "Okay. You people are killing me!" She rubbed her eyes with balled fists as Angelina put her arm around Miki's shoulders.

Zach crouched down beside Sara and wrapped the blanket around her.

"Zach, I'm so cold." She barely got that out, her teeth were chattering so hard.

"Don't worry, baby, it's normal. It's your first change. It's to be expected."

Sara still grinned. "My first change? You mean I've popped my change-cherry?"

Zach looked at her and started laughing. "Yeah, I guess you could say that. If you're tacky enough to say that."

He picked Sara up in his arms and held her close, making sure the blanket was tight around her.

"Clothes! You people need clothes!" Sara peeked over Zach's shoulder to see a naked Conall standing behind them and in front of a clearly disturbed Miki. *Considering she's just taken out a three-hundred-pound animal with one shot, you'd think she'd handle the naked thing a little better.*

"Go on," Conall said to Zach. "We'll take care of cleaning this up. You take care of her."

Zach nodded and walked into the house, Sara's head resting against his shoulder.

*****

Within minutes, Zach had Sara in a hot bath. He washed the blood off her face and out of her hair. He cleaned her wounds and gently licked the one's on her neck, face, and shoulder. He dried her off with a big towel and carried her to the bed. Laying down next to her, Zach pulled her to him, resting her head on his chest, his arms tightly wrapped around her long body. He nuzzled her, rubbing his nose against her wet hair and kissed her forehead. Sara sighed once and in a few seconds she was asleep.

It was early morning when she woke him, her naked body stretched out on top of him. Her lips moving along his neck and her hands moving down his waist.

Zach took her head in his hands and turned her to look at him. To be blunt, she was all fucked up from the previous night's fight: her left eye black and blue, a deep wound on her neck, a vicious cut across the bridge of her nose. *She is so hot*, he thought. And she was glowing. Clearly she took after her mother more than any of them realized. She was all about the hunt.

"Okay, what? What are you staring at?"

He wanted to tell her. Tell her he loved her. Tell her she was his mate and that together they would rule the Magnus Pack. He really wanted to tell her.

"There's something I need to tell you." Her eyes narrowed with suspicion. "Nothing bad," he added hurriedly. "I don't think."

She pushed herself off of him and sat at the other end of the bed. "Well?"

He cleared his throat. "Um...see, after yesterday...you know, you've kind of... well, you've kind of established yourself as the dominant female... which kind of means... that... uh..." She just stared at him. Okay. So she wasn't going to make this easy. "You see, it's just that...for the Pack it's all about...um... and for me... you know..." Why was this so hard? Maybe it was the way she was just watching him, her arms crossed in front of her breasts. "Uh..."

Then her phone went off. "Hold that thought."

She easily swung herself off the bed and grabbed the phone from the top of the TV. "Hello? Hey, Mik. Whasup? You doin' okay? How's your face today?" Sara flopped stomach-down across the bed. Zach stared at that delectable ass and became completely lost, forgetting what he was talking about. Who she was talking to. He forgot his own name. He forgot all of it. "Good. Me? I'm doin' just fine. Just waiting for Zach to quit dancin' around the bush and tell me he loves me." Zach was startled but couldn't tear his eyes away from her ass. "It's taking him an hour and a day." Sara's legs were lazily moving front to back, her breasts barely touching the sheets, her chin tucked into the palm of one hand while the other held the phone to her ear. "That's a good idea. Hold on." She looked at Zach. "Would it help if I told you I loved you first?"

Zach didn't know what to say. Hell, he was still staring at her ass, so he sort of nodded. Sort of.

Sara went back to the phone. "You're right. Apparently that would help. You're so smart." Sara was silent for a moment, listening to Miki on the other end. "Yeah. You got it." Sara snapped her phone closed and tossed it on the night stand beside the bed. But she tossed way too hard and the phone hit the wall and flew back, disappearing under the bed. "Well, shit."

Zach watched her lean down to search under the bed. She slid half her body to the floor trying to reach the phone, but all Zach could see was her ass bent over the bed, one leg sliding across his thigh. He growled.

Sara had just gotten her hands on her phone when she felt Zach's tongue slide over her left ass cheek. She was so startled she flipped right off the bed.

Cell phone still gripped in one hand, she pulled herself up to rest on her knees. Zach was laying on the edge of the bed, smirking at her. "Could you warn me before you do something like that?"

"You shake your ass at me like that, you get no warning."

She tried to stop herself from smiling, but just couldn't. "I'll keep that in mind for the future."

"You mean the future of five seconds from now?" He grabbed her arm and yanked her onto the bed.

"Hey!" Sara's already bruised and damaged face, slammed into a pillow. She lifted her head and brushed her hair out of her eyes. "You know, you've been tossing me around a lot."

"Uh-huh." Zach moved up behind her. "And that bothers you because..." He grabbed her legs and pulled them apart, then dragged her down until her ass was on his lap.

"I didn't say it bothered me, I just think I deserve a little more respect than that. You know, with me being Alpha Female and all." His head snapped up in surprise and she grinned at him. "Don't look so surprised. I'm not stupid. I knew in the hospital, when you wanted me to yell at the girls. Hey!" He'd just slapped her butt.

"You're a real smart ass, you know that? But I'll let it go because you have such an amazing butt."

She growled. "You know, I'm not your..." She stopped and they looked at each other. They both knew what the next word out of her mouth was going to be. "Okay. So maybe I am your bitch, that doesn't mean I'm your chew toy."

Zach raised one eyebrow, and Sara watched him lean down and lick her lower back. Her hands gripped the sheets. "You asshole, you're trying to distract me again." But his tongue took its time moving across her hot and hungry flesh and it felt so good, it was really difficult to remember what the hell she'd been complaining about.

"What were you saying, beautiful?" he asked as she felt his fingers slowly enter her sex, his tongue lapping at her accursed damaged thigh. Sheets shredded under her hands as she looked back at him. And there was that smug prick she'd grudgingly fallen in love with. The wounds he'd sustained on his face, neck, chest, and back the night before had already begun to heal. He'd gotten every one of those rips and tears because of her and he didn't care. She knew he didn't care. Clearly the only thing Zach cared about at the moment was getting her wet and getting her off.

He caught her staring at him and nipped her ass cheek. "What ya starin' at?" he demanded playfully.

But her reply was deadly serious. "You. I love you, Zach."

He looked at her for several moments then leaned down and kissed her ass. His hands slid under her breasts and, holding them firmly but gently lifted her so that her back was flat against his chest.

Kissing her along her neck and shoulder, he stopped to lick wounds new and old. When he reached her ear, he leaned in closer than anyone before him ever had. "I love you, baby," he whispered softly. "More than anything." Then he was inside her and she forgot about everything else.

Chapter Fourteen

Miki held up a tennis ball, looked at Sara's new Pack, and tossed it out into the forest away from the ongoing rave. They all watched it go, then they turned back to Miki.

"Okay. Go…"

Sara and Angelina slapped their hands over their friend's mouth before the word "fetch" could come out of it.

They pulled her over to one of the food tables.

"*Are you out of your ever-loving mind?* Everyone here *but us* is like Sara," Angelina snapped. "And after seeing them in action I'd rather not fuck with them!"

Miki gave that innocent smile. "It was just a little experiment."

"I don't want to know."

How sweet. Her friends were having one last fight before she left. Tomorrow she'd be leaving with Zach. Back to her original home with the man she loved. She wasn't sure, but she thought her father would be happy about that. She was sure her grandmother wouldn't be. That thought made her giddy.

The last thing they were doing before they would leave was throw this all-night rave for Marrec and his Pack. Seemed only fair after they helped her tear a whole Pride to pieces.

But just the thought of leaving was sending her into a full-blown panic attack. How was she going to leave her best friends? These crazy bitches had risked their lives for her, accepted her for who and what she was, and was there whenever she needed them. She knew she should tell them that. She knew she should tell them how much she loved them. But instead she turned to Angelina and glanced down at the four-hundred dollar shoes on her feet. She looked back at her with one raised eyebrow. "Those are nice gold-colored shoes."

"Actually they're champagne. My signature color. They look fabulous on me, don't they? I just found them…ya know…lying around."

Sara smiled warmly at her two friends and tried to think how she was going to do any of this without them. Already the females of the Pack were waiting for her to give them orders. She didn't know what to tell them, although "Move out of my way" seemed to be quite effective at the moment. And thankfully she knew music and DJs because apparently she was partnering with Zach to take over the club business from Yates and Casey. Considering she had no idea what she was going to do with the rest of her life just the week before, it was kind of startling to suddenly be "in charge" of anything. Especially a thriving business. She didn't want to disappoint them or Zach. But she especially didn't want to disappoint herself. Deep down she knew she could do it. But that knowledge didn't stop the panic from causing her to hyperventilate in the bathroom just ten minutes before.

But maybe she couldn't do this. Maybe she shouldn't leave. Just because she could suddenly shift into a wolf at will didn't mean she should leave what she knew best. It definitely didn't mean she should change her whole life for some guy she just met. Hell, they hadn't even gone on an actual date. Christ, did wolves date? And if they do date where do they go? To dinner at a restaurant or just hunting down some deer? Nope. Nope. She couldn't do this. She was nobody's Alpha Female. She'd just have to tell Zach to forget it. He could just take his big cock and go. Yup, that was the plan. Good plan.

That's how it started in the bathroom, too, and the hyperventilating was just about to begin again when she felt Zach's big arms snake around her body from behind. He kissed her neck and pulled her close against him and suddenly it all felt right. *He* felt right. Him and his big cock.

"Ladies." He nodded at her two friends. "Hope you're having a good time."

They both grinned. "Great little party," Angelina offered with one of her dazzling smiles.

"Thanks." He snuggled closer to Sara. "Dance. Eat. Everything's on the house for you two." He paused. "But please don't ask our Pack to fetch anymore."

Sara and Angelina cringed as Miki rolled her eyes. "It was just an experiment. Honestly."

She turned to walk away but crashed into her own personal shapeshifting stalker. "Hey, Miki." Conall smiled. "I think you dropped this." He handed Miki the tennis ball.

"Dude!" Zach barked.

"What?"

Zach was so disgusted he walked away.

They were polite enough to wait until Conall followed after his friend, asking Zach to tell him what he did wrong, before the three friends burst out laughing.

"No one is safe around you three."

Sara turned to find Marrec behind her. She threw her arms around his neck and hugged him tight. "Thank you so much, Marrec. Thank you for everything." And she wasn't just talking about the fight with the Pride. She was talking about the last twenty years.

"You're welcome. But are you trying to get me killed?" Sara opened her eyes and saw Zach watching her from fifty feet away. He definitely didn't seem too pleased. "Or maybe you're trying to get yourself killed?" Sara looked and saw Marrec's wife glaring at her. Funny, the woman had made her graduation dress and had always invited her to every Marrec family event. Now she acted as if Sara were some hooker on the street trying to pick up her husband.

Sara pulled away and looked at Marrec. "I can never come back here, can I?"

"Sara, you'll always be welcome here. But never as Alpha Female."

Sara gave a half-smile. "So I can never come back here, can I?"

Marrec smiled like a proud father. "That's my girl."

She stepped away from him. "Have a great time tonight. Everything is free for you and your Pack. Enjoy."

"We will." He turned to head back to his mate.

"I'll miss you," she whispered, knowing he would hear her. He nodded once and walked away.

"Are you okay?" Angelina put her hand on her friend's shoulder. All three of them had been close to Marrec, for varying reasons he was the only father the three of them had ever really known.

Sara took a deep breath. "Yeah. I'll be okay." She was feeling such a huge sense of loss she wondered how she could face the rest of the night.

Miki appeared at Sara's elbow but she was glaring at Angelina. "You know, I wasn't doing anything wrong." Clearly she had been arguing with Angelina in her head for the last ten minutes. "Just seeing what their play-drive is like. That Conall guy clearly has a big play-drive."

"They're not dogs, you idiot."

"Um... I know you didn't just call me an idiot."

"Um..." Angelina imitated back, "I think I just did."

Yup. There went that sense of loss. Sara realized when she left the next morning there would be no tearful goodbyes with these two. This wasn't goodbye. These crazy women would always be her best friends. Besides, you never get rid of friends like these. They follow you to hell so they can torture you for eternity.

When Angelina poked Miki in the shoulder with one manicured fingernail, Sara left. Zach had disappeared, but she followed his scent into the woods.

*****

Zach leaned against a tree. He was about half a mile away from the rave, waiting for Sara. And he knew she'd find him.

He smelled her lust even before he could hear her. Shit. His dick went hard again.

"You runnin' away from me already?" Now that she'd healed and become what she truly was always meant to be, Sara moved with a grace and power he found amazing. She was truly becoming the ultimate she-wolf and loving every minute of it.

"Nope. Just trying to figure out how I could live in California all my life and never once say 'dude.' But after hanging out with you three bitches for five days, I suddenly sound like an idiot."

She punched him in the shoulder. "Dude. That's harsh."

Sara grinned and Zach rubbed his eyes with the palms of his hands. "You're going to make me crazy."

"It's a gift."

He decided to change the subject. "Your friends arguing, how long will that be going on anyway?"

"Finger pointing just started. Next there'll be yelling. Then, depending how bad it gets, a good old-fashioned slap fight. So it could take hours."

Her friends were definitely crazier than she was, but only marginally. "Interesting. Any nudity involved?"

Sara nuzzled him under his chin and Zach leaned in and smelled the fresh scent of her hair. "Sorry, mister. No other bitches for you. You're stuck with just me. Golden Retriever Sara."

He laughed. "Who?"

She kissed him. "Forget it."

"Gladly." He ran his hand across the scarred side of her face. She didn't flinch away, but instead leaned into it. "You're sure about this, right?" He'd never asked her if she wanted to go home with him. He'd just assumed, but he was starting to realize assuming anything with this woman was a bad move.

"I don't know. California. Actors. Hollywood." She stuck her tongue out. "Yuck."

"Don't stick that thing out unless you plan to use it. And it's Northern California. Completely different from Southern California. Worlds apart. Besides, you were born there. Not here."

"I may not have been born here, but I was made here. And don't you forget it."

"Is that a yes or a no?"

Sara was busy running her hands over his abs, her hands under his T-shirt, and wasn't remotely paying attention. "About what?"

He sighed, deeply, and for some reason that seemed to make her chuckle. "Are you coming with me?"

"Sure. But on one condition."

Zach closed his eyes. "It involves *them* doesn't it?"

"They're my family. So that means every Thanksgiving, Christmas, New Years, Fourth of July, and because Angelina's Catholic, Easter. You attend dinner and you're cheery."

"I'm never cheery."

"But for me, you will be."

He shook his head in resignation. "Fine. Whatever."

"Good. Then yes, I'm coming with you." She grabbed his hand and began to pull him back to the rave. "Now, feed me, wolf. Your mate's starving."

"Sara. Wait." She turned and looked at him. "I think they want to say goodbye." Sara frowned as he motioned toward the forest. A female, the Alpha of the full wolves, walked into the pale light cast from the rave. Her Pack stood behind her, the dozen pair of eyes watching Zach closely. They still weren't sure he was good enough for her. He smiled. Without even trying, Sara earned a loyalty from man and beast he'd never seen before.

The female brushed against Sara, her big body pushing against Sara's legs. Then she circled them once and returned to her Pack. Zach waited for them to leave, move on silently into the night, but the female had one more thing she had to do before she could let Sara go.

The she-wolf tilted her head back and howled, her Pack joining in. But when the Packs at the rave howled back, both Zach and Sara exchanged startled glances.

"I've never seen anything like this before," Zach whispered in awe as the howling continued. "Three Packs." He ran his hand down Sara's back. "Three Packs howling to you, baby."

Sara turned and looked at her mate, a frown flitting across her beautiful features as recognition dawned. "It was you the other night, wasn't it?" she asked quietly as she brushed his hair out of his eyes. "That howling I heard that wasn't like the others. The one I felt..." She closed her eyes for a moment, the memory washing over her. "It was you," she repeated as her gaze again focused on him. "You called to me."

Zach didn't reply. He didn't have to. She already knew the answer. Instead he gripped his mate tight around her hips, pulling her into him. Sara nuzzled her face against his as she trapped him against the tree with her long body.

"I thought you wanted to go eat?" he growled low as he felt her hands move down his body. A few more inches and she wasn't going anywhere anytime soon.

"You better fuck me first, wolf." Her hand unzipped his jeans and slid inside. "You're mate's starving."

GO FETCH!

Prologue

He sniffed the air again. He knew that smell dammit. He knew it from somewhere and it was going to drive him crazy until he remembered where. He kept moving, tracking the scent through the forest, as the rave went on in the clearing behind him.

He tore through the trees, the branches ripping at his fur. The scent shifted, so he stopped and spun, sniffed the air again and moved. This time he overshot, and they came out of the dark, attacking him from behind. Teeth sunk into his flank. Snarling and turning, he knocked them off before they could get a firm hold. One of his Pack mates and a full-blood joined him, but by the time the wolves turned, they were gone. His Pack mate spun in circles trying to see where they went, what they looked like, and who the hell they were.

They weren't Pride, they weren't wolf, and they sure as hell weren't human. Whatever they were, they didn't belong. They were out of their territory. He just wished he could remember where he'd smelled that scent before. He had no idea what had attacked him, but they were gone now. Their scent lingering, but still unknown.

Conall headed back to where he left his clothes. He'd protected the Pack, now he was ready to get back and enjoy the rave. He realized that, although his Pack mate had gone off to check the area more fully, the full-blood was following him. He let him, because he didn't fear him. The full-bloods let them into their territory because they knew they were there to protect a woman. His Alpha's mate–Sara.

Full-blood wolves howled and the full-blood with him stopped to join in. Conall let the sound wash over him. He loved that sound, more than anything. He stopped in his tracks and, without thought, leaned his head back and released a howl that blended in with the howls of the two hybrid Packs at the rave. He realized this was something that didn't happen every day. Three

Packs howling as one. Sara deserved it, though. The female kicked major ass.

Another scent hit him. A scent he'd been coming to love lately. If she let him, he would roll in it all day. He headed toward that wonderful scent, happily realizing she was near his clothes.

He silently moved toward her. She was sitting on a rock, reading an oversized paperback book. She was squinting, forced to use the moonlight and the light from the rave to illuminate whatever she read.

Up to this point, he hadn't been able to dedicate any real time to his pursuit of her–too busy trying to protect his Pack. The few times he'd approached her, she'd been less than receptive. But now that they'd wiped out the Withell Pride, his time was his own. At least for the moment. So he could give her his full attention. Besides, she looked hot. And for once, she was on her own.

He padded up to her, her scent pulling on him like a leash, so close to her that his nose was just inches from her neck.

Like a flash, her upper body twisted, a good-sized hunting knife in her hand. He shifted and blocked her arm with his. Good thing, too. She could have cut his throat from ear to ear with that thing.

Her eyes widened at the sight of him. Then she glanced down and her eyes widened even more. "What is it with you people and being naked?"

"It's a shifter thing."

"That's fascinating, but if you don't put some clothes on I'm going to have to start chopping at things that are protruding." And he knew she would.

"My clothes are over there."

"Get 'em."

She lowered her arm and slipped the blade back into the sheath at her side. Conall had no doubt she knew how to use that knife. He'd seen her in action. She was an amazing hunter–for a human.

And an even more brilliant piece of ass.

Conall walked over to the pile of clothes he'd left by a tree and put them on as Miki went out of her way not to look at him. He'd seen the woman blow the head off a Pride female with a single rifle shot from a moving vehicle, but his cock seemed to unravel her. *Weird girl.*

He figured he'd have to say something since she was going out of her way not to speak to him. "I'm Conall..." he began.

"We already had this conversation."

"...Víga-Feilan," he finished. Just like that, she cut him off. That was new. Women never cut him off before. They didn't necessarily find him fascinating but they faked it real well. At least until they got laid.

But his last name did seem to interest her, even though she didn't look away from her book. "Víga-Feilan?"

People always said his last name back to him. Like an echo. It was an odd name and one he wouldn't change for the world. "Isn't that Viking?"

He stared at her, his Harley T-shirt in his hands. "How the hell did you know that?" True, it was actually a Norse byname, but Viking was close enough. No one ever knew that. *Ever.* Miki was the first to call it right. Christ he wanted her.

"There are these fascinating places with books in them. They're called libraries. When you're not chasing your tail or balancing a ball on your nose, you should think about going to one."

He watched the sly smile she had on those gorgeous lips and he grinned. Oh, yeah. He liked her more and more every second. A girl this mean would definitely be one hell of a wild ride.

Miki glanced up at his silence and raised an eyebrow at his smile. "You know, when you've got folks out there howling and sniffing my ass, I'd say it's kind of dumb to stand around staring at me. I might snap at any moment."

Christ, he loved her voice. Kind of low and husky, with that sweet Texas accent. It played right across his nerve endings. And he *had* sniffed her ass, but only once. "That sounds promising."

She sighed and went back to her book.

He finished getting into his clothes and then sat down in the dirt to pull his black Harley-Davidson boots on.

"What are you reading?" He didn't really care. He just wanted to hear her say something else.

"A book on wolves."

That did peak his interest. "Really?"

"Yeah. Will it be necessary for Zach and Sara to have sex in front of you?"

Conall's head snapped up at her sudden and scary change of topic. She stared straight at him and he realized she was serious. "What? No!"

"Are you sure? Because according to this, the Alphas are the only ones who can mate and they have to do it in front of the Pack."

"But we're human... sort of."

"But you run around in a Pack. So don't you do other Pack-like things?"

"Well...uh...I...that is, we..." Conall shook his head. "They will not be having sex in front of us. And trust me, we can all have sex."

Her eyes narrowed. "I see." She went back to her book.

Conall finished lacing up one boot and moved to the other. "So, Miki what do you...?"

"I'm reading."

"...do?" He blinked. He'd never gotten dismissed so easily. And this girl was dismissing him all over the place. His annoyance peeked out, his voice heavy with sarcasm. "You're reading at a rave? You really know how to party, don'tcha?"

Without even looking up from her book, she gave him the finger.

Man, she is so mean. He was glad he had his jeans on. He was hard as a rock.

With his laces finished, he sat back and watched her. He marveled at how beautiful she was. Soft brown skin, the cutest dimples known to man, curly black hair framing that gorgeous face, and the tightest ass he'd ever seen.

She seemed to sense him watching her again. She looked at him, and glared. "What now?"

"Just looking at you."

"Don't."

"Are you shy?" He didn't mind shy. He could learn to like shy. Hell, for one night of hot meaningless sex he could learn to like almost anything.

"In what sense?"

What the hell kind of question was that? "What?"

"In what sense are you asking am I shy? There are different types of shy. There are those who are shy of people. Those who are shy of animals. Those who are only shy in certain situations. So which shy are you asking me about?"

"I have no idea now."

"Typical."

Okay, cute wasn't working with this one. He'd have to try something else. He was desperate. They were leaving the next day, and he wanted his last night in this dinky town spent between those thighs.

"You know, if you left the rave because you're nervous, I can take you home." Get her home. Get her settled. Get her wet. Then get her in bed. Yeah, that worked as a plan.

She turned to stare at him, her eyes shrewdly looking him over. "Is that a fact?"

Conall gave one of his patented innocent shrugs. He'd worked long and hard on being the big, non-threatening guy. The guy women turned to for safety. No one ever knew that just below his flesh, he had chained one of the most dangerous wolves known to the Norse gods. A wolf descended from Loki himself. A wolf that was always fighting to let itself out. But Conall fought just as hard not to be like the rest of his family. So he'd chained the wolf. Almost like some people chain dogs to a spike in their backyard. He chained it and left it there. It only came out during the hunt or during a battle. But when he was human, it stayed chained and locked safely away where it could do no harm. A few bad experiences had already shown him there was no female, human or wolf, who could handle the deadly wolf he had buried inside. No female brave enough to face that part of him.

He slowly stood up, watching her eyes travel his body as he moved. He put his hands in his pockets and lowered his eyes to give her what one woman termed the "sweetest, most innocent look" she'd ever seen just before she gave him a killer blowjob. A look that had worked on many, many women before Miki. It would work now. "Sure, Mik. It's no problem."

She stared at him for a full minute before she burst out laughing. "You are so full of shit!"

Conall frowned and his body tensed. "Excuse me?"

"You heard me. You think I buy into this innocent act of yours? 'Oh, sweet Conall. He's just a big 'ol teddy bear.' " She shook her head. "Teddy bear my ass."

Conall was shocked. For the first time in a long time, a woman had shocked him. "You're serious?"

"Dead serious." She marked the page in her book with a leaf, stood up, and walked to him. She tilted her head back so that she could see him clearly. "I've known you less than a week and I already see you, Conall. And you're nobody's teddy bear. I don't care what line of crap you try and sell everybody else." She studied him closely and he couldn't stop looking into those brown eyes of hers. She still had a bruise from where one of the Pride males slugged her when she tried to protect Sara. He'd snapped that fucker's neck himself.

"I see it in your eyes," she continued. "You're all wolf. But there's something more. Something…" She stared up at him and it felt like she was walking around his backyard, examining his chained wolf, and he wasn't sure how he felt about that. Actually, he thought he'd locked that gate.

She nodded. "You're more like your name. A Viking. But you know what, Viking? I'm not some British Isles for you to conquer. So go find yourself some nice wafer-thin girl who'll happily buy your bullshit. Whose heart you can break without a seconds thought. I'm off limits."

She stepped away from him but he couldn't stop staring at her. He'd never wanted anyone more in his life. Suddenly one night between those thighs didn't seem enough.

"Miki?"

She looked at him, one eyebrow raised. A small smile sliding across her beautiful lips. She was enjoying herself. "Conall?"

He stepped up to her and was impressed she didn't back away. "I just wanted to tell you something."

"Oh, yeah? What exactly?"

"That you're absolutely right."

"Am I now?"

"Yeah." Conall slid his hand behind the back of her neck and leaned down so their faces were close. "I ain't no teddy bear."

He snatched her to him, lifting her completely off the ground. Then he kissed her. The kind of kiss he'd wanted to give her since he first saw her. A raw, brutal kiss that, to his surprise, she returned. Her mouth opened and his tongue slipped in past her lips. She gave a moan that felt like nails ripping across the flesh on his back and made him so hard his cock hurt. His hands on her waist held her flat against him. He made sure his erection pressed into her as his tongue stroked hers, and he felt her warm hand through his T-shirt. But when her fingers clutched the fabric, trying to pull him even closer, he knew he had to have this woman.

He finally released her, lowering her back to the ground, but he kept his hand possessively on the nape of her neck and his forehead pressed against hers. He had to bend down to reach her, but he didn't care. Especially when all he wanted to do was rip her clothes off, flip her on her stomach, and mount her. He wanted to fuck her until they both screamed.

"Take me home, Miki." He was so desperate for her he could barely see.

She was panting, and if her heart were to beat any faster it would come out of her chest. He knew she wanted him. He could smell it.

Miki pulled her head back and looked him in the eye. She smiled. Not a forced one he'd seen her give others, but a real smile–warm and all his.

"Not on your life." She pulled herself from his arms and headed back to the rave without a backward glance. "Goodbye, Viking. Have a good life."

His cock was rock hard and he could still feel every place she'd touched him. He stood up to his full height and fought the urge to snatch her out of the rave and back to the closest hotel.

He heard a low growl, and turned to see the full-blood wolf in a copse of trees near by. He, too, watching Miki.

"Back off," Conall growled, causing the beta wolf to slowly back away. He returned his gaze to that fine ass moving through the crowd. He grinned as his canines extend. "This one's mine."

Chapter One

Six months later…

Miki's eyes snapped open and she realized she already had her hand around the shotgun she kept against her nightstand. She sat up, the gun still in her grasp. She had to shake her head to bring herself back to this reality. She didn't sleep. Not much anyway. But on those few times she actually did get some sleep, it was a helluva thing to actually wake her up. Especially lately. She'd been having these intense dreams…she shook her head. She couldn't go down that road right now; she needed to focus.

She could hear crunching sounds coming from the front of her house. Well, Sara's house really. She'd rented it to Miki for practically nothing.

Miki slid out of bed in her T-shirt and sweatpants and steadied the weapon in both hands. She silently slipped from room to room, checking every corner as she went. Finally, she arrived at the front door. Taking a deep breath, she snatched it open and aimed.

"Howdy, Miki."

Miki lowered her gun. "Dammit, Eddie! What the hell are you doing here?"

Deputy Eddie Fogle continued to eat his chocolate-covered peanuts and seemed oblivious to the fact Miki was damn good and ready to blow his head off. "Just watchin' out for ya, darlin'." Smooth-talking bastard. The man was leaning back against her porch railing, his incredibly long legs stretched out in front of him. She briefly wondered if he had to have his cowboy boots specially made. His feet were enormous.

"Did Marrec send you here?" Marrec had become like a mother hen since they'd kicked Pride ass six months ago. He was constantly checking up on Miki and Angelina. Not that she didn't appreciate it, but sitting out on her front stoop in the middle of the night seemed a little excessive.

"We just want you to be safe."

"Well, that's sweet and all…"

"You know, Miki," he cut in smoothly. "I'm so glad you're getting out of town for a bit. You deserve it. But I hope you won't be involving yourself with those Seattle city folk like before. I'd really hate it if you upset Sara and Angelina or shame everybody in town. Again."

Miki shut her eyes in exasperation. Boy, Feds drag you out of Advanced Trig in handcuffs just once and some people never let you forget it. Besides, hadn't she already paid her debt to society? And exactly how long had the man been out here? She'd talked to her buddy Craig over five hours ago. They'd planned on meeting at a bar when she hit town and depending on her mood, maybe going to one of Craig's infamous house parties. Craig had hinted at maybe getting back into the Game, but she'd told him no flat out. Damn wolves with their damn wolf hearing. Well, it didn't matter. Her days of risking federal prison were long over. She had bigger plans. So it didn't really matter what Fogle heard.

"My only plans are to help my friend celebrate her twenty-ninth and to become Doctor Kendrick, PhD."

"Good. Good. That's really nice to hear."

Miki watched him for several moments. She sighed. "You're not going anywhere, are you?"

"Not tonight. No. Some strange activity in town. But if it makes you feel better we're also watching Angelina's house."

"It doesn't," she responded flatly.

Eddie chuckled. "When you see Sara, could you give her my love?

"Of course."

"I sure do hope those Magnus boys are being good to her. Not sure about that Zach Sheridan fella." Miki fought the urge to roll her eyes. They'd all babied Sara. Of course, she now knew why.. Sara had been one of them. Not of their Pack but a shapeshifter like, it turned out, most of her town. Apparently, she and Angelina were two of the few non-shifting humans within a one-hundred-mile radius. "And we sure do miss her 'round here."

"Yeah. Me, too."

"Well then, it's about time you got that pretty little ass of yours over there, huh?"

"I haven't been avoiding her, Fogle. I've been working on my dissertation. And she understands that." They were all like a bunch of old women. Chastising her. She could practically see them shaking their collective paw at her.

"I didn't think you were avoiding Sara... maybe that other fella, though."

"Who? Zach?" She snorted. "I'd rip his balls off and wear them as a necklace."

"Nah, not him. The other one. The bear. Conall, I think his name is."

"Oh give me a fuckin' break."

"Uh-huh." Eddie looked back at her with those wolf eyes that reflected light just like a dog's. "Did you know you moan Conall's name in your sleep?"

The man couldn't have startled her more if he'd punched her in the stomach.

She didn't have an answer, so she stepped back into her house and slammed the door. It didn't help she could still hear his laughter through the thick wood.

She put her free hand to her face to rub her eyes in exasperation, but she smelled her scent on her fingers again. Dammit. She was masturbating in her sleep again. Masturbating to Conall.

Well this is spiraling out of control.

*****

Conall Víga-Feilan, direct descendent of the Viking Overlord Sven Víga-Feilan and the Víga-Feilan Pack, dropped face down onto his bed. He was still wet from his third cold shower of the night. *Well this is spiraling out of control.* How could one woman completely dominate his thoughts for six freakin' months? He hadn't masturbated this much since junior high.

But, Miki wasn't just some woman. She was the meanest woman he knew. And her meanness talked to him on a level he never experienced before. She brought out the wolf in him, which he'd learned to control a long time ago. But just thinking about her made his cock hard and his canines grow.

His whole life he'd had to accept the fact he wasn't like the other Víga-Feilans. His father had been too nice. Loved his Irish female too much. His uncle and grandfather had made his father's life a living hell while he lived with the Víga-Feilan Pack. It wasn't until he met Bruce Morrighan that everything changed. Bruce introduced Conall's father to the Magnus Pack. They had a lot of members and they were always looking for new ones. Jarl Víga-Feilan took his wife and newborn son and left the Víga-Feilan Pack. Since then, they'd been trying their best to get Conall to return to the fold. To become one of them. His cousin, Einarr, was especially determined to see him return. But there was no way he'd leave the Pack. Especially not now.

And not because the Pack needed him during this time of war. Or that Pack life really rocked with Zach and Sara in charge. He wasn't leaving because Sara's best friend was the woman of his dreams. A mean, sassy Texan with the sweetest smile he'd ever seen on a woman. He loved that smile. Loved to think about what that beautiful mouth could do to him.

Conall growled. Wrong thought. He shouldn't have gone there. He stood up and headed back to his shower when a knock on his door stopped him.

"Yeah?"

Jake stuck his head in. "I smelled something on our property. But it wasn't Pride."

Conall frowned. "Are you sure?"

"It was different. But nothing I recognized."

Conall groaned. That had to be the same damn scent from the night of the rave. The scent he couldn't remember for the life of him. The whole thing was making him insane.

"Anybody else up?"

"Jim and Kelly."

"Get 'em. Bring 'em out with you. Kill anything that isn't one of us."

"You got it."

"And Jake? Don't hit on Kelly. She'll crush your windpipe and suck the marrow from your bones."

Jake looked so disappointed Conall almost felt bad for him. But not really.

Once Jake was gone, Conall stood in the middle of his bedroom wondering why he was standing in the middle of his bedroom. Then he remembered Miki. Well, Miki and oral sex. With a sigh, he started off again to the bathroom.

Zach was going to kill him when the water bill came.

*****

"So is Conall picking you up at the airport?"

Miki's hands balled into fists over her keyboard and her teeth clenched together. How many times were Sara and Angelina going to mention that man? It was bad enough she couldn't forget him. Bad enough she was jacking off to him in her sleep. The hardest thing she'd ever had to do was walk away from him that night at the rave. But she knew what guys like him could do. Guys with innocent smiles and all the right words. They came into your life, turned it completely upside down, and then left you. Alone, pregnant, and bitter. At least that was how it worked for her mother.

"If you mention that motherfucker one more, goddamn time I am going to kick your ass all over this fuckin' airport."

Angelina calmly stared at her over her Sour Apple Martini. "Hmm. Those sound like the tense cuss words of a woman that needs to get laid."

Miki snarled. She seemed to do that a lot around Angelina these days. Mostly because she wouldn't stop mentioning "Sweet, adorable Conall."

How anyone could think that man was sweet was beyond her. Not with those eyes of his. Those beautiful blue eyes were anything but innocent. The man was a marauder. A conqueror. And he was looking at Miki like unclaimed territory in ancient China.

"We're not having this discussion again."

"Okay. Fine." Angelina was silent. For about fifteen seconds. "But you do know that a vibrator can't really be your boyfriend."

Miki dropped her head into her hands. "I will not discuss Mr. Happy with the likes of you."

Angelina sighed. "I find the fact that you named your vibrator disturbing on so many levels."

"Best relationship I've ever had."

Angelina sipped her martini and eyed Miki over her glass. Miki picked up her Shirley Temple and stared back.

"I didn't know insanity ran in your family, Kendrick."

"We got it from yours, Santiago."

Angelina crossed her legs and Miki immediately looked around to watch the men watch Angie. It was remarkable. The woman had the ability to distract every man in the room and she never seemed to notice. Or care.

"So, did you talk to Sara today?"

Miki was relieved Angelina decided to back off the Conall discussion. She'd hate to hit a beautiful woman in the face with her laptop computer. "Like four times. You'd think I wouldn't be seeing her in a few hours."

"I don't know why you're going to her house first. Why aren't you flying straight to Seattle?"

"Sara booked the tickets. She arranged this little stopover. I guess she misses me."

"Well you'll like her place. It's nice. Just needs a porch."

Angelina had already been to Sara's new home in Northern California. Miki hadn't gone, instead opting to stay in Texas and plow through her thesis rewrites. She knew Sara understood, but she also knew Sara had been hurt. She missed her two friends, almost as much as they missed her.

"Whatever. At least I'll have a place to relax before I head up to Seattle. I'm already so stressed about all this shit. I keep re-reading my notes and analyzing my thesis."

"And writing lists." Angelina gave her a warm smile. "Don't worry, Mik. You're going to be great."

"And what if I blow it, Angie?"

"What if you do? So? The world won't end."

Close enough. She had her whole future riding on this. Angie would never understand. Everything always came so easy to her. And Sara, being the canine that she was, never really asked for much. But Miki was being left behind and she knew it.

But not anymore. An assistant professor position at the university was hers once her dissertation was completed. She simply had to make sure she didn't blow it. The fact they wanted her at all still amazed her. Her and her Seattle friends were infamous. Not only in the university where she got her undergrad and graduate degrees. But in schools across the country. From the time she dumped her clothes on the dorm room floor her freshman year she'd been up to all sorts of hijinks and shenanigans.

Surprising to many, Miki only got busted once. In high school. The judge could have sent her off to juvenile detention or even tried her as an adult, but her mother had died the year before and the entire town turned out to make a plea on her behalf. Sara had even shown up using crutches. She'd never used crutches before in all the years Miki had known her up to that point. And now she was making a tearful plea for Miki while leaning on her pitiful crutches. It was quite the display. Miki would have laughed her ass off if she hadn't been scared to death she was going to prison.

In the end she got one year of house arrest and three years of no computer or phone use. You would think that would have been enough to get her to keep the hijinks to a minimum once she got to college. But when you're eighteen, you always think you're untouchable. And for some unknown reason, she had been. They just couldn't find anything to nail her with and they'd tried. Then Miki disappeared. Well, not really. She just went home. She had just started working on her graduate degree when her grandmother became ill. She was twenty-one and had no idea what the hell she wanted to do with the rest of her life and could easily finish her degree long distance. She thought a year home would help.

But it was eight years and two master's degrees later and Miki was still trying to figure out what the hell she was going to do with her life.

"Trust me," Angelina insisted. "You'll be fine."

"Yes, ma'am."

Angelina grinned. "You know a massage would really help you relax."

Miki liked the sound of that. Maybe she had a few extra bucks in her tragically poor bank account to hit one of those fancy spas up near Sara.

"And dirty, filthy monkey sex with a hot guy like Conall is good, too."

Miki slammed her drink down on the table. "All right, let's analyze this, shall we?"

Angelina's head fell back. "Oh, god. Not the analyzin'."

"Let's say I go and have hot monkey sex with the Viking."

Angelina looked at her. "Who?"

"Conall."

"Okay. You do. You work him out of your system and then it's over. And then everybody can go about their day and you can learn to fuckin' relax."

"Problem is that unlike you and Sara, I have a problem with just fucking whatever comes along."

"Hey! I think I was just insulted. Bitch."

"No really. I get attached. Emotionally. It's this flaw I have. So, then I'll have to see this fucker every holiday I go up there. He and his wolf buddies will nudge each other and give me that 'I had her' look. While I'm forced to pretend that I'm okay."

"You have analyzed this."

"That's what I do, Angelina."

"Fine. You wanna live life alone and bitter, be my guest."

"Trust me. Fucking the Viking isn't going to change the living alone and bitter thing one bit."

"Whatever."

Miki heard them announce final boarding for her flight and the relief almost floored her. Hopefully by the time Angelina arrived in Northern California, she'd have found a new topic. She really would hate to have to kill such a close friend.

"Come on, sassy girl. Let's get your ass on a plane." Angelina finished off her drink.

Miki slipped her computer into her bag and stood up.

Angelina did the same and slammed into a businessman trying to step around their table.

"Sorry, darlin'." Miki *felt* that voice. She looked up and continued to look up at what her grandmother would have termed "a tall drink of water." Once her head was firmly all the way back, she finally saw his face. He was breathtakingly handsome. Dark, dark hair with hints of red and a few streaks of white, but he was definitely their age maybe a year or two older. Gold eyes with green flecks, the lids slightly slanted. And a sexy smile. Basically, trouble with a penis. But he was well groomed. Clearly wealthy if his ten-thousand-dollar titanium watch and alligator-skin briefcase were any indication. And, not surprisingly, he was clearly interested in Angelina. What was surprising was the two men with him. They looked just like him. Clearly all brothers. Which meant that somewhere out there was a couple who created these three gorgeous specimens. Amazing.

"You all right, sugar?" Didn't help that sexy voice was Southern. Miki would place him around the Carolinas or Alabama. Georgia maybe. Wherever he hailed from, guys with Southern accents did things to her and her two friends that any other accent simply couldn't touch.

Angelina stared, "Uh…"

Miki's eyes widened. Never, *ever*, in the twenty years she'd known her, had Angelina been at a loss for words over a man. Any man.

Miki slung the bag over her shoulder. "Sorry about that. We need to get to my plane."

"No problem. Y'all can slam in to me any time."

He may have said "y'all" but he clearly meant only Angelina. Who still hadn't quite found her voice yet. They called Miki's plane again. She had to go or she was going to miss her flight and never hear the end of it from Sara.

But she couldn't leave Angelina. Not with this one. And definitely not with all three.

"Hey, Ang. We need to go." She grabbed her friend's arm and tugged. When that didn't seem to work, she yanked.

Angelina snapped out of her stupor. "Uh… oh, yeah. Yeah. We better get moving." She glanced at Southern Charm. "Sorry."

"Not at all." Then he and his tailor-made suit walked off. Miki knew it was tailor-made because they simply didn't make suits in that size for off-the-rack. His two brothers, with a leer at Miki, followed.

"You all right?"

"Yeah." Angelina shook her head. "Yeah. I'm fine, dude."

"I couldn't leave you with him, ya know."

"You think every tall guy is either Pride or Pack."

"I don't know what he is. But Sara and her Pack have pissed off some major players."

"And yet you're trotting off to Seattle by yourself."

"First off, I don't trot. And second, I can take care of myself. Always have. Always will. I don't need babysitters. Besides I'm not the one in danger of becoming the love slave of some shapeshifter."

Angelina finally snapped back. "You're kidding, right? With Lassie on your tail?"

"Shut up."

*****

Conall checked his watch. Again. Soon his personal wet fantasy would be here. He wondered if it would be inappropriate to tackle her in the hallway as soon as she arrived and drag her up to his bedroom. Probably. Damn human etiquette.

Conall heard the glass doors leading to the back of the house slide open, and then he heard Zach. "Either you control that mutt or I'll have him go play fetch on the freeway. You're choice, woman." He slammed the door shut.

Zach walked over to Conall and, with a heavy sigh, sat down on the bench beside him.

But Conall wasn't buying it for a second. "Don't even try and pretend like she annoys you."

"She's making my life a living hell."

"She's the best thing to ever happen to this Pack. And God knows, she's the best thing to ever happen to you."

"Yeah, I know." Sara Morrighan had only been Zach's mate and the Pack's Alpha female for six months. But it had been the best six months the Pack had known for years. She wasn't normal. Even by wolf standards. But her odd view of everything was infectious. The females worshipped her and feared her in equal amounts. And the males knew not to push her patience, but they appreciated the fact she took the jagged edges off Zach. He was still a ball buster, but a much friendlier one. She'd even gotten the respect of the older wolves who didn't live in the main house, which was usually damn near impossible.

Conall checked his watch.

Zach chuckled. "How long before she gets here?"

"Two hours. Six minutes. And thirty-four seconds."

"Well, I'm glad you're not all wound up about it."

Oh, I'm wound all right. Tight. He never stopped thinking about her. Wanting her. He was dying to know exactly what kinds of things got her off. Sucking her nipples? Licking her clit? Or something more simple? His hands in her hair? His tongue in her ear?

Zach had thrown every available female from the club scene at him. He wanted Conall to lose interest in what he termed "Sara's big-mouthed friend," but none of the women held his interest. Conall only wanted Miki. And he couldn't wait until her tight little butt was naked and on his lap.

"She'll come around."

"She's human, Conall. You should go for a nice wolf girl."

Conall looked over at his best friend and the Alpha Male of the Magnus Pack. Bite marks and bruises riddled the man's body. And he knew from when they shifted after hunting claw marks covered the man's back. It was true, Sara rocked Zach's world. But she also chewed the shit out of him while doing it. Conall would rather have sex that didn't involve bloodletting. At least not as much. "I'm not looking for marriage here, Zach. I just want to fuck her until one of us dies."

"Well…that's a goal. But if you ask me she's rude. Loud. Short."

"She's direct. Confident. Petite."

"Man, do you have it bad." Conall didn't bother denying it because they both knew it was true.

"By the way," he decided to change the subject since talking about Miki was only making him hard. "We had some visitors on our property last night."

He could feel Zach tense next to him. His only objective was to protect his mate. He'd destroy anyone who threatened her.

"Who?"

"Not sure. But it's the same scent as the one from the rave."

"Great. Just what I fucking need."

"They weren't here long. Jake's stupid but he was on them pretty fast."

"On who pretty fast?"

Conall and Zach looked up to see Sara standing in front of them, a stack of mail in her hand. She'd really gotten stealthy lately. She'd learned how to stay downwind.

"Nothing," Zach grunted.

Sara sighed and squeezed in between the two of them on the bench. "You're lying to me. I really hate that." She laid her head on Zach's shoulder. "You might as well tell me now, mate. I'll just get it out of you later."

"I'm never sure if those are threats or promises."

With a low growl, she bit Zach's shoulder. Zach winced as she drew blood. "It's both." She retracted her canines.

Conall knew if he didn't say anything he'd have to witness their idea of foreplay. Wrestling. All they were missing were the ring and the announcer.

"Something in our territory last night. Just not sure what."

"Bunnies?" He heard Zach growl but he laughed. Sara always made him laugh. She was a wacky girl.

"Probably not. Not too many bunny shifters."

"So you say. Well whatever was in our territory should be dead. Are they dead?"

Zach and Conall looked at Sara, then at each other. The woman was dangerous. She didn't tolerate outsiders on the Pack's property. She didn't tolerate threats to her Pack. She didn't tolerate anything she deemed a danger to who and what she loved. She wasn't a hunter like Conall or Kelly or any of the other Pack members. She was a stone-cold killer. And she knew it.

"No, but Jake scared them off."

"I want Angie and Miki safe when they're here."

"They will be," Zach assured her.

"And you better stay close to Miki for me, Conall. You know. For safety."

Zach groaned. "Very subtle, mate."

"I don't know what you mean. I'm only thinking about my friend's safety." If you didn't know her, you would have thought she was being completely sincere.

Sara handed a stack of mail to Zach. "Here." Then she handed a small card-sized envelope to Conall.

Zach examined the stack in his hand. "Why are there bite marks on these?"

"Roscoe got to the postman before I could."

There was that deep sigh Zach seemed to do a lot. The palms of his hands rubbing his eyes. Sara smiled and winked at Conall.

"Did he bite the postman?"

"No. He just ripped the mail from his hand. And then the postman ran away–like a little girl."

"Get rid of that dog."

"No."

Conall opened his envelope while Zach and Sara had their weekly fight over "the dog" as Zach called him. He glanced at it, crumpled it up, and tossed it into the bushes. It took him a minute to realize he now had Zach and Sara's full attention.

"Everything okay?"

Conall shrugged at Zach's question. "It's from my cousin."

Just like that, Zach stopped caring. He knew Conall's family. And he didn't like them. Instead, he began to open the stack of bills. But Sara was a different story.

"What's wrong with your cousin?"

"Nothing."

"Again with the lying. You know I hate that."

Zach grinned at that.

"What was the card about?"

"He wants me to visit the family. But I think I'd rather set myself on fire."

"That seems extreme. But it doesn't matter. We're your family. Fuck them." Sara Morrighan was quite the delicate flower. "Do you want to go see them?"

"No."

"Then I'm forbidding you to go. Because I'm Alpha female and apparently I can do that." Not that she ever would unless he wanted her to. Right now, though, he wanted her to.

"Damn you, woman," he playfully chastised. "I guess I'm stuck here, huh, Zach?"

"I'm not facing those friends of hers on my own."

"What did I say? I want you to be cheery when you see my friends."

"I don't do cheery."

"You will if you want to *do* me."

To Zach's annoyance, Conall laughed at that. The woman never gave Zach an inch. And Conall knew Zach wouldn't have it any other way.

Sara turned back to Conall. "Now I'm insisting you be here because my birthday's coming up and I expect a party. I'm thinkin' Texas barbeque and line dancing."

Zach growled again. "I am *not* line dancing."

Conall nodded. "Then line dancing it is!" He ignored Zach's glare as Sara bumped him with her shoulder and he bumped her back. The woman was like the psychotically dangerous little sister he never had.

Zach stared at the paperwork in his hand. "What the fuck is going on with this friggin' water bill?"

*****

Miki stepped out of the limo and stared. "Are you sure this is the right address?"

"Yes, ma'am. I do all the pick-ups for Mr. Sheridan."

"But this isn't a house." A mansion. A castle. A palace. But not a house.

"I'll get your bags, ma'am."

Miki nodded as she continued to stare at Sara's new home. A huge building on its own sprawling range of land. Next to the house was an enormous garage filled to overflowing with choppers of every shape and description as well as a couple of pick-up trucks and SUVs. She recognized Marrec's bikes immediately. Seemed the Pack was giving Sara's surrogate dad a ton of business.

She couldn't believe this. How could Sara be living here? Sara who was happy with a book and soda. Sara who happily worked at Marrec's place for fifteen years and "C'd" her way right through high school and junior college. How could that Sara now be living in a place where the drive from the gate to the house alone took almost ten minutes?

Miki remembered one of Angelina's last comments to her: "You'll like her place. It's nice. Just needs a porch."

A porch?

The front door opened and Sara appeared. Physically, she was a little different. Leaner. And her hair was much longer, almost to her waist. But she was still Sara with her worn jeans, battered Harley-Davidson T-shirt, and old cowboy boots. Sara's face lit up as soon as she saw Miki and Miki hated herself for waiting so long to come see her friend.

"Dude!" Sara charged down the stairs and straight to the limo, tackling Miki and knocking them both back into the vehicle.

Sara's laughter and excitement were infectious and, before Miki knew it, she was hugging her friend back and squealing right along with her.

"You bitch! I thought you'd never come!" Sara stood up, grabbed Miki's hand, and dragged her back out of the car. She hugged her again.

At the same time they both said, "Your hair's longer."

Then they started laughing.

"Where would you like me to put the bags, Mrs. Sheridan?"

Sara froze, a vicious growl bubbling up from low in her gut. "The name is Ms. Morrighan. You call me Mrs. again and I will squeeze your balls until you're dead. Now throw the fuckin' bags in the hall."

"Yes, ma'am." He hustled Miki's bags away.

"Well, I'm glad to see you finally got your aggression under control."

Arms around each other they walked back toward the house. "I think he does that shit on purpose."

"What's the big deal? You are going to marry him, right?"

"Why?" And Sara actually meant that. "I mean, we're marked. It's not like either of us is going anywhere. Besides…" She held up her right arm, a stunning tribal tattoo covered most of it. "We got matching ink."

Sara and Zach were definitely an interesting couple. Miki was still recovering from Sara's call five months before when she excitedly told her friend she and Zach had "done the deed." Miki thought that meant they'd rushed off to get married. But leave it to Sara…they'd both gone to the hospital and gotten sterilized. Perfectly matched shapeshifters who never wanted to breed. It was kind of sweet in a bizarre paranormal kind of way.

"Such a beautiful declaration of love. You're like rock stars now."

"Sarcastic bitch. God, I missed that."

Sara grabbed Miki's jacket and dragged her into the house. She'd never seen Sara with so much energy. And the woman couldn't stop smiling. She'd finally found where she belonged and Miki was truly happy for her.

"So what'cha think of the house?"

"I think it's a fuckin' mansion."

"Yeah, I guess. But it needs a porch."

Once inside, Miki gawked, her mouth open in awe. It was more amazing inside than it was out. Their hallway actually had marble floors and mile-high ceilings. A winding stairway sat opposite from the huge oak doors that led into the sunken living room.

"Your room is up those stairs. Second door on the left. This is the living room. It's got a gigantic TV. I watch all the football games on that." Sara dragged her down the hallway. "This here's the kitchen. Nice, huh?"

"Shame you can't cook."

"Excuse me, but I make a mean chicken and dumplings."

"And that's all you make."

Miki suddenly found herself in another Sara hug. The girl had really gotten strong. She was about to crack her ribs. "I missed you so much. And I can't wait until Angie gets here. Then the three of us will be back together again."

"You're killing me."

"Oh. Sorry." Sara quickly released her. "Hey. I gotta introduce you to somebody. Hold on." Sara ran outside. Miki looked around the stainless steel kitchen with its Italian tile and whistled.

"I'm glad you like it."

She screamed and jumped back about three feet. "Fuck, Zach!"

"Get used to it, sweetness. We all do it."

They both sneered at each other.

Zach looked her up and down. "Nice boots."

Miki picked up an orange from a bowl on the counter. She tossed it across the enormous room. "Go get it, boy! Go get it!"

Zach gritted his teeth as he glared at her. She wondered what Sara had made him promise to keep him from coming across the counter for her. This could prove to be fun.

"So, Zach." She grinned. "Where are Yates and Casey? Or did you just kill 'em, eat their carcasses, suck the marrow from their bones, and then roll around in your own filth in an orgy of blood and death?"

Zach glared at her.

"What?" She shrugged innocently. "I'm just askin'."

"They're in DC opening a new club, you psychotic little…"

Miki chuckled, ignoring whatever he was calling her and turned back to the glass sliding doors. She saw Sara calling something over.

"Oh, dear God!" Miki spun away, turning to Zach in horror. "What the hell is that?"

"That's her dog."

"Dear God, man, what were you thinking? You can't let that thing in your house. It's a mutant!"

"She found it on the side of the highway. Had to have it."

"What's wrong with it?"

"Nothing, really. Except for his short stubby front legs, his very long back legs, and freakishly large head. His sloping back. And, of course, he's missing an eye."

Sara returned, tragically with the dog. "And this is your Aunt Miki." Miki stared down at the beast. "Mik. This is Roscoe T. Budsworth."

"Roscoe T. Budsworth? That's the best you could do?"

"That's a wonderful name. It has prestige."

Zach looked down at the dog. "No matter what you call him that is still one ugly fucking dog."

Sara glared at Zach as she leaned over and covered up Roscoe's long, floppy ears. "You be nice to him!"

"You're lucky I'm being nice to her." Zach glared at Miki. "Later, Tinker Bell."

"Later, jackoff."

With one last glare, Zach walked out of the kitchen.

Sara crouched down next to Roscoe and rubbed his shiny coat. "You told him to go fetch, didn't you?

"I didn't actually use those words…"

Chapter Two

Miki fell face first onto her bed. Huge and so soft, it would be like sleeping on clouds. And it smelled wonderful. She buried her nose into the comforter and breathed in deep. Okay. She'd admit it. A body could get used to living like this. Easily.

She'd spent the last four hours with Sara in the kitchen. They ate biscuits and drank buttermilk while playing with that amazingly sweet but disturbing-to-look-at dog.

And not once had Conall stopped by. Which was good, dammit. No matter what Sara and Angelina thought, she wasn't about to hook up with Conall Víga-Feilan, present-day Viking. No way. No day.

She'd learned the hard way that love and sex and all the rest of it was bullshit. A distraction from the bigger picture. Her mother had been planning on college in the hopes of going to medical school. Then she'd met Miki's father. One illegitimate baby later and she was working herself to death to put food on the table while her own mother took care of Miki. But Miki had no intention of going down that road. Ever. So her bigger picture would be the next three days. Everything else would take a back seat to that.

At the moment, the Pack was downstairs ordering Chinese food and Miki had taken the opportunity to come up to her room and take a shower. She felt grungy after her day in the airport and on the plane. And she still had a full night planned. They were all going to one of the Pack's clubs for some serious dancing and partying. She'd tried to back out of it, but Sara fought her hard. She kept insisting she needed to relax. But she couldn't relax until she was done. And since she would probably only get two or three hours of sleep anyway, killing some time at a club couldn't hurt.

She thought about the Pack. They were all so sweet to her...except Zach. And they seemed to really love Sara...especially Zach. She got the feeling life with the old Alphas, Yates and Casey, was a little too stifling for the Pack.

Zach tossed around the phrase "free choice" a lot. And Sara didn't like to be bothered with what everybody was up to as long as the Pack was protected.

She realized now she'd foolishly stayed away from her friend all these months. Being back with Sara, talking and bullshitting, was all she really needed to make her feel one hundred percent better. Now she felt ready to defend her dissertation and start her new life.

But that was later. Right now Miki wasn't ready to do too much of anything. So, still lying face down, she tried to kick off her shoes. But they were boots and she'd laced them up pretty tight. She grumbled in annoyance and for some idiotic reason still kept trying to kick one off with the help of the other, feeling way too lazy to actually get up and take her shoes off like a civilized person.

But when she felt strong, firm hands wrap around her boot and begin to unlace it she jerked in surprise. She pushed herself up on her hands and looked over her shoulder. Conall was at the foot of the bed on his knees untying her laces. She had no idea how long he'd been standing there watching her, but her entire body got warm at the thought.

"Hey, Miki." He didn't look up. Just kept untying her laces. And, even though he couldn't see the fronts of her boots, was probably taking a lot longer than was actually necessary.

"Hey, Conall."

"How's it going? You have a good trip?"

Miki had to swallow to get the words out. "Yeah." Okay. One word. Apparently that was the best she could manage at the moment...spitting out one word. All the guy was doing was helping her off with her boots. Of course, he was on his knees doing it. She kind of liked him on his knees.

Get a grip, Kendrick.

She needed to start talking. Now. "How's it going with you?"

He still didn't look up; instead watching his own big hands slowly remove one boot then start on the other. His hair was thick and almost white blonde. And, like hers, it was longer than when she last saw him. Just brushing across his shoulders. His hair reminded her of silk and she wondered if it would feel that way against her skin.

"Pretty good."

He slid the other boot off and placed it aside. He leaned back on his haunches and, running his hands over her calves and feet, stared at her. He had the lightest blue eyes she'd ever seen. "Anything else you need help taking off?"

Miki almost said "everything" but caught herself. She pulled her feet away from Conall's wonderful touch and pulled herself up on to her knees. She smirked. "No. I'm fine. But thanks." He slowly stood up, his eyes never leaving her face. Still on her knees, she moved back away from him as his body kept rising. She'd forgotten exactly how tall he was. And exactly how big. In some respects, the man *was* a bear.

She was so busy staring at him and trying to stay away from him she fell right off the bed.

"Miki?" She looked up to find him on the bed, hovering over her. "Are you okay?" He didn't even try to stifle his laughter. Great. Now he could see exactly the level of her geekiness. It was off the charts, she knew. Well, that should convince him she was definitely not the woman for him. A guy like Conall should get some vacuous super-model babe who couldn't complete a full sentence or even spell sentence.

"I'm fine." She sat up, but before she could struggle to her feet, Conall moved around the bed to stand behind her. His hands slid under her arms and lifted her off the floor as if she weighed no more than a bag of chips. "Uh...thanks," she bit out as her feet touched solid ground. She tried to pull away from him, but he wasn't letting her go. Instead, he pulled her back until he held her against his chest. His arms slid around her body and he leaned in close, gently trapping her arms against her sides. And if this were anybody else, she would have completely flipped out. They'd be lucky if they had their eyes when she was done. But she couldn't even concentrate when Conall had his hands on her.

Husky, against her ear, "I missed you, Mik."

The man was killing her. "Conall?"

"Miki?" He nuzzled her neck as one of his *huge!* hands slid over her breast. Immediately her nipples hardened. She blinked. *When the hell did that start happening?*

"I think you need to back off." At least she was pretty sure that was what she said. She was having trouble concentrating. Especially with his tongue sliding up across her neck to her ear.

"You *think*?" His hand squeezed her breast and her back arched. "Or you *know*?"

Oh boy, he's good. Miki was sure that, with very little effort, Conall could turn a nun into a whore. Of course, she wasn't a nun.

She yanked her body away from his and it was as if her skin started to yell at the loss of him.

Miki backed away. "Conall. Don't get the wrong idea."

"And what idea is that?"

"I'm not going to sleep with you."

He took a step toward her. "I am so not talking about sleeping."

She backed up again. "You're not going to make this easy on me, are you Viking?"

He took another step forward. "Not on your life, Kendrick."

She backed up once again and slammed into a dresser. She held her arm up as if to ward him off. "Stay!"

And he did.

"Look, you're an unnaturally large, good-looking guy. I'm sure there are a plethora of women out there who would be perfect for you."

"Personally, I like women who can successfully use 'plethora' in a sentence."

Dammit, the bastard made her smile. She hated that. Especially when he smiled back. He was truly gorgeous. And as dangerous as they come.

Forcing her smile under control, "I'm going to take a shower. So you need to piss off." She walked to the bathroom and just as she stepped into the luxurious and huge room, she realized Conall stood behind her. Okay. Now this was just getting creepy.

She turned around. "Is there something else?"

"No. Not at all."

"Okay. Well, I'm going to take a shower…by myself."

"Great." They stared at each other. She couldn't understand what the fuck he was grinning at. Then, finally, with a low chuckle he asked, "You do know this is my bathroom?"

Miki closed her eyes. "What?"

"Yeah. In fact, this is *my* room."

She gritted her teeth. Great, that wonderful smell on the neatly made bed had been him. And who the fuck made their bed these days anyway? Miki didn't make her bed unless she was changing the sheets.

"She told me it was the second door on the right."

"Actually, yours is third. Right next door."

"Of course it is." She was going to *kill* Sara.

"But, please, feel free to stay. Take all the showers you want. I can help with the soap."

Images of that danced through her besotted brain and it felt as if someone squeezed her lungs because she was having a lot of trouble breathing.

"Well, that's very neighborly of you, Viking. But I'll just go to my own room."

He wasn't completely blocking her way, but she had to slide against him to get out of the bathroom and she felt that connection all the way down to her toes. She almost moaned.

"Well, see you at dinner," she squeaked out.

Then she ran.

*****

Conall didn't care how his Alpha felt about it; he was going to give Sara the biggest kiss he could. Coming back to his room only to find his ultimate sexual fantasy spread eagle, face down on his bed was more than any man could ask for. And when she started smelling his comforter, he thought he might come in his jeans.

The woman did things to him without even trying. It was like he had no self-control around her. When he first saw her, he'd had no intention of touching her. In fact, he'd purposely stayed away when she arrived. Sara told him if he met Miki at the airport or greeted her at the door, she'd freak. So he wanted to give her a chance to relax before he pounced. But once he smelled her again, he just couldn't keep his hands off her. If this got any worse, he might start humping her leg.

He closed his bedroom door and took a deep breath. Just the scent of her got him hard. And it didn't help she looked so good. It had only been six months, but he was positive she actually looked even hotter. Her curly hair was a little longer, now reaching just above her shoulders, and her skin looked just as soft if not softer then when he last saw her.

Miki simply looked…beautiful. And her body felt amazing. When he held her and when she brushed up against him on her way out the door…he just kept imagining that body naked and in all sorts of positions with his.

And the thought of her in his shower… him soaping those breasts, those legs, that ass.

Damn. Wrong thought, he growled to himself as he headed to his shower.

*****

Miki had just pulled on a pair of sweatpants and a sweatshirt, pushing her wet hair out of her face, when Sara knocked on her door and stuck her head in.

"Hey. Dinner's here."

Miki grabbed Sara by her T-shirt, snatched her into the room, and slammed the door.

"What the hell?"

"You sent me to Conall's room, you bitch!"

"Did I? Huh. How did I make that mistake?" Sara ducked as a bottle of shampoo flew at her head. "Jesus Christ, woman! Calm yourself!"

"Stop trying to set me up with him!"

"I'm just trying to get you laid… put it down!" Miki debated whether to chuck the hairbrush in her hand at her best friend. After a good thirty seconds, she lowered her arm. Sara smiled. "So you went to his room. What's the big deal?"

Miki glared. "He found me face down on his bed smelling his comforter."

Sara choked then exploded into laughter. Miki raised her brush again. "Okay. Okay. I'm sorry. Dude, I'm so sorry. I didn't think you'd get so... comfortable so quickly."

"Bottom line is you and Angelina need to back off."

Sara took a deep breath. "Darlin' I don't see the problem. He's hot. He's straight. He's disease free. Next to my Zach he's walking perfection. What is the deal?"

"The deal is guys like him suck you in, make you theirs, then fuck you over. It's like in their DNA or something."

"Now you're just talking about your father."

"I prefer the term sperm donor. And I'm not going to end up like my mother."

"Of course not. Especially 'cause you're not a sixteen-year-old virgin, screwed over by a rich townie, and left pregnant. So, already you're ahead of the game."

Miki glared at Sara's sarcasm. "I already had this goddamn conversation with Angelina. And if you two whores want to have meaningless sex with some guy you just met... like getting head at a rave from a biker... that's your choice."

"Hey! That's not fair. And it was hardly meaningless. I'm practically married to the guy."

"Don't care. Back off."

Sara sighed. "Fine. Fine. I'll back off."

"Thank you."

And Sara backed off for a total of fifteen seconds. "Although a vibrator does not a life partner make."

Miki growled. "Why are you two obsessed with Mr. Happy?"

"Maybe because you actually named it."

"Whatever." Miki turned back to her suitcase, stopping when she saw something she knew she didn't pack. She pulled out a brown paper bag. "Dude, I didn't pack this." Visions of international spies using her as a transporter flew through her mind. But the expression on Sara's scarred face told a different story.

"*You* may not have packed it..."

Miki frowned and opened the bag. There were boxes of condoms inside. And a note lay right on top. Immediately she recognized Angie's perfect handwriting. "Really, isn't it time you got laid? –Angie."

"I hate both of you."

"Now. Now." Sara backed up toward the door. "Angie and I just want you to be safe. You're not on any birth control. Sometimes people get lost in the moment. Angie did it with the best of intentions. We care about you and just want you to be happy."

"Fuck her. Fuck you. And, for that matter, fuck your intentions."

"See. Those are the tense cuss words of a woman that needs to get laid."

Sara ducked the bag of condoms just in time, tore the door open, and ran.

Miki sat down on the edge of her bed and dropped her head in her hands. This was going to be a long, long trip.

*****

"Forget it."

Sara shrugged. "Okay. You can ride with Zach."

"In hell."

Sara didn't answer Zach's bark. She just reached back and punched him in the chest.

"I'm not riding with…" Miki smiled sweetly, *"him."*

"Then you better get your ass over there."

Miki glanced over at Conall. He leaned against his bike, looking as casual and innocent as always. It didn't help he was wearing black jeans, black boots, black Tee, and a black leather jacket. He looked fucking phenomenal in all black.

He gave her that innocent smile and she couldn't stop the little whimper that came out. He was just not going to make this easy.

"Would you just go?" Sara spun her around and shoved her toward him. She saw the predatory gleam in his eye, but she wouldn't let him see her being weak. Not if she could help it anyway. So, steeling her resolve, she marched over to him.

"All right, Viking, a few ground rules."

He seemed curious. "Such as?"

"No inappropriate touching. No grinding yourself into me. No leaning back into me. No doing stunts on your bike so that I have to grip you tighter. Are we clear?"

Conall chuckled. "I keep forgetting you were raised around bikers." He leaned in to her. She recognized his scent from the comforter. She really liked that scent. *Damn him.* "Look, sweetness, just get your tight ass on the bike."

Miki glared at him. "Maybe I don't want to go."

His head was so close to her it almost touched her cheek. Almost. "We can stay here if you want. I'm sure we can come up with all sorts of things to do in this big house. Alone." Then he leaned in closer and sniffed her neck. She felt a bolt of electricity going right from her groin up her spine and landing somewhere in the back of her neck. "God, woman, you smell good."

She stumbled back away from him but he caught her arm.

With a firm grasp on her, he straddled his bike and gently pulled her close. "Get on."

She forced herself to slide in the seat behind him and took the helmet he handed to her.

Bastard. He was getting to her and he knew it. She put the helmet on her head, tightened the strap. He kick-started his bike and waited. She knew he was waiting for her, but she didn't know why.

"What?" she demanded over the roar of the chopper's engine.

"You going to put your arms around me or what?"

"I was thinking 'or what'."

He leaned back against her and immediately her nipples hardened. Already he was breaking one of her rules. "Either you put your arms around me or I start poppin' wheelies on this thing." And she knew he meant it.

With a silent groan, she wrapped her arms around his waist. He pulled her tighter; making sure her chest was right against his back, which didn't help the hard nipple situation one damn bit.

He pulled out of the driveway and followed the rest of the Pack that had left a minute before.

This was so much more difficult than she thought it would be. The guy was like a dog with his bone. He was holding on even though she kept saying, "Drop it. Drop it now."

She needed to get to Seattle. And she needed to get away from the Viking before she did something she would regret the rest of her life.

His bike pulled up beside Zach's as they cruised down the street. Miki watched Sara. Her friend was finally in her element. She had her arms wrapped around Zach and was yelling something to him over the roar of the motor that was making him smile... well, actually, it was more of a leer. The two seemed to truly enjoy each other's company.

Miki sighed. She suddenly realized she was jealous of her best friend.

"You okay back there?"

Again with the wolf hearing. How did any of them feel comfortable doing anything in that house when they could hear everything?

"Mik?"

"I'm fine. I'm fine."

"Liar." He kept one hand on the handlebars while he used the other to rub her arm. "What's up?"

"Just got a lot on my mind."

"You need to learn how to relax. You know, I'm pretty sure I can help with that."

She just bet he could. "No thank you."

"Really? You sure?"

Miki crossed her eyes, but couldn't help but smile. The man really was shameless. "*You* really don't need to do anything for me. Ever."

"Spoilsport."

Chapter Three

Miki didn't know a shapeshifter could be so boring. The man was just rambling. About himself. Even his name was boring. Bob. She silently began to call him Bob the King of Boring. She let him ramble as she looked around the club.

True, it wasn't much. But that was because wolves didn't need much. A dark, moody room, with a big bar, room to dance, and some alcoves where they could make out with the fellow shapeshifter of their choice. This was neutral ground. A place they could all get together, dance, and have a great time.

Of course, this wasn't the entire club. This was just the wolf part. Just one flight down was one of the hottest clubs in Northern California. A place where the rich and famous met up with the vapid and thin. She read about Sara's club in one of the magazines at the bookstore. The place wasn't only hot it made money hand over fist, starting new trends. All that shit.

And Miki was finally coming to the realization she still had a hard time dealing with.

Sara was fucking rich. Not a little rich. Not sort of rich. *Fucking* rich.

According to Kelly, her new little confidant, Sara not only had Pack money access, she had money left to her by her parents. Her grandmother refused to touch it, forcing her granddaughter instead to work for every little thing she ever got. Although, Miki was kind of glad the woman did. She could just imagine a rich, snotty shapeshifter Sara. She probably wouldn't be friends with that Sara. But cool, still wearing her Jockey For Her underwear Sara was definitely her friend. Her best friend. Just like Angelina.

And it was apparently this Sara that had become quite the truce maker, able to pull together Packs that at one time couldn't stand each other.

Miki's eyes searched the dance floor until she found her. She still couldn't believe six months ago the girl could barely walk. She'd been in constant pain and lonely beyond belief. And as much as Miki envied her now she felt overwhelming happiness for her too. She watched as Sara, her favorite black cowboy hat in place, moved her body against Zach's. She moved with grace and precision and, not surprisingly, Zach couldn't keep his hands off her.

Bob was still rambling. And the tragedy with her brain was that she could still listen to him even when she was thinking about twenty different other things. Her grade school teachers told her mother it was a gift. Gift her ass; if she had to listen to Bob talk about how great he was all night. Thank God he wasn't part of Sara's Pack.

She suddenly realized Bob was moving in on her. He'd gotten closer and she didn't like it one bit. She felt naked with only her steel-toe Docs. Because she had to take a plane into Northern California, she had to leave all her precious weapons back home. Miki had learned a long time ago that a woman her size definitely needed an advantage.

Glancing around for a beer bottle to smash and then use on Bob should it be necessary, Conall suddenly stalked out of the crowd. He grabbed Bob by the back of the neck and slammed his head down on the bar, then he lifted him up and tossed him, sending the man flying across the floor and hitting the opposite wall.

Conall grinned as he sat his big body down on the stool next to her. The one he'd just forced poor Bob to leave. "So, you having a good time?"

Apparently, they wouldn't be discussing Conall's way of getting a man to back off. She wondered briefly if he'd done that because Bob was making her uncomfortable or because Bob was making him uncomfortable being so close to her. She hated herself for hoping it was both.

"Yeah. Downstairs sucks, but this place is great."

"This is for family only." And she knew he saw all wolves as his family. For some unknown reason she liked that.

"You want something to drink?"

"Water." Miki watched as he leaned over and spoke to the bartender. Man, was his body long. Long and big. He'd taken off his jacket and stowed it along with hers behind the bar. He wasn't dark like Zach. But at the same time he wasn't pale. His black T-shirt was sleeveless and she marveled at the size of his shoulders and arms. She focused on the thin black bracelet he wore on his wrist. It looked like something a kid made. It was just a couple of pieces of wool braided together. Yet, it had to be the sexiest thing she'd ever seen *in her life.*. She couldn't explain it. It just was.

Okay. She needed to stop this right now. *Right now.*

Miki slid off the stool she'd been perched on and stretched her neck. Her whole body was tight. Tight and cranky. Angie was right. She was a tense mess. But she had so much on her mind. She hadn't been bullshitting when she told Conall that. She had more on her mind than anyone would imagine.

A bottle of water suddenly appeared in front of her face and she realized she'd drifted to stand in front of Conall. The thought of him watching her stretch her neck and shoulders made her warm. Again. She needed to get control of that. She had enough on her mind without worrying about uncontrollable hot flashes.

Miki grabbed the water and looked up to find Conall hovering over her. "Christ, you're tall. Is everyone in your family so fuckin' tall?"

"It's the Nordic thing."

It was funny, the music was amazingly loud, but the wolves had no trouble hearing each other. She, however, couldn't hear shit over the industrial techno blasting from the speakers unless someone was screaming at her.

Miki drank some of the water and tried to ignore Conall standing behind her. She could feel the heat coming off his body, and it was starting to feel really nice.

*****

Conall stared at the back of Miki's neck. Watching her stretch the tight muscles in her neck and shoulders almost sent him over the edge.

Wearing a tight tank top that showed how long and refined her neck was, her shoulders were small but strong, her back straight and lightly muscled. He could tell she was a girl who knew how to handle herself. He liked that. Liked the fact that she wasn't a little wimp waiting for some knight to come rescue her.

By the time the knight made it up to the tower of the castle, she'd have devised an elaborate pulley system to extract herself to safety. He found her brain so sexy. Well, her brain and that ass.

Unable to resist, he took his thumb and stroked the back of her neck. She stiffened but she didn't knock his hand away. Taking that as a good sign, he continued to knead the tense muscles of her neck and watch her body's response. It didn't take her long to relax a little, so he let the rest of his hand settle against her throat. His fingers spread out across her collarbone, gently stroking the sensitive flesh there.

Her back was still to him, but he was almost positive she'd closed her eyes when she dropped her head forward. He massaged other areas of her neck where he felt tightness. He kept it up until he heard her moan. And that sound almost killed him.

Gently, Conall pulled her body into his, her back against his chest. Wearing her low-heeled Doc Martens, the top of her head just about reached his chest. Yeah, he could make that height work quite nicely for them both.

He leaned down next to her ear. "Wanna dance?"

She turned and stared at him. "Are you kidding?"

He wondered if she was concerned with the fact that she was an amazingly lousy dancer. "What's the problem?"

"I'm not even five-five and what are you? Nine feet or so? We'll look like idiots."

"I am *not* nine feet." He moved around in front of her, finally releasing the hold he had on her neck. For a split second, she actually appeared disappointed.

"You know Kendrick, I'm unimpressed."

"With what exactly?"

"I thought you brilliant types were a lot more creative." She frowned but that quickly changed into a look of surprise as he bent down, slid his hands under her ass, and lifted her off the floor. She was wearing a sexy leather miniskirt and he could feel the panties she was wearing. *Satin. Nice.*

"Are you nuts? Put me down!" But she was smiling and didn't seem all that pissed.

"No way. We're going to dance. Wrap your arms around my neck." She did that quickly since he pretended to almost drop her. "Good girl. And wrap your legs around my waist."

She raised an eyebrow and smirked.

"Get your mind out of the gutter, Kendrick." She rolled her eyes, but wrapped her legs around him just the same. Her ankles locked at the small of his back and her pelvis pushed against his groin. And he wished with all his heart they were back in his room doing this. Naked.

*****

Miki couldn't believe she hadn't punched him yet. She should have. But, she grudgingly had to admit, he felt really good between her legs.

He was staring straight at her as he walked them both to the middle of the dance floor. It was awkward for Miki, his heated gaze tearing right through her. No one had ever looked at her like that before. At least not so she'd noticed. She didn't know what to say or do in such a situation, so she glanced around the room instead. She felt him move and her eyes almost rolled into the back of her head. She *liked* how he moved. She briefly wondered if he moved like that in bed.

Bad thought. Bad thought. Bad thought.

She caught sight of Sara watching her. She expected her to be all cocky and triumphant, but instead she gave her the sweetest look, which only made it worse. She didn't want to get Sara's hopes up over nothing.

But she knew Sara just cared. The woman had cared about her since she'd picked Miki up off the playground floor all those years ago after some evil little boys had knocked her down and called her a freak. Sara'd helped her up and Angelina had kicked their asses. She smiled at the memory of those boys running for their lives by the time sweet, girly Angelina had gotten done with them. Since then they'd been protecting each other. Even risking their lives for each other. But sometimes Sara and Angelina's concern for her could get a little stifling.

The skin of her neck was nipped and she turned her head to look at Conall, that aqua blue gaze of his trapping her immediately. *He is sooo trouble.*

"Where did you just go?"

"What?"

"Come on, Mik. You were two thousand miles away. Where'd ya go?"

"Nowhere." She shook her head for emphasis. "Just thinking."

"You do that a lot, huh?"

"Yeah. I guess."

"Like what? What do you think about?"

"You don't want to know, Viking."

"I like when you call me that."

Well that was the last thing she wanted to hear. She called him that to annoy him. *You idiot, what guy gets insulted being called Viking?*

"You really want to know what I'm thinking?" Perfect. She knew exactly how to scare him off. It had scared off many men before him.

"I asked, didn't I?"

"I was thinking Sara needs to stop looking so happy about us dancing together. And I wondered if Zach was going to fuck her on the dance floor or whether he'd wait to drag her off to the bathroom. He's had his hand down the back of her jeans and his groin pressed into hers for the last ten minutes. I was also wondering whether I should wear my blue suit to my dissertation defense or my dark green suit. Or if I should wear a suit at all. Or just a dress. Then I remembered that I don't have a dress. Then I was wondering if I were hungry or not. I decided not. Then I wondered if I could come up with a way to cancel the government's deficit without taxing the people."

Conall, not surprisingly, stared. "Wow."

"Well, as you said, you asked, didn't you?"

"As a matter of fact, I did." He studied her closely. "Do you ever *not* think? Or, at the very least, only have one thought at a time?"

Miki thought about that for a moment and shook her head. "No."

"Really?"

"I don't distract easily."

The Viking leered and she had that ancient China feeling again. "I bet I could distract you."

With a snort, and before she could stop herself, "Promises, promises." Miki froze and so did Conall. "Uh…"

"Too late. Can't take it back now."

"But…"

"Nope. The gauntlet has been laid." She felt his hands tighten on her ass and she let out a little squeak. "And I'm just the man to pick it up and run with it."

Okay. Exactly at what point did her nipples start hardening without it being cold or someone actually rubbing them? Plus, much more of this, she'd have to change her underwear before the night was out. *When the hell did that start happening?* And what happened to her resolve not to get involved with anyone, especially giant shapeshifters?

I should have added his ass to the List!

"You're vibrating."

"*I am not*!"

"Your *phone* is vibrating." He jokingly tsk-tsk'd her. "Again, we're wallowing in the gutter. What is it with you?"

Suddenly her face felt as hot and uncomfortable as the rest of her.

She pulled the phone off her hip and held it up. "I need to deal with this."

With obvious reluctance, he slowly lowered her to the ground and led her away from the dance floor. "Make your call. I'll be back in five minutes." She watched Conall walk off toward the bathroom. She liked watching him walk off.

What the hell was she doing? This was ridiculous. *She* was ridiculous. She should be worrying about her dissertation not about how his ass looked in those jeans.

Miki flipped her phone open. "Hello?"

She knew from caller ID it was Craig. But the reception sucked in the club. So she closed the phone and headed down the stairs and out of the building.

*****

Conall washed his hands and thought about Miki naked. Basically, that's what he did these days. Think about one small woman naked. There had never been a woman before Miki who distracted him this much. He and Zach had burned their way through a lot of strippers, waitresses, and bar sluts. Girls who knew how to get you hot and suck you off in no time. Girls who really didn't expect you to call them the next morning.

But Miki wasn't anything like those girls. She was hot and sexy without even trying. She never wore makeup from what he could tell and she didn't need any. She wore those same damn Doc Martens every time he saw her. He wasn't sure she had any other shoes. But she always seemed to pair them with the hottest little miniskirt or shorts. Tonight she was wearing leather. She looked really good in leather.

The woman was a walking, talking contradiction and he was starting to really worry he was falling for her. Still, she was skittish. There was no way she could handle him. Not really.

Conall dried his hands and headed toward the bathroom door. Before he could touch the knob, the door opened in and his almost exact replica followed. But his cousin Einarr had hazel eyes and always looked pissed off. The man wasn't pleasant and, after all these years, Conall still hated his guts.

"Hello, cousin."

*****

Miki had to walk away from the club and go half a block down to the corner to get a decent reception. She speed-dialed Craig back.

"Whatcha want?"

"That's not friendly."

Craig was such a bonehead. "Craig."

"Okay. Okay. Just kidding. I just wanted to make sure you were going to be here tomorrow night as planned."

"Yeah. Why?"

"Everybody's psyched about seeing you. Right guys?"

Miki laughed as she heard chanting from the other end. "Miki! Miki! Miki!"

"Okay. Okay. I'll be there. And you're all idiots."

"Meet us at Patty's Pub."

"When?"

"Anytime after ten. We'll be there until closing." Of course they would. Her Seattle friends were the hardest drinkers she knew. "Don't flake out on us, Queen of Despair and Pain, ruler of the dark underworld known as Texas." Miki closed her eyes. Her friends were such geeks. Which meant she was a big ol' geek herself because they often called her their queen.

"I said I'd be there. Don't pressure me."

"All right, my lovely. See you then."

She hung up her phone and hooked it back to the holster on her hip. Then she wrapped her arms around her body. She was freezing. It got cold at night in Northern California. Why couldn't Sara's Pack live in Southern California where she heard it was warm all the time?

Miki headed back up the street toward the club. As she passed an alley she stopped. She had to. They'd called her name.

She stared into the deep recesses of the dark alley. Miki heard it again. A female voice. A couple. Calling her name. She faced the alley, but didn't enter. She wasn't about to. She wasn't stupid. Instead, she'd go back to the club and get Sara and Zach.

But a hand suddenly grabbed her arm. "Don't leave."

She looked up into the face of a woman...or a man...or a she-male. To be honest, she really didn't know. Pretty but androgynous. Yet with a grip on her arm that was causing Miki some serious discomfort.

"Let me go."

"Don't leave, sweetness. We were just ready to get the party started now that you're here."

That's when she tried to drag Miki into the alley. Miki remembered taking a self-defense class once and she never forgot the instructor's words. "Never let them take you to a secondary location. *Never.*"

To Miki that alley *was* a secondary location. There was no fucking way she was going in there. She reached up and grabbed the woman's hair–*this was a woman, right?*–and yanked so that they both stumbled back slamming into a parked car. The car's alarm went off while Miki yanked the woman's hair again. Then she did it again until Miki ripped hair from her head. The woman let out a screech that would have freaked Miki out if she wasn't busy trying not to get taken to the secondary location. Of course, the returning yelps from the alley just spurred her action.

With hair still gripped in her fist, she punched the woman in the face. Then used her steel-toe Docs to kick her in the groin. Man or woman, she knew that would hurt. As the woman dropped to the ground, Miki snatched her arm away and ran.

*****

"What do you want, Einarr?"

"Can't a man just come and see his cousin?"

"No. And you know Zach doesn't want you here." Especially after what happened last time. There was still wolf blood on the walls from that little get together.

"A lackey for that Irish Wolfhound. How do you look at yourself in the mirror?"

Conall rolled his eyes. They'd been having this conversation for over ten years. It was a boring conversation just as Einarr was a boring man. Truly, the only thing his cousin had inherited from their Viking ancestors was his name and his viciousness. Other than that, he wasn't much of a Viking or a wolf. Just a petty little asshole.

"Move, Einarr."

And to his surprise, Einarr did. Yet he never took his eyes off him as he left the bathroom. Conall went back out to the main bar. They were all over the place. Víga-Feilan wolves. Not good.

Conall walked up to Kelly. "Where's Zach?"

"The office, maybe. I really don't know."

Conall headed off to the office before things spiraled out of control. This was why Zach was Alpha. Left up to Conall, he'd snap his cousin's neck as human and start a Pack-Pack war just before being shipped off to prison. Probably not a good idea. At least for the moment, it wasn't a good idea.

*****

Miki slammed her way back into the club, to the backstairs, and right into the arms of one of the wolves guarding the door.

"Hey. Hey. Are you okay?"

Miki looked behind her. She didn't see anyone following her. She took in huge gulps of air and tried to calm herself down.

"I better get Sara."

Miki grabbed his arm. "Don't you dare!"

She had enough problems. Involve Sara and all hell would break loose. "I'm fine. Really."

"You're bleeding, honey."

Miki glanced down at her forearm. There were four deep gashes across it. *Great. Paw marks.*

"I'll take care of it. I'll be fine." She headed up the stairs, stopping at the bar to get her leather jacket from behind it. She slipped it on and headed to the bathroom. Thankfully, she didn't see Conall or Sara. She could only imagine how the two of them would blow this out of proportion.

She went in search of the women's bathroom, finding it pretty easily. How could she miss it? It was actually marked "Bitches." She went in as some females came out. She went to the sink and caught her reflection in the mirror. Except for being a little sweaty, she still looked in control. Good. She slid the jacket off one arm and ran her forearm under the cold water. She winced from the pain, but was thankful the cuts weren't too deep.

She took paper towels and carefully wiped the damaged area. So intent on what she was doing, it took her several minutes to realize there was a woman standing behind her. Staring at her.

She saw her reflection in the mirror. The woman seriously resembled Conall. Funny, he never mentioned a sister. But the woman was just staring at her, smirking. And Miki was in a considerably foul mood.

"What?"

"Just trying to figure out what my cousin's doing with a little midget like you."

"Maybe you should ask him that. And calling someone a 'little midget' is redundant. Midget implies little." The woman stared at her and Miki couldn't resist. "I'm sorry, should I speak slower? Perhaps sound words out for you?"

The woman growled at her as Miki slipped her jacket back on. And, being Miki, she simply couldn't leave it alone. "You know there's no shame in having special needs." She leaned in and whispered conspiratorially, "The short bus can be fun."

With that last shot, she walked out the door, but the woman clamped her hand around her already wounded arm. Miki let out a pained bark, but it only lasted a second. Because suddenly Conall was there, lifting the woman up and slamming her against the far wall.

*****

"I should tear your throat out."

"You don't have the guts, cousin."

Conall growled, his canines extending to deadly points.

Then he heard a snarl and felt hands slide under his arms and loop around the back of his neck. "Let her go or I'll snap your neck."

Einarr. But Conall was too pissed to let her go. She'd hurt Miki. That was all the wolf in him knew. That was all he needed to know.

"Fuck you."

Einarr's grip tightened as he distantly heard glass breaking. Then he felt Einarr stiffen.

"Let him go or I cut 'em off."

The three Víga-Feilans looked down. Miki was behind Einarr. Crouched low. A broken bottle shoved between his legs and up against his groin.

"What the fuck?" Einarr wasn't used to women facing off against him. He was big and imposing and used that to his advantage. But clearly, Miki didn't care.

"Let him go."

"Get the fuck away from me...hey! Cut that shit out!" Conall would have laughed at his cousin's obvious discomfort if the man hadn't tightened his grip on his throat.

"Miki. Go."

"No way." She looked around Einarr's legs at Conall. "I'm having way too much fun." She glanced up at Einarr. "You ever seen a horse castrated? I have."

He could smell Einarr's fear and panic. And he loved it. But he wanted Miki safe.

"Hey, Conall. What's going on?" His Alphas. He loved how Sara was always so calm. Calm seconds before she started to really hurt someone.

"Just a little disagreement."

"Really?" Sara crouched down next to Miki. "Whatcha doin'?"

"Playing let's turn the stallion into a gelding. Of course, in his case I guess it's really turning a dog into a bitch." He heard Einarr grunt and knew Miki was having way too much fun with that broken bottle.

"You know, Mik. We can take it from here."

"He's not your Pack, right?"

"Nope."

"Then as a Texan I have no choice but to help out in thanks for your kind hospitality. So until he gets his hands off Conall... his balls are mine."

Sara stood up. "You heard her." She leaned in. "And if I were you, I'd do it. She helped on a ranch for two years when she was twelve. The girl is not afraid to get bloody."

He felt Einarr's hands release him.

"Good boy." He could hear the condescension in Miki's voice. "Now sit pretty."

Sara slapped her hand over Miki's mouth as she shoved her back with the rest of the Pack. He really was surprised Miki had lived *this* long.

He felt Sara's hand on his shoulder. Heard her cool, calm voice in his ear. "Who's this?"

He tried to rein in the beast. If he let it loose now, he'd kill the bitch in front of him. Sara probably smelled that. She knew her Pack well.

He released her. "This is my cousin. Gudrun Víga-Feilan." That was all he could manage at the moment. Not a problem. Sara pushed him back and the two females squared off while he and Einarr continued to glower at each other.

Sara took a protective stance in front of Conall. Kind of funny, since he towered over her. But he'd seen this woman in action. Gudrun, however, had not.

"Pretty scar," his cousin sneered.

He would have launched himself at her again, but Zach grabbed his arm and held him back. He realized Zach didn't want him involved. Not because it was two females fighting, but because the man loved watching Sara do damage. It made him hard.

"Wow. That was witty. I've never heard that one before."

Gudrun's eyes narrowed. Conall could tell his cousin was annoyed that her insults weren't bothering Sara. And they really weren't. The girl had lived with worse for years. Hell, she'd lived with her grandmother for years. That alone made her tough.

So, seeing that Sara wasn't an easy target, she looked back at him. "That little midget." She glanced in Miki's direction. "So weak. So vulnerable."

Sara snorted. "She almost took your brother's balls off and wore them as ear muffs. And 'little midget' is redundant. Midget implies little, dumb ass."

"I told her that," Miki announced from behind Jake.

Gudrun couldn't stand being made fun of and that weakness seemed to make her irrational. She punched Sara in the face.

A long stretch of silence followed as Sara stared at Gudrun, her hand rubbing her jaw. Yet leave it to Miki to solidify the moment. "She is going to kick your fat ass."

That's when Sara moved. She grabbed Gudrun and slammed her head first into the wall. Then she brought her back and down while bringing her knee up. He heard his cousin's nose break. Smelled Gudrun's blood. Then Sara wrapped her hand in the woman's short blond hair and dragged her past them all.

"Time for you to go, sunshine. You and your Pack are no longer welcome." Gudrun's Pack followed closely behind and the Magnus Pack followed the Víga-Feilans. Miki was right next to him as Sara dragged his cousin down the stairs, making sure she hit a few walls and stairs with the woman's head along the way. They went out the side door and spilled into the alley beside the club. That's when Sara lifted the woman up and threw her out on the sidewalk.

She looked at Einarr. "Get this bitch off my territory. I see any of you back here again, I'll kill you. Not them." She motioned to the rest of the Víga-Feilans. "You. Now get the fuck out of my sight." Einarr stared at her. He tried to stare her down. But Sara didn't flinch. She didn't look away. Conall was pretty sure she didn't blink. And they could all feel it. That moment when she would lose it and tear the man's throat out. No one stared at Sara too long for just that reason. Well, no one but Zach.

Einarr backed away still staring at Sara. At this point, it was his only way to save face with his Pack.

Carrying Gudrun, the Pack went to their vehicles parked across the street, and disappeared.

Conall closed his eyes. He couldn't look at Sara or Miki. His family never failed to embarrass the living hell out of him.

He felt Sara's cool hand on his cheek. "Hey, stretch. It's okay."

"I'm sorry, Sara."

"I'm the one person you never have to apologize about family to. Remember that."

He smiled at Sara. How could Zach *not* have fallen in love with her? And, apparently, Zach felt that way, too. He slid his arms around his mate's waist and nuzzled her neck. Then he grabbed her left thigh and just like that tough, fearless Sara freaked.

First she squealed. A real girly squeal. Then she backed away from her mate. "Don't you dare, Zacharias Sheridan!"

"Come here, baby."

She burst out laughing and ran back to the club, Zach following slowly behind her. He didn't have to run. He knew he'd catch her and then he'd drag her back to their office. Probably so he could fuck her brains out.

The Pack looked at each other, then headed back to the club. They'd never understand their Alphas. But really, they didn't have to.

Miki looked up at him. "What the hell was that?"

"Do you really want to know?"

Miki went quiet for a second, then shook her head. "Probably not."

"Look, Mik. I'm sorry about my cousins. And thanks for threatening his balls for me."

Miki shrugged as if she hadn't challenged a man who could have ripped her apart. "No problem."

"You know you were protecting me."

"See. There's that Viking grin. And that really unnerves me."

"I don't know what you mean."

"Yes you do. And what I did in the club doesn't mean anything." He moved toward her and she backed away. He was really starting to enjoy this little dance of theirs.

"It means everything to me."

She took another step back, tripped over her own two feet and fell back. Conall caught her before she hit the ground. Both arms around her, holding her. And that's when he smelled it.

He leaned in and sniffed her again. "Where the hell have you been?"

"No where." She tried to pull away, but he gripped her tighter. "I smell something…and blood. Are you bleeding?"

"It's that time of the month, is all."

He stared down at her. "Miki. We know the difference between open wounds and menstrual blood. Don't bullshit me."

"Mind your own business, Viking. Now let me go."

She pulled out of his arms and turned to walk away. With a growl, he grabbed her jacket and snatched it off her back. When she spun around to yell at him, he saw the bleeding wounds on her forearm. Something had pawed her. Whatever owned that scent had touched her. Hurt her.

He grabbed Miki around the waist, ignoring her "You asshole! Get your hands off me!" And carried her back into the club.

Chapter Four

Conall held her close to his side. He could smell her blood. He could smell *them.* They'd touched her. They'd touched what he considered his.

He took her back to the Pack part of the club. As soon as they walked in, all the wolves stopped and looked at him and Miki. He didn't stop, though. Instead, he continued to carry her back through the club to Sara and Zach's office. He banged on the door.

"What?" That from Zach. At the moment, he probably had his dick so far inside Sara she could taste him in the back of her throat. But Conall didn't care.

"It's Conall."

"Hold on."

Normally he'd never interrupt the two of them, pretty much because he liked not having his throat torn out. But this was different. After three minutes, the door opened. A sweaty Zach glaring at them. He could smell Sara all over the man.

But Zach took one look at Conall's face and Miki's arm and stepped back, letting them in.

Sara was just zipping her jeans up when she saw Miki. "What's going on, Mik?"

"This asshole won't get his hands off me!"

He released her, letting her drop to the floor. She had to grab his arm to stop herself from falling on her ass. "Someone attacked her."

Sara walked over to Miki and stared at her arm. "Gudrun?"

"No," Conall answered before Miki had the chance. That earned him a glare.

Sara took Miki to the couch. "Sit down. Zach, in the drawer."

"Yeah. I got it."

Sara looked at her friend. "Okay, girl. What the fuck happened?"

*****

"She got grabbed," Conall answered for her.

Miki glared at him. "I can talk for myself. They didn't rip my tongue out."

"More's the pity." Zach muttered as he stood over her with a first-aid kit. She would have been angry but she realized that, in his own Zach way, he was teasing. She grudgingly appreciated his attempt to make her feel better.

"I needed to use my phone and reception sucks on this block. So I went down the street a bit. It was when I was coming back I heard them calling to me from the alley."

Zach frowned. "They called to you? They knew your name?"

She nodded.

"You went into the alley?" Conall barked.

Miki glared at him. "Yeah. I said, let's go see what's in the dark, scary alley all by myself. Because I'm stupid like that."

Conall growled and turned away from her.

"So what did happen?" It was starting to concern her that Zach was the rational one in this conversation.

"This person grabbed my arm. So I handled it."

Zach and Conall frowned as they looked at her, but Sara smiled.

"Is there blood on your Docs?"

"Nah. But I did my best to shove balls through roof of mouth." *If the she-male had balls.*

Sara gave her a thumbs-up, then proceeded to clean off her wound.

"Was there only one?"

"I don't think so. There were more in the alley."

Conall growled again, but she didn't have time to react because her best friend was sniffing her.

"What's that smell?" Sara asked as she took a couple more sniffs off Miki. "Besides blood."

Miki pulled away from her. "Dude, you're freakin' me out. I wish everybody would stop fuckin' sniffin' me!"

"Don't know. But that's what was in our territory," Conall offered.

Sara gently held Miki's wounded arm. "Were they Pride, Mik?"

"I don't know."

"They weren't Pride." Zach leaned against the desk she was almost positive he'd just been fucking Sara on. *Horny dogs.* "That scent is definitely not Pride."

"So then we have another player in the game. Just great."

Miki frowned as Conall suddenly started pacing. He looked like a dog trapped in one of those kennels. She expected him to start barking and running in circles or start chewing at his leg.

"Well, luckily this isn't that bad or that deep. It could have been a lot worse."

"I know."

"Any chance I could talk you into delaying going to Seattle?"

Miki knew this was coming, and why she originally had no intention of telling Sara anything. "No. There isn't."

Sara covered the wound with Neosporin and a bandage. "Then can I strongly suggest…"

"I'm coming with you."

Miki and Sara looked up startled. Even Zach stood up a little straighter and stared at Conall.

Miki shook her head. "I appreciate the offer, Conall. But no. That's okay. Thanks anyway."

Conall looked at her like she'd lost her mind. "I'm not asking you."

She heard Sara sigh as she felt the blood rushing to her brain. She tried for calm. "I don't care if you're asking me or not. I'm politely turning you down."

"I'm going. It isn't up for discussion."

She glared at Conall as Sara finished up the bandage on her arm. "Perhaps you didn't hear me clearly."

"No. I heard you. And I'm ignoring you. I'm going. So get the fuck over it."

Sara cleared her throat. "I need you to move your fingers."

"What? Why?"

"I need to make sure the bandage isn't too tight."

Miki lifted her hand up and gave Conall the finger.

"Well, that works." Sara leaned back on the couch.

"I don't need a babysitter, Conall. And I especially don't need you."

"You're not going anywhere without me. Not until we know what's going on."

"Back off."

"No."

Miki stood up and walked up to Conall. She stared up at him. "You so don't want to play this game with me, Viking. You just don't have the brains for it."

*****

Well that hurt. Of course, he wasn't being rational. He was egging her on. But Goddammit. Seeing her in pain. Knowing they touched her. That they could have killed her. As it was, he was barely holding the wolf in. The wolf that wanted to start tearing through the streets looking for the assholes who did this to her. The wolf that wanted to drag her back to his den and keep her safe forever.

But none of that would happen. Whatever attacked her was long gone and Miki wasn't letting him drag her anywhere now. He was still surprised she let him get away with it this long.

Conall leaned down, his face inches from Miki's. "Bring it on, sweets. I'm more than ready for you."

They stared at each other for at least a full minute. Then, with a snarl, Miki stalked off. She opened the door, but Conall's voice stopped her.

"Maybe I wasn't clear. You're not going anywhere without me. And I mean anywhere."

Miki glared at him. Then she slapped her leg. "Well come on, boy! Come on. Time for your walk." She stormed out the door. "And don't forget your leash!"

Out of the corner of his eye, he saw Zach wince. But he didn't flinch.

Sara stared at him from the couch. "You know, you could have just *asked* her if you could come along."

Of course, he hadn't actually thought of that as an option.

Sara shook her head. "Asshole."

*****

Miki stared at the pathetic excuse of a dog watching her from the foot of her temporary bed. "All right. If you must."

The beast clamored on top of her bed and settled in at her feet. She'd never had a dog before. She'd always left that up to Sara. Yet, especially in the mood she was in, she found him quite comforting. Considering what Sara had to live with when her grandmother was still alive, she wasn't surprised her friend always made sure to have a dog. And she understood why her heart went out to the abused, the deformed, and the freakish of the breed.

She turned the light off and settled in. Her anger had tired her out and she would probably get a few hours sleep. Good. She didn't sleep often, but she was glad when she did. It was a respite from her brain.

She felt the dog jump down from the bed. "Hey, Roscoe. Where ya goin'?" She thought he'd spend the night. Keep her company. "Oh, whatever." She settled back down and was just drifting off to sleep when she felt Roscoe return. He jumped up on the bed and settled down right behind her. His snout against her ear, his furry forearm across her waist.

"Watch the wet snout, beast." Then she was asleep. Oddly comforted by Sara's freak dog.

*****

Conall nudged Miki's door open with his muzzle and walked out into the hallway. He had a couple of hours before they had to leave for the airport and Miki's alarm was just about to go off.

Zach was heading back to his and Sara's bedroom with two bottles of water when he stopped to stare at Conall. "Have you no shame?"

Conall shifted and quietly closed Miki's door. He shrugged and smiled. "Not when it comes to her. No."

"You better be careful. That woman's deranged. And mean."

"Zach," Sara called from their bedroom, "get your tight ass back in here!"

Conall crossed his arms in front of his chest. "Yes, O Great leader. And yours is so stable."

Zach snorted. "At least *I'm* getting laid."

With that, Zach disappeared back into his bedroom.

"Asshole."

He glanced back at Miki's door. It felt so nice sleeping beside her. Even as wolf. She talked in her sleep. She kept spouting equations and formulas. She'd just bark them out of nowhere. It was entertaining, in its own twisted way. He smiled. She'd get over this little anger thing eventually. See that he was trying to do what was best for her.

Hell, how mad could she be?

Chapter Five

So far, it had been the longest day in his recent memory. From when Miki "accidentally" spit Cheerios at him during breakfast. To when she "accidentally" told the airport cops he was carrying heroin. To when she "accidentally" told the check-in staff at the hotel she was only 13 and that Conall was her pimp. Oh, and that she was planning to bring a few "johns" into their four-star hotel. Would that be okay?

And no matter how much he wanted to wring her neck, he wouldn't. Even though she was making him friggin' nuts, he'd be damned if he let her see she was getting to him.

Although she was. And not in the way she wanted to either. If anything, he wanted her more. He liked that she didn't take shit from anybody, especially him. He liked that she was mean as a snake when provoked. He liked how she smelled when she was pissed off.

And she was royally pissed off.

He wondered how much longer she could be mad at him. A day? A year? A lifetime? He wouldn't put it past her. He sensed the girl could hold a grudge.

He pulled a pillow over his head and tried to think about anything or anyone other than Miki Kendrick.

But that lasted all of five minutes. Then he was obsessing over how hot she was.

Just a dog with a bone.

Well, she had to eat sometime. And except for the Cheerios, half of which ended up on the first T-shirt he wore that morning, she hadn't eaten a thing. She'd even passed on the airplane peanuts.

He threw the pillow off and went to the door that connected the rooms. He took a deep breath and knocked.

"What?"

The fact she answered him at all was a darn good sign.

Conall pushed the door open. He'd made it clear she better not lock it. If anything happened he needed to get to her. Of course, that was the time the heroin incident came up. Thank Loki he had connections in the police department; otherwise, he would have endured a very unpleasant experience with a man wearing a surgical glove.

As always, she was on her laptop again. Her wounded arm, un-bandaged and already healing, did not prevent her from hours and hours of typing. She'd been on that thing since they'd arrived at the airport back home. He was surprised the fucking thing hadn't fused with her body.

"Hungry?"

"No."

He took in a breath to control his desire to wring her neck. He gazed around the room. She hadn't really unpacked. She just had her suitcase open, clothes already lying around. A messy girl, his Miki. He did notice the garment bag she'd hung up. He assumed those were her clothes for her meeting. Underneath them were two pairs of pumps. Both black. One had heels that were about four inches high, the other five inches.

He looked away. He had to look away. If he started imagining those great legs of hers wearing those shoes, he was going to do something really stupid.

"You gotta eat, Mik...and don't throw anything at me." He could tell she was looking for something to chuck at him.

"Fine. I'll eat."

"Good. I'll order something in. We'll eat together."

"I don't want..."

"Must you argue every fuckin' thing with me?"

"Fine. Whatever. Let me know when it's here."

She went back to her laptop and it was like he no longer existed on her planet.

*****

He was like a rabid dog. Her own personal Cujo. Constantly lurking around. Constantly watching her. He was driving her nuts.

She was still so pissed she couldn't see straight. It was like he'd taken over her life. He was the big man and he was going to take care of the weak human female. She would have punched him in the stomach, but one look at that body and she knew she'd only hurt her hand.

Of course, if she had her brass knuckles...

Sara had thrown that "big ol' bear" theory at her again before she left with him for the airport. "He just wants to protect you."

Were these people blind? Could they not see past those rugged good looks, innocent smile, and that rock-hard ass? Clearly not. Clearly, she was the only one who could see him as the predator he truly was. He was the wolf and she was the cottontail just trying to make it back to her burrow...unsoiled.

Not easy when he smelled so good. Looked so good. God, did he look good. Miki didn't understand this. She'd believed herself immune to any man's charms.

"Dead below the waist" was how her last boyfriend put it. At the time, the insult had been devastating. She didn't cry about it, mostly because she didn't cry about anything. But Sara and Angie knew something was up and they quickly dragged it out of her. She should have known their silence was not a good thing. When the guy woke up with no body hair and his penis glued to his stomach, Miki didn't ask questions. She merely pointed the cops to the bar full of bikers she'd been serving that night and comfortably settled down to a life of computers and Mr. Happy for those rare occasions when she felt an overwhelming need. Then Conall kissed her that last night Sara's Pack was in town. Suddenly Mr. Happy was going through an enormous amount of batteries, and when she was asleep her fingers were getting quite the workout.

It wasn't fair really. Why couldn't she have this reaction to a nice guy? Not a predator *pretending* to be a nice guy. What more could she be to him anyway, other than a challenge?

Well, he'd started this. He thought he could treat her like one of those vapid whores he fucked who couldn't think for themselves. But everybody knows or should know...you never mess with a woman from Texas.

*****

Two hours and a crap load of Italian food later, Conall was starting to feel a whole lot better. She didn't make it easy, though. But he found a way in. He screwed up facts. It absolutely drove her nuts. So he did it often. First about politics. Then about stuff Sara had told him about the three friends growing up together. Before she knew it, Miki was talking to him and beginning to relax.

And soon she was asking him questions. She asked about his family. About Pack life. About Zach and Sara. And a lot of questions about being wolf. What did it feel like to change? What was different when he changed?

She was the most curious female he'd ever met. Constantly thinking. Constantly analyzing. He wondered what it was like in her head since it seemed like there was non-stop activity.

He also asked her some questions about herself. He liked hearing her talk. Hearing her views on the world. And she had many. She also mentioned something about a photographic memory and being in one of those high IQ clubs until rude behavior got her tossed out. Not surprising. The woman was amazingly blunt. There were very few things she wouldn't say.

It was late. Almost midnight. They'd finished eating and were now sitting at the small table in his room. Miki'd leaned back and put her feet up on his chair, right by his thigh. She was wearing her Doc Martens and white sweat socks with baggie black shorts and an army green T-shirt. He loved it when she wore shorts. He loved her legs. While they talked, he began to run his hands along her calves and he took it as a good sign she didn't slug him.

"So what you're telling me is that you're kind of a hacker?"

"No. No. I *was* kind of a hacker. But that is long behind me. I'm a nice respectable girl now. As soon as I get my doctorate my life is going to start really rolling."

"So what did you do?"

She shrugged. "Moved some stuff around. Infiltrated a few…" she sighed, "…government organizations."

Conall raised his eyebrows. He couldn't help himself.

"But," she quickly added, "I never stole anything."

"Is that why you didn't do any hard time?"

"Well, that and my age. Thankfully, they expunged my record when I turned eighteen. But let me tell you, no computer for three years. To somebody like me that *is* hard time.

"But you know," she continued. "It was always about the hack. It was about proving we could do it. It was always about that. Not money or stealing anything from anybody." She shook her head. "But those days are over for me. No more hacking. In fact, no activity that can get me arrested."

"That's always a good plan."

She smiled then and he immediately got hard. It was amazing really. Almost like she'd stroked him. She had both her legs on one of side of him, so he took one and pulled it over so that her legs boxed him in.

"Having fun with my legs there, Viking?"

"Yup."

He stroked her legs and stared at her. She looked away once and then, after a deep breath, looked back at him. He ran his fingers lightly along her calves and across her knees. He could hear her breathing change. Hear her heart beating faster.

"Conall?"

"Miki?"

"Don't get any ideas. As it is, I'm still pissed."

"Anger can be quite the aphrodisiac."

She laughed. "Men are so pathetic. They will come up with any bullshit to get laid."

"Do you want me to stop?" He massaged the muscles in her calves.

"What if I do?"

Conall stopped and pulled his hands away. "Then I stop."

Miki rubbed her neck and stared up at the ceiling. She was trying to look unaffected, but he wasn't buying it for a second. Especially when she said, "I didn't say you *had* to stop. I just asked what would happen if I did ask you to."

"So do you want me to start again?" Miki shrugged. "That's not an answer, Mik."

She locked eyes with him. "Don't try and bulldoze me, Viking."

"I wouldn't dare."

He leaned forward in his chair and ran his hand on the inside of her thigh. "How about you tell me if you want me to stop."

"I bet you're praying I temporarily lose my powers of speech."

"Only for a few hours."

She smiled again and shook her head. When she smiled her whole face lit up and he couldn't take his eyes off her.

"God, Miki. You're so beautiful."

That seemed to surprise her. "Okay."

He stroked his hand up her thigh and inside her baggie shorts; he felt gooseflesh break out over her soft skin. "Don't you believe me?" His hand played along the very edge of her panties. *Lace. Yum.*

"It's not that I don't believe you. But it's all perception, isn't it? One man's beauty is another man's coyote ugly. I mean, it's all about society's views and..."

"Miki?"

"Yeah?"

"Stop thinking."

"That's a cute idea and all, but I don't think I'm actually capable of...of...oh God." Her hands gripped the arms of her chair as his fingers slid past her panties and his middle finger slid inside of her.

"You were saying?"

*****

Miki was trying to stay in control. Trying to keep her wits about her. But with his finger slowly stroking in and out and his eyes never leaving her face, that was starting to become a freakin' impossibility. "What?" He'd asked her something and for the life of her she couldn't remember what. Her with the fuckin' photographic memory.

"You were just giving me your theory on beauty and society. Thought you could finish that thesis for me."

"Um...yeah. Sure." *Okay, Kendrick. Focus. Focus. You can do this. He's just testing you. Oh, my God in heaven, that feels so freakin' good!* "You see, it has a lot to do with... um..."

"A lot to do with… what?"

"Well, society and…uh…people…" She closed her eyes. "They are raised to…um…see…" She gripped the arms of the chair harder and wondered if she might just rip the fucking things off.

"See what?" He slid another finger inside of her and let his thumb brush her clit.

She almost came out of her chair with that. Instead she let her head fall back. Her breath coming out in short, hard gasps. "Uh…"

"Miki?"

Okay. He won. She couldn't think of one goddamn thing at the moment. Nothing but him and that big talented hand of his. Unable to stop herself, she moaned out, "Oh God, Conall."

She got the feeling that was what he'd been waiting for. Conall slid off his chair and kneeled in front of her. Leaning forward, he brought his mouth to her breast and sucked on it through her T-shirt. She gasped and wrapped one of her hands in his thick hair, pushing him forward so that he could get a better grip on her nipple. And she had been right. His hair did feel like silk against her skin.

Shit. This had so not been a part of her plan. At all! But then he'd started touching her and she couldn't believe how much she loved it. Nothing had ever felt that good before. Now Mr. Happy was more than twenty-three-hundred miles away and she was about to come without him. She never had before, but Conall was bringing her there. Her own live Mr. Happy.

Closing her eyes tight as the sensations began to build inside her, Miki brought her other hand up and gripped the back of Conall's neck. She pulled him tight against her as his fingers continued to move inside her. He brought his mouth to her other breast and sucked on the nipple until that was rock hard. Then he moved his tongue across her collarbone and up one side of her neck. She felt heat spreading throughout her body as Conall whispered in her ear, "You smell so good, Miki. Feel so good. I could stay inside you forever."

That was the last bit she needed. Her orgasm burst inside her and she clung to Conall as his thumb rubbed against her clit, drawing out her release until she screamed against his neck.

When Miki's vision cleared, she realized she was still holding onto him. "Conall?"

"It's okay, baby. I've got you." His hand slipped out of her and he picked her up, walking over to the bed. He dropped them both to the mattress. He rolled on top of her, kissing her neck, her jaw.

"Conall?"

He pulled away and looked down at her. "You really are beautiful, Miki."

"Thanks, Conall."

He stared at her a moment longer. Smiled. Then passed out.

Suddenly the biggest guy she'd ever met had her pinned to the mattress. *A really ugly way to die.* She pushed the thought away and dragged herself out from under him. Luckily, he hadn't fallen completely on top of her. It seemed like at the last minute he moved just enough to crash more to her side.

Miki dropped to the floor. *Well, that had been interesting.* She took a deep breath to calm her body down. She was still rolling from that orgasm, but she wasn't going to let that distract her. And she wasn't going to feel guilty either. He'd started this game, was it her fault he'd underestimated her?

She stood up and looked at her watch. Her calculations had only been three minutes off. Not bad. She had to guess the time he'd finally drop based on what Sara had told her about their metabolisms. Thank goodness for Pharmacology 101. Best three credits she ever earned.

She went back to her room and changed into clothes that didn't have Conall's smell all over them. Then returned to her oversized shapeshifter in his bedroom. She looked down at him and realized that asleep he did look like the innocent teddy bear everybody kept talking about.

She checked his pulse and his pupils. He was out cold, but breathing normally. She made sure that his body was in a comfortable position, brushed his blond hair out of his face, grabbed her backpack, and snuck out the door.

Chapter Six

Miki sat with the closest friends she had outside of Sara and Angelina, and realized that after all these years they were still a bad influence.

"You still have Feds coming to your door and yet we sit here hacking into a man's computer?"

Craig grinned, but never looked away from the laptop he was diligently working on. "Yeah. They're like friends now. I make them coffee."

Miki shook her head. "You're nuts."

"Dude, they have nothing on us. They're just fishing."

Miki put down her Shirley Temple. "But you guys are hacking into someone's computer. So you're giving them ammunition." Miki ate pretzels out of a bowl then briefly obsessed over how many hands had actually been there before her. "Who are you going after anyway?"

"Mitchell Leucrotta."

Miki frowned. "Who?"

Her four friends stared at her. All scrunched together in the booth opposite her, they leaned on top of one another trying to see what Craig was doing on the laptop.

Amy glanced at Craig. "*Professor* Mitchell Leucrotta."

Miki groaned. "Are you guys nuts? Have you lost what little bit of your minds you have left?" Hacking into another university was dumb. Hacking into your own was damn suicidal career-wise. And the thought of Craig being the butt buddy of someone in prison was simply not a pleasant thought.

"I'm almost positive he's holding up my grant money." Craig, like her, was still working on his dissertation. But he had his own lab in the biotech school and would probably be a very rich man one day. If he didn't have a weird fetish about feet, she would have dated Craig herself. But, as it was, they were better off as good but strange friends.

"Whatever you find, you can't use it against him. Not legally." Miki shifted around in her seat and Craig stared at her.

"You so want to see what we're doing, don't you?"

Miki turned her head away. "No."

"Liar." Amy Bitter, who loved her name, accused. Amy could take apart and re-build absolutely anything no matter how complex.

"You want to touch the keyboard. You lust for the keyboard." That from Kenny Liu. A software genius who loved creating viruses.

"You're all idiots."

Ben Klein, whose hacking skills made hers look like child's play, raised an eyebrow. "She desires the keyboard as much as she desires to help us with the password."

"I'm not listening." Miki put her hands over her ears. "You can't lead me down this road of evil and prison time."

"This is part of your 'I'm a good girl now' plan, isn't it?" Amy asked sweetly.

Miki took her hands away from her ears. "Yup. I'm a very good girl."

Craig winced. "Don't say that."

"Why?"

"Because to guys it just means you swallow."

"Grow up," Miki snapped as she tried not to laugh. "How about, I'm going to be a very respectable girl with a life."

"We have lives." Kenny grabbed his bottle of ale off the table. "Sad, lonely, bitter lives. But lives just the same."

"But what about our plan to rule the world, Miki? Or at least Microsoft?" Ben pushed his empty bottle of ale away. "You and me. We had big dreams."

"You guys are boneheads." Yet she loved each and every one of them. She connected with all of them in junior high through an online game before online games were hot. Together they'd begun a minor reign of terror against big corporations. But Miki was the only one busted. She never turned them in, even though she could have gotten off scot-free by turning state's evidence. Because of that they were loyal to her. And she knew it was no accident they all ended up attending the same university.

"Okay. Let me make this clear. I'm here for one reason. To get my doctorate and to get a life. Sara and Angelina are passing me by. I don't want to wake up forty, still living in Texas alone and bitter. So, until further notice, I will not be doing anything remotely…" she cleared her throat. "…illegal."

She didn't know what expression she had on her face, but Amy was all over it.

"Except that you've already done something illegal."

"What? No."

Amy leaned forward. "Bullshit, Kendrick. Come on. Tell us. You'll feel better. What was it? Corporate espionage? Credit card theft? Identity theft?"

Miki stared. "The fact that you would think for a second I would ever do that bugs me." Then she shrugged. "I kind of drugged a man."

"Did you kill him?"

"*No!* What is it with you guys?"

"We're bored," Kenny Liu answered.

"Clearly."

"So did you just do this or…?"

She glanced at her watch. "About two and a half hours ago, give or take. Of course, that's when he reacted to it. The actual ingestion of the drug…"

"Miki," Amy cut her off. "Who the hell did you drug?"

"Just this guy. He's an… associate of Sara's." She'd filled them in months ago about Sara's new life, but she gave only the barest of details. To her friends it sounded like Sara had hooked up with this cool biker guy and ran off to live happily ever after in Northern California. Left out was anything about shapeshifters, Packs, Prides, or vicious battles in Sara's front yard. "He insisted on coming with me so he could be my big male protector."

"How did you do it?" Craig didn't even look up from the keyboard. Miki drugging someone didn't even warrant a glance.

"I combined a few things. All tasteless. It was quite effective. He went to get ice and I put it in his pasta. It took about an hour or so to become active in his system. Then he went out like a light." *But not before making me scream like a little whore.*

Amy looked at Miki over her bottle of ale. "Is he cute?"

Oh, God, yes. "He's okay."

"Got a picture?"

"Maybe." Miki grabbed her backpack and dug around until she pulled out a battered picture Sara sent her five months ago. It was a shot of the Pack with Sara and Zach in front. She knew Sara sent it to her so that Miki would know she was okay.

"Here." She handed the picture to Amy. "He's the big blond one in the back."

Amy looked at the picture while Kenny looked over her shoulder. He frowned and stared at the photo in awe. "Jesus, Miki, is this guy standing on a ladder or something?"

"And you're here why?" Amy demanded, incredulous.

"What?"

Her two friends looked up at her, but Amy spoke. "Come on, Mik. This guy is hot."

Kenny shrugged. "I'm annoyingly straight, and I think this guy is hot. Freakishly large, but hot."

"He's a pain in the ass."

"This guy?" Amy sounded unconvinced. "He looks like a…"

"If you say teddy bear, I'm going to kick the living shit out of you."

"I was going to say he looks like a sweetie."

"Well, he's not. Far from it, in fact."

"You're an idiot. I'd be on this guy in two seconds." And she would too. Amy was a geek, but she was a horny little minx.

"I need safe and boring. He's so not that." *Amazing at hand jobs, though.*

"Why would you want safe and boring?"

"Because safe and boring gets you tenure."

"And let me guess who your idea of the perfect safe and boring guy is."

"You don't have to guess. It's Troy. Perfectly suited for me." Her friends groaned in disgust. "What? What's wrong with Troy?"

Amy sneered, "Dude, he's seriously boring. And a bit of an idiot if you ask me."

"No. No. He's just brilliant."

"Miki, he's just smart. You're brilliant. And he could never deal with that. *Ever.*"

Ben took his empty beer bottle and spun it. "I've talked to the guy. He could never deal with a woman who is smarter than he is. And you are definitely smarter than he is."

She didn't want to hear this. She'd already set Troy up in her mind as her "ideal." She didn't want to hear that he couldn't handle her. She was, in fact, hoping to meet up with him again while she was in Seattle. Another reason she didn't want Conall's tight ass with her.

"You guys are just snobs. Someone has to be dangerously unstable for you to find them remotely interesting."

"You mean, like you?" Miki gave Kenny the finger.

"So, your 'new life' as you call it. What does that mean for us?" Craig was again not looking at her as he plugged away on his laptop.

Miki frowned. "What are you talking about?"

"Are we still going to be compadres? Or are you going to dump our collective ass so that you can hang around Troy's elitist prick friends?"

Miki was kind of hurt. "I'd never do that to you guys."

Amy motioned to the waitress for another ale. "Well all this talk about changing your life…"

"I would never do that to you guys. Period. End of story. Understand?"

Her friends smiled, almost in relief. Miki had no idea they'd been worried.

"So, isn't this big scary guy gonna be kind of pissed you drugged him?" Ben spun his bottle again. When it pointed at Amy he leered and wiggled his eyebrows. In response she chucked pretzels in his face.

"I have it all calculated out. I have like six more hours before he wakes up. And when he does, I'm already sitting there like he simply fell asleep."

"Personally, I think he should wake up with you under him."

Miki rolled her eyes. "God, Amy. You're a horny dog."

"And yet I feel no shame."

Craig frowned at his computer. "Christ, this guy has a twenty-digit password to his freakin' email."

Amy raised an eyebrow. "It makes you wonder what he's hiding."

Miki glanced at her watch. It would be "last call" soon. But her friends wanted her to go with them to have an early-morning breakfast. Part of her wanted to go. She could use a good omelet. The other part wanted to get back to Conall. And that was bugging the shit out of her. "Who is he anyway? Professor Leucrotta."

"He's new in the department. Been there about nine months or so. Surprised you never heard of him."

Miki looked up from her empty glass. "Why?"

"He fought Conridge for you. He wanted to take over your thesis and she pulled rank on him."

Miki felt fear lace up her spine. "What? Why?"

Kenny shrugged. "No idea. But he's been asking a lot of questions about you."

A look of panic crossed Craig's face. "Maybe he's a cop."

Miki could only hope.

*****

Miki rubbed her tired eyes and leaned back into the driver's seat of the SUV. She hated driving the fucking thing. She'd rather have a cute little sports car. Something that fit her height a hell of a lot better than The Boat, as she now called it. But Conall wasn't going to fit into anything tiny. He would always need to drive that big body around in trucks or SUVs.

"Sara? Are you still there?"

"Yeah. I just don't know what to say."

"Tell me I shouldn't be freakin' out."

"I can't tell ya that."

Sara would never lie to her and finding out some professor she'd never met before was asking a lot of questions about her wasn't something that either of them would consider "not a big deal." Not right now anyway.

"Just watch your ass, Mik. I want you back here with Conall as soon as your done."

"Yeah. Not a problem."

"Well, whatever you do, keep Conall close to you. I'm serious, Mik."

"Uh… okay." Her mistake was the pause.

"What? What did you do?"

"Nothing."

"You're lying to me, Miki Kendrick." When her friends used her full name, she knew she was in trouble. When they added in her middle name, she knew she'd gone too far.

"I just went out with Craig and the guys without him, is all."

"How? He'd never leave you. I know him. So how did you get away from him?"

"Um…"

"Miki Marie Kendrick! You drugged him didn't you?"

Miki winced. Boy, did Sara and Angelina know her well. "He'll be fine."

"You get your ass back to that hotel and you make sure he is! *Right this fuckin' minute!*"

"Okay. Okay. Calm yourself. I'm already at the hotel."

"And make sure he doesn't say anything to Zach. He barely tolerates you as it is. I don't want to have to fight my own mate every damn Thanksgiving."

*****

She used her keycard to get into her room, easing the door open and sliding quietly in. She figured she still had a good hour before Conall snapped out of it, but no use stomping around and waking the man up before then. She quietly dropped her backpack to the floor and looked through the adjoining door. They'd pulled the heavy hotel curtains closed the night before so it was dark in Conall's room. She crept in, trying to make out the bed. As she got closer and her eyes became accustomed to the gloom…

Oh, shit.

"Looking for me?"

Miki squealed and spun around to see the outline of Conall's body standing behind her. She could barely see him in the dark, but she could see those glinting eyes reflecting the light from her room.

"Uh…Conall.   Um…before   we   jump   to   any conclusions…"

He stepped toward her and she backed away. "You mean the conclusion that you drugged me and then ran out?"

"Yeah. That conclusion." Okay. No reason to panic. Conall wouldn't hurt her. Would he? No. Not Conall. Of course, he did look seriously pissed.

"Do you realize you could have killed me? You don't know how our bodies work. You don't know what you are doing."

"I knew enough to make a good judgment call." Of course, Conall had woken up way before he should have. So how good a judgment call could it have been?

He was still coming toward her and she was still backing away. Now that her eyes had become accustomed to the dark, she could see exactly how pissed he was. And he was really pissed. He looked just like the marauding Viking she'd been accusing him of being. "You're making 'judgment calls' about my life?"

Okay. That was a good point. She put on her soothing voice. "You know, Conall…"

"Don't try and placate me, Miki. Just don't." His voice was calm, which was making her much more nervous than if he were yelling at her.

Miki felt the back of her legs hit the bed. Conall was blocking her way to the door, so she went up on the bed and over it. She stood on one side, he on the other.

Since soothing and placating didn't seem to be working, she decided to just be herself. "You started this shit. I told you to stay out of my life and you thought you could handle it. Guess you were wrong."

"You are such a little bitch."

"Oh, that's a news flash!"

His eyes narrowed and she realized they weren't merely glinting from the light. His eyes had shifted. He was so pissed his eyes looked just like a wolf's. Probably not a good thing.

"You keep moving away from me, Mik. Why is that?"

"Cause I'm not an idiot."

"Really?" She figured he'd come across the bed for her. But instead, he grabbed the headboard with his left hand and with one good yank, tossed the entire bed across the room. The fact that the frame had been bolted to the wall and floor was not lost on her.

Holy shit...

Conall walked toward her, closing the space between them. She backed away until she found herself up against the wall. He moved in front of her, placing his arms on either side of her body, his palms resting flat on either side of her. She crossed her arms in front of her chest and glared up at him.

"What? *What!*"

"You just took this to a whole new level."

"And what's *that* supposed to mean?"

"That the gloves are off."

"Oh, I'm quaking."

His wolf eyes swept up and down her body once. But in that one gaze, it was like he'd ripped off all her clothes. To her surprise, it wasn't really an unpleasant feeling. "You will be."

"Bring it on, Viking. I do so love a challenge."

He smiled and it took all her strength not to run for her life. His incisors had extended. He had wolf eyes and fangs. So not a good thing.

"You really think you can handle me, baby?"

No. But she wasn't about to tell him that. "Already I'm bored."

With a snarl, he grabbed her by the shoulders and lifted her up against the wall. Then his mouth was on hers. It was a vicious kiss. One that drew blood when his fangs grazed against her lips. But she didn't care. Not when she was experiencing the most amazing adrenaline rush of her life.

His tongue slid into her mouth and she tasted him and her own blood. At first, she didn't know what to do. But then it was like her body had a will of its own. Her legs wrapped around his waist and her hands were under Conall's T-shirt, running over all that smooth, hard skin packed with tight muscles, and settling on those narrow hips. Then she felt his hands under her shirt and on her breasts, her bra torn apart in one pull.

For that moment, her friends, her dissertation, Troy, her attempts to dispute the Pythagorean Theorem, all that was forgotten. Instead, she couldn't think past Conall touching her. He felt so good next to her skin. She wanted to be naked and she wanted this man inside her. And it seemed Conall had the same idea. His hand reached under her short denim skirt and snatched off her panties.

She dug her fingers into his hair and groaned into his mouth as he gripped her ass tight. She was sure she felt his claws just beneath his skin, but he hadn't let them loose. Yet.

He stopped kissing her so he could attack her neck. She wondered whether he'd mark her or not. Normally, she'd fight that. She knew from Sara what it meant. But at the moment, rational thought didn't exist for her. Especially once that mouth of his moved down to her breast and she felt his fangs graze across her nipple. Her whole body jerked violently as she gripped him tighter.

Conall undid his jeans and had them and his boxers around his ankles. Miki could feel the heat from his erection as it pressed against her. She knew she should stop him. If for no other reason then to tell him to put a condom on. But she was lost. Hopelessly lost.

Then the knock on the door came. She and Conall froze.

"Hey, Miki?" Craig's voice. *Oh, shit.*

Conall growled. A low, scary one as he glared at her with accusing wolf eyes. "Who the hell's that?"

"My friend."

There was another bang at the door. This time more insistent.

Miki began to say something, but Conall's hand suddenly covered her mouth. "Not. A. Word," he bit out between clenched teeth. "Hold on," he barked at the door.

He took several deep breaths, then slowly released Miki. She slid down his legs, his erection gliding right across her flesh and she let out a little moan before she could stop herself.

"You're killing me," he whispered angrily before he pushed her away, pulled his boxers and jeans up, and went toward the door.

"Conall." He glared at her over his shoulder. "Fangs," she whispered.

He blinked, realizing parts of him were still wolf. He closed his eyes and cracked his neck. When he opened them again, his eyes were his normal blue and his fangs had receded back into normal incisors.

Miki pushed down her skirt and kicked her torn panties and bra across the room and under the bed as Conall answered the door.

"Yeah?"

"We're looking for Miki."

With a grunt, Conall stepped back, allowing Craig, Ben, and Kenny Liu to walk into the hotel room. They gawked at Conall like he was the main attraction at a freak show.

"What are you guys doing here?"

Kenny was the first one who could actually tear his eyes away from Conall. "Um…you forgot something."

No she didn't. She didn't forget anything. Her friends were checking up on her. They'd probably dumped off Amy and then started wondering what would happen to Miki when Conall woke up. She thought only Sara and Angie were that protective of her.

"Oh, yeah? What?" She loved her friends, but she wasn't above giving them a hard time for the hell of it.

"Uh…" Kenny looked at Ben who looked at Craig who finally turned away from Conall to look at Miki.

"Um…" he patted his pants. "The…uh…fifty bucks I owe you." Craig pulled out his wallet and took out several bills. He walked across the room and handed it to Miki.

"That's the best you can do?" she asked quietly with a smile.

"We were desperate," he whispered back. "And should I ask what happened to the bed?"

Miki glanced at the displaced bed and back at Craig. "Earthquake."

"Miki," he whispered fiercely through his teeth. "This isn't funny. Did you know your lip was bleeding?"

*****

Conall was trying desperately to get himself under some control. He'd never lost it like that before. *Never.* This one woman had pushed the beast out of him, but she didn't run screaming like any normal person would have. Instead she'd almost fucked him.

And he almost took her. Right up against the wall. No condom. No rational thought. No thought for consequences. He knew Miki was healthy as a horse–Sara told him often enough. He was surprised the female didn't pull out Miki's blood tests as proof. So that wasn't even an issue for him. But he also knew from looking at her she was a fertile girl. True, he wanted kids one day but right this minute? And with Miki? The woman who had drugged him and left him to go hang with her friends. Really, wasn't he just trying to get laid here?

Maybe not. Maybe he wanted more. More from the one woman the wolf in him seemed to respond to.

But Miki Kendrick taunted that wolf like it was a small Jack Russell Terrier behind a neighbor's fence. *Crazy woman.*

He watched as Miki spoke to that nerdy imbecile. If they had been in high school together, he would have kicked that guy's ass on a daily basis.

Of course, the way he was leaning into Miki at that very moment, he may still kick his ass.

*****

Miki ran her tongue along her bottom lip and tasted her blood. Christ, things had spun out of control, hadn't they? She heard Conall growl from across the room and saw all her friends tense up. She had to get them out. Now.

"I just bit my lip, it's nothin'." She turned Craig around and pushed him toward the door, both her hands against his back.

"You sure you don't need anything else?"

A box of condoms? "No. But thanks. And thanks for the fifty." Which she had every intention of keeping.

She shoved Craig out the door, then grabbed Kenny and Ben by their jackets and forced them out. "Thanks, guys. See ya!"

She closed the door on her friends and turned to face Conall. He didn't say anything. He just stared at her.

"What?"

"Who the hell were they?"

She pushed off from the door and moved across the room. "*They* are none of your business."

"Fine. Whatever." He headed to the door, snatching his biker jacket up as he walked toward it. "I'll be in the diner across the street when you're ready to go to the campus."

With a slam, he was gone.

Chapter Seven

Conall pushed his second helping of waffles away. Clearly he was upset; he wasn't eating as much as he usually did.

Miki. Fuckin' Miki. She'd done this to him. That tricky, sadistic bitch. He couldn't wait to fuck her brains out.

He shook his head. *No. No. No.* She was a treacherous female he should stay away from. He shouldn't be burying any part of himself into any part of her. She was dangerous. Like uranium. But the way she'd moaned his name when she was having that orgasm…

Okay. He was doing it again! He was not going to think about her and the way she moaned anything. Never again. He was never letting a woman get that close to him again. No matter how cute, sexy, brilliant, or dangerously unstable she may be.

In fact, he was done with women all together. There was absolutely nothing wrong with celibacy. It was a fine way to live. Hell, Gandhi did it.

"Well, hello, sunshine."

Conall glanced at the female standing next to him. She was barely taller than Miki. Another mighty-mite. Great.

"What do you want?"

"And the girls told me you were considered the nice one."

No. More like the stupid one. "What does a Pride female care about nice?"

She slid into the bench across from him. "Uh-oh. Someone looks sad." Christ, this woman was the queen of sarcasm.

"Exactly who are you?"

"Victoria Löwe."

"Of the Löwe Pride?" German lions. Great. His day just kept getting better and better.

She nodded. "And you're Conall of the Magnus Pack."

"Yeah." He didn't ask how she knew that. He didn't want to know.

"Well, Mr. Magnus…"

"It's Conall.   Or Mr. Víga-Feilan if you want to be formal."

And just like that, the girl's whole body language changed. He smelled the sudden waft of wariness coming off her. "You're a Víga-Feilan?"

"That's my family name. But I'm not part of that Pack. I've always been a Magnus."

She seemed to relax a bit from that, but was still wary. He didn't blame her. Einarr and his kin had made quite a name for the Víga-Feilans. Pride and Pack alike hated them. Clearly his family still bought into that Viking bullshit. Problem was they weren't floating around in long boats and decimating monasteries anymore. *Asshole.*

"So, what do you want?"

"To talk."

Conall glanced over his shoulder. There they sat. A Pride of Löwe females quietly watching them, waiting to tear him to pieces. They were what he expected from Pride. But this one, she was a bit of a runt. Maybe she had some mountain lion in her.

"And that's why you tracked me here?"

"Oh, honey, don't flatter yourself. I didn't track you anywhere. Actually, my girlfriends and I are going to the rodeo. I'm hoping to find me a cowboy. And then I saw you sitting here all by your lonesome. And one of my girls recognized you."

"Okay. Then talk."

"I heard about your Pack and the Withell Pride. Such ugly business."

He sighed. "I'm bored."

"Personally, I'd rather not have a repeat of that incident, if possible."

"And how do you propose that? By letting the Packs roll over and expose our collective bellies?"

"Dogs. I swear, everything is just so black and white with you guys. It's cute in its simplistic, puppy-like way."

"You know, I've had a really bad morning, and I'm not above reaching across this table and snapping your neck like a twig."

"If you're the nice one, I'm really curious about your Alphas." She shrugged. "I heard your Alpha female's friend got attacked at one of your clubs. I just wanted to let you know that it wasn't us."

He knew that but, clearly, she was worried he didn't. "And you speak for all the Prides?"

She nodded. "As a matter of fact, I do."

For the first time, Conall really looked at the girl. She was beautiful and young. Maybe a little too young to be speaking for all the Prides. Still, he was willing to give her the benefit of the doubt. "So you didn't send them. Then where did they come from?"

"I have no idea."

"And I'm supposed to trust you because…"

"I'm adorable."

Conall chuckled at that. She was adorable. Dangerous and adorable.

"Am I interrupting anything?"

Maybe it was the way Miki was staring at them. Like she caught them fucking on the diner table. But whatever her look, he *did* feel guilty. But why the fuck should he feel guilty? It's not like he drugged her to go off and meet with anybody.

He looked away from her, unwilling to think too much about her and how cute she was when her hair was wet from a recent shower.

"No. No. I was just leaving." Victoria started to slide out of the booth.

"You don't have to go." Okay. Now he was just being a prick.

He heard Miki gritting her teeth. *Good.*

"Maybe she doesn't have to go. But you do. I need to get to campus."

Conall looked at Victoria. "Are we done?"

"I've said my peace. Now I've got to get myself a cowboy." She smiled at him. "Thanks for listening, Conall. I guess you are the nice one."

She stood up and looked at Miki. "He's all yours." Then she walked back to her Pride.

He pulled his wallet out of the back of his jeans and threw money on the counter. By the time he stood up, Miki had already stormed out the door.

He found her by the rented SUV. He unlocked the doors and they both got in.

"Who was that?"

"Victoria Löwe." He started the vehicle and pulled out of the parking lot.

"She was Pride?"

"Yup."

"And you're sitting around chatting with her in a diner?"

"Apparently so."

They didn't speak again until they hit the campus.

*****

As far as she was concerned, that little ten minute trip was the longest *ever.* Conall parked as close as possible to the building she needed to get to. Then he shut off the motor and stared straight ahead. Miki grabbed her backpack, ready to storm off, but his voice stopped her. "When you're done, come back here. Don't go anywhere else. Don't try and sneak off. 'Cause I will find you. And if I have to do that I'll be much less pleasant."

"You're being an asshole."

"Sorry. It must be the after affects of *the drugs you gave me!*"

Miki didn't even flinch when he started yelling. "You're going to hold that over my head forever, aren't you?"

Conall stared at her with his mouth open.

"What?"

He turned away from her. "Don't let the door hit you on the way out."

Okay. Fine. He wanted to be an unforgiving asshole, he could be an unforgiving asshole. *Self-righteous prick.*

She jumped out of the SUV, pulled her backpack over both her shoulders, and cut across campus toward her advisor's office.

"Hey, psychopath!" Miki, halfway to her destination, turned around to see Amy and Craig walking toward her.

"Hey."

"You okay?" Amy knew her well. "I can't tell if you're pissed or sad."

Both. "It's nothing. I'm okay. What are you guys doing up so early? Or did you even bother going to bed?"

Amy sighed. "I gotta teach a bunch of freshman about quantum physics. Three hours of my life I'll never be getting back." She bitched a lot, but Amy was one of the best associate professors the university had. And if they were smart, they'd cough up and give her tenure before MIT or Harvard finally stole her away.

"And I'm here to see Professor Leucrotta." Miki felt a shudder go down her spine and it wasn't one of those cool ones Conall gave her. But one of those creepy ones she got like when she saw a spider crawling around her bathtub.

"Why?"

"Don't worry. He agreed to meet with me about the grant money. Maybe I'll be able to track down his password while I'm in his office."

"Be careful. Don't do anything stupid."

"Who? Me? And where is my fifty bucks?"

She smirked. "I believe you *forgot* to give me that this morning."

"You're not giving that back to me, are you?"

Miki grinned. "Nope. But thanks for checking up on me."

"Anytime. We felt like we couldn't leave you alone with Conan the Barbarian.

"Hey, Mik." Amy nudged her. "Check it out. Your boring dream man." Miki followed Amy's nod and saw Troy Benson walking toward her.

"Miki? Is that you?"

Miki braved a smile at Troy as she quickly slipped her backpack off her shoulders. Nothing geekier than walking around with a giant backpack attached to you. And Troy was so not geeky. Almost six feet tall–a nice *normal* height, unlike some other abnormally large males she knew–with light brown hair and dark green eyes. She'd had a crush on him since Advanced Chem. Not surprisingly, Troy had his arm around some tall, blond babe who looked like she didn't eat without throwing up after, but he kissed her on the cheek and sent her on her way before walking over.

"Wow, you haven't changed. Still my little Miki."

Funny, that didn't seem like much of a compliment.

*****

"Did she say anything else?"

Conall leaned against the passenger door of the SUV, his cell phone against his ear, and stared out at the deserted campus. It was still early and students were just starting to appear. "Said she was trying to get herself a cowboy."

"I don't really think that's helpful."

Conall grunted and Zach was silent for a moment on the other end. "Is everything okay with you?"

"Yeah. Why?"

"I've just never heard you sound so much...like me."

Conall chuckled. "I'm fine."

"Miki still giving you a hard time?"

"Something like that." He wasn't about to admit to his Alpha Male he let some crazy woman drug him and take off in the middle of the night. If for no other reason, he knew Zach would never let him live it down.

"I'm sure she'll get over it eventually. Anyway, did you believe her?" *Yes!* But he was never going to believe short, vicious women again. Especially ones whose whole bodies shook during orgasm.

"Who?"

"Victoria Löwe."

"Oh... uh... yeah, yeah. I did. I believed her."

"Okay. Well, you two be careful anyway. Soon as Miki's done, bring her ass back here before my mate forces me to start drinking. When she's stressed, she paces. It's driving me nuts."

Conall sniffed the wind coming from the direction Miki had headed. He smelled something...it was Miki's scent. But it was mixed with...some other guy.

Conall growled.

"Conall? Are you listening to me?"

"Yeah. Sure. We'll be careful. Gotta go." He shut off the phone and followed.

*****

"So? Still living in Texas, huh?" Miki took a deep breath. She would stay calm. She could do this. Although it wasn't like Miki was exactly Miss Smooth with the moves. In fact, she was kind of a doofus with men...except Conall. With him she didn't seem to have any problems wrapping her legs around his waist while he slammed her against a wall.

"For now. I'm going to be finishing my doctorate this week. And Conridge mentioned an assistant professor position."

"That would mean we'd be working together. Not bad. And Conridge is tough." Boy, was she. Professor Conridge was notorious throughout the university. People feared her. When Miki decided to finally finish up her thesis, her old advisor had gone to another university and Conridge volunteered to take her on. To this day, she had no idea why. She thought the woman hated her. Of course, she seemed to hate everybody.

"So that'll be great for you, huh?"

She should have noticed the look of fear on Craig's face and the look of lust on Amy's. She should have noticed the fact that the most enormous shadow had just fallen over her. But all she'd noticed was Troy and her lame attempt to get him to notice her. "Well, you know, it's definitely time for a change." She stopped talking because Troy had obviously stopped listening. She was about to see what horror was standing behind her since that seemed to have everybody's interest, but big long arms wrapped around her and suddenly she wasn't going anywhere.

"Hey, baby." Miki froze as warm lips pressed against her ear, sending a delicious and treacherous tingle down her spine and straight to her clit. "I thought you were going to see your professor. You're going to be late."

She looked up to see Conall holding on to her. He smiled. An evil wolf smile. The kind they gave just before they took down a deer.

Sonofabitch!
"What the hell..."

He squeezed her tight and Miki fought just to breathe.
"You just have to make sure Miki's doing what she needs to do
otherwise she gets totally lost."

Miki looked at Craig and Amy but she could already see
they were enjoying this way too much to do anything about it.

Conall nuzzled her neck and she thought about digging
his eyes out of their sockets. "So, you going to introduce me to
your friends, baby?"

Baby?

She tried to pull away, but he wasn't letting her go
anywhere. And Troy looked way too freaked out by Conall to say
anything. He just stared at him.

She was so going to make him pay for this later.

"No. I'm not."

Amy jumped in before Miki could start slamming her
boot into his instep. "I'm Amy. This is Craig. And this is Troy."

Miki stared at his neck. It was a big neck. Might spurt a
lot of blood if she cut it.

"Hey, Craig. We met this morning in our hotel room."

Our?

"But it's nice to meet the other friends of my honey-
bear."

Amy almost spit out her gum while Craig suddenly
became interested in what was halfway across campus. Troy
looked a little disappointed as he stared at Miki. She could see her
future slipping away.

"Troy…" she began. But one of Conall's big hands slid
under her T-shirt and suddenly she felt claws. His claws, running
lightly across her stomach.

I am going to kill him.

"Baby, we better get you to your professor's office or
you're going to be late. Nice meeting you, Amy. Craig. Trey."

"It's Troy."

"Whatever." Conall's hand gripped Miki's and dragged
her away. She barely had a chance to grab her backpack before
she was stumbling behind him.

"Which building?" he bit out.

"Fuck you!"

He suddenly pulled her into his arms. To anyone else it probably seemed affectionate, but she knew better. And, as it was, she was way too pissed to feel anything but homicidal rage anyway. He leaned in close, his hot breath in her ear. "Keep it up and I'll make you wish they'd finished you in that alley."

"That one. Over there."

Conall again started moving, pulling Miki behind him. He walked into the building, found a stairwell, and dragged her inside it. As soon as he released her hand, she slugged him in the chest. Then cursed up a blue streak when she felt the pain all the way up her arm. Of course, he didn't even flinch.

"Are you done?"

"Sonofabitch! What the fuck was that shit!" She shook her hand out, worried she broke a knuckle. Conall suddenly caught it and rubbed the knuckles between his two hands while he glared at her. She was almost positive he didn't even realize he was doing it.

"Who the hell was that guy anyway?"

"Who? Troy?" Was he jealous? Well, then, she shouldn't disappoint. "*That* was the future Mr. Miki Kendrick."

*****

Wrong! *He* was the future Mr. Miki Kendrick. Not some lame, tiny man with tiny little hands. He took one look at the guy and knew he was an asshole. There was no way he was letting Miki anywhere near him. True, she was a vindictive bitch. But she was *his* vindictive bitch. He knew that now. No more bullshitting around. No more debating about what he really wanted. Miki Kendrick was his.

Clearly, though, he needed new tactics. The usual wasn't working with her. Mostly because she was nuts. But he was flexible. And mean enough to go after what he wanted.

"I think you need to stay out of my life, Viking." She tried to yank her hand out of his grasp, but he wasn't letting go.

"And I think you fail to realize that I now have the upper hand here."

"What? For drugging you? You expect me to believe for a second you'd hurt me or turn me into the cops?"

"No. But who knows what I would do to *him*."

Miki froze. Those big beautiful brown eyes staring up at him. "You. Wouldn't. Dare."

"You spit food at me. You set me up with the cops at the airport. And you *drugged* me. Do you really want to test the 'you wouldn't dare' theory now?"

He could see the muscles of her jaw clenching and unclenching. She was so pissed off, which only made her smell so tasty.

"Leave him alone, Conall. He didn't do anything to you."

He kicked her backpack out of the way. "But what about you, Mik? Does he have you?"

"Nobody has me."

He stepped toward her until she backed herself up against the wall. He'd never worked so hard to be menacing before, but Miki kept bringing that out in him. And it didn't help that every time he did it, the smell of her lust punched him in the face.

"But I want you."

"So I gathered."

"And if I'm busy chasing you around, I can't exactly be kicking the living shit out of him, now can I?"

Miki crossed her arms in front of her chest. "I guess."

"So then maybe we make a little agreement."

"What kind of agreement?"

"You give me until Friday."

"To do what?"

He placed both his arms on the wall above her and leaned in. "To get close to you. After you defend your thesis, if I haven't gotten between those sweet thighs of yours by then, it's over. I never bother you again. I won't even look at you."

"You have got to be kidding me."

"When it comes to you, I don't joke around."

He was expecting her to kick him in the nads. But she didn't. *Interesting.*

"At least give me a shot, Mik." He gently pulled her arms away from her body and leaned in to her. She watched him closely, but didn't try and stop him either. "See? That wasn't so hard, now was it?" He leaned down and kissed her. A small one. His lips against hers. She didn't pull away, so he nipped at her bottom lip until her mouth opened and she let him in. His tongue moved slowly over hers, savoring the taste of her. She tried to pull her arms away, but he held them tight, moving them so that he had them flat against the wall over her head. He pinned her with his lower body, his knee sliding in between her thighs.

She moaned and he knew he had her.

*****

What in hell was she doing? Had she lost her mind? Was she actually making out with the Viking in the stairwell of the biotech school? This was definitely a new low. It was early, but there were already professors and students everywhere. Sooner or later, they'd get caught. This was insane. She was insane. How exactly could she expect to get tenure at the school if she got caught getting all hot and bothered with some guy in the stairwell?

She needed to tell him to stop. She needed to push him away. She definitely didn't need to moan. In fact, she really had to *stop* moaning.

Conall pulled out of the kiss and leered at her. "Yeah. That's what I consider letting me get close."

If she had the strength, she would have punched him again. In fact, she was all ready to risk her knuckles just for the hell of it.

But before she could deck him, Conall kissed her cheek, stepped back, and pulled her out from under the stairs where he'd trapped her.

"Miss Kendrick. I hope I'm not interrupting anything."

Conall and Miki looked behind them and up. At the top of the stairs stood the dragon lady herself. Professor Irene Conridge. An imposing forty-ish woman, wearing one of her plain blue suits and a pair of killer fuck-me pumps. The woman was a total dichotomy.

"Really. I know how busy your schedule is. And as all I'm doing is running an entire department, please feel free to keep me waiting for another fifteen minutes."

Miki snatched her arms away from Conall and pushed past him. "Professor Conridge. I'm so sorry. I lost track of time..." *Because I was busy getting fondled.*

Miki grabbed her backpack and yanked Conall's hair as she ran by, but she got the feeling he would only see that as more foreplay. She charged up the stairs, but Conridge had already walked off.

Miki stopped at the top of the stairs and looked back at Conall as she hauled her way over-packed bag onto her shoulders. "I don't know how long I'll be."

"It's okay. Take your time. I'll be here." Of course he would. Because he was torturing her.

"*Miss Kendrick!*"

Miki shook herself out of her stupor and charged off.

Chapter Eight

Conall sat on the stairs and worked really hard to control his raging hard-on. Man that woman was a little firecracker. It didn't take much to get her worked up. To get her hot and wet. For him. He growled and forced his wolf back on its chain.

Nope. There was no one else that was going to be good enough for him. He wanted Miki. Not for a night. Or even a week. But for a lifetime. And he was going to have her too. He'd just have to convince her. And hell, how hard could that be?

Conall frowned. There was that smell. The same smell from the rave. The same smell on Miki after her attack.

This time he'd smelled it as soon as they'd moved into the stairwell, but Miki had him totally distracted. Now he couldn't ignore it.

It was faint, so he didn't think any danger was near, but still...

Conall sniffed the air and realized it was coming from another floor. He followed the scent, letting it lead him up one flight of stairs. He could tell Miki was on this floor. He could smell her delicious scent above all others. He went up another flight. There were several labs on this floor. He walked past them. Past a bunch of classrooms. Then he found an alcove with professor offices. He followed the scent until he reached a door. He tried the door without success. Locked. He stuck his nose right up against the wood and sniffed. Then he sniffed again. He knew that smell. He knew it from somewhere. He sniffed again. A deep long one.

Then it hit him. Right between the eyes. He couldn't believe he hadn't thought of it before.

"Hyena!" he barked out triumphantly.

Conall turned away only to come face to face with Craig. "Hey."

Conall nodded. "Hey."

They stared at each other for another moment, then Conall walked off, positive the man watched him sniff the door like a bomb-detection dog that had located a nuclear weapon. He wouldn't worry about that now. He was too busy thinking about hyenas. The natural enemies of lions.

Conall never believed in coincidences and he wasn't about to start now. He remembered the professor's name on the door. "Leucrotta." He'd have to ask Miki about him.

*****

Conridge crossed her long legs and stared down her nose at Miki. "Well, I believe you are as ready as you're ever going to be."

Of course, that was better than what she'd told other grad students–"Pass you? You're lucky I haven't killed you."

"Anything else I should do?"

"You reserved a classroom, yes?"

"Yes, ma'am."

"And you double-checked all committee members know the time and place?"

"Yes, ma'am."

"Then, Miss Kendrick, you should be all set. Just make sure you're ready to seriously defend your thesis. This isn't the time for you to get tongue-tied. Although I'm certain if that happens then life as we know it will cease to exist."

Miki smiled. "Yes, ma'am."

"So go get some rest and I'll see you on Friday at 3:30."

"Yes, ma'am."

Miki stood up and gathered all her papers together. She knew Conridge was watching her, but she was too afraid to ask why. The woman was the true Dragon Lady.

"So, Miss Kendrick, who was that nice young fellow you were fondling on the steps?"

Miki dropped the half ream of paper that was the last version of her thesis. She dropped to her knees and quickly began to scoop the papers together. She'd worry about order later. Anything to stop this conversation. There was no way she was going to talk about the weirdness that was going on between her and Conall. She didn't understand it so how was she going to explain it? She especially wasn't going to explain it to Professor Conridge. Phi Beta Kappa. Rhode Scholar. And all around bitch.

"Just a friend, ma'am." Anytime she was around Conridge, she felt like she was in the military. Yes ma'am. No ma'am. Please don't flunk me, ma'am.

"Do you get forced against walls by all your friends?" Holy shit, how much did this woman see? Or, even worse, hear?

She felt her face getting red. "We were just talking, ma'am."

"I see. To be honest, I'm amazed you could get him behind those stairs. He is a big boy. Even for Pack."

Miki had half her papers gathered together, but she dropped them on the floor again. She sat back on her haunches and stared up at Conridge. "I'm sorry, what?"

The woman smiled and came around to the front of her desk. She slid onto the top of it grabbing a silver picture frame and handing it to Miki.

"My husband. Niles Van Holtz. Of the Van Holtz Pack."

Miki didn't know what shocked her more. The fact that Conridge's husband was Pack? Or the fact that she actually had a husband? She gawked at the picture. The man was gorgeous, she'd give the woman that. It was a picture of Conridge, her husband, and four happy-looking kids.

Miki looked up at her. "Van Holtz?" She frowned. "Of the Van Holtz restaurant chain?" She'd never been in one. You had to be as rich as God to be able to afford a side dish.

The woman rolled her eyes and smirked. She seemed embarrassed by it all. But not by the fact that her mate pissed on trees and could scratch his ear with his back leg. *That* didn't seem to faze her.

"Is that why you offered to be my supervisor?"

"Of course. I know how hard it is to be human among shifters. And I heard about your friend becoming Alpha Leader of the Pack. And your involvement in the Pride war. I'm impressed. I always knew you were smart. I never doubted that. I just had no idea the damage you could do. You'll make him a good mate."

Miki stood up. "What? Conall? No. I'm not going to be his mate. Ever."

Conridge appeared confused. "And why ever not?"

"Because."

"Because…why?"

"Because I'm not getting that involved with him." Exactly how many times would she have to explain this to people? And why did they keep freakin' asking her?

"But you do realize the way he was looking at you just now is kind of the way Niles still looks at me. And, gosh, we've been together now twenty-three years." She had the warmest expression on her face and Miki realized she was seeing another side of this woman. Conridge loved the man she was talking about. A lot. Miki suddenly regretted calling her a "cocksucker" when Conridge kicked back the first draft of Miki's thesis with so many red marks the paper looked like it had a bleeding disease.

"But Conall doesn't feel that way about me."

"And you know this because you are so in tune with normal society."

Conridge was right. Miki wouldn't know normal if it came up and spit in her face. And she was starting to feel that no matter what she did or how hard she tried, she would never be normal.

"I…I…" Miki sat down Indian style on the floor, the wind knocked out of her. "I have no idea what I'm doing."

"There's nothing wrong with that. We all go through it. Even me."

"Really?" Miki had a hard time believing that. Conridge always seemed so put together.

"Of course. Do you think I *wanted* to be a wolf's mate? The man tackled me from behind and marked my back. So I hit him with a two-by-four. He needed eight stitches in his head."

Miki stared at her and she shrugged. "He was still doing his take-what-he-wants thing. I've trained him not to do that anymore…and to roll over on command." The two women laughed and Miki wondered if she were looking at herself in another fifteen years.

Conridge adjusted her stockings. She actually had the kind with the line down the back. Very 1940s and still very hot. "Look Miki, what you are going through is a normal human emotion. And every once in a while, even people like you and me have those."

Miki grinned. The woman was quite a piece of work.

"You don't trust yourself yet," Conridge continued. "You don't trust your instincts. But you should. You're not just some brain with legs. You've got some nice survival skills. Wolves find that sort of thing incredibly sexy."

Miki smiled as she pulled herself into a crouch and began pulling her papers together. "I guess I just don't want to blow this. My life, I mean."

"You won't. You're smart. You're mean. You'll be fine."

Miki laughed as she stood up, her thesis in a messy pile in her arms. "Well, thanks for the pep talk."

"My pleasure. You know, my husband says I'm not good at pep talks. I think he's wrong."

Conridge pulled her office door open, just as Miki kicked her big, heavy backpack in front of her. It slid out the door and hit what she was almost certain was a man...or maybe a woman...it was something.

"Well, well. And is this the infamous Miki Kendrick?"

Miki glanced back at Conridge. Her professor's distaste for this person clearly written on her face. "Miki Kendrick. This is Professor Mitchell Leucrotta."

So it was a guy...sort of. The guy who'd been asking way too many questions about her. He was a weasley little fellow. Not quite Sara's height. Thin but well muscled. What her mother would have called a "scrapper." But there was something so predatory about him she began to wonder where the hell Conall was. Wasn't he supposed to be protecting her or something? *Asshole.*

Miki nodded her head, but kept her distance. "Professor Leucrotta."

"Well, I'm off." He secured his computer bag on his shoulder. "I'm avoiding this little cretin student. I hate when they're needy."

Now Miki really hated the guy. She was almost positive he was talking about Craig. One of her best buds. And a helluva lot less creepy than this guy.

He gave a less than masculine finger wave then strolled down the hallway. She looked at Conridge. "I hate him."

Conridge chuckled. "You certainly do make snap decisions, don't you?"

"Am I wrong?"

The older woman shook her head. "No. You're not. He's a scumbag."

Conall appeared suddenly in the stairwell opposite where Leucrotta disappeared. He raised his nose in the air and sniffed. She realized he was casting for a scent. Conall followed his nose all the way over to Miki. He sniffed her. Then he sniffed her again. Miki got that little tingle in the back of her neck, and the next thing she knew, her pussy was wet.

Okay, when the hell did that start happening?

"What the hell are you doing?"

"Hyena," he muttered.

"Jackal," Miki shot back.

He looked at her and frowned.

She shrugged. "I thought this was word association."

Conridge snorted a laugh and Conall looked at her. He sniffed the air again. "You smell familiar."

"I'm married to a Van Holtz." *Boy, the woman says that with a lot of pride.*

"Oh. Yeah, I remember. I met you once. It's nice to see you again. I'm Conall." He reached down and picked Miki's backpack up, throwing it over his shoulder.

"Why did you say hyena?"

"That's the smell I couldn't place. The scent that was on you after you were attacked. I've only dealt with them once or twice when I was a kid. A bunch of them beat the hell out of me in sixth grade." He looked at Conridge. "I was a lot smaller then."

"I see."

Conall looked at Miki and the papers in her hand. "Need some help there, Slim?"

"Just a little."

Conall grabbed a handful. "Do either of you know Professor Leucrotta?"

Miki frowned. "You just missed him. Why are you asking?"

"That's where the scent was strongest. At his office door."

She sighed. "He was asking about me."

"What?"

"He wanted to be Ms. Kendrick's advisor for her dissertation. I politely told him to go to the devil. And he seemed to take that rather personally. I don't like him. But I didn't bring him into the university. The dean did. But there have been lots of activity from the hyena clans lately."

"We hadn't noticed."

"Not surprising considering your hands were full with the Withell Pride. Anyway, you may want to keep an eye out for them. They can be quite barbaric."

"I remember that. I mean, for little kids they were really vicious."

Conridge nodded. "Hyenas aren't as big as lions, but they make their lives a living hell. But the females and the children are especially brutal. So watch your backs.

She turned to Miki. "You've got tonight and tomorrow to relax. I suggest you do just that. Don't panic over this, Ms. Kendrick. You'll be fine."

"If you say so."

"I don't say so. I'm ordering it. Now go away." Conridge went back in her office and closed the door.

"You brilliant types can be awfully abrupt."

"What a ground-breaking observation." Miki headed back to the stairs, Conall right beside her. She wasn't shaking him any time soon.

Once outside, Conall took the rest of the papers from Miki. "Gimme." Since molesting her in the stairwell, he was in a much better mood.

"What's with you? Why are you so accommodating?"

"Cause I won."

"You won what?"

"You. Me. The seduction. In the stairwell."

"I didn't fuck you in the stairwell."

"I didn't say you had to. I just said I had to get between your legs by Friday." He grinned. "And I did."

Miki stopped and stared at him. "You're high! That was not the agreement."

"Yes it was."

Miki was ready to deck him again when Craig walked up. "Hey, Mik. Can I talk to you for a sec?"

Miki wasn't done with Conall. "Can it wait?"

"Go ahead. I'm satisfied." Conall winked at her and walked off, her backpack and dissertation in his big hands.

"Asshole," she muttered after him.

"Dude, it's worse than that."

Miki looked at Craig. "What are you talking about?"

"I found him *sniffing* Leucrotta's door. Really sniffing it."

Miki sighed. *Damn shapeshifters.* They were just not discreet.

"Don't worry about it, Craig. Besides, I've got bigger problems than his fetishes."

"Like what?"

"Everything."

Craig smiled. "That's a lot."

"I know."

"Look your dissertation isn't until Friday. So why don't you come to my house party tonight. Everybody's going to be there. You can even bring the Beastmaster if you want."

Well, at least he didn't call him teddy bear.

"I love your house parties." And she hadn't been to one in ages.

"Then come."

That would give her a little reprieve from being alone with Conall. "Okay. I'll be there."

"Cool. It starts at nine o'clock. Bring any video games." She chuckled. Techno geek parties were the best.

Craig headed off and she walked to where Conall was standing.

She took a deep breath and forged ahead. "Look. Craig invited me to a house party he's throwing tonight...wanna come?"

*****

He'd wondered if Miki would say anything about Craig's party. He could hear the dweeb invite her even though he was a good hundred feet from them. When she asked him if he wanted to go he felt his heart swell a little. "Sure. Sounds great. I'm assuming I'll be your date."

"Well, you're assuming wrong. We're just going as friends."

"Why?"

"Because you didn't win," she bit out between clenched teeth.

Conall watched her walk off, and waited ten seconds before he yelled after her. "Yes I did!" He laughed as Miki raised her middle finger high in the air like a salute.

He was really starting to love that woman.

Chapter Nine

Miki looked up as Conall held out her cell phone. "It's Angie."

Miki took the phone and watched Conall go back into the room, closing the glass door behind him. They'd changed rooms, with the bed no longer attached to the wall. And Conall had been polite enough not to mention how much he had to pay the hotel for that little "accident." But she loved the new room they had. She had a great view of Seattle and a little balcony she'd been sitting on for three hours with her feet up on the rail and her laptop right in front of her.

"Hello?"

"So how's the big, blond pooch? Has he started humping your leg yet?"

Miki didn't answer. She couldn't answer.

"Okay, Kendrick. Spit it."

"It's complicated."

"You fucked him?"

"No. Not exactly"

"What are you two up to?"

"Too much. It's getting out of control."

"Okay. Hold on."

Miki waited while it became quiet on the other end. She assumed Angelina was at work and had a customer.

"Okay. I'm back. And I've got Sara on the line."

"Oh, shit."

"All right, Mik. What's going on?"

Fuckin' Angelina with her three-way calling.

"This is too weird."

"We want details."

"Details about what?"

"She and Conall have been up to shenanigans."

"You fucked him?"

"No. She hasn't."

"Oooh. This is getting better and better."

"I hate both of you."

"You might as well tell us."

"Or I can ask Conall. He *has* to tell me. I'm like totally in charge and everything."

Miki rolled her eyes. Sara's reign of terror. *Bonehead.* "Okay. Okay. We've gotten pretty...involved with each other. But we haven't actually done the deed."

"That was vague."

"I'll put it in Sara-speak for ya, hon. He's either used his hand or his tongue to get her off, but no dicks have made an appearance."

How could she still be friends with these two idiots?

"Yum," Sara growled. "So what's the problem? It's time for you to cowboy up and break in that mustang."

"I can't believe you found a way to work 'cowboy up' into this conversation."

Angelina sighed. "See you need to go into this knowing what it is, Mik."

"Which is?"

"A booty call. The extended DVD version, but a booty call nonetheless."

"But what if..."

"No, Miki. No analyzing. No second-guessing. No obsessing."

"For once in your life just enjoy yourself."

Miki sighed. "To be honest, I don't think I know how to do that."

Sara chuckled. "Bartender-Miki knows how."

"Bartender-Miki? Is this like your Golden Retriever Sara vs. Drunk-Sara theory?"

"No. You, smartass."

"Bartender-Miki is the one who always asks inappropriate questions and says whatever she thinks without caring about the repercussions."

"Bartender-Miki who used to set things on fire in Chem Lab because she was bored."

"Who taught herself Elvish and Klingon."

"Who faced off against my grandmother on more than one occasion."

"Who could kick guys ten times her size out of the bar when they got rowdy."

"Bartender-Miki who the FBI still refer to as 'that bitch.'"

"That's the Miki we both know and love."

Miki blushed. Now she remembered why she was still friends with these two idiots. Because they both actually got her. And loved her in spite of it.

"But I was changing everything. I was supposed to be having a nice normal *respectable* life?"

"Normal? Who wants to be normal?"

"Fuck normal."

"I say fuck Conall. But in a good way."

"Would you two idiots focus."

"All right, Miki. Listen up." This from Angie. "Is Conall around somewhere?"

"Yeah. He's in the other room."

"Can you see him from where you are?"

"Yeah. Why?"

"Okay. Do me a favor. Look at Conall. But don't look at him like Miki who wants to have a respectable life…"

"We'll call her boring Miki." Sara chimed in.

"Instead look at him like Bartender-Miki."

"Okay." Miki thought about her night's bartending. She was always in control and she never took any shit. She ruled Skelly's bar with a mighty fist and was respected. She knew what she wanted and what she didn't and she acted accordingly. She felt like she'd knocked that Miki out for the last six months but she was awake now. Awake and looking at Conall like a prize-winning bull at an Austin auction.

Stretched out on the bed, on his stomach, watching TV. The Viking's big arms wrapped around a pillow. Her eyes dragged across every inch of that long hard body; taking in the muscles of his arms, the line of his body, how friggin' huge his feet were. And that outstanding ass. Plus, he was wearing that goddamn black bracelet again.

He seemed to feel her watching him. He looked at her and smiled. A smile that, deep down, she knew was for her and her alone. Instead of turning away, like she always did, she smiled back. And his smile actually got bigger. Then he winked and went back to the TV.

Miki sighed. "Holy shit…"

"We've been trying to tell ya."

"What do I do?"

"Be yourself."

"Are you two high? That scares off most men."

"He's hardly most men, darlin'."

"How about you do me a favor," Angelina asked.

Uh-oh. "What?"

"You've got, what? A couple of days until you have to do that thing, right?"

Miki crossed her eyes. "You mean my dissertation? Yeah. Just a couple of days until 'that thing'."

"Then why don't you just enjoy yourself?"

"Don't worry about work."

"Or school."

"Or bills."

"We've got your back. We'll take care of everything. Just relax and see what happens."

It had been years since she could do that. Just relax. In fact, she was pretty sure the last time she did it, she was about fourteen. Just before her mother died. Since then she'd never taken any handouts. She'd always worked for everything she had. And she realized it would be nice to have a couple of days where she didn't have to worry about anything.

"I guess I can."

"Good."

"What's the worse that could happen?"

"But I'm not promising you two bitches anything. There's no guarantee anything will happen between me and him. I've never actually done the booty call thing, and that's all a guy like him would want."

"You don't know that."

"And it doesn't matter if that's true," Angelina cut in. "The point is not to worry about it. It's your choice what you do with him, Mik. I just want you to relax and not worry."

"Think you can handle that?" Sara asked.

Miki took a deep breath. "I'll give it a shot."

*****

He hadn't been able to stop looking at her since she'd walked out of the bathroom. It wasn't dramatic or anything. A cropped T-shirt, black denim mini-skirt, and steel-toe Doc Marten's. But it was the stockings. Dark thigh-high wool ones with garters. And you could see the garters. It was the total punk, geek-girl outfit, but on her…it made his whole body hard.

She hadn't said much to him since Angie called. But he could tell something happened. She didn't seem unhappy or stressed or much of anything. For Miki that was pretty major because she was usually some kind of extreme. She didn't even complain he'd only gotten one room for the two of them since they had to move. He was waiting for her to bitch, but she seemed more concerned with the great view. He'd had to pay some serious cash for that, but it was worth it just to see her smile.

And he couldn't stop thinking about the look she'd given him when she was on the phone with Angie. He'd been minding his own business, trying to watch TV and not think about fucking her on the balcony when he realized she was staring at him. All he could figure was that she and Angie had been talking about him. But, for once, she didn't look mad or annoyed. In fact, she'd smiled at him. And he couldn't help but think that smile was for him and him alone.

The woman was making him crazy. He wanted her so bad he was afraid his palms would start to sweat. As it was, he was having trouble keeping the wolf under control. Every time he smelled her. Every time she came near him, he just wanted to bite the back of her neck and mark her as his for eternity.

They parked close to Craig's house and jumped out. As Conall came around the SUV, he found Miki crouching down adjusting the laces on her Docs. He growled. He couldn't help it. Seeing her legs in those stockings was fucking killing him.

"I heard that." She stood up and grinned at him. "Try not to start howling during the party."

"Wearing those stockings, woman, I can't promise you anything."

She shook her head and moved toward the house. As she passed him, she grabbed hold of his wrist and dragged him behind her.

She'd touched him. It was the most innocent of touches, but it was the final nail in his coffin. Now he was hooked. And nothing would save him.

As soon as they walked into Craig's house, he knew that Miki was in her element. When the standing-room-only crowd saw her the entire place erupted into a chant. "Miki! Miki! Miki!"

Vintage eighties music pumped through the enormous standing speakers, as well as some recent tech. And there were enough high-tech geek supplies to take over the Pentagon. Everyone was playing games on the giant TV screens or giant monitors or they were dancing…well, trying to dance. He realized that in her world, Miki was a great dancer. Because these people were the worst.

Of course, he was the biggest one there. Several guys were as tall or taller, but they were usually skinny. Like they hadn't eaten in days. Or extremely overweight. Like they never left their computer chairs.

Conall tried to ignore the guys hugging Miki as she made her rounds. She was being friendly. They were groping. But when any of them got out of hand, she handled them expertly. She actually twisted one guy's arm behind his back and slammed him up against the wall.

Conall loved watching her kick ass.

*****

Miki had just finished singing "Love is a battlefield" with five drunken skateboarders when Amy tackled her from behind.

"My best, best, best friend, Miki!"

She was toasted.

"Dudette. How much liquor did we have tonight?"

"Two beers." Then she began to giggle hysterically.

Just like the bartender she was, Miki pulled the bottle of ale out of Amy's hand and dragged her to the coffee pot.

"Drink coffee now. Or we're going to have to give you a cold shower." That way she could be a wet drunk.

"Maybe I like cold showers."

"I'll make Ben do it." Since Ben had been trying for about ten years to get into Amy's pants, Miki was confident she wouldn't have to "make" Ben do anything.

"Bitch. Where's the loyalty?"

Miki handed her a paper cup filled with coffee. "I have loyalty only to the Pack." Then Miki laughed at her own joke.

Amy watched her with narrowed eyes. "You're awfully perky, you know, for you."

"I'm having a good time." And she was in a good mood. Listening to Conall growl every time she moved had done wonders for her ego.

"It's that guy, huh? Masters of the Universe's He-Man." She had such geek friends. She'd already heard Conall referred to as Wolverine, The Punisher, Captain America and, her personal favorite, "One of those blond German guys from 'Die Hard'."

"Don't be an idiot."

"Oh, come on. I'm surprised the guy didn't piss on your leg this morning when he saw you talking to Troy. And it's been quite entertaining watching him watch you. While you do your damn best to ignore him."

Kenny came up behind her. "What's going on?"

"I'm drunk and Miki's got Conan the Barbarian on her butt."

"It has been quite the display between you two."

"What are you talking about?"

"Show her, Ken."

Kenny suddenly hugged her. A big, friendly one. Completely asexual. When he pulled away, they all looked at Conall. She could see his glare from clear across the room.

"That's what we're talking about."

"All of you are idiots."

"Deny everything. Admit nothing. Demand proof," her friends stated in unison.

Miki gave them the finger and walked away. Seeing Conall's face had made her toes curl. This night was getting stranger and stranger.

*****

Conall couldn't stop watching her. He liked the way she moved. He liked the way she acted with her friends. He liked her. More and more with each passing second.

"You know some in law enforcement consider watching someone that closely as stalking."

Conall looked down. Miki's three male friends surrounded him. Craig. Ben, and Kenny Liu who she always called by his entire name.

Conall crossed his arms in front of his chest. "Is that a fact?"

"Yeah," Craig continued. "You may be bigger than us."

"Freakishly bigger," Kenny Liu added.

"But we can do things to you that you can't even imagine."

Ben adjusted his backward baseball cap. "Real shame if something happened to your bank account."

"Or if you ended up on the FBI's most wanted list."

"Or if you were listed as dead."

Conall stared at the three men. He had to admit, he was impressed. He didn't think they had any balls. He'd been wrong.

"So," Craig finished up, "If you hurt her, we'll make your life a living hell."

"And we'll enjoy every minute of it." Kenny Liu reached up and patted Conall on his shoulder. "Remember that Conan."

Conall watched them walk away. True, he could tear their throats out, but he liked the fact Miki's friends felt that strongly about protecting her.

His eyes moved across the crowd and he caught sight of her again. She was playing a video game with some guy. It was one of those fighting ones. He and Zach had to stop playing those because they kept getting into real fistfights over them. Whatever Miki had done, she clearly won because she threw the game controller on the ground, brought both her arms up, and screamed "*In your face!*" Then she did a sad, but hilarious little victory dance.

Conall sighed. "Sure, Conall. Why go for a normal girl?"

He was about to hit the food table again when he smelled it. Cutting through the throng of people. It was a she and she was moving fast. He caught sight of her dark spiky hair as she pushed through the crowded living room.

He glanced over at Miki. Craig had pulled out a karaoke machine and they were dragging Miki up to the front. She'd be fine. She had her dangerously psychotic friends protecting her. He followed the spiky head outside and around the side of the house.

He grabbed her by the scruff of her neck and lifted her off the ground. "Where do you think you're going?"

She fought back, her claws coming out. He tossed her fifteen feet before she could slash him. She hit the ground and slid. Then she flipped herself over and stared at him. She was young. She'd dyed her golden hair black. But she couldn't hide those gold eyes or that Pride smell.

She hissed like a house cat and backed away from him. Conall frowned and slowed his pursuit. Any other Pride female would have gone for this throat by now. This one was running from him.

"Stay away from me!"

Conall stared at her and, for a moment, he was sure she was about to burst into tears.

"I was just here for the party. I...I don't want to fight you."

"Why aren't you with your Pride?" He looked around, expecting them to suddenly appear. Females attacking from every side.

"I'm not part of the Pride anymore."

"Why not?"

"That's none of your business." She scrambled to her feet. He sized her up. She was the alternative queen. All black clothes. All silver jewelry. Deathly pale skin. And black eyeliner and shadow. She was a Goth chick. He could bet she didn't get along too well with some of the other Pride females.

Conall nodded. "Sorry about that. I thought..."

"I know. You thought I was going to fuck with you because you're Pack. No offense, but I could give a shit. That's not my life anymore." She wrapped her arms protectively around her body. "And maybe you shouldn't attack people without being sure they're actually trying to kill you. Asshole."

Then she headed up the street.

*****

Miki went to the food table and grabbed some carrots. She'd tried to go for a brownie earlier, but Conall had nearly broken her wrist getting her to drop it. That's when she knew they were Craig's "special" brownies. It was like having a drug-sniffing dog at her disposal.

Miki ate her carrots and looked around the room. At first she didn't see Conall. She felt a moment of annoyance at his absence. Then she felt a moment of annoyance at her moment of annoyance. And was even more annoyed at herself when she felt relief at seeing him come back in the room.

He walked over to her and took a carrot out of her hand. "Well, I've hit a new low."

"What happened?"

"I just beat up a little girl."

"Compared to you everyone's a little girl."

"She was Pride."

"Oh, yeah. The Goth chick with the gold eyes, right?"

"Yeah. Her. You saw her?"

"Yeah."

"Why didn't you say anything?"

Miki shrugged. "I didn't think about it. She's one of Amy's teaching assistants."

"You think and obsess about everything else but that doesn't seem like something you should tell me about?"

Miki was about to get good and pissed off, but then she realized he was right. "You're right."

Conall choked on his carrot. "What?"

She shrugged. "You're right. I should have said something."

"All right. What are you setting me up for?"

"Nothing." She would have been hurt if she hadn't drugged him once. His eyes narrowed and she felt kind of guilty for making him so paranoid. "Really. I'm just telling you that you're right. I swear."

"You been eatin' the brownies?"

Miki rolled her eyes. "No."

"Drug the carrots?"

"No."

"Drug or eaten the Jello shots?"

"No. I didn't drug anybody or anything."

Conall backed slowly away from her. His eyes never leaving her face. "I'm watching you, Kendrick."

She stared at his body as he walked across the room to talk to a bunch of snowboarders.

He was watching her. She liked the sound of that.

*****

A sloppy round of "Video Killed the Radio Star" with some guys who actually made money playing video games for a living, and Miki was ready for a break from the people and the heat of the room. She headed to the back of the house and went out on the stoop. It was surprisingly dead in the back but, not surprising in Seattle, it was raining a bit. There were several couples in the trees behind Craig's house. She stared in their direction but she wasn't really paying attention. Watching other people fool around had never been very interesting for her.

She felt a presence next to her and turned with a smile to see…Troy. And just like that, her smile faded. "Oh. Hey, Troy."

"Hey, Miki." He sat down next to her on the stoop. She scooted over because he was a little too close. "Where's your pit bull?"

It took her a moment to realize he meant Conall. "Inside. He seems to get along well with the skateboarders."

"I'm glad you're back, Miki."

She frowned at him. "Really?" She never thought the man even noticed her.

"Yes. I'm really hoping you'll take the job Conridge offers you."

"She hasn't offered me anything yet."

"She will."

Miki shrugged. "Whatever."

She stared at her boots. She had nothing to say to this man. In fact, she wanted him to go away.

"You know, Miki," his hand was on her knee. "I've been thinking about you all day."

Miki turned to look at him and, suddenly, Troy's lips were on hers. She could taste the liquid courage he'd been guzzling to make this move. But he took her by surprise and that was always a mistake with her. She shoved him so hard he flipped off the stoop and landed in a heap.

Miki leaned over. "You okay, Troy?"

He lifted his arm. "I'm fine." But it was muffled since he went face first in the dirt. "I'm just going to lie here for awhile. Don't mind me."

Christ, how did she ever think this guy was cute or sexy? Just the touch of his lips against hers made her want to spit.

As she wiped the back of her hand across her mouth, a bottle of water appeared in front of her.

This time she didn't even have to look around to know it was him. He'd been taking very good care of her all night. Making sure she ate, stayed away from any cleverly hidden drugs, and that she was always hydrated. She grabbed the bottle and made room on the stoop so he could sit down beside her. She realized she didn't mind him sitting close. Of course, with Conall she really had no choice. He took up a lot of space on the stoop. At least his shoulders did.

"Feel better now?" she asked as she opened the bottle.

"Yeah. I've recovered from my random act of violence." He looked at her. "Are you okay?"

"Yeah. I'm fine. I almost killed a man, though."

"What?"

She pointed and Conall leaned over her to see. As soon as his body touched hers, she had that same damn reaction. Hard nipples. Wet pussy. It was getting ridiculous.

"What happened?"

She had to force herself to focus. "He kissed me. But it took me by surprise."

She felt the growl before she heard it. Miki dropped her water bottle, accidentally hitting Troy in the back of the head, and grabbed Conall's shoulders before he was off the stoop and tearing Troy apart.

"Don't you dare! Sara will kill me if you go to prison."

He let her pull him back. His arm brushed her breasts and the gasp was out of her mouth before she could even think about stopping it. His eyes locked with hers. She still had her hands on his shoulders. On a whim, she slid them up his neck, cupping his chin. He was so gorgeous. She felt the strength of him under her hands. The power of the wolf just inside his skin. He was a piece of ass and he was interested in her.

Maybe she'd been looking at this the wrong way. Maybe she should go to what she knew. Science. How did attraction work? Why could one man force her to knock him on his ass, while another made her want to drop to her knees? Well, there was only one way to find out.

She took a deep breath and pulled him toward her.

Conall was staring at her mouth and it didn't seem like he was breathing at all. "Miki..."

"Sssh. I'm testing a theory." And then her mouth was on his. And, yeah, this was definitely different from when Troy kissed her. She'd felt nothing but panic and the slightest trace of revulsion. But when her tongue connected with Conall's all she wanted was for him to crawl inside her. She leaned back against the stoop, Conall right there with her. Over her. His hands sliding around her back. His arms wrapping around her. She realized he was keeping her back off the hard stone stoop. And every time his tongue stroked hers, she felt it all the way to her clit. She wanted this man. In fact, she had to have him. Preferably now.

She pulled her mouth away from his. She needed to say something sexy and romantic with a mere hint of her vast intelligence. Something that would entice him into bed.

But what came out was, "I wanna fuck."

Conall groaned and buried his face in her neck. "You're killing me, Mik," he finally managed. "Don't do this if you're just messing with my head 'cause you're still pissed or..."

She rubbed her cheek against his silky hair and decided to just go for it. So what if he probably wouldn't want her after all this was over? At least she could say she had a good time. And she knew Conall would be a good time. A *really* good time. And she was tired of being respectable and normal. It was boring. And she *did* need to get laid.

So what would Miki the Bartender do here? Easy. She'd be honest. "Do you know what one of the wolves protecting my house back in Texas told me?" she whispered in his ear and she felt his entire body vibrate against hers. "He told me I moaned your name in my sleep. And I realized my hand smelled like I'd been masturbating all night long. No one's ever done that to me before you. No one but you."

Conall slowly untangled himself from her. He didn't look at her. Instead, he pulled away and sat on one of the lower stoops. He dragged his big hands through his hair and she watched him stretch out his big shoulders. Miki sat up and reached her hand out to touch him.

"Don't. Touch. Me."

Miki frowned, a little bit hurt.. "Why?"

"Because I'm doing my best to control myself. And if you touch me I'll fuck you right on this stoop, and I don't want to do that to you in front of your friends. So, don't touch me right now."

"I see." She scratched her neck. "But you know, we can go back to the hotel and then you can fuck me anywhere or anyway you want."

Yeah. That was clear. The next move was his. Miki stood up and walked back into the house. She got as far as the coffee pot before she felt herself lifted off her feet and thrown over Conall's shoulder. The entire room cheered as they left. She waved at Amy who drunkenly gave her a thumb's up.

Conall arrived at the SUV in what seemed like seconds, then he opened the door, dumped her in, and stopped only long enough to say, "Not another word from you. Not one."

She watched as he went around the SUV to get in. She was almost positive he had no idea his fangs were out.

*****

Surprisingly, he wasn't pulled over. He used to ride sports bikes that could hit 200 miles per hour and he was pretty sure he'd never gone as fast on one of them as he did in the SUV.

But Miki finally pushed him over the edge. He was praying she didn't back down now. He wasn't sure he could take it. He'd almost dragged her into Craig's bathroom and took her there, but he forced himself to get under some kind of control. Although the wolf was having a full-on fistfight with the man in him.

Tires squealed as he turned into the hotel parking lot and took the first spot he saw. He got out, went around to the passenger side, and dragged Miki out. She didn't say a word as he tossed her over his shoulder and went into the hotel. The hotel staff watched him quietly. He knew they wanted to say something to him about carrying a woman into their four-star hotel as if he were a cave man. But he knew none of them had the guts to say a word. He could only imagine the expression on his face.

He didn't even wait for the elevator. He took the stairs up ten flights and wasn't even out of breath by the time he got to his door. He swiped his keycard, went in, and tossed Miki on the bed.

She seemed unfazed by it all as she watched him with those inquisitive brown eyes. He didn't want to make the same mistake he'd almost made that morning. So he went to his bag, dug through the few clothes he had packed, and grabbed the brown paper bag of condoms Sara had shoved in it as he was walking out the door. At the time he thought she was simply being hopeful.

He tossed them on the floor by the bed. Miki started to say something but he cut her off.

"Not a word."

She surprisingly fell silent, watching him as he moved to the bed. Her eyes dragged along the length of his body as he dropped to his knees in front of her.

"Lay back."

She shook her head. "I wanna watch you."

He growled as he slid his hands under her skirt and dragged her lace panties off. He left the garters and the Docs on. He'd been thinking about going down on her dressed like that since she'd come out of the bathroom. He leaned forward and licked the inside of her thigh just above the stocking. She remained quiet until he pushed her thighs farther apart and his tongue skimmed along the folds of her sex. That's when she gave a low moan as her head fell back. She used one arm to keep herself propped up while the other grabbed the back of his head and pushed him forward.

He pulled back a bit. "Miki." Her eyes focused on him. "You said you wanted to watch me. So watch me."

From the way her breathing changed and the expression on her face, he had a feeling he'd pushed her that much closer to coming. Which was good, because he wasn't sure how much longer he could hold out. He needed to be inside this woman before he lost his mind.

His tongue slid inside her tight pussy. It was wet and hot and tasted so good. Miki's hand tightened in his hair, pulling him close as his hands slid under her to cup her ass. He pulled her close, his hands gripping her tight. She moaned in response, one leg over his shoulder, the other propped up on the bed.

Limber girl, he thought happily.

He licked her slowly, enjoying the sweet taste of her. The smell. He felt her body begin to shake as her orgasm broke around him. She made low, guttural sounds from the back of her throat as he used his tongue to stretch out her orgasm as long as he could.

When she tugged on his hair, trying to pull him up, he knew she was ready for him. He leaned back on his haunches, and stared at her. He needed her to make this move. He needed to know this was what she really wanted.

She ran her small hand across his jaw and down his neck. Then, slowly, she leaned forward and began to lick her own juices off his mouth and chin.

I'll take that as a yes. He slid his hands to her waist and lifted her shirt up, pulling it over her head and tossing it across the room. She pulled away from him, backing up on the bed to yank off her skirt, the stockings, the Docs, all of it. Which was good. He wanted her completely naked. And completely his.

*****

Miki tossed her Docs across the room as Conall pulled his T-shirt over his head, then he tackled his jeans. She'd never been this horny for anybody before in her life. She was almost desperate. Which was good because when he dropped his pants and she saw the size of his raging hard-on, she knew she was in for quite the workout.

But something inside her had changed. Here she was kneeling on the bed, completely naked, and she didn't care. For the first time in her life, she really couldn't give a flying fuck about anything or anyone except Conall and his huge dick.

She smiled and crooked her index finger at him. He didn't need any more prompting than that. He whipped on a condom and was in her arms within seconds. They both fell back on the bed as his hot mouth sucked at her breast. Every time his tongue swiped across her nipple, she felt it all the way down to her clit.

She heard growling, but it wasn't Conall. It was her.

*****

When she growled, he thought he was going to finally snap. He wanted to wait a bit. Make it all special and romantic, but who the hell was he kidding? He was wolf and she was fucking hot. He rose over her, his arms on either side of her body. Miki's body arched up to meet his as he thrust inside of her, embedding himself deep.

She seemed so small under him. Small and beautiful. Miki looked up and gasped in surprise. Her hand reached up and touched his forehead. "Wolf eyes," she whispered. His eyes must have shifted. But she wasn't frightened. She leaned up and, unable to reach his mouth, she kissed his chest and neck. He trembled, holding his body rigid. His cock still buried in her tight pussy. He wanted to stay this way forever.

Her legs wrapped around his waist, her ankles locking at the base of his spine. Her fingers digging into his ass, keeping him deep inside her. When he couldn't wait any longer, he began to stroke in and out. She felt so good, he thought he'd come any second. But he held on for her. Of course, it didn't help when she began moving her hips and moaning his name. Yup. The woman was definitely trying to kill him.

Her tongue swiped across his nipple and he almost unraveled. "Oh God, Miki baby. Don't." He was holding on by a thread.

She smiled against his flesh as she sucked his nipple into her mouth. He felt his canines extend, and he desperately fought his desire to mark her. He didn't want to do that to her. She was full human and he needed to know it was what she wanted. But he knew no other woman had ever made him like this. This crazy. This desperate. He'd worked so long and hard to control his every instinct, and this one clearly unstable woman had completely destroyed all that.

As his claws ripped the sheets underneath them, he knew at that very moment he loved her.

*****

She could hear the sheets ripping under her. His claws were out. His fangs. His eyes had shifted. Who knew this would be such a turn on? And it was. It was like her entire body was on fire for him. And only him.

She liked making him crazy. As crazy as he was making her. She bit into the flesh of his chest and he moaned and snarled all at the same time. He pounded into her harder, a delicious punishment for working so hard to make him come.

Her orgasm slammed into her like a runaway train. So hard she ripped flesh off his back with her nails and screamed in release. He came a moment after, his back arching, a howl torn from his throat. Knowing she made him howl...no, you really couldn't get cooler than that.

He dropped on top of her. His whole body clearly too devastated to move. She didn't complain. She didn't realize how much she'd like such a big guy lying on top of her. She felt warm. Cozy. Safe. After a few minutes, he rolled off. His warmth gone, the sweat on her body chilled. She almost told him to roll his ass back.

They were both silent for several moments. Then she chuckled. She couldn't help herself. Then he started to chuckle. Then they both started laughing outright.

"I was right," she finally managed. "Viking."

With a playful growl, he launched himself at her, knocking both of them off the bed.

*****

"Mmmhm, Conall."

Conall's eyes snapped open. *What in hell?* He turned over slowly and looked at her. He could see her clearly in the pitch-black room. She was on her side, facing him. And she was asleep.

He raised an eyebrow. The woman was definitely out cold, but he'd heard her voice. Was she dreaming about him? They'd just had several hours of seriously hard-core sex, she should be just sleeping. And she definitely shouldn't be having wet dreams about him still.

She suddenly stretched, turning so that her back was against the bare mattress. The ruined sheets had hit the floor hours ago. While she stretched, her back arched, presenting those adorable breasts of hers to him like an offering from the gods. He leaned down and licked one. Just a slow swipe. Her back arched more and again she moaned his name.

He stared at her, loving his wolf eyes because he could see her without turning on a light and ruining the moment. She was the most beautiful woman he'd ever seen. Yet it wasn't simply her looks. Hell, those could go and he wouldn't miss them. It was something else. It was her. She was raw and rude and who she was. The wolf in him loved that. Loved her. When she was around, the wolf in him wanted to lie down and put his head in her lap. And he didn't have to hide who he was. She seemed to relish the rawness he'd always worked so hard to keep bottled up.

"Conall?" It sounded almost like she was pleading with him. Christ, what exactly was his dream self up to? He noticed her arms were still over her head, like someone was holding them in place. He growled and she smiled in her sleep, her lust reaching out and grabbing him around the cock.

He reached over and ran his finger gently across her nipple. It hardened further under his touch but she didn't wake. He pinched the nipple between his thumb and forefinger. She wiggled a bit, but she was still asleep.

Yeah, he liked the way she slept.

He brought his mouth down to her breast, grasping her nipple gently between his teeth. He let his tongue flick over it again and again and then he sucked. She made desperate sounds from the back of her throat, but miraculously she was still out cold.

He ran his hand down her stomach and in between her thighs. She moaned as his forefinger circled her clit then flicked it. She almost came off the bed, so he grasped her arms and held them down.

He briefly closed his eyes. He never thought he'd meet someone like Miki. Someone strong enough to be his woman. His mate. But she was. She was everything he'd ever hoped for. And it didn't hurt she was one wicked fuck.

He worked her clit with his fingers and her breasts with his mouth and tongue. But whatever was happening in her dream was bringing her halfway to climax. All he was doing was providing the last little push she needed.

She shuddered. Actually, her entire body did. Then her legs began to shake. She was coming, and he pulled back just enough so he could watch her. She always came hard and loud, and looked beautiful doing it.

He stayed with her until her body settled down. Then she smiled in her sleep and sighed...his name.

If he physically could have, he would have come himself. That's what the woman did to him. Instead, he decided right then and there. He was going to marry Miki Kendrick. He just had to convince her. And, hell, how hard could that be?

*****

Miki felt warm lips against hers. She sighed and opened her eyes, giving them a few seconds to adjust to the darkness. His lips moved gently down her neck and she felt that wonderful hair of his rubbing across her flesh. God, she loved the feel of his hair against her body. She wanted to run her hands through it, but she couldn't since her arms were pinned above her head.

"Um...Conall?"

"Um...Miki?"

"What's the deal with my arms?"

"It was the only way to keep you pinned to the bed?"

"See, statements like that really freak me out."

"You started it."

"I started what?"

"A woman moans your name in her sleep, it's really hard to ignore her."

Now this was getting embarrassing. "God, did I jackoff in my sleep again?" This wasn't a mental disorder was it? Like being a sociopath or a schizophrenic.

"No. But I thought you could use a little assistance with that."

"Oh." She thought she had dreamed all that. She was glad she hadn't because it fuckin' rocked.

He kissed her mouth again, released her arms then sat up, his back against the headboard. He reached over to the side table and grabbed something. She heard a tearing sound and realized he'd grabbed a condom.

"What are you doing, Viking?"

"Get up here, Kendrick."

"I'm sleeping."

"Not anymore you're not. Let's go. Haul it out."

"Well, you are quite the romantic." She pulled herself up and crawled into his lap.

"You want romantic? How about 'I wanna fuck.' "

"Asshole," she muttered as she straddled his waist and lowered herself onto him. She was already wet and his big cock slid in easily. She let go a rough moan. Christ, he felt so good inside her.

"You okay?" His voice was rough like hers now. She couldn't see him very well in the dark, but she could see his eyes. And she could feel him.

"Are you kidding?"

He licked her neck as he grabbed her around the waist. "I wanted to fuck and kiss you all at the same time without arching my back, and I was thinking this might be the best way to do it."

He didn't seem bothered by their height differences. In fact, it seemed as if he enjoyed the challenge.

"Kiss me, Mik."

She leaned forward, her arms around his neck, her breasts against his chest. She slowly ran her tongue along his bottom lip, then slid to the top. He tried to capture her mouth with his, but she pulled back, drawing one of his growls. She was really enjoying teasing him. He leaned back and waited. She touched his lips again with her tongue. He tasted so good. But when he tried to kiss her, she pulled away.

"What the hell are you doing?"

"Having a little fun."

He groaned. One of frustration, his head rubbing against her cheek then her neck. "Dammit, woman. Kiss me."

"All right," she laughed. "Don't whine."

She kissed him and she felt his hands tighten on her waist, his cock expand even more inside her. She dug her hands into his hair and pulled him closer. It was like they were both trying to slide into each other's skin.

He held her tight as his tongue stroked hers. She felt how much he wanted her. Needed her, even. No one had ever reacted this way to her before. Or made her feel the same.

She slowly began to ride him, her hips moving against him, her pussy tightening around his cock. He moaned and his fingers dug deep into her flesh. It hurt, but in a good way. A damn good way.

She didn't rush it and he didn't ask her to. It seemed like they were both just enjoying the moment. Enjoying each other.

"Miki-baby?"

She liked when he called her that. She realized it was his nickname for her. And she liked that she had a nickname. "Mhhmm?"

"You don't have any school plans tomorrow, do you?"

"No. Why?"

"Just wondering what would happen if we kept this going for the next four or five hours."

Miki chuckled. "I don't sleep, Viking. Not really. So it wouldn't matter to me."

He licked her neck. Nipped her earlobe. And she kept riding him. "You just need somebody to wear you out."

She snorted. "Yeah. Good luck with that."

They both froze. *Dammit.*

"Uh, Conall..."

"Too late! The gauntlet's been laid. I accept your challenge."

"No. No. Now let's be rational about this." She tried to squirm away from him, but his grip tightened like a delicious vice. He wasn't letting her go anywhere and she loved every minute of it.

"Dogs aren't rational, baby. We're dogs. We just want a job." He squeezed her ass and she squeaked. "And I just found mine…"

Chapter Ten

Her damn cell phone ringing woke him up. He wondered where she was and why she hadn't answered it yet. Then he realized she was asleep on his back. Not against his back. *On* his back. Out cold. It took some work, but he'd finally worn her out enough to get some sleep. He had to admit, though, it was quite the party getting her there.

He gazed at the clock. They'd been asleep for about six hours. Not a big deal for him, but he knew she only got about three or four hours of sleep a night, if she were lucky.

He loved having her on his back, her soft breasts pressing against his flesh. Her arms thrown loosely over his shoulders. Her legs stretched out on top of his, although her toes barely passed the back of his knees.

The phone stopped ringing. But now it kept making a beeping sound that made it clear there was a message waiting. That would get on his nerves real quick. He hated to wake her, but she should get her phone and he really had to pee.

"Miki-baby." She stirred a little. Her head turned and her lips pressed against his naked back. Immediately he got hard again. How? His cock should have fallen off with the work out it got last night. "Mik."

"Mmmhmm?" She sounded sated.

"Your phone's beeping."

"What?" He felt the top of half of her body lift off his back and his skin barked at the loss of her. "Oh."

She slid off his back, her groin briefly dragging across his ass. He was pretty sure nothing would ever feel better than that.

She flipped the phone open and quickly checked her messages. She frowned and speed-dialed a number.

"Hey, Craig. It's me. Whasup?"

Conall sat up. He watched her move as she held the phone. He liked watching her move.

"Yeah. I can meet you. But not now. How about breakfast at the diner across from the Watson Suites? Yeah. Yeah. That works. Cool. See ya." She closed her cell phone.

"Everything okay?"

She shrugged. A casual move. All the tension she had when he'd touched her at the club seemed to have drifted away. "Not sure. Craig is weird. It could be something serious or something he thinks is serious that isn't. It's always a crapshoot with him."

She yawned and stretched. He watched her body go taut and heard the little high-pitched noise she made at the back of her throat. Before he knew it, he'd slipped out of bed and was heading for her. But she saw him coming and stepped away.

"I don't think so."

He almost groaned. She wasn't going back into "stay away from Conall" mode again, was she?

"Oh, yeah?"

"Yeah." She walked to the bathroom. "You've got something else to do."

"Which is?"

She looked at him from the bathroom doorway. "Help with the soap."

*****

One shower and three orgasms later, they'd made it to the diner. Conall kept staring at her over his orange juice while they waited for their food. She tried to ignore him but the man didn't make it easy. Especially when he kept growling.

"Stop doing that."

"Stop doing what?"

"Growling."

"It makes you wet, doesn't it?"

She tried to glare at him over her cup of coffee but one look at that beautiful, wicked face and it took all her strength not to nail him right there in the booth.

"Bastard."

"Not according to my mother."

Conall was deep into his third helping of waffles and bacon–the man could really pack it away–when her friends showed up. They all tried to squeeze into the booth, but with Conall on one side that was just not happening. So Ben and Craig pulled chairs to the side and Miki made Kenny and Amy sit next to her. There was no way she was letting Amy anywhere near Conall.

"So?"

Her friends exchanged glances and immediately she began to worry.

"What?"

"I'll tell her." Amy looked at her. "Now don't freak out, but we found a password-protected folder in Leucrotta's computer. It had your information in it."

"What do you mean? What information?"

"Everything. Social Security number, bank accounts, gym membership."

Kenny Liu leaned forward. "Plus a detailed list of your daily activities the last five or six months. And by the way, you live a really boring life."

"We did a trace and it seems like he hired a PI. Someone local to you," Ben added.

Conall pushed his nearly empty plate away and leaned back in the booth. He wasn't saying anything, just calmly listening to her friends.

"We also found a folder for Angelina," Craig muttered softly. "It had the same kind of info."

She should have been freaking out. She should have been screaming her head off and seeing all possible disastrous scenarios that could occur. And although part of her brain was working on contingency plans should things get out of hand, she didn't feel the need to start any kind of global panic. She knew Conall and the Pack would do what they could to protect her and Angelina. She also knew she was too mean to take crap from anybody. She liked the fact that she was finally starting to enjoy that part of herself. It's what made her who she was.

Miki nodded. "Okay. Thanks."

"That's it? 'Okay. Thanks.' That's all we're getting?" Amy looked at her. "You're not freaking out, which tells me you're not surprised."

"I'm not surprised. But that's all I can really tell you."

"Bullshit."

"I'm not going to argue about this with you, Amy. So let it fuckin' go."

"What else do you need us to do?" Kenny Liu cut in before Amy could start ranting.

For the first time since her friends arrived, Conall spoke, "Nothing. Don't do anything. And clean up your tracks. They should never know you were there."

"They? Whose they?" Craig was all over that. He was the king of paranoia. But she knew she couldn't tell him the truth. It wasn't her truth to tell. So she lied.

"Mafia."

Conall's head snapped around and stared at her. She gave the smallest eyebrow raise.

"Mafia?" Amy turned her body in the booth so she could stare Miki in the face. "*The* Mafia? You expect us to buy that the Mafia is out to get you?"

Conall leaned forward, his most innocent expression on that dangerously misleading face. "Hey. That's not something we'd lie about."

Miki looked at Amy. She had to. If she stared at Conall a second longer, she was going to start giggling hysterically.

He looked back at Craig. "And if they find out you were there, we'll find your body in the back of a Cadillac with your tongue cut out."

Miki bit the inside of her cheek and kicked Conall under the table.

She watched the range of emotions pass over her friends' faces. Ben had stopped listening. He was bored. Kenny Liu appeared truly concerned. Craig looked like he was about to pass out from the panic. And Amy restlessly tapped her fingers against the Formica table and glared.

"You must be insane if you expect us to buy that load of shit."

"There's a lot about me you guys don't know."

"You're lying, Kendrick. You *and* Conan the Barbarian."

Miki and Conall looked innocently at each other than back at her friends.

She shook her head sadly. "It hurts me that you think I'm lying."

Conall sighed. "It hurts us both."

She would have really lost it then if she and Conall weren't busy kicking each other under the table.

*****

"The Mafia? Was that the best you could do?" They'd started laughing as soon as Amy and the rest of them left. Ten minutes later and they were still laughing.

"Dude, I was desperate. I needed something and Amy wasn't backing off. I know her."

"Fine. Whatever." Conall grabbed her hand. "Let's go back to the hotel and fuck some more."

"Actually, I have another idea."

Why didn't he like the sound of that? "A *better* idea?"

"Probably not." She held up a small slip of paper. "But an idea just the same."

"What's that?"

"Leucrotta's address. Let's do a drive-by."

"Shooting?" He wouldn't put it past her.

"No, you nut case. Let's go check him out."

"No way, baby. Something happens to you, Zach will have my ass because Sara will have his." He looked down into that adorable face of hers. "And I might miss you a little myself."

"Gee. Thanks." Miki smirked at him. "Look. We can do this one of two ways. We can go there now. Together. Check it out for our amusement. Or you can find yourself passed out in a pool of your own vomit in the bathroom while I risk life and limb going there by myself."

Conall stared down at her. "You'd drug me again?"

"Sure. I'd only have to wrap it in bacon."

Conall wanted to be insulted, but she was just so damn cute. "I can't afford to have you traipsing that tight ass of yours around a Clan den."

"And I have no desire to get too close. I have no guns. No knives. No hand grenades. I'm defenseless. But we need to check out the enemy. We need to find out who these people are. I don't believe in spending my life hiding or running."

He believed that. He saw why Sara was friends with Miki. She was as tough as any wolf he knew. Miki simply found a different way to survive. But still, he didn't want her to get hurt. "I don't know, Mik."

She smiled at him and he felt his cock rear its ugly head. "Please, Conall...baby. For me."

He laughed again. "You're fuckin' shameless."

She took the car keys out of his jean pocket. "Come on, baby." She jangled the keys at him. "Come on. Let's go for a ride!"

"I swear to God, woman. You make one crack about hanging my head out the window..."

She frowned and he could tell she'd been all set to do just that. "Damn."

*****

She wondered how long they would play twenty questions as she led him to Leucrotta's house. She'd memorized every street map of Seattle and the surrounding areas. Didn't take much. She only had to examine a map once to know every detail.

"Where did you learn to shoot?" Again with more questions. Why was he so interested? They'd already gone through these types of questions just the other night, but then he was still trying to get into her pants. Now that he was in, she wasn't quite sure why he was still so curious.

Are booty calls supposed to be this chatty?

"The Marines."

"You were in the Marines?" He didn't have to sound so shocked.

"No."

"Did you date a Marine?"

"No."

He seemed relieved by that answer, which confused her even more.

"Was your father a Marine?"

"I don't know. I didn't know the man."

"Really?"

"He tried to contact me once after high school. But I told him to go to hell. I really had no desire to meet a man that at twenty-six dated a sixteen-year-old girl, got her pregnant, and then dumped her."

And it was a good thing she didn't meet her father then. She was nineteen, in college, with full access to the biotech labs. Between that and her association with Craig and the rest of them, she would have hurt the man. As it was she remembered a late night of hiding one of her creations in what was now Craig's personal lab. Had to. The military wanted to get their hands on it. Of course, Sara and Angelina still thought she was delusional when she said Black Ops would be coming for her one day.

"I can understand that. Did your mother love him?"

"Tragically, yes."

He was surprisingly silent on that point and apparently decided to let it go. "Angelina dated a Marine?"

Miki rolled her eyes. "Nope. They're on the List."

"What List?"

"You know, it's right in your face. You just refuse to see."

Conall stopped at a red light and looked at her. Then he grinned. A big, beautiful grin. "Your mother was a Marine."

"And finally my Cro-Magnon man enters the Twenty-First Century where women are in the military."

"*Your* Cro-Magnon man?" She stared out the window so she didn't have to see his Viking grin. She wasn't going to start liking him. Not really liking him. A passing "I don't hate you enough to kill you" association was fine and dandy. But liking him like she liked Sara or Amy or Angelina or even Craig was out of the question.

The light changed and he moved forward. "Okay. So I missed it. The obvious. So she taught you to hunt?"

"No. I learned to hunt from my grandmother. Her father was a tracker and moonshiner. My mother taught me how to shoot. Every Marine's a rifleman, ya know." She shrugged. "By the time I was twelve, I'd skin my own kills."

"That's lovely."

Miki nodded, ignoring his sarcasm. "I'd cut off the pelts. Strip the flesh. Freeze it. We'd have deer meat for weeks." She looked at him. "And sometimes I'd make little hats from their heads."

Conall pulled over on a quiet suburban street. "Okay. This conversation's ending now." He shuddered. "Freaky woman." He glanced around. "We're getting near. I can smell them."

"We're not going to get any closer?"

"No way." He shut off the car and handed her the keys. "If I'm not back in twenty minutes, leave and don't go back to the hotel. Understand me?"

"Yes, my liege."

He glared at her. "Smart ass."

"What are you going to do?"

He shrugged. "Stay downwind."

Then he was out of the car and disappearing down the street. Miki put her feet up on the dashboard and waited.

*****

Conall dumped his clothes behind an empty house with a For Sale sign in the front, shifted, and trotted the rest of the way to Leucrotta's house. He knew as soon as he hit their street. The smell almost overpowered him. It took him a bit to discover the disgusting scent came from the pasty white secretions on almost every tree and home he passed. *When these guys mark their territory, they really mark their territory.* He soon realized almost every house on the street belonged to this Clan.

The street was pretty deserted and Conall assumed the majority of members were at their day jobs. He slipped into a backyard and tracked his way to one of the houses where he actually heard activity. There was a high fence, but he found a tear in the wood he could look through. It was a good-sized property with a pool and seemed like any other normal high-priced suburban home. And yet he was witness to one of the most disturbing things he'd ever seen.

Four females–*they were females right?*–were in a full-on fistfight. Blood was drawn. And he could hear bones breaking.

The other females, about fourteen of them, watched impassively. But even more freakish was the vicious brawl going on between the children. Not just a shoving match or putting little Johnny's head in the toilet, but teeth and claws used to cause permanent harm.

He thought about growing up as wolf pup. He remembered wrestling with Zach. One time, when they were no more than six, Zach accidentally knocked him down a flight of stairs and the poor kid cried for hours until Conall could walk again and remember his first name.

But what Conall was watching now was a brutal display of pure, unadulterated aggression. These were definitely not people to fuck with lightly.

Then the wind shifted. The fighting stopped. The aggression stopped. And all attention focused on him at the fence.

He took several steps back, spun around, and took off. It was time to call on his Pack.

*****

Miki got tired of waiting in the SUV, so she sat on the stoop instead. She couldn't stop thinking about the previous night. So that's what Sara and Angie meant about getting your world rocked. No wonder people were obsessed with sex. Now she was obsessed with sex. Sex with Conall.

She felt Conall as wolf come up next to her. She didn't even bother glancing at him as he settled down next to her. He nuzzled her arm.

"What are you doing?" He licked her chin.

"Are you going to tell me what happened or not?"

Conall lay down next to her and rolled on his back. She sighed. This was so demeaning.

Still refusing to look at him, she rubbed his belly. Conall clearly loved it. She could feel his whole body wiggling under her fingers as they played across his stomach and chest.

"This is ridiculous. Just shift and tell me what you saw." She finally turned to look at him. His tongue was hanging out, the happiest grin on his face. And it suddenly occurred to her that this dog was not a wolf. And it definitely wasn't Conall. "Oh for shit's sake…"

"What are you doing?"

Miki cringed. She looked up and kept looking up until she could see Conall's face. He was standing on the other side of her. He was human. Wet, like he'd been swimming. Fully dressed. And fully disgusted.

"Uh…playing with this cute doggie?"

"*You thought he was me, didn't you!*"

"Don't get testy. It could have been you."

"It's a Golden Retriever!" he growled. "I can't talk to you right now." He stormed back to the SUV.

Miki looked at the Golden laying comfortably next to her. "Thanks a lot."

"*Are we going?*"

Miki stood up as the dog bolted at Conall's yelled question, his tail between his legs. She couldn't even spare him a glance. She walked back to the SUV and over to Conall. Normally she wouldn't care if she hurt someone's feelings, except maybe Sara and Angelina's but they had hides made of stone. But for some reason, having Conall mad at her gave her a lousy feeling.

She stood in front of him. "I'm sorry."

"I'm not a dog."

"I know that. I just wasn't paying attention. I didn't even look at him."

"You know, we don't all look alike." She didn't bother to point out that they were all part of the *canis lupus* family. That would probably just piss him off more.

"I know." On a whim, she wrapped her arms around his waist and laid her head against his chest. She felt his body grudgingly begin to relax as his arms wrapped around her. She had never been an affectionate person, but for some reason she found it easy and kind of nice with Conall. "I'm really *really* sorry. Really."

He chuckled. "Not sure you said enough reallys."

She felt the dampness of his T-shirt. "Why are you wet?"

"Wind shifted. I had to use someone's pool to get them off my scent."

"Smart. So what did you find out? Was Conridge right?"

"They're more than barbaric. They're scary. Scarier than I remember. Maybe you could do some research on that computer of yours. See what else you can find out."

But she already had some knowledge, so why wait? Miki closed her eyes. She could visualize one of her favorite books. *Encyclopedia of Mammals.* She saw the pages turn as if she had the book in her lap. She flipped to the section on hyenas and read what was there.

"They're matriarchal. Extremely aggressive, which we already know. They don't get along like wolves or Pride, though. There is a lot of in-fighting. Well, this explains a lot. The male-female sex organs look very similar. At one time it was believed they were hermaphrodites, but they're not. Oooh."

"What?"

"The cubs are born with a full-set of teeth and they start fighting from the time they are pushed out of the womb. Sometimes two will fight while the mother is cleaning off a third. How freaking interesting is that?"

*****

Conall frowned. He should be mad. She'd mistaken a Golden Retriever for him. Not even a German Shepherd or a Husky, but a Golden. But he was too busy loving the feel of her arms wrapped around his waist and the sudden realization she just pulled hyena knowledge out of her pretty tight ass.

"How exactly did you know all that?"

"I have a good memory."

"It sounded like you were reading from a book. You were, weren't you?" He could feel her get uneasy. "You just read a book in your head, didn't you?"

"I'm not sure what you…"

"Exactly how high is your IQ anyway?"

Miki cleared her throat. "One hundred and seventy eight."

Last he heard one hundred and forty was hitting genius level. *Damn.*

"Why didn't you go to some special school or something?"

"My grandmother didn't believe in them. But I always took advanced classes and some college courses." Her body was tense against his. She was waiting for some kind of weird repercussion to her admission. She didn't seem to realize he really could give a shit. As far as he was concerned this only meant their kids would be smart shapeshifters.

"Well, so you don't get too cocky, I myself often complete the *TV Guide* crossword puzzle." He puffed out his chest. "In pen."

Miki burst out laughing. He loved making her laugh. Her entire body became involved. Kind of like when she had an orgasm.

Conall kissed her forehead. "Let's get out of here before they...Oh, shit."

"What?" She pulled out of his arms and turned to see what he was looking at. Not a pretty sight. The hyenas had done something he'd never seen before and he hoped to never see again.

They'd sent their children to hunt them.

*****

There were six of them standing in the middle of the street in front of them. A quick look behind them and she saw three more.

It was broad daylight in a nice, quiet suburban neighborhood. And yet she felt trapped in a desert in the dead of night.

Miki didn't mince words. "Let's get in the car and run the fuckers down."

Conall gaped at her. "They're kids. I can't hit kids. And I'm really hoping you can't either."

Miki sighed. No. She couldn't mow down a bunch of kids. But she wished she could. Because they may be children, but they were the scariest fucking things she'd ever seen. She always wondered what kind of kids were home schooled. These guys must make up a huge percentage. She had a feeling the fangs they were showing couldn't retract until they were much older.

"Fine. You want to be Mr. Nice Guy and not hit the kids, then that leaves only one option."

"Which is?"

She quickly snatched the door open to the SUV, dived inside to dig into her backpack, and pulled out her house keys.

"Now I don't want you to take this personally," she ordered as she scrambled back out.

Conall didn't look at her, since he was too busy watching the slowly advancing cubs. "Take what personally?"

Miki pulled off the small plastic controller attached to her keys. She showed it to him.

"Stop the Bark?" He smirked even as his canine teeth extended and his eyes shifted to wolf. "You're kidding, right? That may work with that Golden you were loving up, but I doubt it will do much to the rest of us."

Miki cleared her throat. "I amped it up a bit in case those full-blooded wolves got a little cranky Sara wasn't around anymore." She pushed the button and hoped Conall could forgive her.

He went down first. His hands over his ears, his fangs bared, a howl torn from his throat. Then the hyenas went down screaming. Even the females watching from the sidelines hit the ground, their androgynous bodies writhing in pain. To her it was silent. She couldn't hear anything and she felt nothing.

Well, at least now she knew it worked.

Miki grabbed Conall by the neck of his T-shirt and tugged, hoping he could manage to get up since she'd never be able to lift him by herself. He dragged himself up and crawled into the SUV. She followed, her finger still on the button. She adjusted the seat so her feet reached the gas pedal, and then she started the SUV. She finally released the button as she drove off, making sure to avoid the cubs lying in the street.

Once they were safely away, she dropped her keys and the device back in her bag.

Conall looked at her. His fangs still out, his eyes red rimmed. "You call that 'amping it up a bit'?"

She shrugged. "Be thankful. It could have been worse. I've been thinking about mating it with a stun gun. You know, for shits and giggles."

He leaned back in the seat. "You're a dangerous woman, Miki Kendrick."

She smiled. She got the feeling he meant that as a compliment.

Chapter Eleven

Conall had been watching her for the last ten minutes. She'd asked for grape but he could only find cherry. A cherry ice pop. He'd handed it to her after getting back with their lunch from the deli next door.

Once they got safely back to the hotel, and his ears stopped ringing, he'd talked to Sara. Filled her in on the information discovered by Miki's hacker friends. Told her about what he saw at the Clan den. She was unfazed by the fact Miki had gone with him on his little excursion. Seemed she trusted her friend as much as he did. And he did trust Miki. That realization kept playing through his brain. Sara told him she would talk to Zach once he got back from hunting, and they'd get some Pack members up to Seattle as soon as possible. Then she gave him a direct command. Something she never did. Protect Miki. She didn't care what he had to do or who he had to kill. She wanted Miki safe.

As far as Conall was concerned, not a problem.

So, he'd settled in to eat the first of the three giant sandwiches with chips and beer he'd bought. But he hadn't taken a bite. Not once he noticed her and that freakin' ice pop.

Stomach down on the bed, she was on her laptop doing more research on hyenas. She had both hands on the keyboard, forcing her to suck on the phallic-shaped ice pop only using her mouth. In and out. In and out. And the slurping sounds...she had to be kidding! And he was almost positive she had no clue what she was doing to him.

Eventually, he couldn't take it anymore.

"I want you to do that to me."

She didn't look up from her laptop. "Do what," she mumbled around the pop.

"Suck my cock like your sucking that ice pop."

She froze, her hands pausing over the keyboard. Slowly her eyes lifted, focusing on him. She stared at him for several moments. Then she pulled the ice pop out of her mouth, making sure to include a wet "pop" sound when she did.

"That's quite the request."

"It's not a request."

Miki grinned, her teeth catching her bottom lip. "I see. A demand." She pushed the pop past her lips, long and slow, and pulled it out just as slowly. "Interesting."

Miki slipped off the bed and walked toward him. Suddenly his cell phone went off. They both looked at it. Then they dived for it. But Miki was smaller and faster. She grabbed it and flipped it open.

"Hello? Hi, Zach."

Conall shook his head and waved her off, his big body dropping heavily into a nearby chair. "Bathroom! I'm in the bathroom!" he mouthed desperately.

"No. No. He's around. Let me grab him for you."

He was going to kill her.

Miki put the phone behind her, using her ass to cover the mouthpiece. She leaned in close to Conall, whispering right against his ear.

"You're going to talk to him. And you're going to be like you always are. And if you can't hold on a conversation. Or if you let him know I'm going down on you…I stop."

He wanted to come from that alone, especially when her tongue reached out and swiped across his ear.

She handed him the phone and slipped the ice pop back in her mouth. He held the phone by his ear but hadn't spoken yet as he watched her kneel in front of him. She undid his jeans and he raised his hips so that she could get them off. He was so busy staring at her, wondering what she was going to do next he completely forgot about Zach until she motioned to the phone with her head.

"Hey, Zach."

"Hey. I just talked to Sara. You guys okay?"

Conall nodded his answer.

Miki pulled the pop out of her mouth. "I don't think he can see your nodding," she whispered.

He tried to focus. "Yeah. We're fine."

Miki ran the ice pop down the underside of his cock and he thought he was going to jump out of his skin. *Evil bitch.*

"Good. All right. We've pulled about eight of our guys to send your way. That should be enough until you guys get back. Sara was ready to head up there herself, but there's no fuckin' way I'm letting her ass out of my sight."

"That sounds...fine." She swiped the pop across the tip and then her tongue swiped right after it.

"I just wish I could figure out what the hell they're doing. Lions are their enemies, we should be allies. I'll talk to the older wolves. See if they can help us out here. And you make sure you watch your back."

He pushed his bare feet into the carpeted floor. "You got it."

Zach paused. Then, "You sound distracted. Is she wearing on you?"

Conall gritted his teeth as Miki's tongue followed wherever she put the ice pop. "You have no idea."

"I warned you about her. And you can do better anyway. She doesn't deserve you." Good old supportive Zach with the worst timing *ever.*

"Is she at least talking to you now?"

Conall's head fell back as Miki sucked the tip into her mouth, her teeth lightly grazing over the ridges, her tongue swirling over it.

"Sometimes," he managed.

"Well, don't worry about it. I'll hook you up with a sure thing when you get back."

"Sure," he barely bit back a groan as she took all of him into her mouth and hummed. "Sounds great."

Zach began to ramble about...something. Who the fuck knew? Conall gave some non-committal noises. Thankfully, Miki let him get away with it probably because he was keeping his voice relatively steady. But he had no idea how much longer he would be able to keep that up. Especially once she tossed the ice pop, wrapped that soft hand of hers around his balls, and lightly squeezed.

"Well, since I've got you why don't we go over the stuff for the new club in Barcelona?"

There was no way he'd be able to stay focused during that conversation. No way in hell. As it was, he was surprised he was still conscious.

"I don't have the stuff with me. Can it wait?" Could Zach hear his panting? He wouldn't be able to hold out much longer. She was working him and knew it, too. She smiled around his cock when she wasn't sucking him into oblivion.

"Yeah. Sure. Sara just came in anyway. Hold on." There was a muffled sound from the other end of the phone. "Uh…Conall. She has a sudden interest in my pants, so I need to go."

Abruptly, Zach hung up. *Thank God for Sara.* Unlike Zach, *her* timing was impeccable.

Conall threw the phone across the room, dug his hands into Miki's hair, and finally let out his harsh groans. He was so close he was growling in climax thirty seconds later.

She sucked him clean and then looked up with a smile. "Not bad. The conversation I mean."

Okay. He owed the little brat. Big. Besides that talented mouth of hers had only made him hotter. Just looking at her was making him hard all over again.

He reached down and picked her up. He kicked his jeans out of his way and took her to the dresser, placing them both in front of its mirror. He turned her so that she was facing away from him, pushing her down across the wood.

She smirked at him in the mirror. "Dude. Nice idea, but not quite sure how this is going to work."

The dresser was for humans of normal height. Conall wasn't that human and his height was anything but normal. Miki wiggled that tight ass at him, thinking he was stuck.

"Again. The lack of creativity."

He walked to the closet, grabbed her black leather pumps, the ones with the five-inch heels. He placed them next to her. "Put 'em on."

He caught her fighting that smile again. "I plan to wear those on Friday."

He leaned into her, his arms on either side, blocking her in. "Do as I tell you and put 'em on."

Miki cleared her throat and stepped into the shoes. She looked at him in the mirror. "Well? Now what?"

He yanked her skirt up and ripped her panties off.

Miki gasped as she held onto the dresser. Conall grabbed a condom from a pile next to his keys and change, and slipped it on. Then he grabbed Miki by her hips and slammed into her from behind.

"God, yes," she bit out. She had her eyes closed, but Conall wanted her to see everything.

He had one hand on her hip to hold her steady while he wrapped the other in her hair and pulled. "Open your eyes, Miki."

She looked into the mirror and their eyes locked in the reflection. "Watch me." His voice low and rough, he barely recognized it. "Watch me fuck you."

*****

She didn't think it was possible, but the man had just made her wetter. But that's what Conall did to her. He made her wetter, hotter. With him she was daring, brave, and kind of slutty. But in a good way.

And he made her feel beautiful, hot. When she'd worn the pumps before she always felt stupid. Like a kid wearing her mom's clothes. For the first time, she felt like she *owned* these shoes.

She watched his face as he began to stroke in and out of her. It was like there was nowhere else he'd rather be. No one else he'd rather be in. That alone was an aphrodisiac.

She picked up his rhythm quickly, as she always seemed to with him, and brought her body back as he surged forward. It boggled her mind she made him crazy like this. "Dead below the waist" Kendrick made someone like Conall, who could have his pick of well-trained bar sluts, out of control.

"Touch yourself, Mik." She moaned as she watched him in the mirror. "Do it."

And what exactly was his deal with ordering her around when they were fucking? And what was her deal with not minding? And she didn't mind. Dammit, she was a feminist! Marched on Washington to protect a woman's right to choose, etc.

etc. But damn if she didn't love to hear him growl out orders. Although it was never orders for orders sake. He always made sure she got off. Always made sure he left her satisfied and smiling. The man was a fucking demon in bed.

"Now."

She reached her hand between her legs and trembled as her fingers found her clit. She began to massage the sensitive, straining nub. Her panting becoming louder, harsher. It didn't help that Conall still had a good grip on her hair and every once in awhile, he'd tug.

Sometimes she felt like the sensations were too much. His big cock inside of her, his hands on her, his mouth. Sometimes she thought she couldn't handle one more second of it. Of him. She never wanted to feel this way about anybody. She never wanted her body to be so responsive to just one person. But Conall the Viking had come into her life and blown it completely apart. And she had no idea what the hell she was going to do.

Conall's hand tightened on her waist as her muscles began to tighten around him. "Conall." She always said his name when he was inside of her. Always.

"Come for me, Miki-baby." He coaxed her with that rough voice of his. "Come for me."

And she did. Another one of her screaming orgasms only Conall seemed to have the ability to force out of her. She rode that feeling, Conall following right behind her.

They collapsed on top of the dresser, their harsh breathing filling the room.

"So," Miki reached back and patted that amazing ass of his. "How's Zach doing?"

Conall gently wrapped his big arms around her and hugged her close. "Evil bitch."

*****

Miki opened her eyes and for a minute wondered where she was. Hotel rooms, with their big heavy curtains, were always a little too dark for her. But then she felt Conall's big arm wrapped around her, pulling her close into his even bigger chest.

She relaxed and glanced at the clock. It was seven a.m. She'd actually slept six hours. Two days in a row she'd slept longer than three or four hours. Of course, Conall kept wearing her out. *Really* wearing her out.

But was it supposed to be like this? He should've gotten bored by now. Start ignoring her. Plotting a way out that wouldn't involve getting his ass kicked by Sara. She thought they'd started down that road the day before when he was watching television and she was on her computer. He'd been quiet for almost an hour and she found herself debating whether he was ignoring her or giving her space to study. On a whim, she muttered something about not finishing what was started against the wall in the first hotel room he had. And before she knew it she was pinned against the wall like a butterfly in a display. Then it continued for hours. Against the wall. Against the desk. Face down on the bed. Pushed over the bathroom sink. Bent over a chair. She was pretty sure there wasn't a stick of furniture in the room her ass hadn't been on.

She was so confused. He was confusing her and she didn't know what the hell she was doing. This was not her terrain. Sara and Angelina handled the social stuff and Miki made sure they passed calculus class and didn't get kidnapped by bikers.

But now it was getting harder and harder to separate her body from her heart. Even though she continued to promise herself she wouldn't go down that road. But she made the mistake of listening to those two crazy bitches. What the hell was she thinking? She knew better. Did she learn nothing from the ninth grade lip-gloss and bloodletting incident?

Yet, she wouldn't trade the last few days she'd spent with Conall for anything in the world. He'd taught her sex was fun, pleasurable, and freakin' amazing.

Just thinking about him inside of her made her want to turn over and grab that big cock of his. But then she remembered what she had to do in just a few hours. Get up in front of a bunch of uptight professors who barely tolerated her, wearing a suit she hated, defending a thesis she really wasn't sure she believed anymore. And how the hell could she defend something she didn't believe in? Unlike Craig's work, her thesis relied on theory as opposed to hard facts from her own lab work. Who the hell was going to approve that?

She felt choking panic weigh down on her but she shook it off. She had to get her shit together. She had lists to write. She slipped out from under Conall's arm, found her notes, and sat down to obsess over her future for the next eight-and-a-half hours.

She thought she was being quiet but thirty minutes into her obsessing Conall woke up. He looked at her with that one eye thing he did first thing in the morning and sighed.

"You're obsessing, aren't you?" Because he'd just woken up, his grumbling voice was even more so. The sound made her wet in seconds. She shook her head and went back to her notebook. She didn't have time for this.

"It's what I'm good at."

Conall stood up, gloriously naked, and walked into the bathroom. He closed the door behind him and, within seconds, Miki heard water running. It was her turn to sigh. *Let the ignoring begin!*

She went back to her notes and was halfway down the page when Conall walked back out of the bathroom and straight over to her. He reached down, took the notebook out of her hand and pulled the T-shirt she had on over her head. He tossed it aside, then picked her up and took her with him into the bathroom.

"What the hell are you doing?"

He closed the door with his foot, and took her to the huge marble tub. The room was steamy from the hot water. The tub filled with bubbles. He sunk them both in and relaxed back. Christ, he hadn't stormed out of the room to get away from her. He'd gone off to make her a bubble bath.

"Conall?"

"Miki?"

"I should be preparing. Or panicking. Or both. Probably both."

"Forget panic. It's a waste of energy. And prepare what exactly? You've got a freakin' photographic memory, Mik. You're telling me you don't already know each and every detail from your thesis, your textbooks, and your notes?"

Bastard. "Okay. You've got a point, but..."

"No buts. You're going to relax if it kills us both."

"Relax? How am I supposed to relax?" Conall pulled her close and began to kiss her neck, his hands sliding over her body. "You didn't answer my question, Viking."

"Yes I did," he muttered against her neck.

Bastard. "So this is your plan?"

"Pretty much. You got a problem with that?" He slid his hands between her thighs and Miki braced her hands against the sides of the tub. God, the things this man did to her. "Miki?"

Christ, she was panting. *When did that start happening?* "What?"

She felt him smile against her flesh. "You didn't answer my question."

Bastard.

*****

Conall snatched the door open and three of his Pack jumped back. "What?"

"Uh..." Billy Dunwich was the only one brave enough to speak in the face of his scowl. "We were just checking on..."

"When we're ready, we'll be down. Until then just wait." He slammed the door in Billy's face. Zach, true to his word, had sent eight of his best wolves to escort him and Miki back home. They were even taking a later flight to ensure the whole group would fly together. But until then, he didn't want anything interrupting him and Miki. And he meant *anything.*

He turned and looked at the woman he loved. He didn't even hide the smile on his face. With Miki he didn't have to. She leaned against the desecrated dresser, wearing nothing but one of his T-shirts. It reached to the middle of her calves. "I see."

"You see what?"

"You. You're a closet Alpha."

"I'm a what?"

"You heard me. You're a closet Alpha. You don't really wanna be in charge, but you love to order people around and scare the shit out of them. You're probably only friends with Zach because he doesn't scare easy. Most likely because he's not the brightest bulb in the batch." Zach was a lot brighter than Miki was willing to give him credit for, but other than that she'd hit it all right on the head. The woman was amazing.

"Is that right?"   Conall walked toward her and immediately she began to back away. He watched her nipples get hard under his T-shirt and he listened to her labored breathing. "What else have you figured out about me?"

"You clearly like to stalk me around this hotel room."

"Aw, Miki-baby, don't say that. I'd stalk you anywhere." She laughed at that as he backed her up to the bed. When her knees hit the mattress, she held her hand up.

"Stay!" He stopped and watched her. "I've got to get ready for...uh...ya know...that thing I've gotta do."

Well, he'd wanted her relaxed.

"We've got three hours before your *dissertation*." He nuzzled her outstretched hand until she gave a little moan, then he sucked her middle finger into his mouth.

"You, Viking..." *Christ, is she panting?* "...are a very bad influence."

*****

Miki looked up at him with those big, beautiful brown eyes of hers. "You know," she whispered desperately, "if I start running now I can be back at Sara's by tomorrow night. Afternoon if I don't get stopped by the cops."

"You'll never make it in those shoes." Amazing. The woman faced down lions, hyenas, wolves. Beings that could rip her apart limb from limb. But four puffed up professors were making her unhinged.

She tugged on her jacket again. "I hate dressing like this. I feel like an idiot."

"Maybe. But you look like a total hottie." *Especially* with those shoes. She ended up wearing the four-inch fuck me pumps with her prim-and-proper business suit.

"Where's everybody?"

"I have them around the building."

He brushed her curly hair out of her eyes, then let his palm rest against her cheek. She didn't push him away. She let him get close. And it was the best feeling in the world.

"This is just great. My throat's sore." She sighed and muttered to herself, "Who knew I was a screamer?"

It took all his strength not to drop to his knees and bury his head between her legs right then and there. And the beauty of it all was she had no idea what a compliment she'd given him. He did love this woman. How could he not? She was so insane.

She nervously glanced back at the room. Conridge stepped out and motioned to Miki. "I guess this is it."

Conall tugged on her jacket and she looked at him. "You're going to be great, Miki."

"You sure about that, Viking?"

"Positive. And as you know my people are never wrong."

"You know, the Vikings were quite influential..."

He cut her off. "Miki. Go. I'll be here when you come out."

"Right here? You promise?"

He stepped back, leaned against the wall, and then crouched down. "I'll be right here. I promise."

She braved a smile and then headed off toward Conridge. He watched her disappear into the classroom, the door closing soundly behind her.

*****

Miki figured they'd asked her questions for about two-and-a-half hours before they felt she had proven herself. Conridge, of course, was the toughest of the professors. But Miki figured she would be and was ready for it. In fact, she had been ready for all of them. She was confident, poised, and on point with everything. Even when she screwed up, she made the professors laugh and they let her off the hook.

It seemed Angie and Sara had been right. Bartender-Miki apparently was the way to go because Normal-Miki would have been crying by now.

When she walked out of the classroom, Conall was crouched against the wall exactly where she'd left him. She got the feeling the man hadn't moved. Just like he promised. She was so startled it took her a second to realize one of the professors was congratulating her. She tore her eyes away from her Viking and finished off her "thank yous."

Once the other professors were gone, Conridge shook her hand. "I knew you'd be fantastic."

"Thanks."

"I'm going to my office. I've got to get out of these clothes. Stop by before you leave with your burly friend."

"Yes, ma'am."

She watched as Conridge walked off. Then she turned and faced Conall. He stood up and took several steps toward her.

"Well?"

She'd planned to just say, "I'm done. Let's go get something to eat." And maybe give him a thumbs-up. But the way he was looking at her…like he really cared how she did. Like he really wanted to know and he really wanted her to do well, that just made her feel…well…special.

Before she knew what she was doing, she'd dropped everything, even her precious briefcase-covered laptop and charged over to him, launching herself into his arms.

"I fucking nailed it!"

Conall held her tight. "I knew you would, Miki-baby. I had no doubts."

She pulled back slightly. "They already told me they were definitely signing off on all my paperwork. They didn't see a reason to make me wait to tell me. I'm going to be *Doctor* Kendrick. Me. How fuckin' cool is that?"

Conall laughed and squeezed her. "We're celebrating."

"Not in these clothes, I'm not." He was still holding her so that they were eye to eye. "Down, Thor." She pointed to the floor. He let her slide down his body and immediately her breath caught. She had absolutely no control around him, but she shook it off. She couldn't get all entangled with him now. They'd done enough elicit activity in the biotech school. "Where's the backpack?"

He grabbed it from the floor and handed it to her. She pulled jeans, sweatshirt, and her steel-toe Docs out of it.

"Can't you keep on the shoes?" He was practically begging.

"Dude, I can't even walk in these things."

"Keep them on and you won't have to walk long." He took a step toward her and she backed up.

Miki's face got hot. "Back off, Viking."

"Come on. For me?"

"No." And just like that, his eyes shifted and he growled. She would have tried to run, but she wasn't going anywhere in those shoes. So she let him pick her up and dump her over his shoulder.

"You son of a bitch! Put me down."

"You do know that I *am* a son of a bitch. Literally."

She knew he was heading toward the bathroom at the end of the hallway in the hopes of having his dirty way with her. And the thought had her tingling from the top of her scalp to the tips of her toes.

He kicked open the bathroom door and walked inside. He lifted her up and gently dropped her to the floor, grabbed the handful of clothes she still had gripped in her hand, and tossed them onto the row of sinks. Then he leaned into her, pinning her against the wall. "I do like when you wear these shoes, Mik. I don't have to crouch as much."

"Are you implying I'm short?"

"I'm not implying anything." He pushed the jacket off her shoulders and kissed her neck. "You are short."

She barked out a laugh and punched his shoulder. "Thank you very much."

He reached down and tugged her skirt up. He gave a combination growl-moan in her ear. "God, woman. You're wearing garters again. What are trying to do to me?"

She reached up and wrapped her arms around his neck. "Make you crazy."

"You get your kicks that way, don't you?"

"No. I just want you to miss me when I'm gone."

She was trying to prepare herself for the inevitable. When Sara's birthday was over, they would both be going their separate ways. And she wanted to be ready for that. She promised herself she wouldn't become attached. And she was going to keep that promise.

But when Conall pulled away, the expression on his face shocked her. He looked angry. Viking angry. "And where the hell do you think you're going?"

*****

Okay. He wasn't being rational, but come on. Miss her when she was gone? She wasn't going anywhere. Not if he had anything to say about it. And, as far as he was concerned, he had *everything* to say about it. She wasn't leaving him. Not now. Not ever. He loved her. And he couldn't imagine one second of his life without her.

"I just assumed…"

"Well, you assumed wrong. You're not going anywhere."

"I don't like to be ordered around, Conall. And I never promised you anything."

He stepped back from her. He had to. She was in heat. That's why he hadn't been able to keep his hands off her in the hallway.

He took a deep breath. "You're crazy about me, why don't you just admit it?"

Okay. Where the hell did that come from? That wasn't what he meant to say. And it was definitely the last thing she wanted to hear.

Her eyes narrowed and she pushed past him. "Oh really? *I'm* crazy about *you?*"

"Miki…"

"No. No. I just want to make sure we have the order of worship down correctly."

This was getting bad and he was having a hard time concentrating with her smelling like that. All he could think about was bending her over the sink and fucking her stupid.

"I didn't mean…"

"You know, I'm glad we're getting this out now before we get back to Sara's house and we give her and Angelina the wrong impression."

"What the fuck do they have to do with anything?"

"Well, they said to give you a try…and that's what I did."

*****

She aimed that one to hurt. Aimed it to cut out his heart and leave it on the ground so that she could stomp on it with her Docs.

At first, he didn't say anything. He just stared at her. Then he pushed her change of clothes at her. "Get dressed. The Pack is waiting."

She snatched the clothes out of his hand and practically ripped her business suit off and put her regular clothes on. When she was done she moved to the bathroom door and snatched it open. But Conall's big hand was there slamming it back.

"Wait."

"Why?"

He was so close to her. His body almost, but not quite touching hers. "Because we're not done."

"We're done because we never started."

Miki pulled the bathroom door open and this time he let her. She marched out into the hallway, Conall right behind her.

"What exactly are you scared of Miki? It's clearly not me. So what is it?"

"We are not about to have one of those bullshit conversations about feelings."

She retrieved her backpack, shoved her business clothes inside it, and slung it over her shoulder. She took her computer bag and placed that over her other shoulder then headed toward the stairs.

"This conversation is over, Conall."

She walked off. She was about twenty feet from the stairs when she heard him growl. Not his usual "You're getting on my nerves, Miki" growl either. Something else altogether. She turned and saw that he'd shifted. Not parts of him. All of him. For the first time since the night of the Pride fight, she saw Conall the wolf. No wonder he'd been pissed about the Golden. There was no way that little pup could be confused with the powerful predator in front of her.

Conall shook off his clothes and then he was charging her. Teeth bared. Hackles up. With a tiny squeak that didn't sound anything like her, Miki dropped to her knees, her arms over her head. She waited for impact but there was none. She looked to see that Conall had sailed right over her and right over the stair railing.

"Holy shit! *Conall!*" She dropped her bags and charged over to the railing. She saw him hit two hyenas on the stairs, knocking them down half a flight. But there were six more and they were all looking at her.

Miki didn't even think about it. She ran.

Chapter Twelve

Conall didn't know what happened. One minute he was arguing with the crazy woman he secretly called "wife" and the next he was wolf and making mad dashes over railings.

As he sunk his teeth into a throat, he briefly wondered what happened to his Pack. But then he heard them. Growling. Snarling. Fighting. It sounded as if they were kicking some ass too, but there were so many of them. As soon as he destroyed one, another two were on his back. Mostly females, but vicious beyond anything he'd ever experienced before.

Then he remembered Miki. Last he saw she was ducking and covering. Had she actually thought he'd hurt her? He was the least of her problems.

Still Conall wasn't worried *about* Miki as much as he was worried *for* her. Because the one thing he knew about his woman was that she could take care of herself.

*****

Miki charged down the stairs on the opposite side of the building. She heard the hyenas coming for her. They had the most disturbing howl she'd ever experienced. She had to force her body to move. All she really wanted to do was hide in a corner and cry. Anything to block out that sound.

She took two steps at a time, and stopped on the second floor. Then ran down the hallway until she hit Conridge's office. By then they were snapping at her heels. She had just enough time to get into Conridge's office and slam the door. She held her body against it and could feel them throwing themselves at the hard wood.

Seconds later Conridge was beside her, adding her body against the door. The woman had thankfully changed clothes. She now wore a pullover sweater, jeans, and running shoes. It seemed she would need the running shoes.

"What the hell?"

"Hyenas."

Even as Conridge locked the door, the two women continued to keep their bodies against it. But it wouldn't last much longer. With every hit the hinges became weaker.

"We've got to get out of here." Conridge's eyes began to search the room for some escape. She didn't have a window, but she had a vent. But Miki wasn't about to get trapped in that with hyenas on her ass.

Her amped-up Stop the Bark tragically still sat in her backpack with her house keys, and there was no way to get to it without heading back toward the hyenas. *No way..* And she needed to kill these things, not incapacitate them.

"Is there any chance in hell you have a gun?"

"Bottom drawer on the left." When Miki just stared at her, "I don't have claws, Ms. Kendrick. So I had to find other ways to protect myself. You know the world does not revolve around the Magnus Pack. The Van Holtz Pack has its own enemies."

Fair enough. Miki left Conridge to hold the door while she tore through her drawer. She almost cried when she found two loaded SigSauer P239s. The P239s were compact and fit her hand pretty well. Both were .357s, so there were only seven rounds per magazine but, bless her, Conridge had extra clips already filled with ammo. She liked this woman more and more.

Miki stuck one gun in the back of her jeans and several already loaded clips in her front jean pocket. Then she stood in front of the door and dropped to her knees. She leveled the weapon in both hands and watched the door as the hyenas on the other side relentlessly pounded away trying to get to her. She watched the movement of the door. The way it buckled and where it buckled. She listened to the sounds they made when they made contact with the wood. Then she waited for that "click" inside her head.

Conridge watched her but didn't say anything. When Miki finally spoke, she was ready.

"Move."

Conridge took several quick steps back and covered her ears. Miki took one more second to clear her mind and body and then she shot three rounds through the door. She heard yelps of pain and surprise and then nothing.

After a minute, Conridge stepped forward and listened at the door.

"I don't hear anything." She put her hand on the doorknob. "Be ready," was all she said before she eased the door open and glanced into the hallway.

"Holy shit."

Miki looked at her professor. It was the first time she ever heard the woman utter anything except "hell" and the occasional "damn."

"You're a hell of shot, Ms. Kendrick."

Miki stood up and went to the door. She pulled it completely open, the gun out but at an angle so she didn't accidentally kill someone important. There were three hyenas dead on the floor. Miki frowned.

"There were six on the stairs that Conall wasn't fighting," she whispered. She pulled the other gun out of her waistband. She offered it to Conridge, but the older woman shook her head. "I'm not the best shot." She gazed at the hyena corpses. "Not like you."

Miki shrugged. She'd been smart enough to learn to shoot with both hands. Amazing what you can get done when you're under house arrest.

She had both guns out and low at her sides. Then she stepped into the hallway. She saw them silently moving at her from both directions from the corners of her eyes. She raised both weapons and fired.

Two went down immediately. One kept coming. So she turned and fired, brain and skull splattering the walls.

"We need to get into Craig's lab."

"I've got keys." Conridge grabbed her purse and put it over her shoulders. Miki re-traced her steps to head back up to the third floor where she could find Craig's lab, Conridge right behind her.

She thought about Conall. She could hear the Pack fighting outside the building. The wolves would be outnumbered. Hyena clans could have up to 40 members. The thought of anything happening to Conall almost sent her skidding into full-blown panic. But freaking out now wouldn't help him or her.

She knew what Craig kept in his lab. She'd put it there herself. And she knew what it could do. Hell, she'd invented it. And if she had time, she'd probably realize that using her invention was the dumbest thing she could do. But she had the feeling that she didn't have time to come up with anything else. Time was something they no longer had.

She walked onto the third floor and stopped cold. It was Leucrotta. He had only shifted partially and was on top of one of the wolves. A female. She was out cold and it seemed that Leucrotta had been sniffing her.

He looked at Miki and smiled. An unbelievably sharp row of small but deadly fangs revealed. He stood up and shifted almost completely back to human...except for the teeth. He walked toward her and she raised both guns.

Conridge was behind her. "He's human."

"So?"

"You kill him now, he stays human." Well, that would be difficult to explain to the cops. And she wasn't sure she was ready to actually blow a human away. That actually might bother her...at least for a little while.

"She's right. You don't want to kill me now, Miki." His voice was like a hiss. The sound went across her skin and raised the hair on the back of her neck. If she had been wolf, her hackles would have been standing straight up right across her back. "Besides, don't you like my little congratulations party for you, Dr. Kendrick?"

"Are you working with the Pride?"

"That'll be a cold day in hell." He was still moving toward her and she could feel Conridge's hand gripping the back of her shirt. The woman was having a minor freak out.

"So then what do you want?"

He shrugged. "How should I know? This fight belongs to the females. They just tell me what to do and I do it because I like doing it. And they told me to tear your Pack apart and to feed on your entrails."

Miki snorted. "Melodramatic bullshit." Then she lowered the gun and pulled the trigger. Twice. Leucrotta went down screaming. Both knees blown out.

She heard Conridge gasp behind her. "Oh, my."

She glanced at the woman over her shoulder. "You said not to kill him. You didn't say anything about his knees."

*****

One of them ripped a good chunk out of Conall's thigh with their claws and he roared in anger. Especially when he felt the poison began to seep into his blood stream.

Fuckers.

He tore its throat out and flipped it up and over his back.

He was lucky. The whole Clan wasn't there. With a full Clan, he'd have been dead. But there was still twelve left. Five he'd already killed where lying in the building. Another three were lying on the ground at his feet. He could only hope that Miki grabbed the SUV keys out of his discarded jeans and made it to the parking lot where he'd left it. He could only hope she would be safe. That was all he cared about now.

Another set of jaws locked on the back of his neck. Billy Dunwich tackled it and ripped its leg off as he hit the ground. Conall faced another one and that's when he smelled her. With her going into heat, it came to him a lot sooner.

"Hi. Am I interrupting anything important?"

They all turned to look at her. Conall gave a warning bark. She needed to move her ass. The hyenas wouldn't be distracted for long. She just surprised them with her sudden appearance.

But it was the look in her eye that caught his attention. And the fact she had her hands behind her back. And she was standing just a little too cutesy for the Miki Kendrick he knew. With one leg cocked slightly in toward her other leg, her head tilted. Like a little girl.

Then it hit him. She was *trying* to look non-threatening. But why? He decided not to wait to find out. He looked at the other wolves and, as one, they turned and ran.

*****

Miki had their attention and it was damn scary. Those cold animal eyes staring at her. Sizing her up. Wondering what bits to eat first. But she needed Conall and the Pack to move. Now. But if she warned them then the hyenas would know, too. She knew from Sara shifters could understand everything. They thought, heard, and saw as if they were still human.

Then, suddenly, Conall and the Pack high tailed it out of there. She didn't know what clued him in, but she wasn't going to worry about it. A few of the hyenas watched the Pack run. They weren't a stupid breed. In fact, they were the exact opposite. They would know something was up, so she had to move now or lose her opportunity.

She raised her two guns. The hyenas stared at her for a moment and then began...laughing? It took every ounce of inner strength she had not to curl up into the fetal position and start crying for her grandmother. But, her grandmother was a strong, mean woman and she would have told her to get her shit together anyway.

But she knew what they were laughing at. She didn't have enough bullets in those two guns to take out all the Clan members in front of her. She may kill a few, but the rest would just tear her apart.

And she already knew that.

"Now!" The female wolf that Leucrotta had been sniffing stepped out of the shadows and tossed a mason jar, filled with the clear liquid Miki had created so many years ago, into the air. Miki raised one of the guns and fired. The jar exploded over the hyenas and, within seconds, flames covered their bodies.

A chemical flame that as soon as it touched the fur on the first hyena spread over the entire body within seconds. As it tried to shake it off, it got too close to another hyena and the flame spread. That was the beauty of her concoction, and one of the reasons her government had tried to get her to produce it for them. It wasn't like regular fire. It almost took on a life of its own, jumping from victim to victim as long as they were in a ten-foot range. And it only went after flesh, fur, or skin. The buildings, trees, even the grass would be largely unaffected except for a few burn marks she never could figure out how to get rid of before she stopped working on the experiments all together.

The hyenas began to go up in flames as the wolf female tossed the other bottle on the opposite side and Miki shot that one as well. Then the female lobbed one to the right and left of the hyenas. Miki shot all of them without any problems. It was like skeet shooting. She only needed four bullets for that.

A ring of fire surrounded the hyenas. A fire that wouldn't spread out but in. Once again, a little extra "thing" about her concoction. By the time the fire department showed up, they'd find a pile of hyena ash and a fire that would go out in about five more minutes without water or a fire extinguisher.

"Go!" The female took off running. Two hyenas, untouched by the flame, charged Miki. She fired both guns then. One crumpled on impact. The other flipped head over tail.

Miki ran. Two hyenas still on her ass. Unfortunately they hadn't been close enough to the fire to get hurt. If she stopped to shoot, they'd take her down. She saw Conridge pull up in a mini-van. A typical mom car. Thankfully it had automated doors that slid open at her approach. Miki dove for it but hyena teeth grabbed onto her calf.

She had on jeans but those strong jaws went right through to the flesh beneath. "Motherfucker!" Miki kicked with her free foot, but the hyena wouldn't let go. It yanked and dragged her out of the van, flipping her to her back. That's when she fired. She couldn't get a clean head shot without shooting herself in the foot, so she shot it in the ass. It yelped and danced away. The second one came for her. She aimed the gun, her finger about to pull the trigger. Then suddenly the female who had been helping her shifted back to wolf in mid-flight and took the hyena down. She twisted its neck and snapped it.

Miki struggled to stand, but strong hands grabbed her from behind and lifted her to her feet. She looked over her shoulder and frowned. She'd assumed it was Conall but it was another Pack member.

"Where's Conall?" He didn't answer her, but lifted her and threw her into the van. The rest of the Pack, some human and some still wolf, followed in behind her. He slammed the door and

Conridge was moving. The woman drove like she taught. Dangerously.

"Wait! We're not leaving without Conall!" She had the guns and they all knew she'd use them in a heartbeat.

"He's back here." One of the females motioned to her.

Miki clamored over the seats and around the Pack members, doing her best to ignore the pain in her calf. She could hear sirens blaring as cops headed their way. They'd probably gotten out just in time. As she stumbled to the back, she found Conall in the rear boot. He was still wolf. His shoulder torn open. His struggles to breathe obvious.

"It's poison," the female next to her explained. "We need to get him some place safe."

Conridge spoke from the front, "You'll come to Van Holtz territory. You'll be safe there. And our doctor can help him."

Miki slid into the back with Conall. She petted his head.

"Miki? Is that cool with you?" Miki looked up. The female, Patty was her name maybe, was staring at her. Waiting for an answer. It took her a second to realize the Pack was waiting for her decision. When Zach and Sara weren't around, Conall was in charge. With Conall down that meant the next strongest was in charge. She suddenly realized that was her.

"Yeah. Yeah. That's cool."

She focused back on Conall, running her hands over his flanks, avoiding the bloody wound on his shoulder.

"Conall. Can you hear me?"

He rubbed his snout against her arm. "I'll take that as a yes." She searched around her for something to wrap his wound. "Baby, can you shift back for me?"

He whined and she took that as a no. At least not yet.

"That's okay, baby. That's okay." She grabbed a kid-sized bottle of water from a box lying next to Conall's head and a small T-shirt she found. She tore the shirt into strips and drenched the strips in water.

She wiped the wound with the wet cloth. She sniffed it, but couldn't recognize what they'd used on him.

Taking him to a hospital was out. Taking him to the vet equally so. She could only hope the Van Holtz Pack would help.

She leaned in close to him. "Conall, will you be able to hold on for a bit?" He licked her arm. "Okay. Good. We're going some place safe."

He licked her face. "Don't worry, baby. I've got ya, okay?" He made a soft sound and she rubbed the fur at the back of his neck. "I've got ya."

Chapter Thirteen

Conall forced his eyes open, wincing at the pain in his head. He glanced around and realized he was in the back seat of some vehicle he didn't recognize. He looked down. He was human. His shoulder hurt. The poison had taken hold and was traveling around his system like a flame on gasoline. But his body was fighting it. He could feel the fever coming on. This would definitely get worse before it got better.

But he didn't care. Not really. He needed to know if Miki was safe. Was she alive? He heard doors opening and felt hands on his body. He tried to fight, but he didn't have the strength left. He heard grunts as they hoisted him up and then he was moving.

*****

Miki limped behind the wolves that had Conall. Her leg was killing her, but not from poison. If she'd been poisoned, she'd be dead by now. She wasn't wolf and she would never be able to fight the affects. Conall was wolf. But whether he would live or not, well no one could give her an answer on that.

When they arrived at Van Holtz territory, she was surprised at the size of Conridge's home. It was huge but extremely modest. She liked that it wasn't fancy. She saw Conridge's husband at the front door. He was even more gorgeous than his picture. A typical wolf. Tall, broad, and devastatingly handsome. And his relief at seeing his wife was blinding. He swept her into his arms and lifted the woman off her feet, hugging her close against his body.

Miki thought about Conall and she felt that tightness around her heart again. The pain worse than the one in her leg. *What if he dies?* She stopped the thought. Of all the things she tortured herself with on a daily basis; this couldn't be one of them. She'd never survive it.

They carried Conall into the house and Conridge motioned for them to go up to the next floor. Miki went to follow, but Conridge grabbed her arm.

"No you don't. I want to take a look at that leg."

"I'm not leaving him."

Conridge pulled her toward the back of the house. "Of course not. But the wolves have him now. Niles called in one of their own. He's a physician. Give him some time with Conall. And while they do that, we'll deal with you."

Miki allowed Conridge to drag her to their spotless kitchen. Funny, Sara's kitchen was spotless because apparently none of them used it. Conridge's kitchen was spotless because someone in her family was obsessive compulsive.

"Don't take this the wrong way, but drop your pants." Miki would have laughed if she had it in her. But she didn't. She dropped her pants and Conridge gently forced her into a chair.

Conridge was on her knees, pulling Miki's leg up to examine her wound when Niles Van Holtz walked into the kitchen. He took one look at his wife and raised an eyebrow.

"Don't go there," she warned without even looking at the man.

"I didn't say a word." His gaze shifted to Miki. "Have you eaten?"

"I'm not hungry."

"So no it is." He went to a row of cabinets and pulled out a pot, a sauté pan, and fresh pasta from the stainless-steel refrigerator.

"He's ignoring me." Miki didn't even recognize her own voice. There was no life in it. And until Conall recovered, *if* he recovered, she'd be dead inside.

"Of course he's ignoring you. He's wolf. That's what they do when they don't like what they hear." Conridge cleaned off the wound, wiped it down with mercurochrome, and wrapped it in a clean white bandage. "It's going to hurt like hell, but it will heal."

"Thank you."

Conridge looked up into Miki's face. She wasn't sure what the woman saw but her face softened to the point were Miki barely recognized her. She actually looked kind of pretty. "I know you're scared, Miki. But they're doing all they can for Conall. He's wolf, he'll fight."

Miki nodded as Conridge got to her feet. "Let me get you some clothes." She spoke to her husband. "And I'm stealing a few things from you for the rest of her Pack." Miki didn't bother telling them they weren't her Pack. She was too emotionally drained.

"I'll be right back." She squeezed Miki's shoulder and walked out.

Miki watched Van Holtz at the stove. She was impressed. The man seemed to know what he was doing. And whatever he was creating did smell good.

"You'll be safe until morning. By then we'll know if Víga-Feilan will..." He stopped and looked at her over his shoulder.

"Survive?"

"I wouldn't worry too much. He looks...well, *really* strong. And the fever has already taken hold."

"Fever?"

"It's how our bodies fight. The fever can last up to twenty-four hours. And you never know what will happen when you're going through it. Sometimes nothing. Sometimes you shift a thousand times in twenty minutes. And sometimes you start flipping out. It's a crapshoot."

"I should be with him."

"After you eat." Van Holtz dumped some sautéed pasta onto a dish, added some extra cheese, grabbed a fork, and plopped it down in front of Miki. "You have to eat it. I usually charge fifteen bucks for that dish in my restaurant."

It smelled great and her stomach suddenly roared to life. Taking a deep breath, she took the fork he held out to her and sampled the food. It tasted as good as it smelled.

"Thank you."

He patted her on the shoulder then walked away. She ate while he cleaned up his kitchen. An obsessive-compulsive wolf. *Odd.*

As Miki was taking the last bite she could manage, a girl walked into the kitchen in shorts and a T-shirt, with a soccer ball under her arm. "I'm back from practice, papa."

The girl reached up on tiptoe to kiss her father. "How did you do?"

"Fine. But the rest of the team is holding me back." She turned and looked at Miki. "Hello."

"Hi."

"Who are you?"

"I'm Miki."

"Kendrick?"

Miki blinked. "Yeah."

"I read your dissertation." Suddenly the girl looked just like her mother. "I found flaws." The girl walked out of the room.

Miki stared at Van Holtz. He shrugged. "She takes after her mother."

Conridge pushed the kitchen door open, but she was yelling over her shoulder. "I said do your homework this minute, mister. And don't you dare bare your fangs at me!" She came in with a pair of sweatpants and a long-sleeved Tee. "Damn wolf children."

Conridge handed Miki the clothes. Without even thinking about the fact that Van Holtz was right there, she changed into them.

Just as she finished pulling the Tee over her head, Billy Dunwich stuck his head in to the kitchen. "Miki, we need you."

Miki moved. She ignored the pain in her leg and followed after Dunwich who was now wearing only a pair of jeans. He took her up the stairs and to a door. She could hear snarling and snapping. She pushed past him and threw the door open. Conall as wolf was out of control. She could see the whites of his eyes as he spun in a circle and snapped at anyone who got too close to him. The one she assumed was the Pack doctor had a needle out and was standing behind several Van Holtz wolves. The other wolves seemed at a loss on what to do.

She walked into the room. "Conall!" The wolf spun around at the sound of her voice. She sat down on the floor Indian style. "Come here, baby." He ran to her. His shoulder was bleeding again and he had a pronounced limp. He came to her and dropped in front of her, his head in her lap. He whined and then shuddered. "It's okay, baby. I won't let anyone hurt you." She

petted his head and waited until he was calm. Then she looked up
at the doctor. "All right. Do it."

The doctor walked over, crouched down beside them, and
quickly shot him up with whatever was in the needle. She glanced
up at Dunwich. "Get him up on the bed." Conall's Pack lifted him
up and placed him back on the bed.

"Everybody out."

"Are you sure?"

She nodded at Dunwich's question. "Yeah. I'll be fine."

The wolves left. The doctor the last to go. "You'll have
to clean off that wound again, but that shot should keep him calm.
He'll probably wake up, though, while in the throws of the fever.
I'll be taking care of the other wolves who were injured tonight, so
I'll be here if you need me."

"Thanks."

The doctor walked out, closing the door behind him.

Miki glanced around the room. It was a huge bedroom
with an adjoining bathroom. She was thankful for that. She didn't
want to leave Conall at all. She never wanted to leave Conall.
And the thought absolutely terrified her.

Chapter Fourteen

Conall felt cold. Freezing cold. He pried his eyes open and looked around the room. He had no idea where he was. But even worse, he didn't see Miki. Where was Miki? He needed to make sure she was okay.

"Miki?" He tried to sit up but his head was pounding.

"Hey. Hey. No you don't, Viking." He felt her warm hands on his chest, pushing him back down on to the mattress. "You're not going anywhere yet."

"Safe? Are you safe?"

"We're both safe, baby. Everything's cool. Just sleep."

He grabbed her hand and pulled her close. "Stay with me, Mik."

"I'm not going anywhere."

He smiled as his eyes closed. "Promise?"

She chuckled. "Yeah. I promise."

He settled back down into the bed, but he still wouldn't release her hand.

"You're not going to let me go, are you Viking?"

"I'm never letting you go, Mik. Besides, I'm cold. I need you to warm me up."

She sighed and he felt the bed dip slightly as she got in next to him. "Okay. Okay. Come here."

She pulled him close, laying his head against her chest. He wrapped his arms around her and held her tight. He felt her kiss the top of his head as her arms wrapped around his shoulders.

"You smell good. You're in heat."

She laughed softly. "Christ, Conall, get some sleep."

Knowing she was safe, he allowed himself to relax. She smelled so good and the heat coming off her body was unbelievably soothing. The last thing he remembered was her hands running through his hair.

*****

Miki brushed Conall's hair out of his face. He was sleeping again. He kept waking up, worried about whether she was safe or not. It almost overwhelmed her, his constant concern for her. She'd always had the love and protection of women. Her mother and grandmother. Sara and Angelina. But never of men. Most men found her either overwhelming or a little scary. Even Craig and the guys seemed to have a healthy fear of her.

But Conall. Conall was different. Did he actually care about her or was it just the fever? How the hell was she supposed to know? She knew science. Math. And some history. She knew how to make an amazing Martini and she had a decent roundhouse kick. That was it. Anything to do with people and actual emotions, she was totally at a loss.

Miki kissed Conall's forehead again and settled down next to him. She was so tired. Not surprising with everything that had happened in the past few hours. But she was sure that with a little nap, just a few minutes, she'd be right as rain.

She closed her eyes and let sleep take her.

*****

He was having the best dream. One of those hot dreams with Miki that he'd been having since he met her. He was enjoying this dream too because she smelled so good. She was in heat.

He was behind her, his arms wrapped tight around her waist. He nuzzled her neck and licked it. She sighed softly and snuggled back into him. "My wolf."

"All yours, baby."

Her hand gripped his thigh. "Make me come, wolf."

Oh, yeah. This was a *great* dream. He slid his hand down her stomach and under her panties. He eased his fingers between her thighs and over her clit. Her body jerked and she gave a little moan as two of his fingers entered her pussy. She was already wet. Wet and hot. She gripped his hand and pushed his fingers deeper.

He smiled as he slowly finger fucked her. She moaned again, her tight ass writhing against his cock. It had already been hard, now it was on fire. It wanted to be deep inside her. As deep as his fingers were. Deeper. He ran his thumb over her clit and she gasped, her head falling back against his shoulder. "God, Conall." He loved when she said his name with that sexy voice of hers. He *felt* her voice all over his body.

The pad of his thumb circled her clit and her fingers dug into his hand. Her body tightened. He licked the back of her neck again. "Miki?"

She pushed herself back into him, her body beginning to shake. "Do it, Conall. Please."

"You sure, baby?"

"Please." She asked again. And he knew it was a dream because Miki would have kicked him in the nuts by now. Not begged him.

He extended his fangs and, turning his head to the side, bit the back of her neck. She gave a little cry but he wasn't sure if it was from the bite or the bone-shaking orgasm she was having. To be honest, he didn't care. As he licked the blood off, he only knew one thing. She was his now. And nothing would ever change that.

At least not here, in his dreams.

*****

Miki was having the most rockin' dream ever. A dream that consisted of one of those screaming orgasms only Conall seemed to have the ability to wring out of her. This time with nothing more than his hands and teeth. In this dream she let him mark her. Practically begged him to, in fact. But it felt so right. And it was a dream, so she didn't have to be scared or worry about getting hurt. Or about being in love.

She could do anything she wanted here. She pulled his hand out of her and turned in his arms. She kissed him, deep and slow. Their tongues connecting, sliding, teasing. She felt his dick against her leg. It was hard and hot and all hers. She reached down and gripped it, her thumb sweeping across the head.

Conall growled into her mouth. "God, Miki-baby." His hands gripped her shirt and pulled it over her head. Her bra went next. Then he was kissing her down her body as he dragged the sweat pants and panties off her. He kissed his way back up, lingering on her breasts. Then her neck. Kissing her mouth again. Taking his time to explore.

His body always felt so good to her. So right next to hers. He moved over her and she felt his dick slide into her. Her back arched almost throwing Conall off.

He felt so good inside her. He wasn't wearing a condom and her muscles gripped him tight, pulling him deep. He growled again and she felt it across her body.

His thrusts were slow and deep and she was completely lost in them. Her body arched against his, loving the feel of his flesh. Nothing had ever felt so right before.

Before she knew it, an orgasm slammed into her and she gripped Conall to her tight. Then he was coming inside of her. Another orgasm rocked her just after the last one ended. She gripped Conall's chest with her teeth and bit down. She tasted blood and, before she knew it, she was licking his wound clean. As both their bodies settled down, she unclamped her teeth and released his flesh, but she held on tight to the man.

"I love you, Viking," she whispered, enjoying her dream moment.

"I love you, Miki-baby." Then her dream man started snoring.

Chapter Fifteen

Conall woke up when the sun hit his eyes through the window. He felt great. Better than great. That was the cool thing about the fever. If you survived it, you usually felt better than you did before you got hurt.

Miki was in his arms and he relished it. Especially since the last thing he remembered from the night before was having a huge screaming argument with her. But he didn't want to think about that now. He pulled her closer and she sighed softly in her sleep.

As right as this all felt, he knew something was wrong. He just couldn't quite figure out what. He looked down at her. Asleep and as beautiful as always, she was also naked and had her limbs around him. It took him a second, but he realized he was inside her. Inside her without a condom.

Uh-oh.

The pillow behind her head had blood on it. He winced as he gently reached around and touched the back of her neck. Then it was her turn to wince from him touching the wound.

He remembered that the day before she'd been going into heat. He leaned in and sniffed her. Her scent had changed. Which meant only one thing.

He closed his eyes. *She is going to kick my ass.*

She stirred underneath him and he immediately got hard again. Boy, was this bad timing.

Miki stretched, her arms going wide, pushing him off and out of her. She yawned and rubbed her hands over her face. She looked around and then seemed to remember why she was...well, wherever the hell they were.

"Conall?" She turned and looked at him. "Conall? Are you okay?"

"Yeah, Mik. I'm fine." She leaned over to him and felt his forehead. Her bare breasts rubbed against his arm and he had the sudden urge to have her again.

"Your fever broke. That's good." She gave him the oddest expression. Then she suddenly launched herself into his arms. He was so startled, he fell back on the bed. He pulled her close as she hugged him tight. "I'm so glad you're okay."

He closed his eyes. Nothing ever felt so right as when this woman was in his arms. And knowing she actually cared about him enough to worry...nothing before had ever made him feel so good.

Miki, clearly not comfortable with showing her emotions, pulled herself out of his arms. She sat on the edge of the bed. "I'm really sorry about yesterday, ya know." She glanced at him, then turned away again. "You took me by surprise. And I just never thought you'd want...I just never had..." She shook her head and he saw her smile. "Forget it. We'll talk about this later. Really talk. You and me. Okay?"

But before he could answer her. Before he could tell her the decision had already been made for them, she slid out of bed and headed to the bathroom. "When I'm done, I'll let Van Holtz and the Pack know you're okay."

Christ, they were on another Pack's territory. Well that explained the strange wolf scent he smelled everywhere.

Conall lay back on the bed and waited. Waited for her to realize what had happened. She probably thought like he first did. That it had been a dream. But he had marked her. She was his. Would be for life. And there would never be another woman for him. Never.

But he knew Miki almost better than he knew himself now. She wasn't going to take this well. She'd feel trapped. And she hated feeling trapped. He was having trouble remembering last night but he knew they'd been caught up in something primal and older than most of the gods. In fact, he was almost positive she'd told him to mark her. Knew what he intended with out him actually saying it. The wolf in him wanted her. Knew she was the mate for him. And she was. She could have run yesterday. Taken off with Conridge and never looked back. But she'd faced down a vicious Clan of hyenas to protect him and his Pack mates. She hadn't even been worried about herself. Only him. Those were the actions of a mate. *His* mate.

He heard the toilet flush and Conall counted. "Five. Four. Three. Two..."

"*Conall!*"

"One." He sighed and waited.

Miki stormed out of the bathroom, wearing only white sweat socks and a really pissed off look.

"What the fuck is this?" She pointed at the back of her neck. He didn't bother to look. Not when she was standing in front of him naked.

"My mark."

She stared at him. He waited for it. The explosion of anger. The rants. All of it. He knew it was coming.

But it didn't come. Miki just stared at him. Then she silently grabbed her clothes off the floor and returned to the bathroom, quietly closing the door behind her.

Okay. That was *definitely* not the reaction he was expecting. He expected rage. Rage he knew how to deal with. Whatever she was going through at the moment, they didn't even have a name for.

He got off the bed and pushed the bathroom door open. She had gotten on her shirt and panties but that was it. Now she sat on the edge of the bathtub holding her sweatpants in her hand and staring down at the floor.

"Miki?"

She looked up at him. Her dark eyes glittered in the well-lit bathroom. "You just couldn't let me decide for myself, could you?"

This was controlled rage, and this worried him. When she was ranting and raving, he knew she was simply being wacky Miki. But this...this was Miki who blew the head off a lion.

"It wasn't like that Mik and you know it."

She sighed. Calmly. He was getting more and more freaked out by the second. "I'm going back to Texas, Conall."

He crouched down next to her. He gently laid his hand on her leg. "No." He spoke softly. He wanted her to know she was safe. Safe with him. "Not until we talk about...*ow!*"

She'd punched him. Right in the nose.

"What the hell was that for?"

"Because you're a lying sack of shit! That's what that's for!" Yeah. There was the Miki he knew and loved. "I'm going back to Texas and you can't fucking stop me!"

Conall stood up, crossed his arms in front of his chest, and blocked the doorway. "No. You're not."

*****

She stared at him. Those big, giant arms, crossed in front of that big, giant chest. His big legs braced apart. He was completely blocking the doorway. Hell, he was completely blocking her. And she didn't like it one damn bit.

"I wasn't asking you, Conall."

"You're not running away from this. From us."

Us? At what point did the booty call turn into an "us."

She dropped her head in her hands in pure frustration. He was making her nuts. "There is no 'us'. There will never be an 'us'."

"Why?"

Okay. Why did that question throw her? "Because."

"Because why?"

Christ, it was like talking to a ten year old. "Because I said so."

He smiled. "That the best you can do, Miki-baby?"

"Don't call me that."

"It never bothered you before."

She stood up and pulled on the sweatpants. "Well, it bothers me now."

He stepped toward her and she stepped back. "And why is that?" She backed up against the stainless steel sink as he moved in front of her. "Because I usually say that when I'm inside you? When you're coming and screaming my name?"

Okay. Why couldn't she breathe? He was so close. And he smelled so good. No. This wouldn't do. She needed to go. Somewhere. Anywhere. Away from him. She needed time to think. To analyze. To plan.

"Last night you told me you loved me." *Oh, that he remembered.*

"I was asleep."

"Not too asleep to fuck me."

"Christ, Conall." She wanted to push him away, but she knew she couldn't touch his skin. If she touched him, she'd be lost.

"Tell me you don't care about me, Miki." He leaned in, his mouth so close. "Tell me and maybe I'll believe you."

"I don't care about you." That would have been much more convincing if she hadn't whispered it while staring at his mouth.

His lips were inches from hers. "Liar." Then he was kissing her. His lips on hers, his tongue sliding into her mouth. His hands tangling in her hair. Immediately her body responded. Her arms went around his neck. Her body pressed into his. And her desire to drop to her knees and take him into her mouth almost overwhelmed her.

He pulled back slightly, but his hands were still in her hair and his upper body still had her trapped against the sink. "Stay with me, Miki."

"I can't think about this right now." Panting. She really had to stop panting.

"Then don't think at all." His mouth captured hers again and she became wet for him. Nipples became hard. All the usual. She had no control around him. None.

When he dropped to his knees, she almost exploded. Why was he doing this to her? She was trying to make it easy on him. Giving him a way out. Why was he torturing her?

Because, idiot, maybe he doesn't want a way out. Okay. Exactly when did that new voice make an entrance in her head?

Conall pulled off her sweatpants and panties and tossed them aside. Then he pushed her legs apart and began to lap at her clit.

"Goddamn it, Conall!" He ignored her. What was it Conridge had said? If they don't like what they hear, they just ignore it. And, clearly, that's what her Viking was doing. But his tongue felt so good. And then he growled. A deep one from low in his chest. It reverberated up and through his tongue, hitting right across her clit and sending Miki spiraling out of control. Nothing, absolutely nothing, had ever felt that good before. She gripped his head in both her hands and held him in place. She loved the feel of his hair against the inside of her thighs. She loved the warmth of his body. She loved the way his hands gripped her ass as he ate her out. She loved all of it. All of him.

The growling, the licking, they all conspired to shove her over the edge. And shove they did. The guttural moan she let out as she climaxed sounded like it was coming from somewhere else. From someone else all together.

While her body was still shaking, Conall picked her up and placed her on the sink. Then he was inside her. It seemed she wasn't the only one out of control. She wrapped her legs around his waist and held on as he gripped her hips with his hands and claimed her body. Every time he took her it felt better than the time before.

Her head fell back and Conall's mouth was sucking on her throat. She loved this man. She knew she did. But she was scared to death. She'd always assumed that she'd be alone forever. She'd simply hoped that no matter where Angie and Sara ended up, they'd always have a place for her at Thanksgiving dinner.

But the Viking…

He'd marked and mated her without a backward glance. And she'd told him to. She thought that had just been an astounding dream. An astounding *wet* dream. Now she knew it had really happened. Half asleep or not, they'd connected on a level she never thought existed between people. Now, according to Sara, she was "his." And her fast-moving brain simply wasn't ready to handle that.

Of course, that didn't stop her body from completely exploding as Conall slammed into her. She bit into his unwounded shoulder as his hot seed shot into her. That's when she realized he wasn't wearing a condom and that he hadn't been the night before. Apparently, they were so much a couple now condoms were optional.

And as soon as her body stopped shaking from her climax, she was going to say something about this.

"Hey, Conall. You here?" A male voice. Probably Dunwich. He seemed the only one brave enough to deal with Conall when he was with her. "Van Holtz got your stuff back from the SUV and the school hallway. A few of the cops handling the case are Pack. So we should be cool."

Miki tensed up and tried to pull away, but Conall wouldn't let her go. He held her to him as he got his voice back. "Good. Thanks. We'll be out in a few."

"Uh…yeah. Sure. Okay."

Miki rolled her eyes as she heard that amused sound in Dunwich's voice. *Schmuck..*

*****

Conall kissed Miki's forehead. No way was he letting her go. Now he understood why Zach couldn't leave Sara alone. Because when you find that right one, you don't want to let her go. Even when she was a pain in the ass. Of course, Conall was willing to overlook Miki's ability to be a pain in the ass as long as she kept having those orgasms that almost snapped his cock in two.

"We'll talk about this later, okay? Just don't make any decisions now."

"Conall…"

"Let's just get back to the den, okay?"

She wanted to argue. She wanted to tell him this wasn't right. He could see it on her face. But he wasn't going to let her. Instead, he'd get her back to the house and then he'd fuck her into submission again and again until she finally got the message she was his and he was hers. Forever.

Yeah. That worked as a plan.

He pulled out of her and was surprised she didn't say anything about his lack of condom. He knew it was no longer necessary, but she still didn't. And he wasn't going to say anything about the pregnancy until he convinced her they should be together. He didn't need anything else freaking her out. He was coaxing a high-strung mare. Scare her off now and she'd high-tail that fine ass right back to Texas. If she were going to accept the fact that she was his, he'd have to play this cool. Well, as cool as he could when just her touch on his shoulder made his whole body throb.

*****

He thought the Van Holtz Pack would toss them out as soon as he could walk. Man, had he been wrong. Instead Niles Van Holtz made them all breakfast. The most amazing waffles he'd ever tasted, eggs, bacon, coffee, orange juice, the works. The man was a genius of the kitchen.

He sat next to Miki as she and Conridge talked about how the university management had already begun to successfully cover up the hyena attacks by dismissing them as a pack of wild dogs that found their way onto campus and then proceeded to wreck havoc. And the fire Miki started disappeared so fast that it barely got a mention. And no one had any idea what happened to Professor Leucrotta. Conall forced himself not to react when he heard about the man's knees, although his Pack seemed to be quietly disturbed.

It seemed his mate had done serious damage. To protect him. To protect his Pack. He kept thinking, "She didn't walk away. She didn't walk away." And she could have. She so easily could have.

He looked at his Pack. They all feared her. Even the Van Holtz Pack. And now that they knew she was pregnant, they were waiting to see what she would do if she realized. Even Niles Van Holtz kept looking at him as if to say, "Welcome to my world, buddy."

As if on cue, Conridge's kids stormed into the room. The boys were typical wolf pups. Loud, boisterous, with sharp teeth. The girl was different. She didn't seem more than twelve or thirteen, but she moved slowly. Paced herself. She wasn't dog-like at all, but she smelled like wolf. She would be Pack leader one day. And she already knew it.

She walked serenely after her brothers and headed toward the kitchen door leading to the hallway. But suddenly she stopped and looked straight at Miki.

"You weren't pregnant last night, were you?"

The entire room of people froze. If Conall didn't know better, he would have sworn that the entire universe had frozen. That, like them, the universe wanted to see what Miki would do.

Miki slowly looked up and turned to the girl. "I'm sorry. What?"

"You. You smell pregnant. Papa taught me what that was when I smelled that same scent on my aunt. You didn't smell like that last night. But you do now." The girl shrugged. "I guess you had a busy night." Then, after destroying his entire world, the little bitch left.

Miki turned around, but kept her head down, her hands flat on the stainless steel kitchen table. She began to tap both her forefingers against the metal and Conall watched all the wolves jump. Dunwich waved at him, trying to catch his attention. Then he mouthed something to him.

"What?" he mouthed back.

Dunwich help up his hand. Forefinger out. Thumb up. The other fingers bent into the palm. His hand looked just like a gun.

Oh, shit.

Conall glanced over at Miki and that's when he saw the gun in a holster and attached to her waistband. He didn't even notice her putting it on as they got dressed after their shower. Conridge must have let her keep one for the ride back.

And when Miki suddenly hit the table with her hands, every wolf but him and Van Holtz hit the floor.

Miki pushed her chair back. She looked at Conall. "I'm going to the bathroom. Then we are leaving."

"Miki, I…"

"No. There's nothing to say right now. And I mean *nothing."* Miki looked at Conridge. "Thank you for everything, Dr. Conridge."

"Anytime. Of course, when we take on a clan of hyenas together, I'm pretty sure you can start calling me Irene."

"Thank you Irene. I'll call you tomorrow about your job offer."

"That's fine."

She looked at Van Holtz. "Thank you for everything. I truly appreciate your hospitality."

Simply from the expression on the man's face, Conall got the feeling Van Holtz would be retelling this story until the end of time. "You are more than welcome."

Miki looked around the table and realized that all the wolves had disappeared. She leaned down and looked under the table.   Twelve wolves laid out on the floor for no apparent reason…that didn't seem to distract her one bit. "I just wanted to thank all of you for helping us."

"You're welcome," one of the Van Holtz wolves was brave enough to say.

With that, Miki stood up and walked out of the room.

Conall closed his eyes.   Like his fever from the night before, he was pretty sure this would have to get worse before it would get better.

Conridge leaned across the table and touched Conall's arm. "I wouldn't worry." She motioned toward her husband. "I stabbed him in the leg and set his Mercedes on fire before I agreed to marry him. So she just needs time."

Conall frowned. "Uh…thank you?"

*****

Miki said nothing during the whole thirteen-hour trip that Conall and the Pack turned into a ten-hour trip by doing some seriously illegal speeding and keeping the bathroom and food breaks to a minimum. But really, what the fuck was she supposed to say?

The borrowed SUVs the Van Holtz Pack lent them, pulled up in front of Sara and Zach's place. The Alpha pair already outside, since one of the Pack called ahead.

Miki got out of the vehicle. She was barefoot because she couldn't bring herself to wear Doc Marten boots with sweatpants. She wasn't a fashion maven, but that was too tacky for words. She limped slowly toward Sara, her calf tender but already healing. Her friend's eyes locked with hers as she pulled away from Zach. Sara knew something was wrong. The three friends always knew when something was seriously wrong with one of them without any of them having to say a single word.

As she reached Sara, Conall walked past her. He didn't speak, simply went into the house. Zach followed after him.

"Your leg?"

"It'll be fine."

Sara stared at her. "What the hell's going on?"

Miki glanced back at the Pack members behind her.

Sara motioned toward the house with her head. "Go."

And they did. Once they were gone, Sara turned back to her.

"Okay, dude. What's up?"

Miki looked at her oldest and dearest friend and burst into tears.

*****

Conall had just punched a hole in the wall when Zach walked in. He closed the door and stood behind him.

Leaning his head against the wall, Conall closed his eyes. "She's pregnant."

"I know. I could smell it a mile away."

"She won't stay here."

"She has to. Pregnant with a Pack baby? She'll have every Pride member in North America gunning for her ass. And who the fuck knows what's going on with that Clan. Besides, you marked her. She's yours."

"Not if she doesn't want to be. You know that as well as I do."

"Well you can't go around hittin' walls. The house won't last."

*****

Miki sat at the kitchen table with her head resting on her arms, a glass of buttermilk sitting in front of her, and Sara's nose sniffing the back of her neck.

"What the fuck are you doing?"

"You smell different."

"According to Conridge's demon child, I'm pregnant. And the little bitch found 'flaws' in my thesis."

Sara pulled away, sitting down opposite from Miki. "I'm sorry. What?"

"You heard me. Flaws! In *my* thesis! Can you imagine?"

"I don't mean that, you idiot! I mean the...pregnancy?"

"Oh, yeah. That Cro-Magnon impregnated me."

"Did we not use the condoms Angie and I provided?"

"Yes, *we* did. But this happened during his fever."

"Where were you?"

"Half asleep."

Sara smiled. "Was it good?"

"God, yes." Miki covered her head with her arms. "The man fucks like a god."

"Not everybody can be loved by Thor."

Miki lifted her head just enough to glare at her friend. "Shut up."

"So…am I happy or sad for you?"

"Christ, Sara, I don't know. I wasn't exactly planning on having a baby…you know…ever."

Sara suddenly became serious and Miki raised her head to look at her.

"You know, Mik, no matter what you decide, I'll stand behind you. Always."

Miki almost burst into tears again, and she never cried. But knowing that Sara would always be there for her meant more than she could ever say.

She wiped her eyes with the palms of her hands. "That means a lot to me. But I think…I think…"

"You want to keep it, don't you?"

"I'm an idiot, aren't I?"

"Why would you say that?"

"Because I'm going to end up like my mother. Alone. Struggling with a baby."

"Okay. First off, never ever worry about that. I've always got your back, Mik. And my potential niece or nephew will always be taken care of. *Always.* So that's not even an issue. And you know Angie feels the same way."

Miki wiped her eyes again. She really hoped she was pregnant; otherwise, she was becoming an emotional mess for no reason.

"And second, you'll never be alone. You've always got me. You've always got Angie. And you'll always have the Pack."

Miki snorted at that. "Are you kidding? They're only nice to me because of you."

"That's a load of shit." Sara stood up and grabbed a box of chocolate from off the counter behind her. "They like you."

"Yeah. Right."

Kelly and Julie pushed the glass doors open and walked in. They were both naked having, Miki assumed, just shifted. *If I'm going to stay, I guess I'll have to get used to this whole naked thing.*

She started as soon as she realized what she had just been thinking.

"Hey, Mik. You're back."

"Yeah. I'm back."

"Well, me and Julie are hittin' an after-hours club tonight. You should come. It'll be a blast. We'll celebrate you being all PhD and shit."

Miki laughed. "Thanks. I'll let you know."

"Cool." Kelly grabbed a handful of cookies from a bag off the counter while Julie grabbed two glasses and a gallon of milk. They disappeared through the kitchen door and then came back two seconds later.

Kelly sniffed the air. "Oh, my God! Who's pregnant?"

*****

Conall had his head buried under the covers, but Zach just wouldn't leave.

"I mean, how attached can you be to her?"

"I marked her and she's carrying my baby!" he barked from under his comforter.

"You breeders never fail to make me laugh."

"Just because you want to be childless…"

"Sara and I prefer child*free.*"

"You're an asshole, Sheridan."

"Yeah. I know. And she loves me anyway."

Conall brought his head from under the covers. "And you love her?"

"More than anything."

"Why?"

Zach smiled. "Because she puts up with my shit without taking my crap."

"Miki calls me Viking."

"Well, she definitely has your number. All those other bitches bought into your sweet act. That always drove me nuts. You always got more pussy than me."

"That could be cause you were always a sarcastic asshole. Next to you, I always seem like the 'nice one.' Besides, I would do anything not to be like my family."

"You keep forgetting that *we* are your family. Not those crazed idiots. Besides, I'd kick the shit out of you if you started acting like them."

Without knocking, nine of his Pack mates, all male, walked into his bedroom.

Mac Sumner leaned against the dresser. "So. You knocked her up, huh?"

With a growl, Conall pulled the comforter back over his head. Suddenly, he wished he were an orphan.

*****

"Well, you have to think about this logically."

Miki didn't know when this became a town meeting of the Pack females, but before she realized it twelve of them had joined the conversation. Five she'd never even met before. They all had opinions and they were all supportive. It was the wackiest thing she'd ever experienced. They treated her as if she were one of them and as if this problem was theirs to solve as much as it was hers.

"How logically? Either she loves him or she doesn't. Either she wants to stay with him or she doesn't." Kelly, thankfully now dressed, was short like her. But she was as feisty as a mini-Pinscher on six cups of espresso, and had a low voice like rough sandpaper.

"It's all so black and white for you," Patty snapped. "Maybe she doesn't think that way. You always forget that humans think differently."

"Bullshit. Miki's more wolf than a lot of us."

Miki looked over at Sara. She, too, was clearly enjoying the way this conversation was going. The women had already wrestled the box of chocolate from Sara and now all the females were partaking. Miki desperately resisted the urge to remind them that dogs shouldn't eat chocolate.

"Look," some chick named Ronnie cut in. "This gets us nowhere. We should just ask her if she loves him."

They all turned to her.

Miki stared at them. She had just admitted this truth to herself. She wasn't sure she was ready to announce it to a room full of strangers.

Sara reached over and handed Miki a piece of chocolate. "It's got walnuts."

Miki took the chocolate and stared at it. "Thanks."

"You love him, don't you Mik?"

With an anguished groan, Miki shoved the chocolate in her mouth and put her head back on the table.

"There's no shame in loving Thor." And she could hear the humor in Sara's voice. "He's the god of thunder."

*****

"I think we're avoiding the most important question here. What matters most. What means the most to men like us."

Conall growled at Billy Dunwich's sincere face. "I am *not* telling you if she swallows."

Dunwich smiled. "Just tell me if she's a good girl...or if she's a *very* good girl?"

*****

Sara ended the call on her cell. "I left Angie a message. She'll probably call you later."

"She's only going to give me shit."

"That's her job. Mine is to be the supportive friend."

"Well, supportive friend. What the hell should I do?"

"How the hell should I know?"

"I knew it! You send me off into the desert then leave me alone to die. I should have never listened to you and Angelina. As soon as those fangs started coming out, I should have run for the hills."

Miki glanced up when the room fell silent. "What?"

"What do you mean his fangs came out?"

Damn. She really needed to watch what she said and when. Of course, that only took her twenty-nine years to discover.

She cleared her throat and shifted uncomfortably in her seat. "Sometimes his eyes would change and his fangs would come out."

Sara leaned forward. "During sex or when you pissed him off?"

She again glanced around the room filled with Pack females. "Um...well, both. Sometimes."

Miki reared back when the chanting began. "Miki! Miki! Miki!"

Now she was completely confused. "What? *What?*"

Sara jumped out of her chair. "Dude. You got the guy to extend his fangs during sex. That's amazing!"

Kelly appeared equally impressed. "We're trained from pre-teen years to control that since a lot of us have relationships with humans without them ever knowing. We fuck 'em, but we don't necessarily mate with 'em. Anyway, it's really rare for us to...you know...'bust out' during sex. Even with each other."

"So, if you actually got him to lose control that much..." Ronnie shook her head.

"And this is Conall we're talking about. He doesn't lose it. Ever."

The females actually high-fived each other.

"Wait. Wait." Sara quieted them all down. "So, Mik. What about you?"

"What about me?"

Sara placed her hands flat against the wood table and raised an eyebrow. Miki had the feeling her friend was getting even with her for the rave comment from four days earlier. *Bitch.* "Was your reaction equally as *enthusiastic* as his seemed to be?"

Miki stared at the women, then buried her head back in her arms.

She heard Kelly's voice announce, "Ladies, I do believe we have a screamer."

Her cheeks were burning so bad she was sure they were about to burst into flame. "I hate all of you."

*****

"She's a piece of ass, but once she pumps out a kid, that ass is going to go." Conall glared at Jake. He wondered whether it would really be morally wrong to kill the man.

"I don't care." Conall moved his glare to Zach. He blamed him for this. "If it was only about her ass, trust me I would have fucked her and walked away by now."

"How could any wolf walk away?" That from Dunwich. "The woman took on a hyena clan. She set them on *fire.* Personally, I'd rather have her on our side."

Zach shrugged. "Then it sounds to me like you love her. And if you love her, then tell her she belongs to you and she needs to get over it. Show her who's in charge. That's what I did with Sara."

Zach seemed less than pleased when they all laughed so hard Conall actually fell off the bed.

*****

Miki glanced up as Patty put a glass of milk in front of her. She stared at it in confusion because she hadn't asked for milk.

Patty shrugged and answered her unasked question. "Well, if you're going to keep it, I'm pretty sure you're supposed to drink milk and stuff."

"We'll have to get books. You know. On pregnancy and shit," Kelly suggested.

"And I'm in for the delivery room."

"Yeah. Me, too."

"Me, too."

Miki couldn't believe it. These women were volunteering to be in the delivery room with her. To help her without her even asking. So this was what it meant to be part of a Pack. She felt that sudden urge to cry again, but it disappeared as soon as the wolf females looked at Sara.

She knew what her best friend was going to say before it left her mouth. Miki wasn't wolf, but she could smell the panic and fear coming off the woman. "You must be fuckin' kidding me! Sorry Kendrick, you're on your own once that water breaks."

*****

"You know. This is bullshit." Conall didn't like the sound of that as Zach straightened up and headed for the door. "I'll tell her she's staying."

The males looked at each other then they charged after Zach. As Conall followed, he could see his future with Miki slipping through his hands.

*****

"And what about my career? Conridge offered me a teaching position."

Sara smirked. "First off. You hate teaching. You hate college kids. And second, Northern California has gotten really progressive and they actually have a few colleges. Some universities too. This state is making quite a name for itself academically."

Miki gave Sara the finger as the females began laughing. But when Zach, Conall, and a group of Pack males walked in, all conversation stopped.

Zach looked at Sara. "What?"

Sara's eyes narrowed. "Just wondering what you want?"

"What makes you think we want anything? This is my fuckin' kitchen, too."

"Uh-huh."

Zach went to the frig, and tossed each of the men a beer. Once they each had one, he headed toward the swinging kitchen door, pushed it open, then stopped. "But if I were going to say anything…"

"*I knew it!*" Sara stood up. "You just can't stay out of it, can you?"

"Sara, wait." Miki stood up. "I wanna hear what the brain trust has to say."

Zach glared. "Look, Tinker Bell, I tolerate you 'cause I have to. But Conall, against *my* better judgment, loves your psychotic ass. I don't know why. I don't understand it. But he does. And I have to figure if he loves you, and Sara–who I trust with my life and the life of my Pack on a daily basis–loves you, then there must be something about you besides that big mouth and those tiny elf feet."

Miki's eyes narrowed as she crossed her arms in front of her chest. Kelly leaned in between the two. "Why don't I just take this for now." She plucked the gun and its holster off Miki's sweats.

*****

Conall sighed. He'd had some big plans for his life with Miki. House. Kids. Gun shows. But his best friend was blowing that all to hell and back.

But he'd forgotten about his Alpha female. She was in Zach's face so fast that everyone, even Miki, stepped back.

"*Was that supposed to be nice!*"

"She doesn't get nice. She gets barely tolerated."

"You need to back the fuck off. *Now!*"

"All I'm saying is if she loves him she should just fuckin' stay!"

"And it's none of your business whether she loves him or not. Whether she stays or not."

"Sara, she's already part of the Pack. She protected Conall. You. And now she's carrying a Pack baby…"

Miki cut in then. "*Never* call our baby that again."

"…But if she doesn't want him for the love of all that's holy, put the poor guy out of his misery."

Conall could still hear them going at it, but he hadn't taken his eyes off Miki. He was waiting for her to realize what she'd just said. It took her all of thirty seconds. He knew the exact moment, too, by the look of pure panic on her face when she looked at him.

He smiled. A big, leering, Viking smile, he was sure. And Miki was none too happy.

"That meant nothing!"

Sara and Zach snapped out of their argument as Conall moved in front of Miki.

"That meant everything, Miki-baby.   Absolutely everything."

"You're fuckin' high. It was a slip. Nothing more. I haven't made up my mind about shit!"

The two stood toe to toe. But for once Conall didn't crouch down to meet her gaze.

"Just get over it. I love you. You love me. And we've got baby furniture to buy."

"You're not railroading me, Viking."

"You are so in love with me, you don't know what to do with yourself."

"You are delusional!"

"Marry me, Miki Kendrick."

"Not on your life!"

"We'll have a May wedding. Or September. After the baby or before?"

"I will kill you in your sleep."

"You'll try."

"You are making me crazy and I am sure that's not healthy for *the demon seed I'm carrying!*"

He smiled in the face of her yelling. "Is that any way to talk about our love child?"

Miki let out a strangled scream of pure frustration. And in response, Conall's smile just got bigger.

"That's it!" Miki barked. "Move the fuck out of my way!"

And everyone did. They watched as she stormed out, then they all looked at Conall. He was still smiling. He couldn't help himself. Miki made him smile.

Zach shook his head. "Are you sure you know what you're..."

Miki cut him off, bellowing through the swinging door. "Move your ass, Viking!"

Conall looked at his best friend. "I do love that woman."

"They have treatments for that kind of mental disorder, ya know."

*****

Miki stood in front of Conall's bed and stared at it, marveling at how big it was. He must have had it specially made so that his big feet didn't hang over the edge.

She crossed her arms in front of her chest and braced her legs apart. *Big-footed bastard.*

He walked in and closed the door. He ambled over to her with that Viking grin plastered all over his face. "So whatcha want, baby?"

She gritted her teeth. Could he sound any more smug? "You're just lucky they took my gun."

He slid his arm around her waist and leaned down to whisper in her ear, "You wouldn't really hurt me, would ya?" He nipped her earlobe and a delicious bolt of heat ran down her entire body. "Wouldn't you rather just fuck all night until we can't walk?"

His hand slid under her sweatpants and she pulled herself away from him, scrambling across the room. He took a step toward her and she held her hand out. "Stay!" He smiled at her. The most beautiful smile she'd ever seen. She loved him. She hated him. She couldn't imagine her life without him.

"I don't get you, Viking. Why are you so happy?"

"Cause I love you, Mik." She warmed at his statement. "And because I won." Then she became hot.

She growled. "You did not win."

"I so won."

He wanted to play that game? Fine.

She smiled. "So you think you won?"

"I know I did. I love you. You love me. And I get to keep ya."

Miki nodded. "Did I ever tell you that the FBI has a cork board with my picture on it? Actually, it has me, Amy, Craig, Kenny Liu, and Ben. And our pictures are in this pyramid shape, but I'm at the top. I heard the agents throw darts at it." His smile slipped a little. "The CIA still calls me every six months to ask me if I want to work at their...and I'm quoting...'labs.' They never get very specific, but you've seen the kind of stuff I can create so do the math. And there are several states in this country that I'm not really allowed in for...ya know...ever. And for the next forty or fifty years you'll be busy trying to stop me from saying something rude or inappropriate or you'll be trying to stop someone from killing me because of something rude or inappropriate that I said that you didn't stop me from saying." She grinned. "So tell me, baby. What exactly did you win?"

*****

Sure. He could have gone for a nice, normal girl. Or at least a girl who could shift into something other than human. But no, he had to fall in love with Miki Kendrick. Hacker. Scientist. Nut case. Great lay.

His mate.

The woman who would be driving him crazy for the rest of his natural born life...if he were lucky. She smiled at him. And he realized she was as much a Viking as he was. No wonder she saw through his bullshit. Nope, he was getting just what he deserved. Who knew the gods liked him that much?

"Whatever. Let's fuck." He moved toward her and she backed away from him.

"First some ground rules."

He growled. "Such as?"

"I don't make breakfast. I don't clean. I don't involve myself in any clubs or associations that use the word 'mommy' on their letterhead. At some point I'll actually know what I want to do career-wise which means the demon spawn I'm breeding will be pretty much yours to deal with until he or she is sixteen. By then they're ready for the SATs and that's when I step in. Now, of course I'll talk to him or her before then if I must. And no, this deal does not involve breast milk. I'll make sure to take care of that myself. Now, of course, this is all subject to change if their I.Q.s are higher than 140. Then I'm on deck when they're five. After the baby is born, we can discuss marriage. But I'm not changing my name and the word 'obey' will not be used in the ceremony."

"Is that it?"

She smiled. Yup. There it was. A big ol' Viking grin. "If I stay, I want a concealed weapons permit. And good luck with that since I'm sure all my federal friends will be fighting you tooth and nail on that one." Her smile softened. And it was a smile for him and him alone. "And I do love you, Viking. Just don't try and use it against me."

Yeah. He was definitely the luckiest man in the world. "Now are you done?"

"Yes."

"Good." He proceeded to untie his boots, tug them off, and toss them across the room. She stared at him for a good while before she finally said anything.

"What are you doing?"

"Getting naked." He pulled his T-shirt over his head, then he moved to his jeans.

"Why?" She backed away from him, a smile threatening to spread across her beautiful face.

"So I can have my filthy, dirty, Viking way with you." He kicked his jeans away. "So I can keep everybody awake all night and show 'em how you're a screamer." He walked toward her, and she slammed up against the nightstand. "So I can make you come and come and come until you don't even remember your name."

"That's a hell of a plan." Cool. She was panting again. He loved when she did that.

"I like it." He was in front of her. "Now here are *my* ground rules."

Miki tore her eyes away from his cock to look him in the eye, her arms again crossing in front of her chest. "Which are?"

"When we're in here. You're naked. I don't care if we're ninety. You're naked."

"I don't…"

"Did I argue during your ground rules? Quiet."

She fell silent, but not before growling.

"Back off Zach. He's the Alpha Male, my best friend, and my brother. So no telling him to go fetch unless he started it."

"But he…"

Conall covered her mouth with his hand. "Not. A. Word." She rolled her eyes and glared. "I expect you to always have two pairs of those pumps you had in Seattle. The heel is to be no less than five inches. One pair red and one pair black. They'll only be used in here. And you'll be naked. Also, I make the bed every morning, but feel free to sniff it whenever you feel the need.

And don't get too attached to any of your clothes. Because if they're not off when we get in here, I'm ripping them off. And I really like ripping them off. Because I like you naked."

She pulled his hand away from her mouth. "Anything else, Viking?"

"Just one thing." He pulled her crossed arms apart and stepped into her body. He kissed her neck, her shoulder, her chin. Then he lifted her up. Automatically her legs wrapped around his waist, her arms around his neck. She dug her hands into his hair and pushed her small body up against his. She stared into his eyes and smiled. A smile that was for him and him alone. "No matter where we are. No matter where we go. Or where we end up. That you always...and I mean *always*, Miki Kendrick..." he leaned in close. "Make sure our freezer has cherry ice pops."

Miki burst out laughing as Conall carried her to their bed.

Epilogue

She forced her eyes open. Her head was throbbing. Her back hurt. She felt pain in her arms and her knees. She sat up, slowly, and kept her eyes turned away from the French windows that had bright morning light streaming through them.

She waited until she felt like she could look around without throwing up, then she took in the room. It was beautiful. Gorgeous furnishings. Hardwood floor. Soft bed with a steel frame. This room alone must have cost a pretty penny to furnish. Gold silk sheets covered her naked body.

The bedroom door was open. She wondered whether she should make a run for it, but she was pretty sure she'd start vomiting as soon as she stood up. But she wasn't too worried. Her wounds were dressed. Her body cleaned. The last thing she remembered was something, a lot of somethings, coming out of the trees by her store and charging her. They had resembled dogs almost, but she really didn't know. She remembered going for her gun, then something from behind...tackled her? And that was the last thing she remembered.

She rubbed her temples and tried to piece together the last few hours. And that's when she heard it. It wasn't a growl. Or a roar.

It was a purr.

Angelina Santiago looked back at the bedroom door and watched a 600-pound tiger walk by. It stopped. She could still see its tail swinging slowly from side to side. Then it backed up. It turned its majestic head and looked at her. She looked at it. She was waiting for the fear to set in. And the pure unadulterated panic that comes with it. Then it shifted and spoke.

"Well. Hello, sugar."

She let out a cross between a sigh and a breath. "Oh, shit..."